THREE SIXES

AND A
FORKED TONGUE

OR

COLD MEDICINE
AND A LIAR

James Tyler Toothman

published by **MILLIONS OF COLORS**
Denver, Colorado

BROUGHT TO YOU BY

MILLIONS OF COLORS

AND

THE CULT OF RAY SAWYER

Published by Millions of Colors LLC.

For more information, write to millionsofcolorsllc@gmail.com
or 24 Elm St. Mayberry, NC 27030.

10 9 8 7 6 5 4 3 2 1
Hardcover - ISBN 9798987763209
Softcover - ISBN 9798987763216 pbk

Library of Congress Control Number: 2023932129.

____

Nicole Cooper - Creator of Priscilla's Fungarium (cover image)
John Gay - End paper logo design, Opening and Closing art pieces
(Struggling Angel, I'll Take You There)
Amanda Wotton - Interior art pieces
Jiri Cechak - Graphic design
Shirley Tennant - Inspiration for the story.
Jessica Powers - Editor

This book is dedicated to my late mother,
Pamela Kay McQuain-Toothman.

TO THE READER

THIS

BOOK

WILL

ALLOW

YOU

TO

COMMUNICATE

WITH

THE

DEAD

My mind starts trippin', a tear drops my eye.
—Snoop Dogg

A hasty move, the twitch of a finger,
the smallest of miscalculations—
I suppose we all stand no farther
than that from ruin.
—Larry Mcmurtry

More now than ever you have
the responsibility to speak recklessly.
—Dave Chapelle

A word from Joseph

God created the earth, but he never set foot on it. Not once. He wouldn't dare. Would you? If you created this fuckin' tragedy? If you were God? 'Course you wouldn't. Couldn't, even. Hubris wouldn't allow it. You'd steer as far clear of this here train wreck as yer big fancy Cadillac would let ya. Mind you, you can drive whatever you want when yer God, but when I'm God, I drive the sharpest Cadillac you ever laid eyes on. Yes sir, no doubt about that, sharp and fast. But as it turns out, I ain't God and you ain't God neither, and if either of us was, well, I rightly suspect we might have some explainin' to do. But seein' as to how we ain't, well, I'm just gonna walk my white ass wherever I need to go, 'cause I been poor since I was a boy and I don't pay much mind to shiny things. Like Cadillacs. Oh, but if I was God, I'd paint her red and I'd run her hard, you can bet yer sweet ass on that.

Now to be clear, in case there might be some question, when I mentioned that God created the earth, I was absolutely referrin' to the one and only God of the holiest of Holy Bibles, father of Jesus Christ almighty, and the maker of Adam, the first man. I hate to break it to a lotta folks thinkin' the gospels are just a bunch of bullshit and lies, but you all better get right with Christ and quick or yer gonna fry yer ass off in Hell for the rest of eternity. You mark my words here and now. I know. First hand, I know. I met the Devil twice in my life and I saw God once. Saw him raise the dead, if you can believe that. Spoke to him too. And the goddamned Devil, he done ran off with my best good buddy Priscilla, and I ain't seen her, or him, since.

I do realize up to this point that most of y'all done likely written me off as some kind of Bible thumpin' asshole or a damn lunatic, maybe even some kinda stone drunk Catholic car salesman. Hell, I don't know. Half of y'all probably think I'm just queer and lonely with too much time and spare ink on my hands. Well, I'll go ahead and let ye in on a little secret. I, Joseph Henry Smith, do not give a good goddamn what anybody other than my own sweet momma thinks of me and she's been dead longer than my first two coon hounds, rest their souls. So think of me what you will. Believe what I'm tellin' ya or not. I couldn't give a shit. It comes down to this. Either listen or suffer. The choice is yours. But my advice is you stick around for the entirety of this here story 'fore you make any hasty or…precarious decisions.

Now, like I said, God did indeed create the earth, and shortly thereafter he also created the heavens. He created the earth as, what I once heard the Devil refer to, *a simple gesture of power*. That's what he said alright. A simple gesture of power. And he said God created the heavens to hide woefully above the stalkin' shadow of his creation, the bastard children of the holy Prometheus. He said God gave us fire to watch us burn. And for no other reason. Them is the Devil's words, not mine, mind you, and I ain't even sure I believe 'em, but they always stuck in my brain, and I carried 'em with me most my life.

But anyhow.

Ya see, God never got to read the work of Mary Shelley, at

least not before he started tryin' his hand at creatin' people. He obviously hadn't created Miss Shelley yet, so it stands to reason that he couldn't have possibly read her gloriously hauntin' tale of creation and damnation if she had yet to write it. But had God read about the good doctor and his monstrous work, ahead of time, there is no way the irony of God's own undertakin' could have slipped past even him. And if yer thinkin', Joseph what in thee hell do you know about Mary Shelly, let me go right ahead and tell ya. Partner, I have read a few books in my day and son of a bitchin' *Frankenstein* was one of 'em. Now granted, I didn't know every single word I came across, but my momma kept a copy of Webster's on a shelf in the hall when I was growin' up, and now I keep my own copy on that same shelf in that same hall, if you catch my drift.

I ain't no fool is the point. Not even close. And the Bible ain't the only book I ever read. Matter of fact, it ain't the best book I ever read neither, not by a long shot. *The Blood Meridian, Rant, Still Life With Woodpecker, Carrie, Love in The Time of Cholera,* they was all better. But that should come as no surprise though. God is the architect of existence, not the author. And the real majesty of his creation is found in mountains and streams, and puppies, and children, and good music—shit like that. Not in the pages of a book. A man can learn very little 'bout God by way of readin'. If he wants to learn more than a thing or two, he's gotta take a look around. Spread his wings, ya know? Fly a little.

But I'm gettin' off track all to hell. I'll tell ye all about the true nature of reality later. I just wanted to start at the beginnin' for clarity's sake. Why God created all this ain't the point right now, and neither is Frankenstein. The point at hand is creation itself.

So here's how it went down. The way the Devil put it anyhow.

God created a man and a woman. Adam and Eden. Not Eve. Eden. It was her garden everybody talks about. Eve came later.

But anyhow, God created 'em both, Adam and Eden, in his very own image, the result of splittin' his masculine and feminine counterparts, or some such madness. But Adam, as a result of his superior physical strength, all too often took dominion over Eden, and over time this disparity grew to be less and less acceptable to her, particularly in matters concernin' coitus and cunnilingus.

Now even here I had to stop him—the Devil, I mean. I stopped him and I says, What in the hell is coitus and cunnilingus? And you know after he told me what those words meant, I turned red as a bucket of blood in the sunshine. Christ, I didn't know. I hadn't done a whole lot of readin' up to that point in my life. I was just a kid.

Anyhow, apparently Eden, *rather boldly*, again them's the Devil's words not mine, brought up to Adam that she would no longer accept the lack of reciprocation of snatch lickin', my words not the Devil's, and from time to time she wanted to be on top so she herself could at least occasionally have the chance to get hers, if ya know what I mean. The Devil said that apparently there was a knee-length list of other complaints that Eden took that moment to voice, but her sexual dissatisfaction was an unrivaled precedent in the long list of grievances, and was the focus of her tirade, but after all was said and done, Adam, ever the archetypal man, would not be moved. The Devil said Adam just shook his head and told her no. Then he pushed Eden down in the tall grass and forced himself on her.

I suppose this is a good time to pull back on the reins a little, cause I know what yer thinkin'. Yer thinkin', Why, Joseph, what in the actual fuck are you doin' makin' conversation with the Devil? And what in the hell are you carryin' on about? The Bible don't mention a damn thing about any of this here Eden business. Well, I'm here to tell ye, I've learned a few things about God over the years, and the Bible don't mention quite a few of 'em. And the business concernin' Eden is one. Matter of fact as that. Hell, there's a whole heap of misconceptions what's revealin' would shatter the minds of most folks. The actual truth about God would send folks jumpin' off the side of fuckin' bridges . Yes indeed it would.

Oh sure, there is quite the difference between the Bible and the truth, between what folks believe about God and the actual nature of God. But hey, what the hell can we expect? There are bound to be a few misunderstandin's. What with all the different translations and what have you. All the different kings and popes and saints and all, just pickin' the passages they was keen on, and burnin' the rest. Well, it's a damn wonder how even a single sentence of truth could have survived until now. Oh, but yes indeedy many have. And what's left written down ain't so far off as it won't lead you to the pearly gates if'n you foller it, but I am here to tell you, sure as shit, there are quite a few discrepancies between what is and what is written down.

But I reckon that'll all get made clear as the story unfolds. Come to think of it, I reckon this will all make more sense if we just start from the beginnin' of the story, rather than the beginnin' of time. You see, this story don't start when I was born. It don't start with me at all, and it sure don't start with God. As a matter of fact, this story starts how all good stories start. It starts with a young girl calmly wipin' blood from her face.

———◆———

—◆—

Chapter ONE

G.O.D.

She was sitting on her front porch dabbing blood from her nose and cheek with an old wet rag, and then ringing it out in a tin bucket at her feet. When she pulled the rag from the bucket, tainted water spilled over the sides and was beginning to gather in a muddy red puddle under the porch. Somewhere, birds were singing, but they were too far away for her to hear them. She closed her eyes to fight back tears. A tremor ran the length of her spine. It was Sunday morning.

She licked away the blood on her lip, prodding the wound with her tongue. Eyes still closed, she reached in her mouth and wiggled a tooth. She exhaled. Then she spit blood on to the rotten floor boards, and watched it for a while.

Sadly, this was not the first time her father hit her. In fact, he hit her fairly often. Usually with his hands, or a belt, sometimes a paddle, but usually it was his hands. He liked to use them when he could. Her father had big hands, big hard hands, scarred hands, hands that shoveled coal for ten years, hands that served in the United States Army, hands that turned wrenches, hands that chopped firewood, hands calloused and blistered and sliced from years of toil, and when his temper turned, those hands became fists, fists that beat men into unidentifiable gore, that shattered mirrors, left holes in walls, and that broke the cheek bones, bruised the bodies, and brought forth the blood of those closest to him with terrifying regularity.

At night her father would sit in his favorite chair, drinking beer, smoking, and listening to local country music on the radio. During commercial breaks, he would admire his scars. Slowly turning his hands, he would study the disfigurements from different angles and think about all the men he'd beat and all the hard work he'd done to acquire them. His only source of pride or satisfaction, he cherished the scars and all that they represented.

When it came down to it, Everett Carpenter adored his hands. His daughter feared them. His wife would have hacked them off with a hatchet if she'd had even the slightest confidence that she could succeed in the act. Never mind the notion that she alone would somehow be able to provide food and shelter for herself and her children. But either she never possessed such confidence or if she had, it was beaten out of her long ago, and any hope of escape, if it were to ever happen, had come and gone, or been taken.

And so it was written, mother and child would have to endure.

A faint breeze blew, and the girl opened her eyes. She looked at the blood on her hands, and at the bucket and the rag. Then she looked up at the sky. She thought for a moment about God, and if God had a plan for her. She wondered if God really loved her like all the old folks at church said he did. It sure as hell didn't seem like it. Maybe he was too busy. Or maybe he forgot about her. She hoped that wasn't true, but she couldn't be sure. She wasn't angry with God though. Just disappointed.

Like God's light, the sun rarely shone where she lived. Most days found the sky in shades of ash and heavy with moisture, and this day was no different. It rained often, but between the coal dust and the mountains, the sun could hardly cast a shadow even if the clouds were to part permanently. And tucked back into a hollow the way her father's house was, she felt the warmth of sunshine less often than most. This deficiency showed in the paleness of her skin and in the brittleness of her hair.

The faint breeze subsided and the girl's gaze fell away from the sky. She would find no comfort up there today. No warmth either.

At length, she stood. A rotten floor board squeaked. She collected the bucket and rag, and stepped down off the porch. There was pain in her hip now and her cheek still bore a sharp ache. There would surely be bruises.

She emptied the bucket in a patch of weeds on the side of the house, and used water from the well to rinse her blood from the rag. She put the rag in the bucket and hung it on a nail on the side of her father's shed. She did this all very carefully. Her father had no patience for his things not being where they belonged. If he had found the bucket laying in the yard, instead of on the nail where he'd left it, he would have likely waited until she returned from church and hit her with the bucket. He'd done that once before.

Even though only a moment had passed since she hung the bucket up, after a few steps, unsure of herself, she looked back to be certain that it was indeed on the nail where she had just left it. She let out an uneasy breath. The bucket hung in place.

She turned back toward the house as several coal trucks passed by, and she watched them lumber down the road until they were out of sight. The mine never stopped digging, not even on Christmas. The trucks would barrel up and down the road in front of her house, and the only thing that ever stopped them was a heavy snow. They would come in empty and leave full. Truck after truck. Each outbound truck trailed by a thick billow of coal dust rising up from its bed. Day and night.

The coal dust would hang thick in the air and then settle harshly on every possible surface. Things were black to the touch. She and her mother couldn't even consider wearing white dresses, and neither could any of the other women at church either. "Weren't no point," the women at church would say. "It would just be black by the end of the service."

And so, the discoloration caused by the mine was suffered by all. Coal dust covered everything. From the dishes in the kitchen to the clothes on the line, nothing was safe. Nothing was clean. Not even the space between things. The air itself was so thick with coal dust that lungs couldn't filter it, and the insides of the people living in Clockmaker, West Virginia were turning as black as the hands of the men who mined.

She sat back down on the porch. All was silent inside the house. Another pack of trucks rolled by with empty loads. She listened close over the roar of the engines and droning jake-brakes, and still she heard nothing from inside. The blood around her nose and eye, and the little bit that had leaked from her ear canal, had crusted over. She picked at it a little. Her head throbbed. She could smell copper now, in addition to the smells of burnt wood and engine exhaust to which she was normally accustomed. She pulled up her shirt and examined her hip. It was purple and yellow. She wondered where the bruise had come from. She couldn't possibly have known, however, because the bruise was created when her father kicked her, and that was after he had knocked her unconscious.

She considered that her father's paddle had possibly created the bruise, but quickly dismissed the thought upon recollecting that the paddle had been in the house at the time. He would never walk that far when he could bludgeon her with any object in arm's length. Though it would have made sense if he had used the paddle because the marks that it normally left were indistinguishable from the ones she now wore.

Her father was fond of the paddle and he seemed to relish in wielding it, despite being horrifyingly inaccurate. His blind rage often sullied his aim, needless to say, and there were many times when swinging for her backside, he would miss his mark and hit maybe her hip or perhaps her head. The paddle, like the bucket, like an odd many of her father's things, hung on a nail, but it hung in the house, behind the door that led to the basement, where it was more convenient to access. The paddle was thick and shaped like a small oar. It was made out of birch, and it had holes drilled through it to decrease wind resistance. It was painted red, and it had two names carved into the handle. One of the names was hers. You could barely make out either name by then however. They had all but worn away from use.

Once, piss-drunk and furious, her father had missed with the paddle and grazed her chin. This 'mistake' sent three of her teeth scattering across the kitchen. Lucky for her, they were baby teeth. Two years later, new ones grew back in their place. She never could talk the same though. Her jaw had fractured and healed crooked. A doctor could have set it to mend properly, but she wasn't taken to see one. Her father wouldn't allow it. That's what her mother told her, and it was the truth. So that night, while her parents slept, she crept from her bed, and in the darkness, on her hands and knees, she located each of her three scattered teeth. She didn't expect the roots to still be attached to them. The sight turned her stomach. In the stillness, she moved to the far wall and behind the wood burning stove, she removed a loose floor board and dropped the teeth into the place that she kept the few things she didn't want her father to destroy.

She thought she would maybe try to put the teeth back in later—when her father wasn't around. No one had ever told her she would grow new ones, and nothing she personally intuited granted her insight into this biological oddity either. She was but a child then. How was she supposed to know that a person couldn't just put teeth back in? No one ever told her. She fumbled with this question as she ever so gently massaged the darkening bruises on her thigh, and she felt disgusted with herself. Child or not, she shouldn't have been so stupid. *Of course you can't just stick yer teeth back in.* That's what her father would have said if he had known about it. *Little girl, you must be goddamn stupid.* In her mind, she could hear him saying it. He may as well have been standing right beside her.

It wasn't long after the baby teeth incident, when her father was away, that she knelt down behind his shed and realized the hard way that one cannot simply reinsert their teeth after they've come out. Not without severe anguish anyway. At the time, she thought there still might be a chance if she could stand the pain, but the nerves were too raw, and the pain too extreme. So she put the teeth back under the floor behind the stove and that is where they stayed.

Something felt wrong to her about throwing them away. Even as a child, she felt like maybe she would be throwing away pieces of herself. Vital pieces. Pieces that, once lost, could never be re-covered. So she kept them. In a jar, under the floor of her father's house, she kept the three teeth, for reasons perhaps only a child could understand or perhaps in preparation for some strange rainy day.

After losing her teeth, her head hung in her father's presence. On instinct, she maintained distance, spoke softly, and never met his eyes. And since that day, she had been particularly careful to never spill milk on his sofa again. In fact, she didn't go anywhere near it. She sat on the floor by the wall or at the kitchen table whether she was in possession of liquid or not. Never the sofa. Sure, most of this behavior was based on instinct, but the rest was an absolute certainty that if he knocked out the teeth she now had, they would not be growing back.

She heard a door slam inside the house and it made her shudder. After a moment, she heard the radio come on in the living room. Hank Williams carried a melody out the open window. It was her father. She could picture him sitting in his chair. Ash dangling from his cigarette. Bottle of beer resting firmly between his legs. Occasionally picking at his teeth or biting coal from under his finger nails, she could never tell which. Eyes dead and cold. Staring hard at the wall. She could picture his eyes most of all. They were ugly eyes, small and glassy. Menacing. The iris exploded off the pupil in a chilling baby blue. Their mere visualization made her skin crawl, and she forced from her mind such wretched a thought and replaced it with prayer. "Lord, watch over me," she whispered. "Lord, watch over me and keep me safe." She whispered so quietly that even God couldn't hear. Then she tasted blood in the back of her throat and she spit it out.

Thinking of her father made her think of her mother. She would most likely be in the bathroom putting on makeup. She couldn't leave the house without it. It always took longer if she had to cover bruises, but bruises or not, she didn't set foot on her own front porch without spending a few minutes in front of the mirror first. Ain't no one outside her immediate family ever seen her real face. That's what her father once said, anyway. He also said, If the Lord almighty woulda known people were gonna spend so much time worshippin' mirrors, he never woulda created 'em. He said mirrors were a sin. Makeup too. But he allowed his wife to have them both so that the rest of world wouldn't know how wicked of a man he was.

More than anything in the whole wide world, despite all of the woman's shortcomings and bad decisions, she loved her mother. On mornings when her father was working, she liked nothing more than watching her mother apply her makeup. Her father wouldn't allow her to watch if he was around, makeup being a sin and all. She would pull the seat down on the toilet and sit quietly as her mother gazed long into the mirror, the smell of nail polish and hair spray in the air. Shading and softening and defining, she would watch her mother as her mother gazed, hands in constant deliberate motion. Watching her transformation in front of the bathroom sink, a bare thirty-watt bulb shining down, she would sit in a state of perpetual awe and adoration at her mother's unequivocal beauty and grace. Oh, how she adored her mother. It warmed her heart just thinking of her, and she longed for the not-so-far-off day when she too would be old enough to darken her eyes in front of the bathroom mirror.

She didn't necessarily understand this desire to change, to evolve, but she did feel it. It was nothing new to her, this feeling and not understanding. It was something she had been noticing more and more as she grew older, but it had always been there. She didn't quite understand why her father disapproved of makeup so vehemently, and she didn't understand why God so rarely answered her prayers, but she was beginning to suspect that there were far deeper meanings behind the things that she didn't understand, and that life may very well be just as confusing for her parents as it was for her.

For all their experience and age, she sensed they were lost, her parents. She could somehow feel it. There was something else going on, something she could not quite yet wrap her mind around, but that nonetheless arose in her as certain as a fever. There was something more to living, to being alive, and sitting there on her father's porch, with bits of dry blood flaking off her face, she realized for the first time in her fifteen long years on earth that if she was going to figure out what that something was, she was going to have to do it alone. The hair on the back of her arms stood up.

Another pack of coal trucks was about to pass, but they were still around the bend. She could always hear them before she could see them. They were unnervingly loud. The engines would roar and the beds of the trucks would slam against their frames as their drivers failed to navigate potholes and wash outs. Between the shifting loads, stuttering brakes, and roaring engines, a thought could hardly be heard. Or so she thought. As the trucks grew closer, she covered her ears. Her head still throbbed, and the sound made it worse.

Earlier that morning, the dog had gotten loose. It was her father's dog. His name was Shit Eater. Her father named him that, and only her father called him that. He was a filthy and mean dog, and her father left him chained to a railroad stake under a tree in the backyard so that he would have something to starve and occasionally sink a boot into. That's the way it seemed to her, anyway.

Once she saw her father hit Shit Eater with a rusty piece of rebar so hard that the dog went permanently deaf in both ears and vomited blood for a week and a half. He would have died too, but for a month straight, whenever her father wasn't around, she fed the poor animal whatever scraps she could save from her own meals, gave him plenty of water, and in time, when the animal finally allowed it, she held him and petted him, and scratched hard behind his ears the way he liked it. And through these selfless acts of courage and love, the poor animal's life was spared, for without the girl he would have surely perished at the hands of a far lesser creature.

Shit Eater was mean as they come. The few people who shared that small expanse of hollow with the Carpenter family would have likely said he was vicious and needed to be put down, and they were likely right, but the hound had come to know love, and vicious though it may be, since that day, that dog wouldn't harm even a single hair on Everett Carpenter's daughter's head. By means of tenderness and compassion, Shit Eater had quietly turned on his master and found a new allegiance in his master's offspring, an allegiance which Everett Carpenter would one day find out about the hard way. The day Shit Eater broke his chain.

She pulled her hands from her ears when the trucks were in the distance. She didn't watch them disappear this time. She studied the blood under her nails, and thought of Lucky—she couldn't refer to or even think of the dog as Shit Eater. He was far too wise an animal to be called something so vulgar. So as she cradled him those many years ago, as she nursed him back to life, she had privately renamed the dog Lucky. For no particular reason other than the name came to her when she put her mind to it. And now, sitting on her father's porch, she wondered where Lucky was. He'd been gone at least an hour, if not more.

She hoped he was okay. More than anything, she hoped. And indeed she prayed, but hope and prayer were no match for the sudden dread that overcame her when her mind suddenly drifted to the reason that Lucky had broken free, and that she had dried blood under her finger nails.

When she woke up earlier that morning, she could hear the chainsaw running behind the house. A single gnarled limb of the old crabapple tree had grown out of control and been threatening to come through the roof of Everett Carpenter's home for some time now. He was sure the next good storm would bring it crashing into his bathroom, probably while he was trying to take a shit, and he would be goddamned if that was going to happen, or so he told his wife before he went out to his shed and began greasing the chain on his saw.

By the time his daughter was waking up, Everett had almost finished with the tree and his wife was frying bacon to go with biscuits. The sweet smell of fried pork washed over her as she came into the kitchen and she sat down eagerly at the table. She still had bits of crust in her eye and she dug at them while her mother poured her a glass of milk.

"Mornin', Momma," she said.

"Mornin', sugar," said her mother. "Finish up 'at plate quick, then get on out back. Yer daddy wants you to help him. He's in a mood."

"Yes mam," she said.

She finished the meager portion quickly, as her mother asked, except for one small piece of bacon which she stuffed into her pocket to save for Lucky. That old dog loved bacon almost as much as her. Then she put on her boots and hastened outside. Her father would be waiting, she was sure.

As she came down off the porch and made to round the house, she heard the chainsaw engine die away, and for a second she paused. Now she could hear her heart beating. In fact, that was all she could hear. The birds were still too far away. *Shit*, she thought. *Here we go*.

By the time she made it to the back of the house, her father was leaning against a stack of used tires smoking a cigarette and surveying his work. He wore a look of smug satisfaction. *Pride's a sin*, she thought, defiantly, but what she said was, "Mornin', Daddy."

"Pick 'ese chunks of wood up and throw 'em in the burn pile," he replied. "Stack the big ones against the shed."

"Yes sir," she said. "Momma says yer plate's in the oven when yer ready for it." He'd been drinking. She could see it in his eyes.

"Took her fuckin' long enough," he said. Then he flicked his cigarette into the grass. "Get to pickin' up 'at wood. Move what ye can. I'll worry 'bout the heavy 'uns." He hadn't looked at her even once. It was like he was telling the apple tree what to do.

Lucky the dog had spent the morning laying at the base of the tree in the shade, nervously watching his former master prune, but the instant that she came into the backyard, the dog was on his feet. And when she wandered close enough, in collection of wood, he sauntered over to her for his usual affection. Now by her side, something like happiness could be seen in the old dog's eyes. She gave him a firm series of pats on the head, and he responded by letting out the softest whine of elation.

Apparently, this faint noise, however pleasant, did not register well with her father. Apparently, it didn't register well at all, because, out of nowhere, he snuck up quick from behind, brushed her aside, and sent a size thirteen steel toe boot sailing into the side of Lucky's head.

Lucky did not see the attack coming. The blow sent the dog onto his side with a yelp, and before either the dog or the girl had a chance to process the violence, Everett had turned his attention to his daughter. She couldn't breathe. His eyes were fixed on her. She could feel his cruel stare, drunken with rage, burning into her and she dared not meet it. She would rather have had a thousand vultures peck out her eyes, a little at a time, than spend even a moment staring into his glittering baby blues. So she kept her head down, gritted her teeth, and waited for the worst.

But the worst never came. Instead, there was a voice. It said, "Go get Old Red."

He meant the paddle. She knew Old Red too well, and her heart sank at its mention. But she didn't move. She only stared at her boots. She felt like a child.

Louder this time, and savoring every word, he said, "Girl,

if'n you don't get yer little ass up in the house and get th—" He paused mid-threat. His eyes lowered to the ground at his feet, and his voice went flat. "Never mind Old Red," he said, "I got a switch right here."

Everett bent at the waist and snapped off a small but sure limb from a piece of fallen timber. His daughter stood frozen and trembling, staring at her feet. He grabbed her by the back of the arm with one iron hand, forcing her to her knees, and with the other hand, he raised the switch. But instead of bringing the stick down against her as intended, Lucky leapt up from near death, and with his rotten and decaying fangs, he snatched the switch and half of the hand that held it.

Everett fell to the ground screaming. Blood sprayed, though he tried desperately and frantically to contain it. He curled into a ball with his wound at the center, and with his good hand, he attempted to squeeze off the flow, but warm fluid still gushed from the wound. "Fuuuck," he screamed. "Fuuuck. Ahhhh! Fuck. Fuck." He writhed and kicked, and spat profanities and cursed God and his dog and his daughter. "Whore, fuck, fuckin' mutt, God cunt fuck. Ahhhhh!"

But at long last, his will to live overcame his agonizing pain, and the solution to his problem became clear. Still laying in the dirt, he quickly reached in his back pocket and removed the handkerchief that he used to blow his nose, and with some struggle, he managed to get it tied around his mutilated hand, cutting off the flow of blood. He cried out when he cinched the knot tight, and he stared at the wound for a while. He laid there on his side and stared at it. The dog had taken three fingers and most of his palm. All that was left was his thumb and pointer. He cursed again, mostly to himself. Then he rolled over in search of his daughter.

As soon as Everett hit the ground, she'd run to Lucky, and

now she sat under the tree hugging the dog and watching her
father, transfixed by the horror that was surely to come. A piece
of her hoped he would lay there and die, that he would bleed
out, and it would be over. Which was a terrible thought to have
about her own father, but she didn't have time to feel bad about it
because Everett had rolled over, and he was now getting up, and
any thought of repentance was washed away by the pain she saw
in her soon-to-be future.

'Seasons in the Abyss' by Slayer plays

He meant to kill her, and he meant to kill Lucky. She could
see it in his eyes. They were crazed. Stark raving mad. Baby blue
gone black. He started to reach for a log, but when he did, Lucky
began to growl and snarl. Everett paused and looked at the dog.
"Don't like sticks, do ye," he said. He nodded his head, knowingly, and looked down at his mangled hand. For a split second,
she thought he might cry. Instead, he turned, took a step, bent,
and picked up his saw.

Standing there in front of his young daughter and supposed
best friend, he pulled the chainsaw up to his waist with his good
hand, and with a snarl of his own, said, "Time to fuckin' die." Then
with the remaining fingers of his other hand, partially wrapped in
his snot rag and still dripping blood, Everett pulled hard on the
starter rope and the saw came alive.

When she saw him move forward, saw buzzing, she panicked, and in her panic, she had forgotten one crucial detail—the
chain that Lucky was wearing around his neck was fastened, on
the other end, to a three foot long iron stake that had been driven
deep into the ground. Her mind was so focused on keeping the
dog from harm that, without any thought of the chain, she looked
directly at Lucky and pointed at the forest, and though the animal

TWO ZERO

could not hear, when she shouted run, Lucky burst off in the direction she was aiming.

But something unexpected happened. When Lucky got to the end of his chain, instead of being violently jerked on to his back with a strangled yelp, his momentum sent two shattered quarter-inch steel links sailing into the air, and by the time they hit the ground, Lucky had disappeared into the tree line.

She watched the dog until he was nearly out of sight, and she felt some relief, but before she had a chance to consider her own safety, her father brought the chainsaw down on her head, engine first, and she went out like a light.

When she woke up, she was still laying in the dirt beside the tree, like an apple. She carefully got herself to her feet and brushed the dust and grass from her clothes. She touched her face and her curiosity left blood on her hand. She started to cry. But only briefly. She never allowed for much self-pity.

And so, with tears still in her eyes, she made her way to her father's shed and found a tin bucket and an old rag. She filled the bucket with water, then she sat down on her front porch, and calm as she could be, started wiping away the blood that covered nearly every inch of her face.

Patsy Cline took over for Hank Williams as she sat there staring at her finger nails. 'Crazy' was the name of the song. The breeze that blew earlier returned and it cooled her cheeks. Another truck rolled by. This time the driver of the truck looked up at her and waved. She returned a faint gesture. Then the truck was gone.

She let out a long, lonely sigh. Then she thought of something, and began digging around in her pocket. At the bottom, she found the piece of bacon. She gathered it into her hand and clutched it but did not withdraw it. When she did this, a strong sense of well-being came over her and she closed her eyes to embrace it. She tried to picture Lucky, and that last look he gave her, but the image that emerged from the blackness of her own mind was not that of her beloved and gentle dog, but the head of a disgusting and vile goat. Bright and vibrant. Cartoonish and neon. Its eyes were spirals, and its horns twisted on forever into the depths of her inner workings. Giggling. Spiraling. Bleating. The goat licked its snout and beckoned to her.

Utterly shocked by what she envisioned, her eyes shot open. A rare strain of terror coursed through her bones. Pure terror, she was all too familiar with, but this terror was not pure. It was mingled with something. Something that seemed inseparable from its host, something that she could not quite put her finger on, something powerful, something… seductive. It was a feeling unlike any she had ever felt before. A feeling that seemed to echo solely from her loins, and give rise to the strange sensation that her entire body had been dipped in warm gooey caramel and that somewhere between her legs now existed whipped cream and a cherry.

A violent chill went up her spine. This new feeling that surrounded her, that overcame her so completely, was beyond tantalizing. It was all-encompassing. It was bone-rattling. From far beyond the furthest birds, a chilling and beautiful song began calling from within her, and she unexpectedly squealed aloud, in response. Deep down inside of her… something was happening.

Confused and shaken, she tried to stand in an attempt to collect herself, but her mind, seemingly against her will, turned to the goat once more and without her even being aware that she had let go of the bacon in her pocket, she fell back on to the chair and both of her hands began drifting between her legs. Within moments, the vision of the goat enveloped her completely. Her eyes, open or closed, it made no difference. There existed only the goat. The goat. The goat. The goat. In all directions, further and beyond. Its horns twirling and bending into fractals, its eyes multiplying and spinning, its teeth rotten and jagged, there was only the goat.

A master and slave to her own pleasures, her hands pressed on and she writhed against them. The goat's Fibonaccian eyes, yellow and sickly, burned in her vision, deeper and deeper, and she gasped hard for air, but it was with this gasp that she became completely untethered from reality, succumbing to the bestial phantasm completely. So much so that she could now feel the warmth and smell the stench of its breath. She could feel its heart beating, and she could feel the cold blood running through its veins. It repulsed her. And for her repulsion, her body spasmed intensely, then went stiff with confused delight.

And just like that, it was over. The goat had vanished. It was nowhere to be found, eyes open or closed. She had a sudden feeling of being watched and she looked all about her. She saw no one, and she sunk in the chair. Her legs were quivering and twitching. Her knees were weak. She looked down at her lap and realized she was going to need the rag again. Just not for blood.

Then she heard her mother call from inside the house. She said, "Priscilla, sweetheart, get in here and get ready for church."

'Stop the Wedding' by Etta James plays

C**HAPTER** two

I was into whips and things, she was into pain.
And I would beat her black and blue when she called me names.
I chained her to the basement wall where she went insane.
'Cause I was into whips and things, and she was into pain.

—*David Allen Coe*

A harsh cold wind swept in from the east like a judge, making it ever so difficult to light a cigarette. The morning sun had vanished behind the clouds and the day had gone grey. There would be rain before noon.

Priscilla and her mother had walked the nearly two mile stretch of dirt road that led to the Mount Zion Methodist Church without speaking a word, and now, just in sight of the old white shack, she watched her mother struggle and curse as she desperately attempted to get a cigarette lit. She had been drinking. No amount of wind or perfume could cover the smell.

Knelt down beside a rusty livestock gate, burnt matches strewn about her feet, her mother cursed everybody from God to Abraham. She even cursed her long dead Aunt Charlotte whom she claimed to love dearly, but who also turned her on to the foul, finger-staining habit to begin with, and Priscilla had a sneaking suspicion that somewhere under her mother's breath, her own name was being dragged through the same mud as God's and her Great Aunt's.

Priscilla shook her head a little as she watched. She felt pity for her mother. She would never get the thing burning with the wind blowing the way it was. She was not a smart woman. Even at Priscilla's ripening young age, this fact was becoming all too clear. She knew for sure that her mother didn't know how to read or cipher, and standing there in the road watching her wrestle with the matches, Priscilla was reasonably sure that she didn't know how the wind worked either. Priscilla shook her head again and sighed, then she made her way to where her poor mother crouched.

Standing over her, Priscilla said, "Let me help you, Momma."

Without the slightest acknowledgment, her mother struck another match between her knees and another fatal gust instantly extinguished the flame, blackening the stick's end. Her mother glared at the burnt match, then she took a deep breath and closed her eyes, defeated. Without opening her eyes, she handed the box of matches up to Priscilla. She pulled the cigarette from her lips and she handed that up too.

"Make yer momma proud," she said. And after a few moments, for the first time that day, she opened her eyes and actually looked at her daughter.

Priscilla, without responding or the slightest hesitation, stuck the cigarette between her lips, and let the shawl loose from around her neck. Pulling the breast of her Sunday dress away, she ducked her head inside through its neck, cigarette and all. Then, with an equal lack of hesitation, she hiked her dress to her waist and brought the box of matches in through the dress's bottom. Effortless as that. Head and hands inside the dress, she retrieved a match from the box and struck it. Uninhibited by the breeze, the match stick roared within the confines of her bosom. Careful not to let the fire get too close to her dress or her skin, she steadily brought the flame to the end of the cigarette and sucked hard.

◆

Lavinia (pronounced luh-ven-ee-uh) watched her daughter carefully as she performed this deed, and when, all of a sudden, Priscilla's head reappeared on top of her shoulders in a cloud of smoke, lit cigarette dangling from her lips, Lavinia wondered for a brief instant if perhaps she had mistaken an apparently hidden set of skills for outright magic. If Priscilla had followed up that feat of prestidigitation by pulling a fluffy white rabbit from under her dress, instead of the nearly empty box of matches, she would have regarded her with no less astonishment.

Crouched there by the gate, looking up with amazement and pride at her daughter, Lavinia Anne Carpenter did something she didn't do very often: she smiled. Years of poor oral hygiene had left her teeth a wreck and when they started falling out, she stopped smiling nearly altogether. The inside of her mouth was the most white trash thing about her, at least that's what her husband would say. *Seen cleaner teeth on a nigger*, he would say. On odd occasions when she couldn't help but laugh aloud, she covered her open mouth with her hand while she struggled to close it.

The rare glimmer of a smile and the illusion of magic were, however, quickly dashed away. With the parting of the cigarette smoke came the revealing of the yellow and green bruise that had been forming and darkening on Priscilla's face since early that morning. A light yellow hue covered her entire forehead and it deepened to green as it neared her hair line. There were bits of dry blood still visible on her scalp. Lavinia gave the faintest whimper at this revelation and struggled to swallow. There was no fluffy white rabbit. No hidden aces, nor levers. No trap doors. No astonishment. No surprise. No illusion. Lavinia had been a fool, and a blind fool at that. But now, crouched in the dirt off the side of rural route eight with tears welling up in her eyes, the truth of the matter became painfully clear, and she spoke it in a barely audible whisper. "Everett." The word was a mouth full of broken glass.

She hadn't actually taken notice of Priscilla all day, or maybe it had been days. She couldn't remember, and that pained her. Years of mental anguish and vodka had left her manic, and at times completely self-absorbed, but by the color of the bruising on her daughter's face, she could tell the wound was fresh. *That son of a bitch*, she thought. *That son of a mother fuckin' bitch, I should'a known when he came whistlin' into the house this mornin'. Whistlin' like he won the big bucks. The sick bastard. Only thing makes him happy is someone else's mis'ry. But oh my sweet God. What kind of goddamn mother am I? I shoulda noticed. I shoulda did somethin'. I shoulda…*

Then she thought about killing Everett. She thought about cutting his throat, in his sleep nonetheless. She thought about using his own hunting knife. She thought about faking sorrow, and—. Her murderous thoughts were interrupted by the sight of her daughter slowly coming back into focus. At first she thought Priscilla was attempting to hug her. Both of her arms were extended as such. But upon further scrutiny, and the blinking away of tears, it became evident that Priscilla was not reaching down to embrace her, but to return the box of matches in her left hand and the burning cigarette in her right.

"Here ya go, Momma. You alright?"

Lavinia carefully accepted the cigarette and the box, and in a soft voice said, "I'm just fine, sweetheart. Must be somethin' stickin' in my eye." She gave Priscilla a small sad smile, then she tucked the box into her purse and stood up. She pulled long and hard on the cigarette then dropped it on the ground. "Come here," she said, exhaling smoke, "let Momma take a look at you."

Priscilla moved closer and Lavinia began to inspect her head for damage. "How's yer head feel?"

"It hurts a little."

"Does it hurt when I touch here?"

"Yes mam. I tried to clean it up best I could."

Lavinia parted her hair where the dry blood was caked. "Oh Jesus Christ on the cross."

"What is it, Momma?"

Her mother sighed. "He got you pretty good. Might need sutures. You feelin' dizzy at all, baby?"

"No mam."

She tilted back Priscilla's head to inspect her eyes. "Seein' any spots?"

"No mam."

Lavinia nodded her head in consideration. The next question, she hesitated to ask. She already knew the icy truth, but she had to be certain. Every single part of her unconscious being yearned for an answer that would soften her step in this world, an answer that would renew some faith in what she had long deemed a cruel and vicious existence, but the part of her that had been present and awake for the last thirty-four years knew damn well better, and simply needed to hear the cold hard facts. That part of her maintained a direct and solid link to mankind's ancient desire to not only confirm but to bring shape to its own worst suspicions, to solidify the existence of things most hideous and dark that walk formless upon the earth, to know what lies motionless within the hole. And so she asked the question.

"Priscilla honey, yer daddy, he did this, didn't he?" She could hardly choke out the words. She always blamed herself when Everett hurt Priscilla, and rightfully so, she often decided. The choir of angels mourning over Christ's crucifixion couldn't have felt more shame and responsibility.

Priscilla's answer came slow, and without sound. She only nodded.

Lavinia pulled her daughter close and gently squeezed her

into her womb. Her motherly mind labored to thoughts of her husband and their life together. She considered where it had all gone wrong, or if it had always been wrong and she just hadn't seen it for what it was. She supposed in the very beginning, things had been different. Her father had liked Everett well enough, and though now it pained her to admit, she had liked Everett too. But her mother had always known. From the first time her mother met Everett, she hated him.

Everett had moved down from Ohio with some money his father left to him and after it ran out, he was forced to work in the mine. That's when he started with the bottle. He loathed the mine, and he took it out on his family on a daily and sometimes nightly basis, depending on what shift he was working. Most of the time, retribution was dealt by his boot heal or the back of his hand, but on occasion, when the notion took him, he would turn insanely violent.

He had almost killed Lavinia a number of times, but rarely did he act so hostile when dealing with Priscilla. Though there was the time when he had knocked out Priscilla's teeth with Old Red when she was a toddler, and the time he tried to drown her for not draining the tub. If Lavinia had not intervened, Everett would have left her floating face down in dirty bath water, she was certain of it.

Then she remembered the time Everett lost Priscilla in a game of five card draw, deuces wild, when Priscilla was only a few months old. And with that thought, Lavinia squeezed Priscilla a little tighter, careful not to aggravate the wound on her daughter's tender, fragile head. Lavinia was a fool. She was a fool and she knew it.

Everett had always been an evil bastard. The only thing different in the beginning was how blind she was to recognize the beast of a man that he would always be.

THREE ZERO

After some time, Lavinia looked down at her daughter, meeting her face to face. She gathered both of Priscilla's hands into her own and kissed them, then she looked her hard in the eyes, and said, "I wanna tell you somethin', Priscilla."

Priscilla nodded, but did not speak.

FLASHBACK

Lavinia met Everett when she was fourteen years old. Already close to fully blossomed, Lavinia was devastatingly beautiful, and was in possession of curves so dangerous that they bent the minds of the men who dared to follow them. Most men gazed along these curves tightly, winding along her thighs, edging ever closer to the ditch as they wound, leaning hard into the corners of her hips and then accelerating wide open along the arch of her navel until finally easing off the throttle at the crest of her budding breast, only to hit the brakes hard and quick at the face of undeniable adolescence. For though she was ever becoming a woman, she indeed maintained the face of a child. And for most men, the ride ended there and with a shiver, but for Everett Carpenter, this was not the case. His mind eagerly bent well beyond her curves, and the innocence in her face made it warp.

Lavinia's father, Sam Fisher, or Fish, as he was known to most at the time, was the proud proprietor of The Broken Key, otherwise known as the Clockmaker Tavern, because that is what the sign on the front of the building read. The Broken Key didn't have a sign. It was in the basement. The Clockmaker Tavern was the first tavern ever built in the town of Clockmaker, and still it had no competition.

The church and the government had long since run all the other booze joints out of business, and the whore houses too for that matter, but Fish never did take too kindly to the church or the government. The last time the law came knocking, Fish slammed the deputy's legs in his own car door when he was radioing for back up, and the last time the Lord came knocking, well, he grabbed the Bible out of the ladies' hand, opened to Proverbs, ripped out a page, wiped his ass with it, and then chased the lady up the road, cackling and howling, with the stained scripture outstretched toward her.

Needless to say, neither the law or the Lord ever knocked on the door of The Clockmaker Tavern again, not as long as Fish owned it, anyway.

The Clockmaker tavern was open every day of the week, even on Sunday, from six in the evening until eleven at night, and when the tavern closed, that's when The Broken Key opened. And it stayed that way until dawn. The basement of the tavern could be accessed by a door on the rear of the building, and when the lights went out upstairs, they came on downstairs, and people would start lining up out back. If a man had an automobile of some kind, though it was rare he did, he would have to pay his tab at the tavern and drive up to the mine to park, then walk back down to The Broken Key through the woods. 'Out of one hole, and into another,' some miners could be heard saying, after a long shift underground. The Broken Key was known for fast women.

The basement of the tavern wasn't anything special. It had dirt floors and low ceilings, but it allowed gambling, and the bar served not only beer but whiskey, and moonshine liquor as well, and on the weekends, Fish would bring in different bands and musicians, even Negro ones, sometimes from as far away as Huntington and even Pittsburgh. Most nights would see maybe a dozen patrons, but on the weekends, the bar was lined with blackened and haggard-looking miners and their painted and haggard-looking wives. Both card tables were full and tense, entire paychecks disappearing into thin air, and the dance floor would jump like a Baptist revival. The bacchanal would go on all through the night, and often times, the sounds of horns and laughter were the only things to be heard for miles. Maybe there was an old owl hooting or a cricket chirping somewhere, but not much else, just a little horn and a little laughter echoing through the hollow.

Lavinia and her mother spent most nights there. Lavinia would sweep the floor and clear empty mugs and the like, and her mother would tend bar. Her mother, Priscilla Fisher, was, hands to the ground, the sweetest woman on planet earth, but behind the bar, she was a ruthless ball-breaker with the mouth of a sailor. She didn't take shit from anyone, man or woman. She was bold, and she was quick to tell a drunk to go fuck himself, but rarely without a grin. She had nicknames for most of her regulars. They had names like Dickless and Dog Breath, Shit for Brains Sam, Slutty Patty, Slutty Marge, Old Toothless, Dummy, and Nig Dad, but she never gave a nickname to somcone she didn't like, no matter how regular they may be. She got along rather well in this manner, and truth be told, most people were actually quite fond of her.

Young Lavinia loved working at The Broken Key. She loved everything about it. She loved the people, the smells, the laughter, the card games, she even sort of loved the way people behaved when they were drunk, unless they got mean, that is. But more than anything else, she loved the music. God in Heaven, did she ever love the music. She wasn't much for dancing, she would mostly sit on the cooler behind the bar and sway, with stars in her eyes, but she loved to watch and she loved to listen.

THREE THREE

But more than just the music, she was captivated by the entire scene, and more accurately, by the long list of men who made the scene what it was. These drummers and fiddlers, these smokey-eyed, calloused-fingered, iron-lunged vagabonds, these Appalachian instrumentalists, these guitar-pickers, they were Lavinia's entire naive world. They were her heroes when she was six, her idols at ten, her crushes at twelve, and by the time she turned fourteen, she had fooled around with two guitar players, and a saxophone player, and one of them was a Negro.

Do consider, mixing races got people killed in those days, especially when it came down to a white girl and a black man, and Lavinia knew that. She was young but she was well aware of the danger and she didn't take it lightly. If she were caught parked in Pine Holler with some unfortunate black man, they would likely be beaten to death or shot. Well, she personally might have gotten off with just a beating, depending on who caught them, but despite the dire consequences, on that one particular occasion, Lavinia could not help herself. She had never heard anyone play quite like Tyrone Whitaker.

Tyrone bled for his work, it could be heard in every note. Head back, eyes closed, sweat pouring, music came through him like a wide open channel. Lavinia was mesmerized by his sound, and the passion with which he performed. No matter his color of skin, he could have been three foot tall and covered in scales like a lizard, and she still would have given every piece of herself to him, race be damned. Lavinia liked boys and men just fine, but musicians made her salivate.

She would watch them come shambling in as she wiped down the tables and bar. Occasionally there would be a woman, and once three young sisters showed up to play, but on most weekends, only men would perform. She would watch them come in early, before all the patrons, when the bar was still dark and quiet, carrying their old guitar cases and horn cases, and often carrying the instrument itself, a violin perhaps, naked or wrapped in cloth. These men, these curious and talented men, with their strange clothes and strange accents, who came from strange places, places far away like Pennsylvania and Ohio, would come to her father's tavern and down into his basement, smoking their cigarettes and cloves, their cannabis, and drinking from different small bottles. They would smile and wink at her, and she would feign shy and her mind would race with fantasies of running off with one of these strange, sometimes rather handsome men, and being swept away to some strange and exciting city where there were things like sidewalks and soda bottles and fancy dresses and the like. But in the end that never happened. They always left her in the morning and often in the dead of night. They never asked her to come, never swept her away, and never came back. She was sure that it was because they were so much older that they always left her behind, and partly she was right.

Everett had seen Lavinia once before, but the first time they met, Lavinia was walking home from a late shift at The Broken Key early one Monday morning. The sun was rising all around her and the day was already hot. She was tired as an old dog and her feet and back ached, so when Everett pulled up in his shiny new Thunderbird, offering a lift, she simply could not resist. Although she should have known what kind of man Everett was by the color of his car, periwinkle, she could only think about how much her feet hurt, and she couldn't see the car's color through its shine anyway. So she opened the door and stepped inside. And just like that, sore feet sealed Lavinia's fate.

Everett stayed for breakfast that morning, and he met Lavinia at the tavern for a late supper the following evening. He said all the right things and made all the right moves. He hid his insidious motives quite well over the following months, courting Lavinia like a proper gentlemen, impressing her father with his inherited bank roll and good ol' boy wit, but no matter what Everett did, he could not get past Lavinia's mother. She could see right through his flashy car and even flashier smile, and she wasn't shy about voicing her opinions of him either. She pointed out his shortcomings and called him on his bullshit at every turn, and Everett loathed her for it, silently of course. Not until after they were married did he start referring to Lavinia's mother as 'the cunt up on the hill.'

Everett was twenty-two years old at the time, or so he claimed. He was actually thirty-two, but no one, not even Lavinia, would find out until long after they had tied the knot. There were almost eighteen years between them. It was just another of the many lies she was told in the beginning. He also promised to take her places and show her the world, but the first thing he did was buy land from her father and set to building a house on it, and the only time they ever left Clockmaker together was the one occasion he took her to see Elvis Presley. The smitten feeling that Lavinia carried with her during their short courtship quickly dissolved with the reciting of their wedding vows and was replaced by a kind of weight, like lead, that she began to carry like a cross.

As soon as they were married, Everett made her quit her night job at The Broken Key. He allowed her to work at the tavern during the day, but only four days per week, and only as long as she came straight home afterwards. Lavinia objected of course. She didn't mind not working but she would have to miss all the music too, and that she would not accept. She could not accept. She tried to explain this to Everett, she tried to make him understand how much she loved music, how much she needed and cherished it, how it was vital to her very survival, but Everett did not understand, or if he did, he must not have agreed because he punched her hard in the stomach, bruising a rib, and stealing the breath from her lungs. Lavinia fell to the floor and curled into a ball, gasping for air, tears streaming. Everett didn't say another word. He turned and walked out of the kitchen. That was the first time he hit her.

The following day Lavinia told her father that she was going to quit The Broken Key, and though he was reluctant, and despite having little choice in the matter, he gave her his blessing, but he added one small request that she work one more weekend so that he would have time to find her replacement. Everett allowed as much. He was, after all, 'a reasonable man.'

That Sunday night was to be Lavinia's last night at The Broken Key. When her father picked her up for work, he asked Everett if he wanted to come along. There was supposed to be a hot act coming in from Lexington, with a high and lonesome sound, that he was sure would be right up Everett's alley, but Everett declined, claiming to be too busy. The truth was that Everett simply hated people, and only chose to be around them when he needed something. Backing out of the driveway, Lavinia's father waved to his new son-in-law who was standing on his newly built front porch, watching the truck pull away. Lavinia did not wave. Everett squinted one eye for the sun and raised a hand to the sky, and when the truck was out of sight, he spit in the grass and walked back inside his house.

That night, the band arrived early. Lavinia was alone in the dark, counting the register behind the bar, when the basement door swung open and they came strolling in, silently carrying their instruments. They were each wearing matching black wide brim Gamblers, white button down shirts, black pants, and black suspenders. Obscured by shadow, Lavinia could hardly make out the faces under the hats. The first man through the door, a large bearded man, paused briefly and scanned the room, then he made his way to the stage in the back. The other three men followed him. They set down their cases and began to unpack an assortment of musical paraphernalia. Lavinia reached under the bar and switched on the stage lights and the band looked up from their tasks to find a sweet young lady sitting on a barstool behind the bar, staring back at them.

"Thank ye, mam," said one of the men, and they all set back to their work, all but one of them anyway. The man crouched beside his guitar case, with long feathery blond hair, was incapable of looking away from Lavinia. She was the most beautiful thing he had ever laid eyes on, and it wasn't until she blushed and gave an uneasy smile that he realized he had been staring and the trance was broken. Turning a bit red himself, the man turned quickly back to his task, pulling his bottom E string true across the bridge of his guitar and then twisting the tuning key.

After Lavinia finished with the register, she commenced to wiping down the bar. She could hear the patrons filing out of the tavern upstairs to line up at the back door. She had ten minutes, maybe less, before her father would let them in. She was putting a little elbow grease into something brown and sticky on the edge of the oak bar when she was overtaken by shadow.

She looked up to find two of the band members pulling up stools and sitting down. One of them was the blond man who had stared at her so curiously. Lavinia could not help but notice that he was incredibly handsome and seemingly younger than she had first suspected, much closer to her own age. The other man was the big fellow with the beard and although he wasn't necessarily what Lavinia would have called handsome, his face was jovial and gentle and unscarred, and despite his intimidating size, she took an immediate liking to him. Another thing she noted was that they were both very clean—a rather unusual sight in Clockmaker. There wasn't a single bit of dirt or coal under either of their nails.

The big man offered a giant's smile from deep within his long scruffy beard and slapped a strong meaty hand down on the bar. "Evenin', mam," he said. His voice was pleasant and surprisingly soft. The other man gave a half smile and nodded, boot gazing, in a futile attempt to not stare.

Lavinia, rather sheepishly for her, said, "Evenin'." She felt awkward and was unconsciously fiddling with her hair.

The big man said, "Woudn't be too much to ask for a beer and a whiskey for me and the boys, would it?"

"No sir," said Lavinia.

"Good," he responded, "these boys don't play for shit without a little taste in 'em, and nor do I. Say, what's your name, little lady?"

Lavinia told him her name.

"Well that damn sure is a purty name," said the big man. The other man nodded absently but he stayed silent. Then the big man said, "Lavinia what?"

"Fisher."

"Fisher? This ain't yo daddy's place, is it?"

"Yes sir."

The big man continued, "Well no shit, pleased to meet ya, little lady, my name is Phillip Marshall Davis, only son of Reverend Willard Marshall Davis, from Woodford County Ken-fuckin'-tucky, little lady, and this here is my oldest boy Duane Richard Davis. Those two ugly sons of bitches back there are Wyatt Simmons, and Dale Noble, and we are yo humble entertainment for this evenin'. The My Sweet Lucille Boys."

Lavinia flashed a smile. "My pleasure, I'm sure, gentlemen," she said. She felt her tension ease a little. The bearded man had a way about him that young Lavinia found disarmingly charming. She set several mason jars upon the bar and began preparing their drinks while Phillip Marshall kept on. "Hell, last time we was here, I can't even 'member, we got s'damn skunked. That mountain hooch yo daddy got don't get no better, little lady. I done fell out in every holler from here to Californee and I'm here to tell ya, Rockies, Ozarks, Smokies, don't none of them old boys have shit on yo daddy's liquor. Now they make a fine wine west of Denver, don't misfigure me, but that there in yo hand is the good stuff, from God's own private stash. Tell ya the truth, it's the only damn reason we play this far east. But my son here, he ain't never had Old Fish's liquor. He's heard plenty 'bout it. Probably good'n damn tired of hearing my old ass yap about it. So, way I figured it, now that he's playin' lead in the band, it t'was high time we get on back to Clockmaker, so he can find out what all the fuss is about. Say, little lady, would ya mind puttin' them on a tray? We'll take our drinks on stage."

Lavinia arranged the glasses on a small round tray, and slid the tray toward Phillip Marshall, careful not to meet Duane Richard's eyes. She could feel him watching her.

"Band's first round still on the house, little lady?" asked Phillip Marshall.

"Long as these walls stand," said Lavinia in a vaguely mocking tone.

Phillip Marshall smiled wide and said, "You sound just like yo daddy."

Every bit of intimidation inflicted by his general size and appearance melted away under the brilliant beam of Phillip Marshall's pearly white Kentucky smile, and Lavinia found herself briefly wishing that he were her father and not somebody else's.

"Don't I know it," said Lavinia, raising her eyebrows. She'd heard the comment many times before and her inflection made that fact obvious.

The great bearded man started to turn back for the stage with the tray of glasses balanced professionally on one hand, when he stopped, and over his shoulder, said, "Son, give little Miss Lavinia a quarter tip, she's earned it ten-fold, I'm sure." Then he turned to Lavinia and said, "Thank ye, mam," and gave a slight tip of his hat. The two men on the stage clapped and howled at Phillip Marshall's fruitful return.

Duane pulled a turquoise blue velvet pouch from his trousers and from it he retrieved a shiny new quarter dollar coin. He was just about to place it in Lavinia's palm when from somewhere near the stage behind him, one of his bandmates, either Wyatt or Dale, shouted, "You better hide that woody in yer pants 'fore you walk away from that bar, boy!" The men on the stage burst into a roar of laughter, Phillip Marshall included.

Duane, as a direct result of this comedic jab, turned red as a freshly painted barn, dropped the coin on the bar, opened his mouth to say thanks, hung his head in shame instead, and walked away.

Lavinia grinned and watched him retreat to the sound of belly laughter, his tail tucked. *He sure is handsome*, she thought. Then she thought about Everett, her new husband, and went back to wiping down the bar.

It wasn't long before the place was packed and Fish got on stage and introduced the band. Their name was The My Sweet Lucille Boys, and Fish couldn't have been happier to have them, or so he said, and with that, the four men took the stage.

What followed was described by many people in many ways, but it left Lavinia without words and incapable of speech. She loved Everett, or so she thought, and even if she didn't, she was now his wife and she was committed to him and him alone, and when it came down to it, Lavinia wanted, wholeheartedly, to be an honest and upstanding woman and a faithful partner, but she was not at all prepared for what Duane Richard Davis was about to do to her mind with his guitar.

FOUR ONE

To say he twisted or warped her mind is an understatement. He fractured it. Just like that. Like a bone. In a matter of moments or notes, Lavinia was transformed from the ever faithful wife into the dripping wet whore of Babylon. It took one song. That's it. Just one song. Later, when Lavinia told her mother what happened, she made no excuse. All she could manage was 'God, Momma, could he ever play.'

That night, in the dirt and again against the side of a rusty Ford, Lavinia let Duane have her. And from that brief encounter, a child was conceived. Duane told Lavinia many things that night, about the places he had been and the things he had seen, but among the many things that he told her, it was what he said last that she never forgot. 'I'll be back,' he said. With a parting kiss and a gentle smile. 'I'll be back.'

When Lavinia became aware of her pregnancy, it was assumed by everyone except Lavinia and her mother that the child belonged to Everett, and neither woman ever bothered to clear up the misunderstanding. Lavinia let Everett believe the boy was his, for obvious reasons, and the years went on that way. Everett named him Jeremiah, after his own father. He was fond of the boy at first, but Jeremiah was prone to clinging to his mother and eventually Everett's fondness for the child turned to a severe and savage resentment. By the time Jeremiah was three, Everett referred to him as Mommy's Little Faggot.

And still, time marched on.

Then one day, some six odd years or so after Lavinia's last night at The Broken Key, Duane Davis did something that none of the others ever did. He came back.

'Melissa' by the Allman Brothers softly plays

His hair was longer and blonder than before, and finished

halfway down his back, and the clean-shaven, almost boyish face that Lavinia remembered had been replaced by chiseled features, and a soft-flowing and kempt beard. He had grown considerably in the years since they last met, but his eyes were the same, and his voice was the same, and when he looked at her and spoke her name, she came apart all the same. He had become a big and beautiful man with a generous smile and a countenance of ease and equanimity. Duane Davis was surely and without doubt or question his father's son.

Everett had just left for the mine, Jeremiah was in school, and the morning sun was bright orange. Lavinia was hanging clothes on the line. She had just finished with Everett's socks, when past a flapping bed sheet, she saw him emerge from behind Everett's tool shed. At first, she froze, in shock. She did not instantly recognize him. Her mind scrambled to fit the image of this man into her reality, to find placement for a sight so foreign and out of place, and she recoiled with confusion and fear as if she had been dropped into a dream and was now staring down a lion. But within an instant, his memory and the sound of his music washed over her, along with his name, and she spoke it, softly. "Duane."

He came to her without hesitation. His lips were soft and wet, and they were firmly upon hers before she could even think to protest or turn away, not that she would have, had she the time to consider it, nor would she have after it was too late. She hadn't been kissed like that since the last time he kissed her, so many years ago. Everett never kissed her that way. *Oh my God, Everett!* The thought came to her like a direct hit from a bolt of lightning, and she pushed away from Duane instinctively, a strand of saliva stretching wildly from her bottom lip to his. Eyes wide and frightened, Lavinia cast glances all around her, nearly breaking her neck to avoid any possible blind spot.

"It's alright, sweetheart, he's gone. I made sure of it," said

Duane, warmly, if not rather directly. The look of dread on Lavinia's face must have been unnerving though, because despite being previously certain that her husband was gone, he too gave a careful look about his surroundings.

Lavinia made to speak, but couldn't, and in a panic, she grabbed Duane by the wrist and pulled him into Everett's shed. Her heart was pounding in her chest, and she had no idea what she was going to do, but once inside the little rickety shack, she slammed the door shut behind them.

Seeing him there in the dark of the shed, he became real, maybe too real. She had always wished he would come back, but now that he was there, at arm's length, a chimera no more, Lavinia couldn't help but wish that he were gone. Everett would kill them both if he found them together in a church, let alone in his tool shed. She looked around her, at all the possible murder weapons, and they were plenty. Drills, pipes, chains, knives, saws, an aluminum baseball bat, Everett would take pleasure in having so many options to choose from. The thought of him smashing Duane's head to a bloody pulp with the hemispherical end of his ball-peen hammer inspired the next words that would come out of her mouth.

"You shouldn't have came here."

Duane smiled. "Well... I had to, I uh...well, I never stopped thinkin' about you, Lavinia, and I just had to see you again."

Lavinia's bottom lip began to quiver. On many long and cold nights, with Everett asleep at her side, she had fantasized about this moment and about Duane uttering the very words that he just had. And now, the moment for which she had so desperately longed had come, and her heart reacted appropriately, with an immediate and overwhelming gushing of desire and passion. Without a second thought, she kissed him. All considerations of her husband dissipating into nothingness, an offering to the sensual void.

Within a matter of minutes, they had both achieved orgasm. This was a first for Lavinia, and unfortunately a last, though she would have no way of knowing as much. From the very instant that he pressed into her, she could feel her insides brimming and tingling with pleasure, like a hardwood fire was being stoked in her loins. And within seconds, the cast iron cauldron that hung above that fire began to boil over, spilling a warm slimey goo that she could feel running between her butt cheeks and sprinkling on the insides of her thighs. She moaned low and her body shook, and in the softest whisper, she said his name once again. "Duane." The word was sugar on her tongue.

Duane finished, twenty three and a half slow thrusts later, and collapsed on top of her. Lavinia pulled him tight to her chest. She could have laid there underneath him until the sun burned out. She'd never been so happy or so satisfied. But alas, the vulnerability of their situation could not be ignored and so they pried themselves from one another and began to dress.

They spent the morning together in the safety of the woods. Walking mostly, and talking. The day had turned out to be a warm one, and Lavinia walked barefoot. Duane held her shoes. Their conversations were somber for the most part, and carried with them the weight of their unavoidable parting. Duane told Lavinia about how he had given up guitar and started working for the railroad after his father had died from liver failure four years prior. He told her about how he went heavy on the bottle for a couple of years, and he told her about the pain he went through coming off of it. At twenty-four years old, he had never married, and he had never sired children, at least to his knowledge. His life was spent shoveling coal for the B&O Railroad, three hundred and fifty days a year, but he reckoned he was happy.

Lavinia, in turn, told Duane about her life in Clockmaker, what little there was to tell. She told him about her father losing a long fight to breast cancer, of all things, and about her mother winning the first place ribbon for the best blackberry pie at the Logan County Fair, the fall prior. She told him about her Wednesday church group, and about the new Presbyterian church that was being built at the bottom of Plum Hill. Eventually, she told him about Everett and her marriage to him, but she diminished the severity of the abuse, out of shame, and when she told Duane about Jeremiah, she did not reveal to him that the child was his.

Neither of them mentioned the idea of running away together. Both knew, deep down, that the option was not on the table. Duane could not afford to support himself, let alone Lavinia and her child, nor was it reasonable to think that the three of them could somehow live together in the boiler of the number eleven locomotive. And Lavinia was certain that, if she and Jeremiah left, Everett would eventually track them down like wild game, taking hides for his prize. The grim realities were obvious to both of them, and there was no illusion whatsoever to even the prospect of some daring lovers' escape. It was because of this mutual understanding that Lavinia decided to keep matters of paternity concealed. The inevitability of her and Duane's situation was grave enough without that added detail, she decided.

Judging by the sun, it was close to noon, she would have to start preparing Everett's lunch sooner than later or she wouldn't have it on the table when he walked through the door, and that was unacceptable. She told Duane that she would have to go home, and he asked if he could walk with her. Reluctantly, she told him that it was better if he didn't. She told him to keep following the path and to stay left at the fork and that eventually, he would come out on the main road that leads into town.

She started to tell him how much it meant to her that he had come back to see her, but before she could utter a single syllable,

Duane pulled her in close and kissed her, her shoes dropping at their feet. Once, twice, three times he kissed her, then he pulled himself away and gave her his father's best grin and said, "Who knows, Sugar Britches, maybe I'll see ya in another six years." Then another quick peck on her cheek and he was gone.

Lavinia made her way home at last, pausing on her way into the kitchen to remove the clothes and sheets from the line. She was taking down the same sock that she had been hanging when she had first seen Duane, and almost instinctively and with a rather irrational anticipation, her attention stole to Everett's tool shed. But there was no Duane. He wasn't there. And he wouldn't be back anytime soon. Lavinia gave a slight sly grin as she turned back to her chores. *Lord have mercy*, she thought. She would never look at that old shed quite the same again.

Eight months, ten days, and ten hours of painful labor later, like clockwork, Lavinia gave birth to her second child, and she named the child Priscilla after her mother. Lavinia was in love with her little green-eyed angel from the very first moment that she saw her. She had prayed many nights that the child would be a girl, and the Lord had seen fit to answer those prayers. She loved her son endlessly, but to Lavinia, her newborn baby girl was the most pure and true thing she had ever seen in all of her days, more so than baptisms or snowflakes or nightfall.

The countless hours Lavinia spent holding Priscilla, loving her, nursing her, gazing down at the flawlessness of God's design, admiring the perfection of her features and form, Lavinia could never have imagined that fifteen years later, she would be kneeling in the middle of the road, staring at the same sweet child, her skull likely fractured, blood in her ears, and the flesh under her two glowing green eyes growing blacker by the minute.

FOUR SEVEN

SEVENTY-ONE

Lavinia had always been hesitant to tell Priscilla the truth about her conception. She feared that the young girl would not be able to keep the truth hidden, that she would accidentally let it slip, not realizing the gravity of such secrets, as teenagers are often wont to do. If Everett hadn't been so cruel, if he had been a good man, she likely would have never told Priscilla the truth, but as it stood, as Everett was, Lavinia felt that she must tell her, for Priscilla's own sake, if not that of God's.

So kneeling there in the road, church bells in the distance, thoughts of dying, of her own death in particular, circling Lavinia's mind, she decided that now was the time. Lavinia couldn't bear the thought, should something happen to her, of Priscilla living the rest of her life thinking that she and Everett Carpenter were of the same blood. She had to tell her. Priscilla was old enough to know, to keep the secret. She would have to be.

And so, Lavinia squeezed her daughter's hands a little tighter, and in a strong, motherly tone, she said, "Yer daddy ain't really yer daddy. He ain't yer brother's daddy neither. Yer real daddy was a wonderful man that played the guitar."

Priscilla's eyes widened, and her forehead scrunched, but she did not speak. Lavinia could tell that she was struggling to comprehend.

Lavinia continued, "His name is Duane Dav—yer daddy—yer real daddy's name is Duane Davis. Duane Richard Davis. Everett, he—he ain't yer real daddy. I met yer real daddy a long time ago. He was a wonderful man, Priscilla. He was kind and gentle and handsome, so handsome, and…well, but I was already married to Everett, and honey we just couldn't be together, me and yer real daddy. You understand what I'm tellin' you, sweetheart?"

Priscilla nodded wearily.

"Good. Now Priscilla, this here is real important. You can't never tell Everett. He don't know. He thinks he's yer real daddy. I'm scared if he found out, he'd kill me, honey. I know you understand that, right?"

Priscilla nodded again, this time much more confidently.

"I know you do. Now, I'm sorry to put this burden on you, angel. I truly am. Ain't easy for a little girl to keep a secret like this, but I want you to know. I need you to know. Everett ain't no part of you. And you ain't no part of him. All his meanness, and shit, ain't none of it in you. The man who helped me make you was a fine man. He had a big heart and a big smile, and he played his guitar with so much soul, Priscilla, you wouldn't believe it. He was a real dream, he was. And all his goodness, that's what's in you."

Lavinia readjusted Priscilla's shawl, snugging it to her neck, and brushed the light auburn hair from the girl's face. "Maybe one day Everett will die, and we can be free of him. But until then you have t'know somethin'. Everett don't love you. He never has. He likely never will. Yer gonna have to survive him just like yer momma has. I figure yer at the age now, you oughtta know. Now don't cry, sweetness, wipe away them tears."

Priscilla did as she was told, and wiped away her tears.

Her mother continued, "Thatta girl, you be strong now and you listen good. I know this don't seem fair, and it ain't, it surely ain't, but that's just how it is. Now Everett, he's a—well, he's a—a monster. He don't love nothin', Priscilla, it ain't just you. He don't love me or nobody. He don't even love himself. He's all hate and ugly, all the way down. You understand me?"

Priscilla nodded again.

"Good."

FOUR NINE

The church bell rang in the distance. They were late. Priscilla turned her head toward the sound, and Lavinia followed her stare. Pastor Riddle was standing on the steps, ushering in the last of his flock. The bell rang again.

"Don't worry 'bout that, honey," said Lavinia. "Look here. I'm tellin' you this for a reason."

Lavinia placed her hand gently on Priscilla's cheek and turned her daughter's head away from the church. Even with all the bruising, she was still the most beautiful little angel Lavinia had ever observed. And she was growing up so fast.

"You have to know this, Priscilla, cause if somethin'—" Lavinia's words caught in her throat like a railroad spike, and she started again. "Priscilla, if somethin' were to happen to me, heaven forbid, I can't have you livin' yer whole life thinkin' Everett is yer daddy when he ain't, so I just had to tell ya. Seein' you like this, all bruised, and I—."

Lavinia paused. An old rusty truck had appeared from around the bend, and was heading in their direction. Lavinia ushered Priscilla to the side of the road as it drew near. As the truck passed, it crept to a stop in front of them. Through the truck's window, Lavinia could see Carol Wilson and his wife Sue Ellen.

Lavinia had been acquainted with the Wilsons through the church for several years. She knew Carol to be a kind and generous man, though the onset of dementia had, in recent months, begun to wear on his patience, thus quickening his temper with his wife. But then again, Sue Ellen, in her hideous floral print dresses, was an unrelenting, nagging, and demanding bitch, whom Lavinia intentionally avoided, but seldom could, given the woman's enormous size and uncanny ability to endlessly contrive situations that placed her at the center of attention. So maybe it wasn't the dementia that was wearing on him. Maybe Carol was just tired of the old heifer's shit. Lavinia could hear the giant woman chastising her husband before he could even get his window rolled down.

"Mornin' ladies, jump in the back," said Carol. "May as well show up together if'n we're gonna show up late."

Priscilla looked to her mother for an answer, and Lavinia began to decline the offer, but before she could respond, Carol spoke up. "Jesus, Mary, and Joseph, Priscilla, what happened to yer head?"

Though Carol posed the question to Priscilla, Lavinia made to answer, but found herself paralyzed by shame and incapable of speech. Fortunately or unfortunately, depending on perspective, young Priscilla had been through this tired act many times before and so she responded with the most natural and graceful of lies.

"Oh, it's no big deal. I fell outta Old Man Parmore's big oak tree… Me and Joseph was just messin' around. Momma says I gotta be more careful."

"Well, I should say so, young lady," said Carol. "You have got to be one of the clumsiest girls I have ever come across."

Sue Ellen had been staring out her window and away from the Carpenter women since the truck pulled up. She had yet to look their way, and was obviously annoyed that Carol even stopped in the first place, but here she chimed in, under her breath, of course, but intentionally loud enough for all to hear. Of course.

"You know damn well what happened, you old fool," said Sue Ellen. "I don't know why you even bother to ask." And then in a much louder tone, "Now can we get to church 'fore it's over."

Carol Wilson gave Lavinia a forced smile. Lavinia could see that he was struggling to keep his temper hidden. He was clearly embarrassed by his wife's crude behavior, and how he had put up with it so long, Lavinia did not know. Carol had likely thought himself a lucky man in the beginning. Sue Ellen had been quite attractive in her day, and she was half of Carol's age, at that, but for every year they had been married, Sue Ellen seemed to gain ten pounds. And the fatter she got, the meaner she got. Thirty-two years at ten pounds per year. The math was easy. Poor Carol, he deserved better.

"Jump on in, ladies," said Carol, ignoring his wife.

Lavinia stared at the old man for a moment, and at his unpleasant wife who had still yet to even acknowledge her or her daughter, and then Lavinia said, "No thank ya, Mister Wilson, Sue Ellen, but I think we'll walk. Ain't much further, and it's a fine day."

Carol gave the two women his gentlest smile, and said, "Alright then, mornin' to ya, ladies."

Lavinia watched the truck as it drove away. Priscilla watched her mother. Lavinia thought about how much she hated living in Clockmaker. Everyone knew about Everett, but no one ever said anything, not to her face anyway, and they never offered to help. They just pitied her and kept to themselves. They just left her to suffer. And when you suffer, you suffer alone.

With the Wilsons long gone, Lavinia turned to her daughter, who was staring up at her admiringly, and said, "Let me tell you somethin' else, daughter of mine. If you think you can make it on yer own, you go. If not now, then whenever the time comes. To hell with this town. I'll always love you, girl, always, no matter where you are, no matter what you do, but when you feel ready, when you feel tough enough, you get outta this holler. You get outta Clockmaker altogether, you hear me? Outta West Virginia even. You go far as you want to and don't you ever look back. Everett won't come a'lookin for you, but he'll never let me leave. Not never. He'd hunt me down. But you…you can go."

Priscilla considered her mother's advice carefully, and said, "Everett don't scare me, Momma." Everett did scare her of course, but Priscilla's intuition told her that her mother was in need of a strength that at the moment she did not possess. And so once again, for her mother's sake, Priscilla lied. "Not even a little bit," she added.

Lavinia, with tears in her eyes, attempted a sly grin and said, "That's my girl. Say, angel, you think you can do that trick with the matches again?"

Priscilla nodded eagerly as Lavinia handed her the box of matches and then a cigarette. And with the same ease and mystery as the first time, Priscilla magically defeated the wind, and returned the cigarette, lit and smoking.

"Lord, child, you really are somethin'," said Lavinia, and she took a long satisfying pull from the cigarette. As she exhaled, she said, "Alright, let's go," and she began to walk away.

Priscilla watched her without moving, and after a few paces, her mother stopped and turned back. "You comin'?" asked Lavinia.

Priscilla gave her mother a confused look and pointed the box of matches over her shoulder. "Church is thata way, Momma."

"Fuck church today, honey. We're goin' up to see yer Maw Maw."

———◆———

Chaapter threeE

Walkin' on water, and trippin' on blotter,
that's how my Jesus rolls.
—Unknown

Joseph stirred in his seat. Sunday service had only just begun and he was already bored as a Jew on Christmas. In general, Joseph found church to be a waste of time. He could have been in the woods right then, fishing, swimming, checking his traps, gigging frogs, climbing trees, or even breaking bottles down at the salvage yard. In fact, he could have thought of countless things that he would rather have been doing— just about anything really—other than listening to crusty old Pastor Riddle drone on about the majesty of heaven and the rewards that await the saved on the other side. It was all a crock of shit, as far as Joseph was concerned, and for the love of God, he could not understand how he was alone in that belief, when to him, a mere young man of sixteen years, it had always seemed so obvious.

When it came down to it, Joseph went to church for one reason and one reason alone. Force. His mother and father quite literally forced him to attend Sunday service on a weekly basis, and on a weekly basis, as though a fighting chance actually existed, Joseph revolted against their coercion. Each and every Sunday morning, Joseph fought the good fight, railing against the powers that be, or against his loving parents, depending on how one looks at it.

In the name of freedom and truth, he fought against tyranny and oppression, or in the name of laziness and pessimism, he fought against his parents' relentless attempts to simply get him out of bed in time for church. Again, it depends on how one looks at it.

Joseph tried everything from feigning sick to flat out refusing but nothing ever worked. There were times when his father would implore his mother to let him sleep, but his mother would never have it. He had been pulled from bed by his ear, dragged face first on to the floor by his ankles, and once, in a frustrated rage, his mother had filled a bucket with snow and water and then dumped it on him. But Joseph's mattress took a week to dry and developed a funk so terrible that it had to be thrown out and replaced, and so his mother refrained from employing that method any further.

Anymore though, his father was quick to take off his belt, and so Joseph had been finding it somewhat easier to rise on Sundays. Nevertheless, his attendance at church was no reflection of his faith and if it was up to him, Sunday mornings would find him at home in his bed, cozy beneath the covers.

Joseph's longing for his warm bed was interrupted by Pastor Riddle's request that the congregation stand for the singing of hymns. His father gave him a nudge and said, "Stand, boy." Joseph stood, and the singing commenced. Instead of singing though, which truth be told he could do quite well, Joseph began feverishly scratching at his arm.

For the last week, he had been constantly digging at a small spot that had mysteriously appeared on his wrist. It was red and swollen and not much bigger than a freckle, and it itched more than anything had ever itched. It itched worse than all the times Joseph had gotten poison ivy, even that time that he got it on his nether regions. It itched so bad that he hadn't been sleeping for waking up to scratch it throughout the night.

The doctor thought it might be some kind of bacteria, Joseph's mother thought it was the product of some rare strain of stinging nettle. And Joseph himself thought his arm had been possessed by a small demon, spawned from the deepest darkest depths of the itchiest part of Hell. Little did Joseph or anyone else know, but a small hookworm larvae had imbedded itself under the first layer of Joseph's skin and was now migrating, subcutaneously, in circles about his wrist. And it was this migration, this tunneling through flesh, that was causing Joseph's wrist to spasmodically itch with the fury of a thousand flea-infested monkeys.

As Joseph dug at the skin on his arm, behind him the doors to the nave opened and Carol Wilson and his unfortunate looking wife Sue Ellen came down the aisle between pews, each head in the flock turning in their direction, casting judgment for their tardiness. Joseph watched the Wilsons as they made their way to the only two seats with space enough to accommodate not only Carol but a woman of Sue Ellen's size, and those two seats just so happened to be right up front. Joseph swore they left those seats open on purpose, just to make a show of it. Either way, he was glad it wasn't him. He had made that same shameful walk countless times before and he knew, all too well, the feeling of being late for church.

As the Wilsons settled into their seats, Joseph began to scan the pews and he realized that he had yet to see either Priscilla or her mother that morning. The front row on both sides of the aisle always held the same people, and these people were known to consider themselves to be the 'devout' and 'pious' among the parishioners, the 'holy.' Joseph figured they were just like the kids who sat up front in school—a bunch of ass-kissers. He was likely right.

Priscilla and her mother, Lavinia, always sat in the front too, but they weren't like the others. Joseph suspected that Priscilla had swallowed most of the bait, but not necessarily the hook, line, or the sinker, and the same went for her mother. When it came to the Bible, they sort of picked and chose the parts they liked and didn't pay much mind to the parts they didn't. They weren't always going on about God or praying over people or anything of that nature, and it was this inconsistency that had, at one time, puzzled Joseph to such an extent that he simply could not resist the urge to inquire. So one day, while Joseph, age twelve, helped Priscilla, age eleven, and her mother pick blackberries, out of a perfect silence, he said, 'Miss Lavinia, I gotta ask, why do you and Scilly always sit up front at church with the ass-kissers?'

Priscilla's eyes went wide. Joseph, secretly, loved to make his dear friend squirm, and he framed his question with intention, if not deliberation. But Lavinia, to the surprise of both children, only gave a half smile and after a moment said, 'The piano, Joseph. I like to be close to it.'

Lavinia was one of the most perplexing people that Joseph had ever met, but over the years, he had grown quite fond of her. To be honest though, he thought her a strange woman. Sweet, and oddly charming, but strange all the same. She was perceivably sad most of the time, and that was Everett's doing, Joseph was sure. But underneath her misery laid a childish and black sense of humor that surfaced only when she was alone with him and Priscilla, and Joseph found it riveting.

Lavinia didn't say much by and by, but when she did speak, and when only Joseph and Priscilla were around to hear it, she cursed, often and well, and she said things that Joseph had never heard any of the other grown folks in town say. She was raw and direct, but never mean about it. She was gentle in her entirety. She was more matter-of-fact than anything, and Joseph found that to be her most charming quality.

Once she referred to Pastor Riddle as a greedy Bible-whore,

which caused Joseph's jaw to slacken and his eyes to bulge with adoration, and another time she asked Joseph if he liked tits yet. Just like that, she said, "So Joseph, you like tits yet?" Joseph, having just turned thirteen, nervously shook his head. Lavinia then suggested, when the time came, that he ask the middle Layfield girl, Lilly, to see hers. Lavinia said, "I know you don't know it yet cause you ain't took off enough bras, but I can spot a good pair a mile away." Then she gave Joseph an affectionate pat on the ass, and walking away, said, "Just a little womanly advice." And it was about that time that Joseph began to wonder why Priscilla and her mother always sat in the front row.

Among the ass-kissers that day, there was Eddie Baker and his wife Harriet, and their three children, all of them swaying and singing. There used to be four kids, but one died. He hung himself. The Bakers still always sat up front though. Eddie was a foreman at the mine and Harriet used to play the church piano during hymns, but she gave it up after the suicide, and turned the gig over to Kathleen Gibbons. Their two youngest boys were fine enough, but the oldest boy, George, had a chip on his shoulder that Joseph had once accidentally knocked off by punching him square in the nose. Since then, the two boys had not seen eye to eye.

Beside the Baker family sang the Pratts, Ellis and June. Ellis and June were Joseph's closest neighbors, in proximity and relation. They lived in a rather large, poorly built, but well cared for vernacular two story that was constructed to hold the many children they never had. "I guess the Lord had other plans for me." That's what June told Joseph once.

Joseph spent a fair amount of time in the company of the Pratts. Ellis, now retired and living off of a military pension, often hired the boy to do odd jobs around their house, clearing brush, stacking wood, and painting fences. And once Ellis paid Joseph to dispatch of a raccoon that had been terrorizing his garden. Joseph terminated the critter in a deep part of Mill Fall Creek the following morning, and Ellis was so pleased at the pace with which Joseph worked that he paid double and gave Joseph an apple pie that June had baked especially for him.

All and all, Joseph liked both Ellis and June. They preached at him a lot, but even as a young man, Joseph knew that nobody was perfect.

Across the aisle from the Pratts sat Carol and Sue Ellen Wilson, whom Joseph knew very little of, other than the fact that Sue Ellen had, at one time, been one of the most attractive women in Clockmaker. This fact, given her current size, was rather suspicious to Joseph. "Shit, back when she was twenty, I would'a dragged my balls across three miles of broken glass just to suck the dick of the last guy that fucked her." Joseph had heard his uncle Bob say that one time, and he spent a week trying to wrap his mind around what he had meant. Even still, however, looking at her, Joseph was almost certain that he and his uncle couldn't have both been referring to the same Sue Ellen.

Beside the Wilsons were the Layfields and their three daughters. The Layfields owned the only grocery market in Clockmaker. Their three daughters, like their mother, each had long blonde hair and fair skin, and they were each, in their own right, exceptionally beautiful. They ranged in age from thirteen to seventeen, and Joseph was hormonally enamored with all three of them. The only problem with them, in Joseph's mind anyway, was that they were stone-cold bitches who wouldn't give him the time of day if he had been blind and they had been standing under a giant clock.

Take Violet for instance, the eldest Layfield girl. She was a picture of budding teenage perfection, perky as a pussycat, and so ripe that in the summertime, she melted right off the vine.

Only two months prior, Joseph had asked Violet, in all her mouth-watering glory, for a kiss, and with all the earnest sweetness Violet could summon, which was an admittedly unnerving amount, she told Joseph to close his eyes and pucker up. And Joseph did just that.

Only, instead of Violet's supple teenage lips, Joseph's naivete was met with a large steaming cow patty that the youngest Layfield sister, Daisy, mashed into Joseph's poor puckered face. SPLAT. That's the sound it made. Joseph would never forget it, not as long as he lived. He swore it. He could still see them standing there, pointing and laughing at him, little Daisy wiping the shit from her hand onto her dress.

Joseph continued scanning the church in search of Priscilla or her mother, though he was sure he couldn't have missed them. Behind the ass-kissers in the first row was the same tired lot that Joseph saw every Sunday. The Miller family, the Singleton family, the Carmichaels, the Joneses, the Cutlips, Old Man Parmore and his hound, the Elkins sisters, the entire McCauley clan, the Scarberrys, and of course Gwenny Mire.

Gwenny Mire went crazy after her husband died in a mine explosion, leaving her with no money, no hope, and nine of the most ruthless, ill-tempered, ill-mannered, and generally unpleasant children ever shat from a womb. And no matter which order they were lined up in, each one was uglier and dirtier than the next.

All but three of the Mire kids were boys, although the oldest sister Mary, who was rumored to have been struck dumb at birth by a massive thunderclap, was so crudely designed that if it were not for her giant sagging breasts, most would only count two girls among the bunch. She was a beast if Joseph had ever seen one, and he detested her. He detested the entire Mire family. The Mire brothers in particular, all six of them, could burn up in a house fire and Joseph wouldn't so much as whip his dick out if one drop of piss would save them.

For years, Gwenny and Merle Mire's offspring had tormented and harassed both Joseph and Priscilla, along with most every other kid in Clockmaker. Joseph had gone toe to dirty toe with them more times than he could remember. It was a constant struggle, and though on most occasions Joseph would try his best to avoid a fight, he had long ago decided that he damn sure wasn't going to run from one either.

Once, and only once, when he was fourteen, Joseph and Priscilla took the woods home from school, rather than the road, in order to avoid Kester Mire, who was two years older and, at the time, nearly two feet taller than Joseph. Rumors were floating around that Kester had found himself an old knife in his father's dresser and was planning on using it to remove Joseph's scalp, and although Joseph had no idea if the rumors were true, or what, if they were true, he had done to make Kester ever want to remove the top of his head, he decided it best not to tempt the situation, and made for the woods with Priscilla firm on his heels.

Joseph kept his skull cap that day, but by the time he and Priscilla reached his house, he felt as if Kester had sliced off a large piece of his pride, and he was beginning to bleed out. Joseph sat down on his porch steps stewing, and Priscilla sat beside him. In time, he asked Priscilla if she thought he was a coward and she told him that she wasn't sure. Then she asked him if he thought that he was a coward, and he nodded. It was Priscilla's next words that made Joseph cringe, and silently swear to never again cater to his own fears. "Momma says God hates a coward, Joseph." Those words rang in Joseph's ears like a shotgun blast, lead ricocheting through the trees. Even then, Joseph cared very little about what God thought, but if God felt that way, then there was a chance that Priscilla felt that way too, and to Joseph, that chance, no matter how slim, was unacceptable.

The next morning, as Kester set at his desk in his first period science class, clearing crust from the corner of his eye, Joseph walked in, and before the pontificating teacher or the oblivious Kester or anyone else realized what was happening, Joseph, without a word, tackled Kester out of his desk, mounted him, and began pummeling him with a flurry of wild, clenched-fist haymakers. Several of the blows were landing with sickening thuds and it took every bit of strength that the teacher, Mister Pickstone, could muster to pull Joseph from atop the confused and terrified Kester, who was shrieking and shrilly calling out, over and over again, for his momma.

Chokehold firmly in place, Mister Pickstone seized back on Joseph's neck, but Joseph wouldn't let go. He clung to Kester's hair and clawed at his clothes, and it wasn't until the teacher deepened his hold that blood ceased flowing to Joseph's brain, causing him to go limp in the teacher's arms. Kester continued to sob. The class was silent. Mister Pickstone, still holding the lifeless Joseph, looked around at the overturned desks and debris, and the blood, and at Kester Mire. "Class is dismissed," was all he could manage to say.

After, inside the principal's office, Joseph, though he tried, could not remember anything that had transpired beyond walking into Mister Pickstone's classroom, but he could tell by his throbbing hands and by Kester's face, which he had briefly glimpsed in the hallway as Joseph was being shuffled into the office, that he had made his point.

Mess with the goat. Get the horns.

Joseph confirmed to himself right then and there that he had made the correct decision to never again run. With his pride wholly intact, and his shoes dangling an inch from the ground, his heart felt full, and about him was a sense of strength. And power even. A far cry from the humiliation and shame he had felt the day before as he and Priscilla fled through the woods. His hands hurt like hell, sure, but otherwise, he had never felt better. And to top it all off, he couldn't fucking wait to tell Priscilla.

When it was all said and done, Joseph was suspended from school for ten days and he got a week of extra chores from his parents. Kester was not suspended but he never came back to school after that. Word spread quickly of his girlish cries for his mother, and his shame wouldn't allow him to face his peers, so he spent most of his time at home or lurking around town. Soon after the fight, or attack as it were, each of the Mire kids, one by one, quit turning up at the schoolyard. The constant mocking and teasing turned out to be more than the bastard clan could handle. "Help, Momma, help," was the taunt. Kester had disgraced them all.

Since then, relations between Joseph and the Mire siblings had been turbulent, to say the least. Anytime Joseph ran into them, there would be a fight, but only when they were together. They never approached Joseph one-on-one. They knew better. In numbers, however, provided no adults were around, the Mires never missed an opportunity to exact revenge, and though he tried, no matter their number, Joseph could not win every quarrel that they aimed his way. They had gotten the best of him on more than a dozen occasions but no matter how bad they had gotten him, it was never enough. The Mires had it out for Joseph. Social ostracization, in combination with their willful ignorance of all things substantive, not to mention abject poverty, prevented them from ever forgiving Joseph for his slight against their family, let alone ever simply moving on. And in that vein, a bitter, if not juvenile, feud was born.

And so, though he tried not to, Joseph fought, and often. Over the years he had laid violent hands on each one of the Mire brood. All besides the oldest brother and the youngest sister, Suzy. She was only seven years old, but Joseph figured it was only a matter of time before he would have to let that little cross-eyed half-wit have it too. He had fought both of the older sisters, that was for sure. On one occasion, he knocked Mary Mire out cold for making fun of Priscilla's mother for not having teeth—even though Mary, herself, was obviously missing a canine and two incisors. He hadn't meant to lay her out, just shut her up, but after Mary hit the ground, Priscilla kicked dust on her and said, "That's what you get," and Joseph relaxed a little, deciding that the ends justified the means.

As can be imagined, if not expected, Priscilla, as a result of her regular affiliation with Joseph, had also become an object of the Mire kids' scorn and resentment. The old mine, the drive-in theater, the creek bed, the woods behind the school, no place that kids congregated was safe for either Joseph or Priscilla. There was always a Mire or three loitering nearby, drinking stolen beers, burning tires, or fishing, just in earshot, threatening to ruin a good time. It's not that Joseph and Priscilla shunned these places altogether, they still played in the creek bed and at the old mine, and went to the drive-in on occasion, but frequenting those certain places always carried with it a certain amount of risk. Even danger.

The only places Joseph and Priscilla could go, without worry, were two of Joseph's least favorite places, church and school. Priscilla, on the other hand, liked both church and school, so she thought that was pretty damn funny, but Joseph could not see the humor in it. The reason being, the Mire kids quit showing up to Mt. Zion Methodist about the same time they quit showing up in the classroom. As rough as the kids at school were on the Mires, the kids at church, with their parents around to protect them, were worse. At first, Joseph felt remorse for the Mires, given their self-imposed exile and excommunication. That was never

Joseph's intention, but years of battling with the bastards had left him weary and pitiless for their circumstances.

Gwenny still showed up, though. Every Sunday. Her eyes sunk back, her pale skin pulled tight to the bone like a bat wing, her silver hair frazzled, clothes ragged and worn, the lonely matriarch of the Mire clan resembled a rug that had been walked on too many times, like a horse that had, the day prior, been rode hard and put away wet. Joseph hated the Mire kids, but he only felt a kind of sorry for their mother. He couldn't imagine having to look at their unsightly faces every day. He couldn't imagine looking at them and knowing, like Gwenny, that he had created them. What a soulless feeling that must bring. Joseph supposed the only reason Gwenny still came to church was to pray to God to kill her and take her away from the vile monsters that she spawned.

Joseph scratched at his wrist again as the congregation finished its singing. Still no Priscilla. Pastor Riddle asked everyone to sit, but instead of beginning his poorly prepared sermon, as was customary, he said, "As you all have known for quite some time now, today will be my last day. Doris and I are honored to have served you all this long, but the parish committee or the district superintendent, one, or both, seems to think our services would be better employed among the wretched of Charleston, and they have sent my replacement. So, without further ado, I would like to introduce you all to Pastor Swann."

Just then a man on the far side of the room, previously hidden to Joseph by the Scarberry family, stood and walked up to the altar, carrying a wicker basket. He sat the basket on top of the piano, giving a gentle smile to Kathleen Gibbons as he did, and then stepped up to the podium from which Pastor Riddle had just retired. A large wooden cross hung behind him.

He was a conventional-looking man. He wore black-framed glasses and a grey suit with a white shirt and a navy blue tie.

The suit wasn't particularly nice, but it was exceptionally clean and well pressed, and it fit as though it was made by a tailor. His demeanor was calm as he examined the silent audience and when he finally spoke, his voice was unquavering.

"I would like to begin by thanking Kathleen Gibbons, I believe it is, for her beautiful playing. Thank you, Kathleen, God has given you a wonderful gift.'" Then to the larger audience, he said, "My name is Pastor Swann, Pastor Douglas Swann. Like the bird. But spelled different. The church has sent me here to replace Pastor Riddle, but I assure you that my movement through life has a greater purpose. If I am here with you now, it is because I am supposed to be here with you now. God himself has chosen my path and it is with his hands that I do my work. It is with his grace that I bring forth his tidings of love and forgiveness, and I am honored to be here with you all."

As he spoke, he casually walked back to the piano and removed his jacket. He laid it folded beside the wicker basket, and began rolling up the sleeves on his shirt. Joseph, still scratching, watched him listlessly.

"When I am judged, I will be judged according to my works on earth," Pastor Swann continued. "As will all of you, and it is my job, my mission in this life, to insure that each and ever member of my flock passes through the golden gates of heaven upon their day of judgment. And it is through God's ever loving grace that eleven years ago, on a bus bound for Montgomery, an angel of a man sat next to me. And that man showed me the way. The only way, brothers and sisters."

Pastor Swann's voice began to raise, in volume and intensity, as he picked up the basket and brought it to the podium.

"It is with immense gratitude that I find myself before you all today, to share in the teachings of our holy father. For Hell, my friends, is real, and the wicked among us will be sent there to boil in its fiery lakes! Believe my words. We must repent, my brothers and sisters. Repent! We must demand more of ourselves and our convictions. We must not stray from the path for fear of the vipers that may lurk there. We must face the evil in ourselves… and in the world…"

Pastor Swann lifted the lid on the basket.

'Blood milk and sky' by White Zombie plays

"We must show courage and never question, my brothers and sisters. Never… And these signs shall follow them that believe! Let it be spoken. In thy name, they shall cast out devils. In thy name, they shall speak with new tongues. And in thy name…"

Pastor Swann reached into the basket, and from it was brought forth a knot composed of four actively coiling copperheads, which the pastor slowly raised above his head in a slithering sacrificial gesture.

"…they shall take up serpents."

The flock of parishioners recoiled in terror. There were several gasps and one of the Layfield girls shrieked. Kathleen Gibbons fainted head first on to the piano with a resounding discord that echoed throughout the nave. It was pandemonium, and Joseph watched the entire scene unfold, with giddy delight, from the edge of his seat.

Pastor Swann's eyes rolled back, and his entire body began to shake and twitch. The snakes, still raised above his head, hissed at the air, the scent of repressed sin, gliding like silk across their forked tongues. Outside, a light rain began falling on the tin roof, and thunder rumbled the thin walls of the church. Joseph was no longer bored.

————— ◆ —————

SIX EIGHT

A word from Joseph

Baptists don't fuck standin' up because they're afraid it could lead to dancin'. Methodists don't fuck near rivers because they're afraid they might fall in and people would accuse 'em of bein' Baptist. And Pentecostals don't fuck without a snake in their bed so they can prove to the Baptists and the Methodists who the true fuckin' believers really are. Otherwise, there ain't much difference between 'em, if ya ask me. From the outside, anyhow. But things changed quite a bit after Pastor Swann took over, that's for certain. That son of a bitch was wilder than rabies.

He had damn near a hundred snakes from all over the world, most of 'em poisonous. He collected 'em on mission trips throughout the years, and kept 'em in glass tanks all over his house. Hell, he slept with an African Feathered Tree Viper in a big glass tank above his bed in place of the headboard. And let me tell ya, that breed is deadly as they come, right up there with rattlers. They look like they're part dragon. You could almost call 'em cute, but they'll leave you deader than fuck if they bite ya. Pastor said he found her coiled up in his boot, in Uganda, and that she was sent from God himself, as some kind of sign. He also had a death adder, and a king cobra, a thirteen foot long boa constrictor named

Splash, maybe a dozen vipers, twice as many rattlesnakes, and several other random species, what's name I don't recollect.

Yeah, old Pastor Swann was one crazy motherfucker, alright. He danced with snakes, and preached Hellfire, and brimstone, and he drank strychnine a couple of times to prove to us he was chosen. He also told me I was bound for the lakes of fire on a regular basis, but I always liked him. He was always good to me, and after him and the snakes started comin' to church, I started enjoyin' Sunday service quite a bit more. But no matter how many times I saw him dance with them snakes without gettin' bit, I just couldn't bring myself to believe. I believe that he believed, that's for damn sure. Actually, I never met a man who believed more. He believed with all his bein' that if he loved God, those snakes would not murder him. And he tested God's love weekly. Lots of folks say they believe, but they ain't dancin' around with death adders to prove it, neither.

Ain't no wonder I couldn't believe though. Most of the evidence of God is either insufficient or unverifiable. I reckon I would wager, and I reckon Pascal would too, the reason most folks go to church is because the possibility of spendin' eternity poppin' the blisters on yer own boilin' flesh far outweighs any and all advantages of spendin' Sunday mornin' anywhere else. Ain't hard to believe in God, so fuck it, better'n a red-hot pitchfork up the ass. For a lot of folks, they think that's good enough, just goin' through the motions, and for good or ill, they are correct. If you go through the motions, you will go to Heaven after yer mortal soul perishes. There's other ways, mind you. But the motions will get ye there.

Lookin' back on it now, one thing that's odd to me is that I ain't believe in Christianity before I even knew the reasons why I shouldn't. Ya understand what I'm sayin'? I intuited its falsehood before I had all the particulars. Somethin' about it just didn't sit right with my white trash teenage soul. I mean, for example, I ain't know about the theory of evolution, or how physics works. I didn't know about the logical fallacies, or the historical fallacies, or the moral fallacies, or none of it. I never questioned why the Ten Commandments mentioned takin' thy neighbor's property, but ain't mention takin' slaves for commercial gain. I ain't think about the implications of incest in the Garden. I ain't think about dinosaurs, or Jesus's skin tone, or nothin'. I ain't think about shit. I just knew it weren't right. I felt it.

I was wrong, mind you, 'bout God, anyway. He surely exists. But, I was also right in ways.

The thing is, for all my experience with divine Biblical bein's, I've only come to understand that the religion they inspired has been absolutely corrupted by mankind. So much so, it don't even resemble its origins in the slightest. What we call Christianity today is a complete fabrication. Damn near it anyway. A religion of lies, misunderstandin's, and fairy tales. The Bible of today may as well be kept next to the toilet to clean up a good shit. It would serve a higher purpose. Now, the way to God is indeed within the Bible, but it's buried so deep within allegories and metaphors and outright hogwash nonsense that the average man would need two dozers and a team of Mexicans to excavate it, and a Limey archaeologist to help dust it off.

To clarify, I want you to picture the Bible. Let it materialize in yer mind's eye. Turn it on its side and picture it from all directions. Can you see it? Good. Now realize that the original Bible, in its completion, had ten pages, includin' a foreword from the author. All that depth, all lies. The original Bible, perfect in every way, although worn from age, took me no more than ten minutes to read through, cover to cover, and I couldn't read for shit at sixteen years old. The Devil had a copy of it on his night stand, next to a copy of Erections, Ejaculations, Exhibitions, and General

Tales of Ordinary Madness, which was published the previous year, if memory serves me. I snuck a peek at both books once, while Priscilla and the Devil was busy chattin' in the livin' room by the fire. After readin' the Bible and leafin' through the other book, I came back into the livin' room, and I'll never forget it, the Devil turned to me in mid-sentence, and he kinda cocked his head to the side and smiled, and he says, 'Awfully thin, isn't it...?' Creeped me the fuck out.

Now, imagine how wrong Christianity is about its own God, considerin' the one mere fact that the original Bible, the one actually written by the hand of God, had roughly eleven thousand nine hundred and ninety fewer pages than the bullshit Bible that's floatin' around today. I mean, are you fuckin' kiddin' me, the new Bible is damn near as thick as the Lord of the fuckin' Rings, and not half as insightful. Too many men had their way with the Good Book over the years, plain as that. Fact is, too many men, over the years, done had their way with the entire concept of God. And that, my friends, is why the whole dang religion is now in a state of paranoid mania. The path to God has done been planted over with a thicket of briars, and the trail gets harder and harder to foller as the sun goes down.

No sir, I ain't never believed in today's Christianity, and I still don't. I suppose the reason it never set right with me when I was a boy was because everything I learned up until meetin' the Devil, whether it was in church or from grown folks, was all plain wrong. And somehow I sensed it. But hell, these days, not only do I not believe in it, I tend to loathe it. What Christianity has become disgusts me. It's vulgar and profane, and what's worse is the older I grow, the more I learn to despise it. These days, I say I love God, but I hate his religion. Kinda ironic, don't ya think? Maybe it's not. I never really understood the concept of irony, to be honest with ya. But that's what I say, anyway.

SEVEN TWO

Who could blame me though, really? Buncha' goddamn heathens. What with all the kid fuckin', and the Crusades, and Prohibition, and witch burnin's. Mega chruches. Preachers with private jets. The list goes on and on. That damn religion is the most heinous, inhumane organization on earth, and how people still allow themselves to be swept up in the nonsense, I surely do not know. Women in particular, it's like they have some kinda metaphysical Stockholm syndrome. It's a damn shame, if ye ask me. Christianity ain't done nothin' good since before Christ got crucified, and some way or the other, they still run the show. It ain't no coincidence that the period in time when the Catholic church was at its most powerful is referred to as the Dark Ages. They got it right about creation but they destroyed damn near everything about livin'. How 'bout that, another bit of irony for ya.

Now, I don't mean to go off on a rant, but for thousands of years, these dirty fuckers have not only censored science, but also the most beautiful and true form of expression known to man. Which is fuckin' art, of course. Now, it's one thing to throw Galileo in a cage for his helio centered notions, but when you start fuckin' with music and paintin' and what not, well, buddy, I just can't abide by that.

There'd still be swingin' dicks all over the walls of the Sistine Chapel if it was up to the artist who painted 'em, and there damn well still should be, if you ask me. That artist was Michelangelo, if ya didn't know. His paintin', The Last Judgment, is the finest thing I ever seen. And those Catholic dip-shits had the nerve to try and make him change it 'cause they thought it was lewd. Paint some clothes over them cocks, they said. Can you imagine? If I was Mikey-angelo, I woulda told 'em all to fuck themselves into eternity. But, alas, Mikey-angelo weren't no poor old boy from West Virginia, he was a master painter from Italy, so instead of blurtin' out, "Go fuck yerself, you kid fuckin' old prick," and stormin' off to a brothel, he went back in the chapel and painted the Papal Master of Ceremonies portrait, stark naked, with donkey ears, and a serpent wrapped around him, devourin' his cock. Now, that's how an I-talian virtuoso tells ya to go fuck yerself.

And don't even get me started on music. Jesus fuckin' Christ. If I ever have to listen to another song with the curse words censored out, I'm gonna fly to Rome and beat the pope to death with an original press of the White album. Guess what, ya medieval clown lookin' bastard, the Beatles were bigger than Jesus. It ain't braggin' if it's true. I don't care if you were Christian, or Muslim, or Hindu, or a good old-fashioned devil-worshipper, you knew the words to 'Let It Be.' And I'll tell ya right here and now, girls only scream like that for God when you get a snake involved. I know from experience.

Oh and by the way, 'cause I know what ye might be thinkin', but God don't give a damn what you say. There ain't a word or series of words that could come outta yer mouth, or mine, that could make God constitute us as sinners. God don't listen to them kinda things. Only words that God hears is prayers. That's it. The catch is…the Devil does care what ye say, and he's always listenin'. Ya see, that's how spells and incantations work, how things like voodoo and witchcraft thrive. The difference between the Devil and God is the Devil don't just listen to yer naughty words. He listens to yer prayers too. And to make things worse, the Devil, he's omnilingual. His lexicon is ever expandin' and ever knowin'. He can speak and understand all languages, instantly, upon their very first articulation, on conception even. So, unfortunately for us, my friends, the Devil, he is legion, in number and tongue. When we speak, he hears us. Yes sir, he does. So beware.

And while we're on the subject of right and wrong, I'm gonna go ahead and tell ya. God don't give a damn where you stick yer dick or what ya rub yer coochie on. That's one of them misconceptions I was tellin' ya about. The Devil ain't tell me that neither, I just know.

Alright, anyway, let's reel it in a little bit, and get on back to the story. I reckon I have a tendency to get carried away. To ramble. But that is my nature.

Lookin' back, I remember that day real clear. My momma had her brown pokey dot dress on, and her pearls. She was a pretty woman back then. She's dead now, but back then, she was a real looker. Folks thought my daddy a right lucky man. But, I can remember Momma sittin' there that day, holdin' my daddy's hand. I can picture her singin' and swayin'. Oh yes. Yes, I can.

Know what else I can picture? The look of fuckin' dread that come over her face when Pastor Swann pulled them snakes out. She was terrified. Not as terrified as my daddy though, he feared snakes more than he feared death. That is to say, if given the choice between touchin' a snake and drownin', he'd run to find a crick. He pulled out them snakes and Daddy came outta his seat like he was sittin' on a bee hive. Good Lord, you shoulda seen it. Needless to say, my family started sittin' in the way back after old Pastor Swann showed up.

Another thing I remember about that day is my goddamn wrist itchin' to high heavens. Friends, you have no idea what I went through. I promise ya, the most used whore at the Wool Sock Saloon ain't have a snatch that itched half as bad as my goddamn arm did that day. I was losin' sleep at night for stayin' awake scratchin' at it. Lookin' back on it, I believe not sleepin' was havin' effects on me. I was forgettin' folks' names, and I was havin' hallucinations. Ever' now and again, I'd see bugs crawlin' on the walls, but then I'd blink and they'd be gone. It was fucked up.

Them was strange times, that's for sure. Hell, times is still strange… So I'll quit wastin' yer precious time.

SEVEN FIVE

Oh, but before we get back to it, I just wanna say, them Layfield girls can kiss my hillbilly ass. All three of 'em's still alive, and they all three fat as hell now too.

———◆———

ChAPTR FOUUR

———◆———

I'm nothing. Nobody. I'm a box car. I'm a jug of wine.
And a straight razor if you get too close to me.
—*Charlie Manson*

By the time Priscilla and her mother got back to Fallen Branch Hollow, a light rain had begun to fall, and thunder rumbled in the distance. Priscilla could see her grandmother's house on the hill above her own as they came up the dirt road. However, instead of walking up the gravel driveway that ran between the houses, the two women, without a word between them, made for the hillside, both of them fearful that Everett might happen to look out a window and see them if they took the obvious route.

Although Everett never attended church, he had little tolerance for his wife not attending for any reason. Priscilla, from her bedroom, once heard him say to her mother, "If God wanted me in church, he wouldn't give me so much fuckin' work to do." And then her mother responded to him in such a way that it made Priscilla's jaw fall slack. She responded to him in such a way that as soon as Priscilla heard it, her little heart began to shudder in her chest, because she knew, without doubt, that her mother's response was guaranteed to summon her father's psychotic temper.

Her mother's response was simple. It was laughter. That's all. Just laughter. Simple, jeering, side-splitting laughter. Like she had just heard the funniest joke ever told, or like someone had fallen face down in mud. After all the beatings she had seen her mother take, Priscilla could not believe that she still had the nerve to do something so foolishly defiant. What bravery that must have taken. What foolish bravery. But foolish or not, Priscilla couldn't help but to be proud of her. Of her and her stubbornly resilient nature. Nevertheless Priscilla's intuitions were correct. After a few moments, her mother's cackling fell silent with a hard packing sound.

Her father's presence in church was a subject that Priscilla never heard mentioned again, but the memory of her mother laughing like that was one that Priscilla carried with her always. And it just so happens that Priscilla and Lavinia, both, were thinking of that very day, as they made their way up the hill through the tall wet grass to Maw Scill's house.

BOREDOM

Maw Scill, or Priscilla Anne Fisher, was not only Priscilla's grandmother but her namesake as well. Where the name Louise came from only Lavinia knew, but in a matronymic turn of events, it was the adolescent Priscilla who, at the age of three when she had yet to attain the linguistic capabilities necessary to formulate the words 'Grandma Priscilla,' rechristened her grandmother Maw Scill.

And apparently, young Priscilla's infantile attempt to communicate, though born of necessity, had a ring to it, because the name stuck. Priscilla Anne Fisher—Fish's Old Lady, Fish's Widow—

from then on would be known not only by her granddaughter but by most as Maw Scill. Eventually she even introduced herself that way. Truth be told, she thought it was a proper and fine moniker for a tough old mountain woman of her age and station. She began to identify with the name and embody its implications almost right away.

The old woman had seventeen cats and she hated them all. Why she continued to feed and care for them was beyond anyone's comprehension. As Priscilla and her mother crested the top of the hill, several of the animals came down off of the porch to greet them. They were mangy little critters, but Priscilla adored them, and she kneeled to stroke their matted fur. Lavinia continued into the house, the screen door slamming shut behind her.

Priscilla picked up one of the cats, a grey one with a hairless tail, and carried it up onto the porch. The pain in her head had gone away, though her ribs still ached, and she could still taste metal in her mouth. Looking down at the ugly little critter cradled in her arms, she thought about Lucky. But then she thought about the fact that Everett wasn't actually her father, and she sat the cat down on the porch swing and walked inside.

"I can't believe I ain't see it, Momma. We made it most the way to church before I ev—." Lavinia's self-pity was cut short when Priscilla stepped into the house, several ombrophobic cats circling her feet. She kicked at them. Not hard, not to hurt them. Only to move them.

As Priscilla removed her shoes at the door, Maw Scill came back into the room, carrying towels. The frail, sweet old woman tossed one towel to Lavinia, and then she froze, looking hard at Priscilla. The look of concern that she had previously worn melted into a limp and bitter thousand yard stare, and a deep quiet fell over the room.

Unknotting the last of her laces, Priscilla looked up at her grandmother, and then to her mother, and back to her grandmother again. They were both just staring at her, and it was more than sort of bothering her. Rather self-consciously, she said, "What?"

Maw Scill quickly shook off the stupor that seemed to have overtaken her, and gave Priscilla her most encouraging smile. Then she came toward her, unfolding the towel. "Jesus wept, child, let's get you dried off 'fore you catch the grippe," she said, and she wrapped the towel around Priscilla's shoulders, and led her away from the door, saying, "Come in here, honey, where they's more light."

Like terror, there are many strains of love. Some abundant, some rare. Of the more infrequent forms of love, there exists only one strain of absolute purity. Just one. Only a mortal woman can possess it, and only then after having lived long enough to see her children rear children of their own. It is a love without horizon. Without measure. Infinitely vast in its expanse, it is a love without ambition or pride. It is a love that, knowing all, asks no questions, and that gives endlessly, because it understands that life is terribly, terribly difficult. It is a love that courts death. It is a love that sings like a lonesome violin. It is a love that fills a home with warmth, compassion, and the smell of baked cookies. It is the love of a life earned. It is the love of a grandmother.

And it was with this precious one-of-a-kind love that Maw Scill cleaned and stitched her granddaughter's bludgeoned head and inspected her bruises for breaks. When she finished, she kissed Priscilla softly on her forehead, just below the wound. Then she stood, and said, "I'm gonna fuckin' kill yer daddy."

Priscilla, defensively, and without a second thought, shot back, "He ain't my daddy!"

Shocked to hear the words spoken aloud, her mother blurted out her name, "Priscilla!" and the room was once again quiet.

Priscilla hung her head. No one spoke.

Maw Scill sat back down in her chair and pulled a small floral print pouch from her apron. Priscilla watched as she retrieved from the pouch a worthy pinch of tobacco and a rolling paper, which she quickly combined and set on fire. Then she took several long pulls from the cigarette and watched the dark clouds through the window. The rain was already beginning to let up. Priscilla's mother pulled a factory rolled cigarette from her own pack and struck a match, in response. Both women reminded Priscilla of movie stars. After another puff, Maw Scill spoke.

"Priscilla, honey, darlin', go on out back 'ere, and play with the cats for a few minutes. I need to talk with yer momma."

Priscilla nodded. Not caring to listen to her mother get chastised, yet again, for her poor decision making, Priscilla hopped up and made for the back door. But Maw Scill stopped her. She said, "And Priscilla…honey, don't mess with Old Blacky too much, she's bein' a little snatch. I think she's pregnant, so you let her be. And you let us know if'n you start feelin' dizzy or tired, honey. Alright?"

Maw Scill blew out a cloud of smoke and mashed the butt into an ashtray, then she sat down at the kitchen table with her daughter. Priscilla nodded again and disappeared outside.

Cats swarmed her feet the moment she stepped onto the back porch. Blacky was not among them. Priscilla picked up one of the cats and cradled it in her arms. None of them had names, per se. Most of them were called by their color or their general appearance. A black cat was called Blacky. A striped cat was called Stripes. A cat with no tail was called No Tail. And so forth. The cat Priscilla picked up was called Grey Cat Two, and Grey Cat Two was Priscilla's favorite. Grey Cat One used to be Priscilla's favorite, but he died the year before.

Walking to the far end of the porch, she found Blacky. Sunbathing herself, and swollen as a wino on payday, she was laying in the gutter that ran along the roof of Maw Scill's porch. The fat cat was posted up like a bloated toadstool and to Priscilla, she looked absolutely miserable. But absolutely miserable in an adorable sort of way, so as to make Priscilla shake her head and smile. And she damn sure was pregnant.

For who knows how long, Priscilla watched Blacky. She could simply not get over the fact that the old cat had somehow managed to find the only direct ray of sunlight in sight to bask in.

Cats are some dang wild creatures, Priscilla decided.

When she came back in the house, her mother was gone. Maw Scill was setting at the table, drinking coffee and smoking. Priscilla sat down across from her.

"Yer gonna stay with me for a while again, honey. Yer momma and fuckhead need some time alone. I reckon she's mad at me, but...well, she just don't use her brain sometimes...and with the drinkin', an—ah, hell, no matter...You feelin' alright, sugar?"

"Yeah, I'm okay, Maw Maw."

"That's my angel," she said, then she mashed her cigarette into the ashtray, got up, and moved to her chair in front of the television. She was saying something about Archie Bunker being a fat ass, and Priscilla was just about to get up to sit beside her when her stomach growled like a strangled tiger being churned in lava. She froze in her seat, her eyes wide, horrified that if she moved she would lose what little control of her bowels that she maintained. The churning continued briefly, but then it abated, and as soon as it did, Priscilla stood up and said, "Maw Maw, I'm goin' to the jake."

Maw Scill's jake was an outhouse toilet that stood about eight feet tall and was made out of rickety, rotten boards that had come from an old barn on Bunner's Ridge in nineteen fifty-three. The jake was surrounded by three foot tall weeds, except in front of

its entrance, and its door swung on rusty hinges. In the center of the door, near the top, a small waxing crescent moon that served as ventilation was cut out of the wood. Inside, was a wooden bench with a circular hole cut out of the center. It was a standard jake.

The gaps between the vertical boards that composed the frame of the jake had widened over the years, as the outhouse's foundation had settled into the earth, and it should have been relatively easy for Priscilla to notice someone approaching. But as she sat with her Sunday dress hiked up and her feet dangling several inches from the floor, humming a melody, utterly satisfied, a voice spoke to her from just outside the outhouse. It gave her such a start that she came an inch out of the hole her butt had previously plugged, and she shrieked.

The voice that spoke to her was boyish and coy-sounding but sharp, and Priscilla recognized it instantly. The voice said, "Scilly, you takin' a shit or what?"

It was Joseph. Priscilla cursed him for scaring her, calling him a dick licker and the like. Then she scolded him to leave her alone while she finished her business.

"Alright, alright," said Joseph, from between slats. "Maw Scill said you was takin' a shit, so I figured I'd come find ya. Stifle yerself, Edith, damn. You in a bad mood too? Maw Maw kicked the shit out of that one ugly cat. Oh say, I checked my traps on the way here. Got two dead in a sack. Figured we can take 'em down to the river, and drop 'em off Indian Rock—."

Priscilla's voiced boomed from inside the outhouse, "Joseph, you dickhead, leave me to do my personals!"

With a half-offended look on his face, Joseph sulked away from the outhouse, scratching at his arm and whistling the theme to *The Andy Griffith Show*.

Eventually, Priscilla opened the outhouse door and saw

Joseph sitting on her grandmother's back porch steps. He was drumming on his knees and grinning from ear to ear. Priscilla could tell right away that something had happened, and by the amount of teeth that he was showing, she assumed it was going to be good. He never ceased to gain amusement from informing Priscilla of juicy gossip or humorous and sometimes unfortunate events. As Priscilla drew nearer, Joseph said, "Hey there, ya red-headed retard, everything come out alright?"

Priscilla paused ten paces shy of the porch and glared at him. "I've had a right shitty mornin', Joseph, give me a rest. Everett bashed my brains in with his saw, and Lucky ran away…and… damn goats and…and it turns out I'm a bastard."

Joseph's eyes widened. "Holy shit, did he ever bash yer brains in. Look at them two black eyes!"

Priscilla gave Joseph another tired glare. Then, ignoring his last remark, she said, "I think I had my first organism too."

"What?! Yer shittin' me?"

Priscilla nodded. Joseph's jaw hung slack with disbelief and amazement.

Seven months prior, Joseph's Uncle Bob, his father's broth-er, had come to Joseph's house for dinner. Priscilla was there too. She sometimes ate dinner with the Smith family. Joseph's mother was incredibly fond of Priscilla, and cared for the girl as if she were her own. And as everyone attempted to eat, and to the adamant protest of Joseph's mother, Uncle Bob casually explained to Joseph and Priscilla the finer points of the female orgasm. With bated breath and thirsty minds, both Joseph and Priscilla gobbled up this information. And since that day, the legendary female orgasm had been not only a topic of lengthy discussion between the two friends, but also the overwhelming subject of each of their curiosities, particularly and understand-ably, those of Priscilla's.

"Yer fuckin' bullshitin'," said Joseph. "You mean Everett hit you so hard, you came in yer pants?"

Priscilla said nothing, nor did she laugh about Joseph's joke. She just sat down beside him on the steps. And for the first time, without the sun in his eyes, Joseph could see the damage that Everett had done with his saw. Both of Priscilla's eyes were black and there was one large green bruise covering her forehead. And from the side, he could now see the stitches just above her hairline. Almost instantly, he regretted giving her a hard time.

Finally, Priscilla said, "I ain't bullshitin' ya, and I'll make ya a deal. After we get rid of them two coons, if you help me find Lucky, I'll tell ya all about it."

Then she turned to face Joseph, and said, "And trust me, old pal, there's plenty to tell… Deal?"

Joseph nodded his head in consideration, though he would have helped her had she nothing to offer. Then he spit in his palm and held it out to Priscilla. Priscilla did the same, though she still would have told him about her orgasm had he declined to help her. Nevertheless, their salivas now interlaced, Joseph said, "Deal."

Priscilla withdrew her hand and said, "Done and done." Then she said, "Let's tell Maw Scill we're leavin'."

Maw Scill didn't like the idea of Priscilla going out with her injuries still so fresh, but the two insisted they would be careful, and Joseph promised to look out for her. And eventually Maw Scill finally gave in. She seemed to trust Joseph. She always had, for whatever reason. When Priscilla was with him, her grandmother rarely questioned her.

And so the two of them set out for the woods, Joseph toting a potato sack half full of dead raccoons, and Priscilla with a bright red sucker jammed in her cheek. Most signs of rain were erased from the sky and the sun shone down on them as they breached the tree line. They made their way to Indian Rock, and Joseph dropped the sack into the river. They watched it float downstream until it was out of sight, and when it was gone, Joseph said, "Alright then, Scilly, let's find us a dog."

'Peace Frog' by The Doors plays

———◆———

ChaPtEr FIIVE

Well, it's a big round copper pot with a fire under it,
and there's a pipe that curls round and round like this,
and runs into a little bucket.
—Opie Taylor

Clockmaker, West Virginia, in nineteen hundred and seventy-one, was a forgotten town, forgotten by most who didn't live there, and even still by a few who did. The Clockmaker Number Nine Coal Mine was the chief employer in Clockmaker, and the soul reason for the town's founding and development. Next to the mine, the second largest employer was Shaffer's timber mill, which provided jobs for fewer than twenty. The high school employed ten, and the elementary school employed four. There were a few other opportunities, not many, but a few, and otherwise, people got by in any way they could.

Some of the men chopped, split, and sold firewood. Others traded vegetables from their gardens, or game meat. While some women mended clothes, or waited tables at the diner, or served bar, most women and a noticeable number of men didn't work. Some collected a government check, and others would have rather starved to death than accept a handout from anyone, let alone from the United States Government, but one way or another, all but the dead got by.

The town had one grocery market, Layfields, that also served as a general store, selling everything from loaves of bread and

ELDER TERRITORY
OLD MAN FARMORE PLACE
#9 MINE
MAWSCILL'S HOUSE
PRISCILLA'S HOUSE
UNCLE BOB'S HOUSE
SCHOOL
SHERIFF STATION
MAIN STREET
JOSEPH'S HOUSE
LAYFIELD'S MARKET

BUFFALO CREEK
ROBINETTE
MAW
CROWN
GUYANDOTTE RIVER
THE KNOB
TIMBERMILL

canned sardines to lengths of rope and ten penny nails. There was one bank, owned by the mine of course, and five churches, including Mount Zion Methodist. Of the others, one was Catholic, two were Baptist, one for whites and one for blacks, and the last was Presbyterian. There was one doctor, Doctor Zonts, a rather brilliant clandestine chemist, who, in the basement of his home, unbeknownst to all, synthesized everything from liquid heroin to LSZ. And interestingly enough, a wide variety of sleeping aids.

Additionally, there were two bars that served liquor, and one that sold only beer, the Clockmaker Tavern and Broken Key having long since shut down with the passing of Fish. There was a drive-in theater just outside of town. Other than the salvage yard and the creek beds, it served as the primary source of entertainment for the youth of Clockmaker. There was E-Rundle's Diner, across from the white Baptist church, a post office, a fueling station, and across the street an old brick building that housed the office of Sheriff Maynard White. Unlike the cops on television, the sheriff rarely smiled or laughed, and he most certainly did not play the guitar. He was nothing at all like Andy Griffith. But then again, Clockmaker was nothing at all like Mayberry, either.

The town sat just southeast of the mouth of Buffalo Creek, along the Guyandotte River, and was surrounded by a dense and unforgiving forest that proceeded well into eastern Kentucky and Tennessee. Desolate as it was, there still were available many of the luxuries of city life for a number of people in Clockmaker, but while some drove cars and had televisions, quite a few others had little more than a shack and a pair of shoes. Nevertheless, despite the isolation these differences still divided them.

But it must be understood that, whether or not the people of Clockmaker were employed or vagrant, whether they mined coal or pissed away their days on a bottle of rot-gut, they were a people who were not originally meant for the woods. In the early days, to mine coal in West Virginia was to walk away from the comforts and safety of the developed and civilized world, but for most what was left behind turned out to be of as little value as the things they had brought along, because they had, near all, forgotten to pack an understanding of how to properly survive in such a wild and inhospitable wilderness. They were an industrialized people, lured into untapped mountains by the promise of big money. They were out of tune with the seasons and had no feeling for the ground. And inevitably, they suffered for it. Television rich or one pair of pants poor, they all suffered.

Luckily for Priscilla, this was not the case with Joseph. The woods, the ground, the seasons, they were where the young man shined. Joseph spent nearly all of his waking hours outside, and mostly in the forest. He was a proficient hunter, fisher, and trapper, and recently he had taken to tracking larger game by sign of scat, blood, or earth print. He could climb a tree like a squirrel and swim a stream like a trout. He knew which berries and mushrooms would sustain human life and he knew which ones would extinguish it. He could build a fire in the rain and harvest plants from seed. All but the gardening, for which he could thank his mother, he learned from his father and uncle and grandfather, each avid woodsmen. His grandfather in particular could skin a buck hanging from its hind legs in under a minute, a record that both of the old man's sons had tried for years to beat but never could.

The truth is that Joseph had once seen his father skin a buck in fifty-four seconds, beating his grandfather's best time by five-hundreth of a minute, and when Joseph asked his father why he wasn't going to mention it to the old man, his father told him that there were things in life more important than winning. "Most things in fact." He told Joseph, "Yer grandaddy has been knocked down a peg or two many a time in his life, but he always did his best by me, and by you too. So it seems to me, we oughta just let 'em have this'n. Dignity's hard enough to hold on to as it is, Joseph. Time has a way of passin'. You'll see for yerself someday. We all grow older and weaker."

Joseph held Priscilla's hand as she jumped down from Indian Rock, then they climbed up the river bank to the path that led back to Maw Scill's. Joseph's plan was to stop at The Hideout for supplies, and then start their search for Lucky at the spot where Priscilla saw him disappear into the wood line behind her house.

When they got up to the path, Joseph said, "Hot damn, yer eyes are blacker than pitch now. You sure yer feelin' up to hikin'?"

Priscilla looked at him unwaveringly, and said, "Everett ain't raise no bitch. To the hideout."

And off they went.

On their way, Joseph, outwardly amazed that he had forgotten, told Priscilla all about what happened that morning in church. He told her about the new preacher and his snakes, about Kathleen Gibbons fainting on the piano, and about the sound it made, and how he laughed. And though Priscilla refused to believe him at first, thinking that he was, for some reason, putting her on, she eventually had no choice. The perceived gossip was far too detailed to be a lie, and Joseph was absolutely insistent in his honesty. Priscilla was dumbfounded. "Snakes? In church?"

The Fort, sometimes known as The Hideout, was a poorly constructed scrap lumber shack that was nailed into the branches of a mammoth White Oak. It was so high up in the tree that it was invisible from the ground, and the only two people who knew about its existence were Priscilla and Joseph. There were pieces of two-by-fours nailed to the tree that served as a ladder, but the first rung was nearly fifteen feet off the ground. In order to access that first rung, Joseph had constructed a removable ladder that was kept in a briar thicket, which, once removed from the thorns and leaned against the enormous tree, could be used to gain access to the first length of two-by-four. Once up the ladder, there were two padlocks on the floor entrance to The Hideout that Joseph removed, using a key that was kept hidden in a hollowed out knot at the tree's base.

Inside, Joseph went to the far end of the room and removed a piece of the floorboard, a trick Priscilla had shown him. Then he kneeled down and removed another padlock. Under the floor of the shack, Joseph kept a rifle, a machete, several knives, an old grenade that he stole from his uncle Bob, several sticks of dynamite, and a stack of adult magazines. He removed the rifle and the machete. Then he said, "Well, don't look at me like that, Scilly, goddamn. You never know, we might need it."

Priscilla glared at him, her hands on her hips. "We don't need yer rifle to find Lucky," she said, impatiently.

"Oh come on, we might see a big old buck along the way. The Hideout needs a rack on the wall."

"The Hideout needs more nails in the ladder."

"Aw, that ladder's fine. And it ain't like I'm bringin' the dynamite, shit. We can have a little fun. And the machete we actually need."

Priscilla conceded without another word. She closed her eyes and raised her palm to him. Then she said, "What else do we need?"

Joseph tossed Priscilla a large military issue shoulder pack, a late birthday gift from his father, and started reading to her from a mental list as he inspected his rifle.

"Compass."

"Check," said Priscilla, after locating it under a stack of comic books.

"Binoculars."

They were hanging by the door. "Check."

"Matches and striker."

"Check."

"Ammunition."

"Check."

"Flashlights."

"Check."

Replacing the padlock, Joseph said, "Put the key back in the knot, I'll carry the pack down, we got about four hours 'fore dark."

Priscilla dropped the pack beside Joseph and said, "Real live snakes, huh?"

Joseph look up at her and smiled. "I swear it."

Priscilla stared at him, attempting to read his face, searching for any sign of deceit, and after finding none, she wearily shook her head and proceeded to make her way through the floor hatch and down the ladder.

From inside The Hideout, Joseph heard Priscilla say to herself, "A girl misses one gotdang day of church."

◆

They started their search for Lucky at the tree line beyond the field behind Priscilla's house, and though she was sure that the dog hadn't been too badly wounded by Everett's boot, Joseph found a blood trail almost immediately. Fortunately, the rain hadn't lasted long enough to thoroughly penetrate the forest canopy and wash it away. He followed the trail for some time before losing it, and when he did, he told Priscilla to stay put and he went off by himself. He came back, then disappeared again, this time at a more westward angle. When he returned the second time, he said that he had found more blood and they continued on.

Further and further into the hills, they walked. The day drew on, and the air had warmed some but it was still quite chilly. Joseph untied a flannel shirt from around his waist and handed it to Priscilla. She put it on. Joseph had lost track of the blood trail three times since they began the search, but this time, he was fairly certain that he'd lost it for good. He had carefully scoured the perimeter, fifty yards from the last sign of blood, east to west and over again, and found nothing. He could only assume that the dog's wound had dried up because the blood trail hadn't led to something dead, as blood trails often do. And obviously dogs don't just disappear into thin air, either. But just as he was about to vocalize his defeat to Priscilla, something caught his eye.

It was a small patch of dirt that appeared newly unearthed, as if something had been recently buried there. Joseph moved to it, crouched down, and began gently digging into the soil. What he found, shallowly buried, made him recoil with disgust. He leapt to his feet and stared down at it. He had been wrong about the dog's wound having healed. Lucky wasn't wounded. Not at all. And he wasn't bleeding. He'd been carrying something that was bleeding.

Joseph looked to Priscilla who was watching him from behind a fallen and rotting Sycamore, and said, "Well, Scilly, you want the good news or the bad news first?"

Priscilla's shoulders slumped. "The good," she said with indifference. She couldn't see what Joseph had found from where she was standing.

"Well, the good news is, I don't reckon Lucky's hurt at all. It ain't his blood we been followin'. But I have a feelin' we're still on the right track."

Priscilla raised an eyebrow. "What's the bad news?"

Joseph grinned. "I found a right nice size chunk of yer daddy's …uh, looks like his right hand."

Priscilla's eyes went wide, but quickly lowered into a scowl. "He ain't my fuckin' daddy, fucker," she responded.

Joseph raised his hands in surrender. "My mistake, my mistake. I apologize," he said. Then he bent down, snatched the mangled hand from the dirt, and hurled it at Priscilla. She shrieked, having barely avoided it, and nearly fell over a bed of rocks trying to move out of the way. As she cursed him, Joseph, through howls of laughter, said, "Hey Scilly, I found a right nice size chunk of *Everett's* hand." Then he said, "Hey Scilly, whoever woulda thought that Everett was gonna give us a *hand*, lookin' for Lucky." And they both had a good laugh at that.

They left the better part of Everett's right hand, which was eaten by a family of birds the following morning, in the pile of fallen branches where Joseph threw it, with the intention of heading back the way they came. Joseph assured Priscilla that their hunt was not over, merely halted by the setting sun, and after school, the following day, they would return to begin their search anew.

On the way home, however, Joseph decided to take what he thought was a shortcut that would bring them out just above the mine, but it wasn't long before they both realized that he had made a mistake. He had gotten cocky, keeping hold of that blood trail the way he had. And because of his arrogance, he had foolishly gotten them so turned around that he could not now determine which direction was the one that led back to Clockmaker. And to make matters worse, the goddamn sun was setting.

Joseph tried the compass. He rotated the housing but the magnetic needle stayed pinned, and wouldn't orient with the arrow. It was busted. "We might be up shit crick," he said, as he continued to spin in circles, eyeing the compass.

Priscilla adjusted the pack on her shoulder and watched him. "So what do we do now?"

Joseph scratched his head. "Welp, best I can figure is we hole up in 'at old cabin we saw back yonder for the night, I seen a stove pipe comin' outta the top of it. You may as well pull 'em flashlights out. Dark's comin' on quick."

"Are you fuckin' kiddin' me? We gotta sleep in the woods?"

Joseph hung his head. "I don't see another choice."

Prisicilla dropped to one knee and began undoing the pack's draw strings. The cabin would have to do. Its windows were broken out, and a part of the roof was caved in, but it would have to do. It was getting cold. Priscilla threw one of the flashlights to Joseph and then she attempted to turn on the other one, but it was dead. Joseph tried his. Dead too.

"Jesus Tap Dancin' Christ," said Joseph. "We really gotta' start inspectin' our gear a little better 'fore goin' on missions, Scilly."

Priscilla closed her eyes and hung her head over the pack. Grinning down at her, Joseph said, "You prayin' the matches'll work?"

Priscilla looked sternly up at Joseph. She was not amused. "I'm prayin' for the strength to not kick you square in the nuts. Now let's go."

'John the Revelator' by Ralph Stanley plays

◆

In nineteen hundred and three, a man named Clayton Doty came to West Virginia with the intention of killing someone. No one in particular, just someone. He'd wanted to do it for as long as he could remember, but he could never quite summon the courage, for fear of Hell. So at the dismal old age of seventy-six, Clayton came to West Virginia and went far up into the mountains, where he built a small cabin. He lived there, alone, for one year. In that time, he read the Bible twice and built a rock garden. Then he killed himself. He hung himself from a rafter with his own belt, and on the cabin's only table, he left a note that said, *Better me than you.*

Clayton was an unextraordinary man who lived an unextraordinary life, but the cabin that he built would simply have to do, because by the time Joseph kicked its front door in, all light had vanished from the sky and night was upon them.

In the dark, the cabin appeared haunted, though Priscilla did not mention that fact. When they passed it during the day, it simply looked abandoned and in need of repair, but at night, vaguely visible by the light of the moon, the cabin took on a demonic appearance, as though occupied by the worst kind of ghosts and ghouls. Its boards were decaying, and its foundation had sunk on one side, causing the cabin to warp to the left and sag at its central gable. It was surrounded by weeds and a dense undergrowth, and unbeknownst to Priscilla, Joseph had quietly slid a shell into the chamber of his rifle as they approached it.

The door of the cabin now open, Priscilla and Joseph stared into a tomb of pure blackness. A netherworld of children's worst fears. Nothing inside the cabin could be seen. Priscilla was waiting for some hideous monster to come slithering out of the darkness to eat them. But when Joseph struck a match and stepped into the cabin, she could see through the cobwebs and dust that it was uninhabited, and after looking back over her shoulder, she followed him inside.

Joseph instantly moved to a potbelly stove in the corner of the cabin, beside which was a small pile of firewood and some old newspapers, and began building a fire. Priscilla was glad for it. A fire would certainly help. The air had gotten cold since the sun set, and it wasn't much warmer inside the cabin. The two of them could have survived without shelter, but without some sort of walls to fend off the wind there would have been little in the way of comfort or sleep. Joseph had been right, the cabin was necessary.

While Joseph tended the fire, Priscilla walked about the cabin, searching for anything that might prove helpful in their situation. There was a single table and a single chair, and in one corner of the room there were several empty glass bottles of different sizes and shapes, but the quick inspection found nothing of any true value. Spent matches, dead bugs, an old shoe.

After Joseph got the fire roaring, he and Priscilla laid down on the bare floor beside the stove. They talked for a while, mostly about their misfortune that day, and briefly about Priscilla's morning, and obviously her *organism*. With the firelight dancing around the room, the cabin was far less scary than it had been when they first arrived, and Priscilla felt sort of silly for having ever feared the old place.

By and by, Joseph fell asleep, and Priscilla rolled on to her side, toward him. How she adored Joseph. He made her feel so safe when they were together. She would have been absolutely terrified to sleep in that cabin without him. And laying there on the floor, beside the fire, she watched her friend as he slept, and she thanked God for him, and for his presence in her life. She added a prayer for her mother and for Lucky, and for Maw Scill. Then she closed her eyes.

But just as Priscilla was about to drift over the edge of unconsciousness, there came a sound from outside the cabin. At first, she didn't move, only listened. But when she heard the sound again, she shot up right, certain that the sound that she was hearing was that of cautiously approaching footsteps. CRUNCH. Then she heard it again, twigs breaking under foot. SNAP. She began shaking Joseph, and whispering to him to wake up. All the while she could hear the footsteps slowly growing closer. CRUNCH.

When Joseph awoke he must have been able to tell from the look on Priscilla's face that something was wrong, because he spoke in a whisper. 'What is it?'

"Someone's here," Priscilla whispered back.

Joseph bolted upright and pulled his rifle on to his lap, and he slid over in front of Priscilla, positioning himself between her and the cabin's entrance. For a moment, they waited, and there was nothing. Then there was another noise. It sounded uncannily like a tongue clicking twice against the roof of a mouth. Which meant whatever was outside was likely human. It could have been a vampire of course, but whatever it was, judging by volume, it was right outside the cabin door.

Joseph, still seated on the floor of the cabin with Priscilla at his back, lifted his rifle into a firing position, and waited. They could hear the faint electric hum of the night, but otherwise nothing stirred. Nothing moved, save the still flickering fire in the stove. Then after what seemed like forever, in terrified-teenager-time, the door of the cabin slowly eased open several inches.

CREEEEEEEEECK

Joseph lowered his finger to the trigger, and Priscilla tightened her hold on his shoulder. But what came through the door was not a person. Nor was it any sort of specter or revenant, either. What came through the door was a voice. A small voice, sounding like that of a young boy. The voice tried to sound authoritative, but to both Joseph and Priscilla, it had failed in that regard, and while Priscilla loosened her grip on Joseph, Joseph loosened his grip on his rifle.

The voice that came through the door had said, "Come out with yer hands up, varmints! This here's my territory, and that there's *my* wood I can smell a'burnin'."

Priscilla and Joseph looked at one another. Then Joseph shouted, "We ain't varmints, fucker. We's lost. Just hole'n up fer the night."

There was a brief quiet before the voice responded, but when it did, it said, "Ye armed?"

"Durn fuckin' tootin'," Joseph shouted quickly, "we armed to the fuckin' teeth."

"Aw heck, ye ain't armed. You sound like a boy," came the voice.

"I sound like a boy? Son of a bitch, you sound like a dang kid."

"That's fair," the voice said, matter-of-factly. "I am." Then the kid said, "How many ye got in there?"

"Five," Joseph shouted, too quickly for his own good.

"Now I know ye's puttin' me on," said the kid.

Joseph's bluff had been called. To himself, he said, "Fuck." Then, aloud, he said, "Alright fucker, there's only two of us, but we's well-armed, I tell ye."

With confidence, and drawing out the last two words for emphasis, the kid said, "You ain't armed, rascal."

With more than a bit of satisfaction, Joseph responded to the kid's smug assertion by pulling the trigger on his rifle and firing it into the ceiling of the cabin. KERBLAM! Debris rained down and Priscilla's ears rang like she was inside a church bell. She was pissed. She smacked Joseph on the shoulder and said, "Dick sucker."

After a moment, the smoke having time to have cleared, the kid, in a much more serious tone, said, "I thought ye killed me for a second." All playfulness had vanished from his voice, along with his wild-west accent. Then the kid said, in that same dour tone, "Alright feller, the jig's up, yen's is armed and I ain't. I don't want no trouble. Don't bushwhack me. I'm just a defenseless kid, true enough, but that there is my firewood I can smell burnin'. I collected it, so I do have some right to it."

By this time Priscilla was standing. This had gone on long enough. She could take part in this juvenile, biscuits-and-gravy western no longer. Joseph was opening his mouth, probably to refute the kid's timber claim, but Priscilla raised her hand to him, and he stopped. And though she was still looking directly at Joseph, she said to the kid outside, "We're sorry we burned yer wood. We was lost, and it got dark and we—."

The kid blurted, "You gotta dang girl in there with ye?! What are y'all doin', you gettin' busy in my mansion? This ain't no dang house of ill repute!"

Priscilla came back hot. "We are—well, I—I got yer house of ill repute, you little bastard!"

Just to her right, in the pale darkness, Priscilla heard a brief snicker, and she turned to see Joseph fighting back a grin, pretending to be casual and innocent. So she took two steps and slugged him hard in his bicep. She did this a lot, punch Joseph. It was the only way to get his attention.

"That's fair," the kid said, from behind the door. Then the kid said, "Y'all for real lost?"

At the same time, Priscilla said, "Yes," and Joseph said, "Sure as shit."

A few seconds passed and the kid said, "Alright, I'm a'comin' in. Hands is up, don't kill me."

The front door of the cabin opened wider now, and out of the darkness of the night came a small, thin, tan boy who appeared to be maybe nine or ten years old. His hair was long and black and tangled, and he had on only a pair of dirty and torn denim bib overalls. He wore no undershirt and no shoes. As he stepped cautiously into the cabin, with his hands raised, he clicked his tongue twice, and Joseph made to raise his rifle at him, but Priscilla took hold of the barrel and pushed it back toward the floor.

Priscilla and Joseph watched from beside the woodstove as the kid came closer, into the heart of the cabin. He was mostly still concealed in shadows, the fire now casting only a faint glow, but as he approached them and his filthy cherubic face became more visible, Priscilla was seized by a sudden sense of dread. It was the kid's eyes. When she looked into them, she saw not the bright, spirited eyes of a child, but the milky dead orbs of a demon. *Dear Jesus*, she thought. *We've been fooled.* At any moment, the kid would sprout wings and fangs, and pounce, draining their blood from their necks. Priscilla braced herself.

But then Joseph, said, "Holyyy shit, you a Elder boy, ain't ya."

The kid stopped, and lowered his hands, but not all the way. He was still a good six feet away, standing beside the table. The kid looked around the cabin, as if he were watching a bird fly by in the distance. And after the bird had passed, his gaze fixed back on Priscilla and Joseph, and, almost serenely, he said, "That depends, who's askin'?"

Joseph spoke up first. He told the kid his name, and then he told him Priscilla's name. Priscilla didn't speak. She couldn't look away from the kid's empty eyes. She was no longer scared so much as mesmerized. It was when Joseph said the kid's name that things started to make sense. Who the kid was dawned on her, and she realized, in addition to his lineage, why his eyes were the way they were, but she could not quit staring at them, all the same. Floating there in the night, all white except for the outer rim of a cloudy grey iris, the kid's pupils were perfectly obscured by a bleached moon, and Priscilla felt as though she were gazing into two reverse solar eclipses.

The kid said, "Carpenter, huh? My daddy knows a Carpenter feller. Maybe my daddy knows yer daddy?"

The question broke Priscilla's trance, and she started to say that *Everett was not her fuckin' daddy* but thought otherwise. Instead she said, "I reckon they might."

The kid took pause to this, and scratched his chin as though pondering, then he said, "Well then, I reckon you two oughta come on back to my place. We got ham to eat, and we can give ye a bed."

Priscilla studied the kid, trying to determine his intentions. She had heard about the Elder clan. Not much, but she had heard that they were all blind and she would hear people talk about staying away from them for fear of catching whatever disease that surely afflicted them. She knew Joseph had heard the rumors too, but when she looked at Joseph, he seemed at ease. Maybe he knew something that she didn't. She hoped he did, and when he looked back at her, she gave him a nod, as if to say, *It's up to you.*

Looking back at the kid, Joseph said, "Alright, to hell with it, let's have a sleepover with the creepy blind kid."

"Yee-haw," said the creepy blind kid, "damp 'at fire out, n' get yer stuff. T'ain't far, two thousand paces, give er take."

Priscilla and Joseph both stared at him. She was sure that she and Joseph were wondering the same thing, but fortunately, Joseph spoke first. "Elder, quick question, how the hell is yer blind ass gonna get us anywhere in the dark?"

The kid didn't answer right away. He allowed the absurdity of the question time to expand before he spoke, and only smiled in a confident sort of way. "When yer blind, Joseph Smith, it's dark always," said the kid solemnly. Then he turned on his heels, and walked toward the door, saying, "I smell glycerin too, y'all packin' dynamite?"

Joseph stopped moving. To himself, Priscilla heard him say, "What in the fuck?"

"Thought you weren't bringin' it," said Priscilla.

Joseph turned to face her, and he started to speak but faltered. Maybe it was the stink-eye she was giving him, or the way she was standing with her hands on her hips, but he fumbled with his words. She was sure he was about to deny being in possession of the Apache dynamite they had found at the rock yard two months prior, or maybe even apologize, explaining his entire thought process for bringing dynamite along to find a lost dog, but all that came out of him, and no longer in a whisper, was, "Well, goddamn, Scilly. What good's a gun without a stick of dynamite?"

Before Priscilla had a chance to respond to such a ludicrous question, the kid, from outside the cabin, began softly singing,

"Joseph and Priscilla, sittin' in a tree…"

Priscilla and Joseph both, once again, responded simultaneously, and this time with nearly the same phrase:

"Go fuck yerself!"

"Ehh, go fuck yerself!"

Outside the cabin, the kid was smiling at being told to fuck himself. He pulled out his last wad of tobacco and stuffed it in his cheek. Then he hooked his thumbs into his bibs and, staring up at what would be the sky if he could see it, he hummed an unknown tune.

◆

The kid's name was Elias Elder, and he was indeed blind. As was his entire family. He was nine years old and he was the son of Mathias Elder, and the grandson of Obadias Elder. His mother, a Siamese woman named Khun Mae, had died while giving birth to his brother, who was now four years old and slow to learn. Elias liked cowboys and soda pop and chewing tobacco and fiddle music. He had one brother, the slow one, nine sisters, and sixteen cousins, and his favorite thing to eat was rabbit meat. He hated snakes, locusts, and liars, and he was born with a third nipple under his arm. And so forth. Or so Elias told them.

The Elder boy prattled on about himself as he led Priscilla and Joseph through the dark woods. Elias also liked climbing trees and playing hide-and-go-seek with his cousins and he said as much. When Joseph queried how exactly it was possible for a blind person to do either of those things successfully, and for that matter, how he was able to lead them through the woods without eyes, Elias told them that he counted his steps a lot, that getting down a tree was always harder than getting up, and that when he clicked his tongue, he could sort of see things. "Mostly big stuff," he added. "People and trees and houses. Stuff like that." And although these explanations were far from satisfying, Joseph did not prod further. Elias talked enough without encouragement.

As they made their way through the chilly moonless night, Priscilla watched Elias. She didn't necessarily have to pay careful attention in order to keep track of him in the dark, but she couldn't help but marvel at how easily and gracefully he navigated the woods. He would occasionally click his tongue and from time to time, he would call out a warning about obstacles that lay in their path, but he himself never tripped or stumbled or even hesitated. He walked confidently and at one point, Priscilla saw him just barely duck a tree branch that would have left a mark on his forehead at the pace they were moving. He moved so fluidly, in fact, that Priscilla was beginning to have a hard time believing that Elias was any blinder than she was.

The journey to Elias's house was longer than Priscilla expected, and far more arduous. Elias seemed to be taking the most direct route, as opposed to the clearest. Instead of walking around fallen trees or large rocks or even briar thickets, he would simply go right through them or over them, whatever was necessary. At one point, when Priscilla had first noticed that Elias's flight path was that of the crow, albeit without wings, she considered mentioning an alternative route along a barely visible creek bank, but then she remembered that Elias was blind, and that she was the one who was lost. So instead of speaking, she scolded herself for having been so presumptuous, and kept walking.

For most of the pilgrimage they had walked uphill, through a dense underbrush that Joseph hacked away at with his machete, removing briars and low hanging limbs as they went. Joseph figured it would make it that much easier for Elias to reach his mansion in the future, and he told him as much. After nearly thirty minutes, the mountain they had been ascending began to level out and Elias stopped and looked back at Priscilla and Joseph. His white, irisless eyes seemed to be floating in the dim night, and he said, "Y'all hear that?"

Priscilla and Joseph both stopped moving and listened. Priscilla could hear the wind, and she could hear leaves rustling in the trees, but nothing else worth noting. She looked to Joseph to see if his hearing was any better than hers, but he only shrugged his shoulders. What had Elias heard? Were they being followed? Was it a bear? A wolf? Before Priscilla had time to panic, Elias whispered, with a smile that no one could see, "Daddy's awake… y'all stay quiet now."

Elias turned and started walking again and Priscilla and Joseph both followed, but it was because Priscilla could not see Elias's smile in the dark that she proceeded with dubious apprehension. Something in Elias's tone seemed cautionary to Priscilla, and maybe it was the dark of the woods, or her experience with her own father, or perhaps it was simply the macabre theme of the day, but with the words 'Daddy's awake,' Priscilla began to fear that following this strange blind boy deep into the woods may have been a mistake. *What have we gotten ourselves into?* was the resounding question being silently shuffled like a deck of cards through her mind as she and Joseph followed Elias. The same forest that had seemed so ordinary only moments ago now took on the sort of spooky quality that only kids can conjure when the unknown gets the best of them.

As they followed Elias, the ground leveled out completely, and in front of them, out of the blackness of the night, appeared a giant rock wall, a cliff face overgrown with trees and vines, so vast that in the dark its edges could not be discerned, nor its height nor depth. And sunk into the face of the rock, like a rusty and forgotten Excalibur, was a large, forbidding wooden door.

Joseph struck a match, and cast a faint light on their surroundings. The door appeared old but strong, and it swung on large iron hinges. Crudely carved into the center of the door were the letters EST and the numbers one nine zero nine.

Elias reached into the chest of his bibs and retrieved an old skeleton key that was hanging by a chord around his neck, and when he turned the key inside the warded lock, a heavy bolt disengaged sharply. Before opening the door, Elias turned to his new friends, his eyes more perceivable and more innocently menacing than ever. And as Joseph's match died out, Elias crossed his mouth with his first finger and said, "Shhhhhh…"

'Nocturnes in E Flat Major, Op.9 No.2'
by Frederic Chopin plays in all worlds

As soon as Elias began opening the door, Priscilla could hear it. The sound floated out of the mountainside like some ghostly lullaby, like the fond memory of some picnic on some sunny day with some lover who has long since passed and will never be met again, like the good intentions that pave the eternally long road to Hell, like the death of an old enemy. She recognized the sound immediately, it was a piano, and she turned to Joseph for confirmation, but Joseph was already looking past her, lost in some trance, hypnotized and fixed within the rock that lay before them and the sweet silvery sound that was escaping its solitary entrance. Joseph's mouth hung open. His eyes were dazzled and dancing with stars, and to Priscilla, he looked as though he were gazing into the eyes of God.

When Priscilla looked back toward the rock, Elias was standing in its doorway with his thumbs hooked into the suspenders of his overalls. He stood there for a moment, just listening, rocking back and forth on his heels, looking down at what would have been Priscilla, had he sight. Then he said, with noticeable pride, "Y'can hear it now, cain't ya?"

To no one in particular, Priscilla nodded. She could indeed hear it. It was beautiful. Priscilla stared into the darkness of the doorway beyond Elias, from which the music was coming, and at first the inside of the cliff face appeared dark and cavernous, but as her eyes adjusted, she could see within the great stone. A glimmer of light that revealed an elegantly constructed corridor with unlit lanterns lining its walls laid before her. The light seemed to be coming from somewhere deep inside the rock, and Priscilla couldn't help but imagine that somehow the music and the light were radiating from the same source.

And in the literal sense, she was wrong, but in ways she was right. Of course the music and the light weren't actually coming from the same place, it's not as if somewhere inside the mountain played some fancy neon jukebox, but the truth is that the same man who had built the fire was indeed the same man responsible for the sounds now echoing out of the rock, and the ultimate truth is that when it comes to all matters metaphysical, transcendental, or divine, music and light are two of three things that spring from a source of absolute and utter purity, love being the third. So, as stated, in ways, she was right.

The music continued playing as Priscilla and Joseph followed Elias through the dimly-lit corridor. The passage through the rock, although narrow, was chiseled to perfection. Priscilla felt as if she were walking through Count Dracula's catacombs. With every step she took, the light that seemed to emanate from somewhere at the end of the winding hall grew brighter, the music echoed louder, and the details of her environment became more clear.

She couldn't believe she was inside a mountain. The walls were lined with green glass lanterns that clearly hadn't been lit or touched in years, their globes filled with a multitude of dead insects and covered in blanketed layers of spiderwebs, some inhabited, some not. Under each lantern, carved out of the rock itself, like canine gargoyles, was the bust of a grave and fierce-looking English Mastiff hound, and as they passed each one, Priscilla watched spiders disappear into their mouths.

The passage through the mountain was maybe forty feet. It wound uphill to the right, and up three stone steps that had also been carved out of the very rock itself, and then downhill to the left. As she followed Elias around the last bend, carried by the sound of wistful melodies, Priscilla felt as though she were floating. Under these circumstances, she would have normally been afraid as any person would in such a vulnerable position, surrounded by spiders and stone hounds, and coerced along through the darkness of what appeared to be an ancestral tomb by some strange, although admittedly charming, demon-eyed hillbilly sprite with a fondness for Herman Munster and an ear for high art—but alas, she was not. No fear stirred within her.

It was the music, or perhaps the melody, that softened the nature of her surroundings, that kept almighty fear at bay. The music carried Priscilla. It cradled her and inspired in her a sense of awe and wonder, where suspicion and uncertainty would have otherwise surely resided. She felt as though she were still asleep in the cabin and that this was all some strange dream from which she had yet to wake. The mysterious tunnel through the rock, the blind child, the darkness, the piano music, all combined to create a dream-like quality that permeated Priscilla's reality so fully that she had to reach out and touch the rock wall to be certain of what was real. And though this simple stroke of stone did indeed momentarily remedy her confusion and curiosity, it wouldn't be long before Priscilla would realize that the presence of physical matter has little to no bearing in the determination of what is real in this world or in that of dreams, and that the only possible way to tell if anything is real in this life is to die.

When they came out of the rock, the music was still playing. Priscilla could smell smoke and the breeze felt cool on her cheeks. They were now walking along a well-worn footpath, cast in the light of some distant and great fire. All around them, everywhere, interlaced with the same footpath, were small wooden shacks. More than Priscilla could count. The shacks were scattered about the woods like carelessly rolled dice, and apparently without deliberation. All of the underbrush around them had been removed, including rocks. There was not a single stone to trip over. However, it appeared as though not one tree had been cut down or even trimmed during the construction of these shacks. They grew strong and tall in the oddest of places.

The shacks sat in between the trees and among them. Some of the shacks had been sitting so long that the trees had grown into them and now added to the overall integrity of the structure. Some of the shacks were raised and some weren't. Some had porches and some didn't. The shacks were of all different shapes and sizes, mostly ramshackle, but they were all dark and still inside. Priscilla noticed as they passed that not a single candle burned in any of their windows, and although she wasn't scared so much as perpetually lost, to herself, as she walked, she said, "Dear Jesus, watch over me."

Beyond the haphazardly-erected hovels was a clearing where a large fire roared. The clearing was only visible in glimpses as they made their way through the shacks and trees. It was obviously where the light was coming from, and Priscilla assumed the music was coming from there as well, but she had also assumed, from its clarity and colorful tone, that the music was coming from vinyl on a turntable. So imagine her surprise when, after following Elias around a Birchwood lean-to and into the clearing, she found the silhouette of a large bearded man tickling the ivory on a nearly decayed grand piano while gazing deep into the embers of a fire the size of a small house.

As they entered the clearing, once again, Elias held his finger to his lips. The man at the piano continued to play, seemingly unaware of their presence. Priscilla looked back at Joseph, whose eyes were wide with excitement and noticeable unease. He hadn't spoken since they entered the rock and Priscilla could tell that he was dying to say something, anything. His nervous tension was palpable, and when Joseph was on edge, he could rarely go a second without cracking wise to lighten the mood. He simply couldn't handle silence and Priscilla thought he sometimes talked too much because of that. And even though he had been quiet up to that point, she could tell that he wouldn't last much longer.

They approached the pianist from behind, and as they drew closer, the silhouette in front of the fire took shape. His hair was wavy, full, hanging nearly to his waist. His arms and back were thick and muscular. He wore a flannel shirt rolled up at the sleeves. From behind, Priscilla watched the man's fingers move across the keys. His movements were graceful, deliberate, and quick, like that of a master, far superior to anything Kathleen Gibbons ever played in church, and beside the man, on the piano bench, was a half-empty bottle of whiskey.

Could this really be Elias's father? Priscilla was watching the man's fingers as they began pounding the keys, a silhouette bathed in fire. *What had he said his father's name was…? Mathias?*

Priscilla thought she had heard the name Mathias Elder on one other occasion, though she couldn't remember the context. It just seemed familiar. She thought maybe it was Maw Scill who had mentioned the name once, but she couldn't be sure. The only other things she had heard about the Elder clan, at church mostly and some in school, were that they were rendered blind by disease or a bad batch of moonshine liquor, no one knew for sure which, and that they didn't pay taxes or believe in God.

Just then, the man swept his hand along the keys from one side to the other, low to high, and when his fingers reached the last white key, he said, without turning to face them, "Evenin', son."

Priscilla and Joseph both froze in their tracks. The man at the piano lifted the bottle at his side and tilted it into his mouth. Elias plopped down backwards on the bench beside him, and while still looking at what would have been Priscilla and Joseph, with a proud smile, he said, "Evenin', Daddy. Joseph and Priscilla, this here's my daddy, Mathias Elder. Daddy, this here's Mister Joseph Smith and a Miss Priscilla Carpenter. Daddy sure does play good, don't he? And I sure am sorry for makin' y'all be so still on the way in, I just love to hear Daddy play. The drunker he is, the better he plays too, that's what everyone says."

As Elias spoke, his father turned slowly on the bench to face them. His face was hard and scarred, and his great beard flowed seamlessly into his tangled hair. His eyes were white like his son's, and with the fire burning massive behind him, he appeared like some ancient Viking. He placed an arm around Elias's shoulder and pulled him close, and for a moment the two blind men, father and son, dully stared at Priscilla and Joseph, their cloudy, lifeless eyes plain to see.

And that's when Joseph's nervous tension must have gotten to him, and he said, "Well…evenin' there, mister…" *Okay, so far so good*, thought Priscilla. "Sure is some right fine playin' you were doin'…" *Still good. He's bein' polite. Maybe we'll make it out of this yet.* "Especially for you bein' drunk and blind and all." *Aaannnd there it is.*

Priscilla hung her head. Joseph grew suddenly quiet. Elias grinned up at his father. Mathias only watched on without expression. It seemed as though he was looking directly at Priscilla, but it was hard for her to be certain with his lacking pupils.

Elias broke the silence. "Daddy, I done found these two holed up in my mansion. They's kids like me. Older, fifteen and sixteen they said. They got lost somewhere over near Betsy's Crick, and I smell't their fire. And I could hear they stomachs growlin' so I told 'em to foller me and we'd fix 'em up with some ham, n' we'd take 'em back to town in the mornin', huh, Daddy?"

Mathias disregarded his son's question, and still looking at Priscilla, said, "Yer last name's Carpenter, is it?"

At first Priscilla didn't know what to say. She wasn't ready for him to speak to her. Most adults made her nervous, and this one in particular. But somehow she managed to nod her head. When Mathias did not immediately respond, Priscilla grew anxious, but then she felt dumb when she remembered that he was blind and could not see her subtle gesture, and so she pitifully forced out the words, "Yes sir."

Mathias turned his head slightly to his right and grinned, and he said, "Yer brother Jeremiah?"

Priscilla was taken once again by surprise. How could this man know her brother? She hardly knew her brother, and she hadn't seen him in nearly a year. She looked at Joseph with confusion, but Joseph, again, could only shrug his shoulders. Finding no help or even comfort, she looked back at Mathias. There had been no suggestion in the old man's voice as to whether or not being related to Jeremiah Carpenter was a bad thing, and so, uneasily, Priscilla said, "Yes sir… Jeremiah's my kin."

Mathias only nodded his head in response. His white eyes seemed to glow in the night. Priscilla felt as though he were staring not at her but through her, or maybe into her, somewhere deep, maybe her soul, and she felt a panic rising up inside her. Unknown to Priscilla, Joseph had been, since the moment Mathias spun around to face them, gripping tight the handle of his knife that hung on his belt, waiting cautiously for a reason to unsheathe it.

Then, with a conviction cool as November, Mathias clicked his tongue twice and said, "Find a vein and fuckin' dig it. Dig into the layers of existence. It's all chemicals and motion, don't you know anything?"

Priscilla's heart sank. Once again, this was not the response she expected, and for the first time, she was glad Joseph carried so many weapons. There wouldn't be enough time to raise his rifle if Mathias moved on them, though. It was slung over his shoulder. Joseph was not a violent boy, by most any measure, but if he had to, he wouldn't hesitate to do whatever it took to keep Priscilla from being hurt, she was sure of that.

But instead of leaping from his seat in a literal blind rage, Mathias leaned back against the piano, causing several of the keys to make a dull, blunt sound, and said, "That's the last thing Jeremiah said to me 'fore he left…" He let his last statement sink in, then he stood up. Priscilla, although immediately filled with questions, remained speechless. As did Joseph, which Priscilla was thankful for.

Mathias placed his hand on top of Elias's head and stroked the child's hair with his thumb, and fondly, he said, "Don't that beat all… Miah's baby sister, Priscilla… Yer big brother's a dear friend of mine, and me and Elias here are real glad to make yer acquaintance. You and yer boyfriend."

Priscilla finally found her voice. "He ain't my boyfriend," she shot back, feeling instantly foolish for reacting with such childish intensity. What, was she ten? It was perfectly reasonable for anyone to think that she and Joseph might be going steady.

Up to this point in the interaction, Mathias's face had shown little to no emotion. His stoic reserve was almost intense at times, and so it was all the more striking when Priscilla watched a warm and hearty smile form on the blind man's face. It was a generous smile, and for an instant, it was a smile that gave so freely that Priscilla could see the life come back into his dead eyes, and all of her feelings of foolishness fluttered away.

Mathias, sincere as he could be, said, "My mistake, little lady. I won't make it again." Then he turned his head in Joseph's direction, and still smiling, said, "You mean to tell me yer out here with a Carpenter girl and you ain't made her yer one and only yet? What's wrong with you, boy?"

It was Joseph's turn to be embarrassed this time, but Mathias didn't drag out his misery too long. Before Joseph had time to respond to the question, Mathias said, "Aw, I'm just givin' ya a hard time, Mister Joseph. You kids come on in the house 'n' we'll pull out some cold bacon for us, what do ya say? Elias, son, grab Daddy's t'baccy pouch off the porch and fetch a bottle of the Number Nine hazelnut too. Reach way in the back, far as ye can. Get the good stuff. We have cause for celebration on this momentous night, son of mine. The many gods done seen fit to bless us with the company of friends."

"Well, shit on a stick," said Elias, coming up off of the piano bench.

Priscilla and Joseph watched Mathias 'watch' Elias scamper off into the night, then he turned back toward them with a grin, and said, "You kids do drink, don't ya?"

Priscilla and Joseph looked at one another, and Mathias gave a chuckle, and said, "What am I thinkin'? 'Course ya do, you Miah's little sis. Foller me to the kitchen, let's get fed. Right this way, kids, foller yer cousin, Mathias. Watch yer step, now. There's roots up ahead. And don't mind the dogs, just shove 'em off ya if'n they jump. They don't bite none."

———— ◆ ————

Chapter SIX

The Elder Clan's compound, as it were, sat on top of
Backbone Ridge, one of the many mountain ridges that interlaced to form the valleys that cradled within them the town of
Clockmaker. If some person were to follow the lone dirt road that
led to Clockmaker, and through it, past Priscilla's house and up to
the Number Nine Mine, that person would find, at the tree line
beyond the mine, a fork in the road. If that person chose to go
right at the fork, they would follow a tight and rocky path, hardly
wide enough for a pull cart, and at the end of the path, they would
find an old man with a shotgun and two dogs sitting on the front
porch of a small, well-maintained hardwood cabin. And if asked
his name, the man on the porch would say, "Parmore, who's ak-
sin'," and he would spit on the ground, and cast a suspicious eye,
and if that person's response wasn't agreeable, then Old Man
Parmore would likely fire a shot into the air as a warning, but only
the first shot would be a warning. The second shot would peel a
person's cap back.

However, if some person were to come to that same fork, and if
they were to decide to go left, instead of right, they would follow
a smooth dirt road, patched with gravel, and just wide enough for

a single car. This road would go for three miles through dense forest, and it would eventually lead to a dead end. At the dead end, there would be a clearing, and in the clearing would be four massive steel shipping containers. These containers, one by one, were originally installed by Obadias Elder and his sons during the early years of alcohol prohibition in the United States. If some person were to unlock these containers, they would find three of the fastest cars that ever gave blur to the open road, and a modified nineteen thirty-six, Bedford flat-bed truck that could drive over top of a revenuer's Chevy in third gear.

This dead-end clearing was as close as any vehicle could get to the Elder compound. From the shipping containers, a foot path led another mile into the forest and up the backside of the mountain to the Elders' land, but by walking, and only by walking, could anyone reach the great, cliff face entrance, through which Priscilla and Joseph had entered. In all the years that the Elders ran liquor, not one of them had ever been captured or caged, their home had never been raided, and not one of their cars had ever been completely totaled. Not one Elder had ever been killed or even maimed in the name of manufacturing or running moonshine in some fifty odd years of operation. And throughout the years, somehow, the Elder name had been kept quiet. Local law enforcement was paid off weekly by Obadias and later by Mathias, but the state boys never once heard the name Elder even whispered in the context of a crime.

By nineteen seventy-one, the Elder clan was twenty-seven in number. Several generations had lived on the plot since Mathias's father Obadias broke ground there in nineteen hundred and nine. Obadias survived black damp and seventy-two thousand pounds of rock in the Monongah West Virginia mine disaster of nineteen hundred and seven, and then, shattered shoulder and all, ventured south into no man's land, terra incognita, a relatively untapped neo frontier, hoping for a fresh start.

Along with his wife Mildred and three sons, Obadias climbed Backbone Ridge and began building. In the early days there was only one house on the property, but as the clan grew, so did the number of homes. To preserve space, they were built small, and Priscilla was correct when she thought the houses might have been built around the trees. Obadias had a fondness for the giant plants that superseded most of his affections, and would not allow any tree on the property to be cut down. Obadias loved trees like he loved his family, and like he loved dogs, Mastiffs in particular.

There were three outhouses, all in a row, at the edge of the property, one large indoor common area beside the circular clearing where Mathias had played piano by the fire, and one large indoor kitchen area where everyone in the Elder clan cooked their meals. And it was in this kitchen where Priscilla and Joseph now sat at a large wooden table, pie-eyed.

Everything in the sparsely-furnished kitchen, except for a few metal tools, seemed to be handmade from wood. There were no modern appliances anywhere to be seen. Besides a few cobwebs in the corners of the room, the area was noticeably clean and obsessively organized. Dozens of jars of different spices and herbs filled one wall, in front of which, from ceiling hooks, hung a dozen or more cast iron pans. In every corner were canvas sacks of different grains, wheat, barley, oats, and cornmeal.

Upon entering the kitchen, Mathias had lit several candles for his guests, and was now stoking the stove. Though he was blind, he couldn't have been more hospitable. Priscilla sat watching him, unconsciously picking at her stitches, and Joseph was fiddling with his compass, which still wouldn't spin. He paused every ten or fifteen seconds to scratch at his arm.

It was all too obvious where young Elias had gotten his predilection for conversation. Mathias maintained a light but steady chatter as he prepared several large strips of fried pork on a cast iron skillet. By the way he went on, it was obvious he didn't get much company. However, Priscilla had to admit, he was quite interesting. He was kind, and sort of funny, and obviously intelligent, and watching him cook while blind was next to astonishing. Much the way Elias moved through the woods, deliberately and without hesitation, so did Mathias in the kitchen. He made no mistakes as far as Priscilla could tell. He chopped the pork quickly and without losing a finger. When he reached for a fork he got it in the first try, then he used it to turn the meat. He sliced and diced and drizzled with flawless fluidity, and all the while he spoke. He asked some questions, but often times moved on without allowing time for responses.

"You kids like classical music? Lots of folks don't. But that's alright, ain't it. You know why they call it classical? Cause the word classical is derived from the Latin word classicus, which means taxpayer of the highest class. Ain't that some shit? That damn sure ain't me or mine. Hell, I ain't paid a tax my entire life. But they was wrong anyway, namin' it that. That music ain't for high class tax payers, it's for high class minds. I've met plenty of rich fools in my day. Plenty of rich fools who wouldn't know Fred Chopin from Elmer Fudd. Say, y'all heard that song 'Ain't No Sunshine' on the radio? Lord, what a song that is. I know the boy 'at wrote it too. Born right here in West By God. Well, I know his daddy, really. Did business with him for several years. Ya'll ever been down to Slab Fork?"

Mathias carried on like this as he cooked, and after a few minutes, Elias returned with a large glass jug and a leather pouch. He carefully laid both items on the table and sat down, smiling, across from Priscilla and Joseph. As Elias took his seat, Joseph looked up from his compass and watched him. Then Joseph's head flinched like something caught his eye, and abruptly, he said, "Scilly, you see that?"

Priscilla turned to Joseph and he was looking up at the ceiling, to one side and back again. Priscilla looked up in the direction of Joseph's gaze, but she saw nothing, and she said as much. Then Joseph pointed at the wall and said, 'There, ya see it?!"

Priscilla looked again and saw nothing, and she shook her head.

"Damnit, Scilly, I'm seein' bugs. Little crawly ones," said Joseph.

Priscilla and Elias both stared at Joseph. Even Mathias stopped cooking and turned to look in his direction.

When Joseph realized everyone was looking at him, he stopped looking for bugs, and blushed. Still digging at his arm, he shook his head and said, "Never mind…just never mind."

Mathias went back to cooking and pleasantly pontificating. "I seen a deer one time when I was a boy so full of bugs and maggots, they was comin' out its eyes and nose. Ain't that some shit, I only seen a few things in my life, 'fore I went blind, and that was one of 'em. It was a big old buck too. Maybe the biggest I seen. I'll never forget it. You a hunter, Joseph?"

Joseph waited a moment for Mathias to continue on, but when he didn't, Joseph said, "Uh, yes sir, I killed plenty deer. Coons, opossums, foxes, beavers, I 'bout killed 'em all, sir. My daddy taught me."

"Who is yer daddy, Joseph? I don't reckon I know him."

"Jimmy Smith, sir. My momma's Lynette."

"Lynette. Lynette, what? What's her maiden name?"

"Hazzard," said Joseph.

"Yer shittin' me? Lynette Hazzard's yer momma, I'll be damned.'"

Joseph nodded suspiciously. *How would somebody like Mathias Elder know Joseph's mother?* Priscilla wondered, and she was sure Joseph was wondering the same thing. Priscilla had never known Lynette Smith to go anywhere except church and the market, and once she had gone to Ohio to see her great aunt before she died, but that's it, as far as Priscilla could remember.

Mathias said, "Don't that beat all, I ain't seen yer momma in nearly twenty years. Holy shit. We used to be drinkin' buddies, you believe 'at?"

Joseph shook his head, and Priscilla couldn't believe it either. Joseph's mother, to Priscilla anyway, had always seemed so…so prudish. So…prim. So sober.

"Yer momma'd come up here every Friday after she got outta school, and we'd get drunker than skunks, me and her. Good God, she'd always bring Sally whatever the hell her name was, and me and my brother Zachy, and them, what a time we had. Yer momma'd get so drunk, she'd run naked round the fire up 'ere. You couldn't keep clothes on her."

Joseph's normally confident demeanor faded. He was visibly shaken. Priscilla, on the other hand, was insanely amused. She would never let Joseph live this down.

Mathias kept on. "Hell, one time she got so drunk, she fell back'ards off the log she was sittin' on. Passed out cold, legs stickin' up in the air, then she pissed herself 'n about drowned. I heard somethin' like runnin' water 'n looked over, 'n it was just comin' right down on her pretty little face. I never laughed so damn hard in all my life. She never told you 'bout that?"

Joseph shook his head for several seconds before he managed to say, "No…no, she never."

Elias started it. It wasn't his fault, he couldn't help it, but he started it, and it was contagious. The blind boy burst out laughing, like a fucking hyena, holding his stomach, and almost fell out of his chair. He cackled and howled and Priscilla could not refrain, nor could Mathias, and all three of them fell into uncontrollable laughter.

ONE TWO FOUR

Elias, in between hysterical sobs, tears rolling down his cheeks, said, "Yo momma…naked…pissed," and then he broke up again, and they all laughed harder. Even Joseph couldn't help but be amused by how comical Elias found his father's story, and Joseph too, begrudgingly, joined in the merriment at his own expense.

Mathias served the pork drizzled with honey and dashed with brown sugar and cinnamon. He also sliced up four juicy pears, and poured four glasses of the creamiest and richest milk that Priscilla and Joseph had ever tasted. Priscilla, herself, could not remember ever eating any one meal quite so remarkable. She was used to canned meat and bland vegetables. She'd drank soda pop on a number of occasions, but rarely did Everett allow for such things. He maintained a tyrant's control over expenditures in the Carpenter household and picked up extras where he alone saw fit. Priscilla's palate had been so poorly stimulated, in fact, that she felt as if she were eating for the very first time in her life. Each and every bite was an experience in and of itself, a gustatory cascade of mouthwatering goodness, and one step closer to Heaven than Priscilla had ever been.

At one point she even heard herself moan, but she was too enraptured by the bacon to care if anyone else had noticed. Every bite of pork Priscilla took, she would wash down with milk and she would finish with a piece of pear, and as each mouthful of juicy pear slid down her throat, her mind was driven back to thoughts of that morning and the goat.

There was little conversation as they all ate, the mark of any truly delicious meal. After they finished, Mathias, in all his blind glory, cleaned the kitchen. He rinsed the pans and utensils in a bucket of water, and packed away the pork and fruit. Then they all went back out to the fire where Mathias broke the seal on a ten-year-old jar of homemade liquor.

Mathias passed the jar to Priscilla and said, "Ladies first."

Priscilla had never tasted moonshine before. Once, she and Joseph had shared a six pack of a German beer that was paid to Joseph for poisoning a dog that wouldn't quit barking, and on another occasion, her mother had let her sip at her wine at a church picnic, but Priscilla had yet to ever imbibe in the hard stuff.

When Mathias handed her the jar, she almost instinctively refused the offer, but there was something about the look on his face and his encouraging demeanor that Prisicilla could not deny. She reached out and took hold of the jar, and Mathias gave a smile, genuine as far as she could tell. Priscilla hesitated briefly, then she tipped the jar up.

She knew when it hit her lips that she was in trouble, but by the time it reached the back of her throat, it was too late. Priscilla swallowed a giant, shivering, fire-breathing, brain-burning gulp of some of the cleanest, most powerful hooch known to man. She wanted to scream, but all that came out, almost in a shriek, and with a sharp exhale was, "Fuck!"

Priscilla chased the drink with a moment of panic. She had never said that word in front of an adult before, and she instantly feared that Mathias would take offense, or worse. But when she looked up at him he was still smiling, just as before. He said, "You alright there, Prisc?"

Priscilla, mouth still on fire, muttered, "Yes sir," and Mathias burst out laughing.

"Woowee," he said, and snatched the jar from Priscilla.

"Little girl, by the sound of the swallow you just took, yer gonna be feelin' like Joey's momma in no time," said Mathias.

"Now, what the shit," said Joseph, and Elias broke up into laughter once again.

Mathias said, "Aw, I'm just kiddin', little buddy," and he stuffed the jar in Joseph's chest.

Joseph took the jar, reluctantly, and gave Mathias a tough

stare. "Now dang it, Mister Elder, now I'll drink with ya but what you say we just leave my momma out of this. I ain't up here talkin' bout yer momma, am I."

Elias stopped laughing and Mathias's smile faded and softened into an honest look of concern. "Joseph, I'm real sorry. Honest. Sometimes I kid too much. And you don't right know me yet. And you don't right know about yer momma and me neither. You have every right to be angry. I'm sorry."

Mathias seemed genuinely apologetic, and Joseph seemed to drop his guard.

To Joseph, Mathias said, "Now. Take ye a pull on that jar. Take two if ye like. And Elias can have a taste, but only one, you hear me, boy?"

"Yeah, yeah, I hear'd ye," said Elias with a grin. Joseph pulled twice, then once again on the jar.

Mathias shifted his position on the log to face Joseph directly. Firelight glimmered in his weary, lifeless eyes, and as he spoke, he rolled a cigarette. He said, "Joseph, I don't know what kind of woman yer momma is today, I know time changes people. But twenty-five years ago, she was the sweetest and prettiest girl in the county. I'm here to tell ye, she was smart and funny and ever'body liked her, and about every man was in love with her. Myself included. I give you a hard time about her but boy, I'm here to tell ya I loved her like I love my family. I don't mean any disrespect to you or her. She liked to drink and get wild from time to time but she weren't never nothin' but good. You understand?"

"Yes sir," said Joseph.

Mathias nodded his head and said, "Good." Then he said, "Now, how is Lynette these days?"

Joseph thought about it a moment and said, "She's okay, I reckon."

"Okay, huh?"

"Yes sir, I reckon. She seems mostly happy. If not, it's normally 'cause of me."

Priscilla chimed in, "Always 'cause of you."

Mathias smiled at that comment, and said, "I believe it, raisin' boys ain't easy, that's for sure... She work?"

"No sir, she don't work," said Joseph. "Spends most of her time at home or at church, well, she used to, I don't know about after today."

"What happened today?"

"We got a new pastor. A feller who likes snakes."

Mathias nodded at this but he didn't say anything. Then he clicked his tongue and said, "I said one, Elias."

"Aw, shit, pop," said Elias. And he passed the jar to Priscilla. She considered taking another drink, but decided otherwise and handed the jar back to Mathias, who reached for the vessel as soon as she made to deliver it. It was as if he could see her reach out to him.

Mathias took a long drink from the jar and finished with a sound like that of an owl hooting from the bottom of a deep well. Then he extended the jar to Joseph, and said, "Tell me 'bout yer daddy, Joseph, is he a good man?"

Joseph accepted the jar and said, "Yes sir. Momma says he spends too much money on drinkin' but they don't fight much. He don't hit her. Or call her names. Nothin' like that. And he's good to me. He busts my ass when I fuck up, but—. Excuse my cursin', sir."

"Ehhh fuck," said Mathias proudly. "Ain't no such thing as curse words, Joseph. Words is just words. It's all in how ya use 'em. You say what you want around me, and you say it how you wanna say it, ya understand? All I want from you, and from you too, Priscilla, is to be yerself around here. I tell Elias all the time, ain't that right, son?"

"That's right, Daddy, no lies, no masks," said Elias.

"So Joseph, if yer old man busts yer ass when you fuck up, I want you to say, 'He busts my ass when I fuck up,' you understand me, old buddy? You be you. Don't wear no masks. No lies, no masks."

"Alright, then," Joseph said, and he took yet another long swallow from the jar. Then he handed it back to Mathias who tipped it up again. Like Mathias, Joseph seemed to be drinking the stuff like water, and Priscilla had no idea how that was possible. She was genuinely impressed.

Mathias said, "Continue, Joseph, you were sayin' yer daddy busts yer ass when you fuck up, but…"

Joseph considered a moment and said, "I was just gonna say… well… He busts my ass when I fuck up, but I know he loves me and I know he loves my momma too…that's all." Another drink and the bottle was passed, and then passed back.

While Mathias was letting Joseph's response sink in, he tilted the jar skyward once again, and drained a sizeable portion of the clear liquid. Then he handed it back to Joseph, who by then was starting to lean on his log.

"Well Joseph," said Mathias, "I can't tell ya how happy I am to hear that. I always hoped the best for yer momma, I surely did. She really was one of my dearest friends."

Mathias looked up toward the sky above the fire, but no stars held his gaze. He said, "I can see her now. Plain as day, she's more clear than most my memories…them golden curls, them eyes, goddamn skies never seen a bluer blue, and that smile…she used to wear this wide-brimmed hat…I can see her so clear…"

Mathias resonated on the memory of Lynette Hazzard's face for some time before he spoke again, but when he did he said, "Ain't no hard feelin's 'bout my jokes now, is they, Joseph?"

Joseph's head spun on his neck and he squinted at Mathias

with one swimming eye, and he said, "Ahhh, say what ya want, ya old blind son of a bitch, I'm fuckin'…I'm fuckin' skunked…"

Priscilla blurted out, "Joseph!"

"Whaaat? Fuuuck," slurred Joseph. "He said no fuckin' masks, Scilly. No fuck— no fuckin' masks…you heard the motherfucker. Do you see a mask on my face? D— do ya? Do you see a mask?"

Priscilla was in shock, but Mathias only chuckled. Elias said, "Daddy, what is it you say about apples fallin' far from trees?"

Mathias smiled. Joseph was too drunk to catch the jab. Then Mathias said, "Elias, I'm gonna put our guests to bed. You get on to the house and get to bed yerself. It's gettin' late."

"You puttin' 'em in the library, Daddy?"

"Yes, indeed, son of mine."

"Okay," said Elias, and he got up and hugged his father, then he turned to Priscilla and Joseph, his white eyes shining and blank, and said, "Goodnight friends, I'll talk at ye in the mornin'. Thanks for gettin' lost. I sure had fun." Then Elias turned and disappeared into the night.

With Elias gone, Mathias turned back to his guests, and said, "Joseph, can ya walk, partner?"

Clearly insulted, and without a word, Joseph scoffed and attempted to stand up from the log, but quickly found that he could not actually do as much. So he tried again, and again he failed and almost fell backwards off the log in the process. Mathias and Priscilla both chuckled.

After several failed attempts on Joseph's part, Mathias handed Priscilla the jar and said, "Carry this, please, young lady."

With both hands free, Mathias hoisted Joseph up off the log and slung him over his shoulder with obvious ease, and though Joseph initially fought being carried, even protested it, he would be passed out cold as a tombstone before they reached the library door. To Priscilla, Mathias said, "Foller me, Miss Carpenter," then he scooped up Joseph's rifle and moved back toward the kitchen. Along the way, a stick of dynamite fell out of Joseph's boot, and clattered to the ground. Priscilla quickly picked it up and tucked it away into her pack. Mathias said, "Was that dynamite?"

Priscilla sighed. "Um…yes?"

"I thought I smelled glycerine. Smells like it's leakin'. You better leave 'at outside. Stick it up 'ere by the squirrel feeder. One of them dogs gets ahold of it and we'll have one hell of a mess to clean up."

◆

The library was connected to the kitchen by a long dark hall. At points, Priscilla could hardly see anything. She did notice that they passed many rooms on the way to the library, but what was inside each room, she did not know. Each of the doors were shut. In the library, a candle was already lit. There was a well-stocked bar, two faded leather fireside armchairs in front of a massive fireplace which still held a large mound of orange glowing coals, two bronzed leather Queen Anne couches, and in the center of the room a nine foot tall statue of Hercules wrestling Diomedes in the nude. "Whoa," said Priscilla as she passed by it. The walls of the library were lined from floor to ceiling with shelves and contained within them were hundreds upon hundreds of dust-covered books, more books than Priscilla had ever even seen in her entire life. Ten times as many books as the public library kept.

Mathias laid Joseph down on one of the couches. He rested Joseph's rifle within arm's reach against the end table, then he lit two candles and he and Priscilla retired to the chairs beside the fireplace. Ever since their arrival, Priscilla had been wondering, in an offhand way, just exactly how Mathias Elder knew her big brother. It seemed so strange to her that a grown man, an old man like Mathias, could know Jeremiah so intimately as he seemed to. Jeremiah was just a kid, only six years older than she, but Mathias was a full grown man, with a beard, and scars, and memories. The question had hijacked the back of Priscilla's mind since the moment Mathias had mentioned her brother, but her nerves were getting the best of her, and she simply could not find the right way to ask the question. Luckily, for Priscilla, she didn't have to find a way to broach the subject at all. As soon as she and Mathias sat down by the fireplace, he brought it up for her.

"I still cannot believe that Jeremiah Carpenter's little sister found her way into Elder territory. You have any idea how serendipitous that is?"

Priscilla shook her head. It simply was not easy for her to talk to adults. Maw Scill, her mother, and Joseph's mother, Lynette, were the only three that Priscilla ever felt comfortable enough around to actually speak without being spoken to first.

"You don't talk a whole lot, do ya, little lady?"

Priscilla shrugged. "I talk some," she said.

Mathias, clearly relaxed, sat back in his chair and steepled his fingers. Then he said, "Everett's still a mean cocksucker, I take it?"

Priscilla flinched. She had never known any adults to speak about Everett that way, other than Maw Scill, of course. Most people never even mentioned his name, let alone referred to him as a cocksucker. It seemed to Priscilla that most people, deep down, were afraid of Everett. But in no way, shape, or form, did she get this feeling from Mathias Elder, not even in the slightest. Come to think of it, Mathias Elder didn't seem like he would be afraid of much of anything. But it wasn't just his size, though he was a formidable man. There was something in his grace that made Priscilla feel this way, something in his gentleness that gave way to an air of fearlessness, and Priscilla found herself in a sudden state of admiration for him. Mean cocksucker, the words were music to her ears.

Before Priscilla could think to speak, Mathias said, "So you understand, little dear, I know all about yer family. Me and Miah done got to know each other pretty well over the years so I know all the trouble yer daddy done put you and yer brother through, yer momma, too… Miah done told me all about that son of a bitch." When Priscilla didn't respond right away, he continued, "I used to know yer grandmomma too, Miss Priscilla, and I did business with yer grandaddy, Fish. Long time ago, long, long time ago… I knew yer momma too, when she was just a little girl like you, 'bout yer age in fact. Maybe a little older… Hard to say. Hell, I first met her when she was just a tiny little baby. She'd always be in the Key, behind the bar in her bassinet. Just cooin'. Never did cry, that I can remember. Boy, Fish would have bands playin' so loud you could hear it down the holler and yer momma'd be fast asleep behind the bar like she was Jesus Christ in a manger, you believe that?"

Priscilla only stared at him. She didn't know what to believe. Her mind was struggling to keep up with current events, let alone historical ones, and her thoughts waxed and waned agnostically.

"I reckon the last time I saw her, she was about yer age… then she married off…or I went blind, I don't quite remember which… It's hard to say, when she was twelve she coulda passed for twenty if you weren't payin' attention, but I'll bet she was just about yer age… Ya know, now that I think about it, I don't reckon she talked a whole lot neither…"

Mathias paused as his mind painted pictures of streams that had long run dry, and as the images danced on the canvas, he retrieved a pinch of tobacco from his pouch and began to roll it. Then he said, "We was already blind so I never seen him, but I met yer daddy once, back in fifty-six, outside of—"

Priscilla interrupted, "Everett ain't my daddy…" She said it without thinking.

Mathias did not respond. He only raised one eyebrow and continued to look at her, his gracious pearly eyes showing signs of confusion.

"And yes sir… he still is a… mean cocksucker… Real mean." Priscilla spoke soberly, as if she were simply stating the facts. She knew she wasn't supposed to tell people the truth about Everett, not about his abuses or that of her own conception, but she was somehow certain that if she lied or even withheld a single fact, Mathias Elder would instantly smell her deceit. And besides it felt good to say those words out loud, especially to an adult, and especially to one who understood the true gravity of her domestic situation. And though Priscilla wasn't prepared for it, upon saying the words mean cocksucker, a defiant if not bashful grin began forming at the corners of her mouth that she could not suppress.

Mathias grinned also, almost as if in return. "No masks, Priscilla…call me Mathias. No formalities," he said solemnly. "None of this sir shit. We don't care about fancy titles on Backbone Ridge, only fancy brains. Fancy hearts. You put yer feet up on that damn table if you want to, you understand? Hell, shoot snot rockets if that pleases ya. Weeeell, outside, mind ya—well, at least not in the library, anyway. Eh fuck, ye can shoot 'em where ye want, just don't let my brother's wife catch ye." And he gave Priscilla a snowy white wink. "You can say fuck, cunt, and cocksucker if ye want, I don't care, they's just words, just plain old words, and sis, look here," Mathias leaned forward in his chair and his tone grew heavy, "you can always tell me the truth, I won't never judge ye. You understand, friend? I won't never judge ye. Not fer nothin'."

Priscilla nodded. She did understand. She understood exactly. She looked Mathias square in his eyes, and firmly as she could, even though everything that came out of her mouth was sweet as berry cobbler, she said, "Alright…you blind motherfucker, no masks."

Mathias got such a delightful kick out of this comment that he brought his hands together, with a fast firm clap. "Woo, there we go, ya little shit. Now ya got it. See, now ye got it. Alright."

Priscilla smiled. She felt like she had it. Mathias's earnestly mischievous nature had finally won her over. *Just like a big old kid*, Priscilla thought. He was even beginning to appear less frightening in the physical form.

At first, same as when she met Elias, she couldn't get past Mathias's eyes. They had stained his entire appearance, lending him a quality that was reminiscent of a living specter. But now Priscilla was beginning to realize that behind the beard and all the hair, and beyond the misty eyes, there existed a man who wasn't ugly or ghostly in any way, merely a sightless man whose attractive features had faded with the passing of time.

In his eyes, Priscilla had previously felt floaty and lost, but now she envisioned chestnut-colored irises looking back at her, and for a brief moment she could see Mathias, not as the man he was, but as the man he had once been, before his sight had been taken, before his mother and father and wife had died, before his eleven children, and before suffering some sixty odd years of making sacrifices and mistakes and living with their consequences. For one brief instant, Priscilla saw past all that, and found the man that Mathias Elder used to be, long before the passage of time had the opportunity to sink its teeth in and rob him of his beauty.

"Now that we got that outta the way," Mathias said, lowering his nonexistent gaze on Priscilla, "what in the hell do you mean, Everett ain't yer daddy?"

Priscilla sighed. *Shit*, she thought. She wasn't supposed to tell anybody, and here she was telling everybody. But she might as well come clean. After all, she was the one who opened this can of worms. Not to mention, the whole no masks no lies thing. "Well," Priscilla said, in a rather impassive way, "he ain't my daddy. He ain't Jeremiah's daddy neither. And honest, I don't know what to think about it, I just found out this mornin'. My momma just laid it on me."

Priscilla's stare got momentarily lost in space, then, wearily, she said, "A lot's happened today, Mister Mathias."

For some time, Mathias seemed to ponder Priscilla's words, then he said, "But…I…yer brother don't know this, Priscilla. Are you certain?"

Priscilla nodded assuringly. "Yes sir, I'm certain—I mean, yes. Yes, I'm certain, my momma told me. My real daddy's name is Duane Richard Davis, he was a geetar player. Momma said he was a real fine man."

Mathias shook his head in disbelief, one of his fingers resting befuddled upon his chin. "Well, I'll be goddamned…Duane Davis…I know just who that is. His daddy, Phil, I believe it was, and yer grandaddy, Fish, was long time drinkin' buddies. Hoooly shit. And I seen Duane—yer fuckin' daddy, I reckon—play guitar at The Broken Key damn near twenty years ago... And I'll never forget it neither. I still don't think I ever heard anyone play guitar like 'at boy. That was the year before we went blind, if memory serves me…and it generally does…*man*…long time ago.'

Mathias was no longer sitting back relaxed, he was on the edge of his seat and clearly enthralled in the conversation. Priscilla sat charmingly in the leather-back chair, her long curly hair tangled and falling down around her. The wound on her head still stung a little, but ever since she took that first, accidentally significant, gulp out of Mathias's jar, both her head and her ribs had been feeling oddly better. In her reflection in the window pane, she could see the dark bruises under her eyes and on her forehead, and beyond them she could see the fire. For the sake of her appearance, she was glad Mathias was blind.

"You said you know my Maw Maw Scill," said Priscilla.

Mathias smiled. "Sheeeiit, do I ever. My daddy and Fish was good friends, good good friends. Miss Priscilla and my momma used to be good friends too, but…then, well, Daddy died and then we all went blind, and then Momma died…But hell yes, I know Scill. She probably whipped my ass more than my own mother when I was a growin' up, my brothers too. Me and my brothers used to play in the woods behind the Key when Daddy and Fish was doin' business, then when Daddy died, I sorta took over, and me and yer granny was good timin' buddies for many a year after that. When you see her next, you ask her about the time her and Mathias Elder got drunk and stole a crate of fireworks off the back of a broke down freight truck. She'll shit her pants.'"

Priscilla smiled and said she would, and she meant it. Then she said, "Can I ask you another question?"

Mathias nodded, "You know it, darlin'."

"How the shit do you know my brother?"

Mathias sat back in his chair, smiling wide. "You got it now, don't ya," he said, then he laughed, hearty and warm.

Mathias pondered the question aloud. "How the shit do I know yer brother? That is a good question, Miss Priscilla. Another good question is, 'Who is yer brother?' Aaannnd another good question is, 'Where is yer brother?' Do you know the answers to either of those questions, little lady?"

Priscilla shook her head. Then because the person she was speaking to was blind, she said, "No."

The fact of the matter was that Priscilla hardly knew her brother at all. Their separation in age had kept them from ever really building any kind of connection or bond outside of their fundamentally flawed and chaotic domestic situation, but Priscilla did, however, know at least a few things about her big brother. She knew he was a good person. He wasn't anything like Everett, she was sure of that. She also knew that her brother loved her. He had done his best to protect her from Everett through the years, and he had been badly beaten many times for his efforts. And she knew that more than anything, he wanted to be famous so that he could leave this shit-hole town and never look back, or at least that's what he had said once, but she knew little more than that. Jeremiah kept to himself and was mostly quiet in Priscilla's experience, and the truth of his daily life, it seemed, was a fact that had somehow slipped past her.

"I didn't think so," said Mathias. "I did not think so. Well, Miss Carpenter, it is my absolute pleasure to tell you everything I know… and I'll start from the beginnin'." Leaning back, he combed through his long tangled hair with his fingers and searched his mind for the right place to start, and when he found it, he said, "Five or so years ago, blindness started gettin' to me… Khun Mae had just passed and I was drinkin' heavy, and I weren't playin' no piano at the time neither. Mostly only drinkin'… Anyhow, one day I was sittin' up in my bed, up the house, mine's the big one when you first come out of the rock, and I was skunked to my wits, mind you, and there comes a knock at my door. It was my little brother, Nehemias, Sheriff White, and Jeremiah Carpenter, yer brother, and he was in handcuffs. Nehemias told me as much when I opened the door. Miah told me, after we'd become friends, that Sheriff White looked me up and down like I was a mangy dog that day. I bet I was a sight though. Starin' at 'em outta one blind eye…Lord. Anyhow, Sheriff White, he tells me to clean up and get it together, take a minute if I need to, and meet him in the kitchen. And that's just what I did."

At this point, Mathias had Priscilla's full attention.

"Now back in, oh say, about thirty-four, I delivered some jars up to New York City, and I got to drinkin' with this Jew feller, a wealthy feller I could tell, he was business partners with the ol' boy I was deliverin' to. What business they had together I can't say, I never asked. Anyhow, before I left, he give me this glass medicine bottle full of pharmaceutical grade liquid cocaine, for the ride home, he says, in case I start to feel a little drowsy. Well, it got me home alright, I don't think I blinked the whole ride, and over the years, I hung on to that bottle. And when Sheriff White says to get it together, I kinda panicked. I shut the door, pulled that bottle out, took me a big old sip and away I went. I still got the bottle but it's empty now, me and yer brother got into it one night and—oh, but I'm gettin' carried away. So I warshed off an—"

"Cocaine's a drug, ain't it?"

"Oh I apologize, yes mam, it is. A damn good one too if ye ask me."

"Ain't drugs bad for you?"

Mathias scratched his chin for a moment, then he said, "Naw, not really. A lot of drugs is bad for ye. Same as booze. A little won't usually hurt ye. You ain't die from that sip ye took earlier, did ya?'"

"No sir, no."

"That's right. Most drugs ain't bad, it's just people can't handle 'em. The real trick to drugs is purity. And that includes liquor too. And it don't get no purer than what drips off the Elder still, but I'll tell ya all about drugs later if yer interested, alrighty?"

"Alrighty," said Priscilla.

"Now where was I? Oh yes right, so Sheriff White tells me to clean up and come on down to the kitchen so I takes me a sip of that cocaine juice—now that's like drinkin' a hundred cups of coffee all at once, Priscilla, you understand, and I warsh my face and hands and zip on down to the kitchen and Sheriff White tells me he done caught yer brother smokin' dope behind the school. Now

Sheriff White, he's long time acquaintances with yer Maw Maw Scill. They was childhood sweethearts, I believe, but I could be wrong. And Sheriff White, he ain't want to burden yer Maw Maw with the knowledge that her grandson was some kind of good fer nuthin' dope fiend, that's how Sheriff put it anyhow, and so instead of throwin' Miah in the jail, he figured maybe I could put him to work, quietly. He reckoned I could have Miah move some timber or dig ditches. He didn't want yer Maw Maw to find out, but he damn sure couldn't let yer brother off without some sort of punishment. He was real clear 'bout that part. Sheriff White don't play when it comes to drugs. He still don't. The fact he ain't beat Miah senseless and toss him in the slammer is a true testament to the Sheriff's affection for yer Maw Maw, no doubt about it. You with me so far, little lady?"

"Yes, I follow, I'll be sure to let you know when I don't."

Mathias gave a grin and put his palms up in mock defense. "Alright, alright. Brazen young thing. Movin' forward… So now, here I am higher than fuckin' Jupiter on cocaine and still half-cocked off liquor and I have the goddamn Sheriff of Clockmaker askin' me to help him punish yer brother fer smokin' a little dope. And for the life of me, I just could not rectify how I could do that without feelin' like a hypocrite of the most worthless kind. Do you understand that predicament, do you know what a hypocrite is?"

"Yes. I understand the predicament, and yes, I know all about hypocrites, I go to church. What's pot make ya feel like?"

Mathias chuckled. "I bet you do and I hope you know I didn't ask you that to condescend, I just want to make sure yer with me…"

"I know it."

"Good. Now, what does pot make you feel like? Well, it makes ye feel all goofy. And it makes ye laugh and think a whole bunch…

it makes ya hungry as a dog. Kinda hard to reckon actually…"

Priscilla nodded. "That's alrigh… You can go on…"

"Alright, well, the way I figured it was if I told Sheriff no, then he would likely find someone else to do the job or some other way, altogether, of gettin' justice out of yer brother. And that didn't sit right with me, bout as much as bein' a hypocrite. So I told the Sheriff I'd help him out. I told him I would work yer brother hard, that I'd teach him a thing or two about respect. And discipline. I told him he picked the right place to come and that I ain't mind helpin' the little dope head form a few callouses, and all that type of hard ass shit. And the Sheriff believed me too, ate it up, and so did Miah for that matter, he told me so later. Said he was scared shitless. But I was lyin', of course. My plan was to let Miah come up here and read books for a few hours every day for a month, maybe help with a few of the chores that are harder to get done when yer blind. Nothin' back breakin', that's for sure. I honest just wanted them to leave so I could continue drinkin', but the Sheriff, he says, 'I'll be back to pick him up come dark. I'll drop him off after he gets out of school every day and you can have him till sundown. Two weeks to a month depending on good behavior, that sound alright to you?' And I told him it did, and he walked off. Now me and Miah, we—"

Priscilla interrupted, "Why you call him that…Miah?"

"Well…uh…endearment, Priscilla. Endearment. And I think it fits him better, don't you?"

Priscilla nodded. She wasn't sure what endearment meant, but she didn't want to ask either. So she said, "Maybe so…go on then."

"Well, me and Miah didn't get along right at first, and since the Sheriff was pickin' him up every night, we couldn't just lounge around drunk like I planned. The Sheriff wanted to see sweat and dirt and callouses. I swear he inspected Miah's hands every night, said he wanted to make sure he was payin' his debt to society, he liked to put it that way. I suspected as much right off, so I set Miah to work the first day choppin' wood, but I went from feelin' like a hypocrite to a slaver real fast. So I decided if yer brother was gonna have to break his back, the only fair thing for me to do was break my own back right alongside him. So I walked on out to the wood pile and picked up an axe and started swingin', and boy, yer brother coulda laughed his ass right off, watchin' me tryin' to split that wood. I'd swing and miss and spin halfway around, fall on my ass. But we kept up and eventually it all got split. Miah had his callouses, and we had some time before dark so we sat down, just he and I, out by the fire, on the logs where you and I sat tonight, and we had a few drinks and we smoked a little dope, and we had the first of what would become many long conversations about the greater questions in life."

Mathias paused, ruminating, then continued. "I don't know what it was that made us get along like we did, a man old as me and a boy young as him. I reckon Miah had a lot he wanted to learn and I had a lot I wanted to teach, or maybe it was the other way around. I'm sure I'll never know… Anyhow, we both worked our ass off for two weeks. We got this place fixed up real nice, weren't a loose board in the place. The Sheriff let yer brother off on good behavior, as promised, and with my blessin', of course. But Miah kept comin' back. Every day. And over the next couple months, he and I got closer and closer. And let me tell you somethin'. I've never met anyone like yer brother. He's smarter than damn near anyone I ever met, and I met a few. He's got a way about him too. Folks like him. Women like him, plenty. He's honest and kind, and he's brave…brave as any man could be. But, well, then—actually, I'm sorry, can I offer you anything to drink, Priscilla?"

Priscilla thought for a moment. "No, then what happened?"

Mathias smiled at her candidness. "Theeen old Mathias went and did it. One day Miah and I was talkin' and I was tellin' him about all the shine the Elders done run over the years and I got to tellin' him how bein' blind put us plum outta business other than local distribution. Theeen I got to tellin' him about the cars we had collectin' dust at the bottom of the ridge. And, well, one thing led to another and I ended up makin' a quick call to Kentucky and me and him went on our first run."

Mathias stood and walked to a small cart that held several bottles and began pouring himself a drink. "You sure I can't offer ye anything to wet yer whistle there, little lady?"

As sweet as she could be, Priscilla declined. Mathias finished pouring his own whistle wetter and sat back down across from her. He removed a rolling paper and a pinch of tobacco from his worn leather pouch and began to roll them together. As he did so, without missing a beat, he continued where he had left off.

"Made five hundred big ones on that one. It was easy and smooth as any run I'd ever been on. Yer brother took to drivin' like a natural, and he loved it. Couldn't keep him from behind the wheel. All he wanted to do was run liquor. Don't get me wrong, he was savin' money, and we were havin' a good time, but Miah loved the thrill of it most. And he liked to go fast. Yes he did, he liked to go fast. So I figured what the shit. I contacted a few old customers and sent Miah to work. He was drivin' all over Appalachia and the Blue Ridges, up to New York regularly, sometimes twice a week, big loads in the truck. I couldn't believe there was still such a high demand for Elder liquor. I still can't, to be honest. But there was. And Miah was makin' money, not a lot mind you, but money all the same."

Mathias paused to pull hard on his cigarette, and perhaps to reflect. Priscilla watched him carefully.

"Anyhow, that went on for a year or so, and then last year,

Miah came to me with an idea about expandin' out to Colorado and possibly as far as California, but he wanted to run reefer. He said he met some fellers in Florida with contacts in both them places. He said they could move as much dope as we could deliver, and he also said he had an idea about how to make it happen. It was a hell of an idea too. The last thing yer big brother is is dumb, I'll tell ya that. We went out and bought a Dodge Coronet, five hundred, sixty-six model, I believe, and painted that baby flat black from bumper to bumper, even the wheels. We swapped the engine and did some work on the suspension, took out the backseats and trunk divider for cargo space, a few other modifications here and there. Yer brother did most of the work. Then we filled the car with as much dope as we could fit and when the sun went down, he climbed in that car and without headlights or a license plate, drove at roughly one hundred and sixty miles an hour, from Clockmaker, West Virginia to Colorado by the light of the damn moon. Seventeen hundred miles in sixteen hours. Full speed in the fuckin' dark. Somehow he made it back in fifteen hours. Goddamn, he loved it… He said it was like travelin' through time. Said he was slippin' through dimensions. Space surfin' worm holes. Called the car his time machine… But…Miah made the trip to Colorado maybe a dozen times, then, a little over a year ago, he started doin' drives that took two nights out to San Fran. Now, Priscilla, I don't know exactly what yer brother was getting' into out there, but he was doin' more than runnin' a little pot, I know that. The west is different. People is different. And smart as yer brother is, the amount of trouble he could get into is endless. So it's hard to say just where he is or what he's doin'… But I ain't seen him in eleven months. And I don't know nobody that's seen him neither…Last thing he said to me was *find a vein and fuckin' dig it, dig into the layers of existence*, it's all chemicals and motion, don't you know anything… Then he gave me that grin he gives and he was off. So if ya ask me where Jeremiah Carpenter is, I would say he's either dead or in California."

Then Mathias leaned in conspiratorially, and added, "But between you and me, I'd put everything I have on Californy."

Priscilla felt like an open sieve, through which an ocean of information had been poured. Between Mathias and her mother and whatever happened earlier with the goat, she didn't know what to think or how to think it, but there was one thought that loomed at the forefront of Priscilla's mind—she couldn't wait to tell her mother. Her mother hadn't been the same since Jeremiah left. Her drinking picked up, she was distracted and distant, and she always seemed just a little more sad than usual. Priscilla had heard her tell Maw Scill once that she just knew Jeremiah was dead, that she couldn't help picturing him face down in a ditch, and Priscilla could not wait to tell her that she was wrong. She had the urge to get up and run to her mother at that very moment, but she quickly remembered that she had next to no idea where she was or how to get home.

Priscilla said, "You ain't just tryin' to make me hopeful, are ya? You really think that? You really think he's in California?"

Mathias smiled. "I know it with all my heart..."

This statement gave Priscilla a deep sense of comfort and ease. Her mother was going to be overjoyed. Her son was alive, and in California of all places. *How dreamy.* Jeremiah was probably dropping pennies from the Golden Gate bridge at that very moment. With his arm wrapped around some pretty girl, he was probably dropping pennies and watching them fall. Priscilla could see him laughing, high above the bay. She could see the pretty girl's long blonde hair blowing in the wind and Priscilla could see that she was smiling, and that made Priscilla smile.

Priscilla stared at Mathias. In the candlelight, with shadows flittering on his face, Priscilla decided that she liked him. He was a good man, this much Priscilla was sure of. She watched him as he rolled another cigarette, but her eyes began to wander along the walls of the dimly lit library. She followed along the shelves, admiring the multitude and variety of books they contained, until the last tattered spine disappeared into the darkness at the back of the room. Her wandering gaze took the long way home, through the ceiling rafters, down to the massive statue, over Hercules's tiny stone cock, and pausing briefly at Joseph's gaping mouth, before finally falling back upon Mathias, who was just setting flame to his newly finished creation.

As Mathias placed the matches back in his pouch, Priscilla said, "Can I ask you another question?"

"You know the answer to that."

"Why you got all these books when yer blind?"

Mathias chuckled. "Don't make much sense, does it?"

"Bout as much as fuckin' a chicken 'fore ya cut its head off."

Mathias burst into laughter. "Holy shit Christ, where did you hear that one?"

Priscilla gave a faint smile, proud at having made Mathias laugh so fully. "Joseph says it some."

Mathias looked toward the couch where Joseph was snoring. "Good God, well, I never… That's a good one. I'm gonna have to use it."

Mathias took a sip from his drink and then, settling his sightless sights back on Priscilla, he said, "We wasn't always blind, honey. I've read a great many of 'ese books. Not half mind you, but a great many. Anyhow, they's mostly all my late momma's. You never met anyone that read as much. Always collectin' new ones too. She'd have everybody bring her books. All the boys we had runnin' shine for us went all over the country and they'd bring her back books…all her friends would find 'em for her, and friends' friends too. Every time someone came up here, they brought a book or four for her…and she would line the shelves… That closet back yonder is full to the ceilin' with books too…but me and my brothers was all big readers. The Elder family was raised to read…Momma instilled that in ever one of us. This here is a smart family…even the kids who was born blind and ain't never read, like Elias, he's smart as a whip. We teach the children everything we know…and we tell stories best we can… Blindness will not hinder this family, you understand. But we ain't always been blind. No, we went blind in fifty-two, a couple weeks after my daddy died…But these books, at one time, used to get read plenty… Lots of fine, fine literature on these shelves… Lots of old literature too. Now they's just wasted paper… You like to read, Priscilla?'

"Yes sir, I mean, yes, I read a lot." Priscilla couldn't quit with the sir shit. Old habits and what not.

"Well, that's good. That's real good. You know the difference between someone who can't read and someone who can read but don't? Not a whole lot, they's both likely fools… What do you like to read, little lady?"

"Well… The Bible mostly. I read some other books at school… *To Kill a Mockin'bird*… I liked that one. And *Dracula*, Jeremiah give to me. I also read *Where the Wild Things Are* when I was little, but mostly I read the Bible… Asshole Everett won't let me have no other books…says they're a waste of money…"

Mathias scoffed and said, "Is that so… Well, I'll tell you the same thing I told Miah, fuuuck Everett. He is a fool his damn self. But forget that asshole, I got a question for ya. You like readin' 'at Bible?"

"Well, yes I like it alright… Ain't as good as *To Kill a Mockin'bird* but…"

Mathias drank and laughed a little, then he said, "Yeahhh, I've read better books too, Pris."

Then he said, "Yeah I don't much care for the Bible myself. I always figured most of it was horseshit… You believe it?"

Priscilla attempted to give consideration to the question but her instincts took over and with more than a little uncertainty in her tone, she said, "Well…sure I do."

Mathias nodded his head in consideration. "Yeah I reckon I believed it at one time too… One last question, this snorin' feller yonder, Joseph, what's his nature?"

"What do you mean?"

"…I mean, what kind of feller is he, what's his nature?"

Priscilla's head tilted to the left and her eyes searched for the answer on the ceiling of the library, as she subconsciously twirled a strand of her hair.

"Well," said Priscilla, "he's nice."

"Alright, what else?"

"Well, he's kind of a rascal, but the good kind. He don't never mean no harm."

"He like to fight?"

"No sir, I mean no, he don't like to fight. He don't take no shit though, but he don't never start it. He don't let nobody mess with me neither, but he don't never start it, I swear."

"He like to hurt animals?"

"Goodness, no. Joseph don't like it at all. He hunts a lot, but he don't like when they suffer. His daddy taught him to kill 'em quick so they don't. He's a real good shot too. And he don't never shoot if he can't hit the heart."

"What about God? He believe in God?"

Prisicilla hesitated, then she remembered who she was talking to and said, "He thinks it's horseshit like you. He thinks everybody's crazy for believin', says it all the time. Sometimes I worry about the destination of his soul."

Mathias smiled, "Is he a Democrat?"

"…A what?"

"Good answer. And he treats you nice all the time, right?"

"Always, yes. Me and him's best pals. I thought you only had one more question?"

"Fair," said Mathias, then he sat down his glass and stood up. "Welp, that suits me. I'll let him keep his gun overnight, but if he starts shootin' up the place, it's on you. Now, a couple things. Them coals in the fire ought to keep it warm in here all night. And you can sleep on the couches or wherever you like in here. But if I was you, I think I'd make a bed right here on the floor by the fireplace. But do what you want. Blankets is over there by the closet. You might wanna throw one on top of yer buddy over there while yer at it. Now, when you two wake up in the mornin', you just stay in here till I come get ya, alright. Don't go out explorin'. Like I said, we don't get many visitors."

Mathias clicked his tongue and walked to the door. "Let's see, there's a pitcher of water on the bar if ya get dry, help yerself. Have some liquor too while yer at it. Drink as much as ya like, aaaannnd I will see you bright and early. I'll cook breakfast before we get ya home, sound good?"

"Yes, that sounds real good. Thank you for yer hospitality. Me and Joseph both really appreciate it."

Mathias didn't respond immediately, but when he did, he said, "I couldn't be happier to meet you, Priscilla. I love yer brother a lot and I have a feelin' I'm gonna love you just the same. Yer at home here, Miss Carpenter. Sleep well." Then he turned and walked out of the library, but before he shut the door, he said, "Hey Priscilla, if ye get a minute, before bed or in the mornin', pick yerself out a couple of books to take home with ye. Take three or ten if ya want, I don't care. I know you'll return 'em. Can't have you readin' that fuckin' Bible all the time, it'll rot yer ripe little mind. Nighty night."

Priscilla watched the door shut, and she listened until Mathias's footsteps receded completely. What a day. For some time, she simply sat there in silence, examining her surroundings and contemplating recent events. She thought some about Lucky, and about missing school the following day, about the fact that Everett wasn't her father, and about Jeremiah, and snakes in her church, and she thought about quicksand too. Where that last thought came from, not even Priscilla knew. Quicksand was a fascination with which she had yet to come to terms.

Starting to feel a bit sleepy, Priscilla retrieved some blankets and made a bed on the floor in front of the fireplace, as Mathias had suggested. Then, again as Mathias had suggested, she laid a blanket over Joseph, who was still sawing enough logs to build another library next to the one they were in. Even in his sleep, Joseph scratched and clawed at his arm. Priscilla eyed him with one raised brow. He was indeed her very best friend, but he was an odd one, if she had ever met one.

The old library was surprisingly still warm without a fire. The hearth itself seemed to radiate heat and even the stone mantle was warm to the touch. On top of the mantle were several old black and white photos in frames. In one of the photos, Mathias and two other men stood beside a creek with fishing poles. Mathias was much younger and his eyes were normal. Priscilla looked at that picture for quite a while. Beside the pictures was a stack of books. She read each title and recognized none of them.

Priscilla counted ten different liquors behind the bar and at least two dozen dead insects in the drawers above. She inspected the walls, on which hung several antlers that she determined to be harvested from deer, and one unknown animal. To the right of the fireplace, on the wall, was a long vertical wooden slat and nailed to it was the outstretched skin of a snake. Beside the snake was a black and white portrait of an old woman inside a barn.

The statue in the center of the room, one of the Many Labors of Hercules, Priscilla found to be quite interesting. She studied it for several minutes. She couldn't determine what the statue was attempting to portray or convey exactly, but the piece excited her, and she decided that she would have to remember to ask Mathias about it in the morning.

'Dogma' by Marilyn Manson plays

Priscilla picked up the candle from beside the bar and began walking toward the back of the library, which had, up to this point, been previously obscured by shadows in most places, and utter darkness in others. Curious, she wandered into the shelves, running the tips of her fingers along the spines of books as she went. Lit by the small flame of the candle, the library proved much larger than Priscilla had once presumed. It could have been her imagination getting away from her but the towering shelves appeared to go on forever into the darkness.

Priscilla moved slowly, careful not to extinguish her source of light, stopping frequently to examine the spines of books for their titles, removing some of them and leafing through their pages before eventually returning them to their spot on the shelf. She was looking for a book, or maybe even two, that she could borrow. Mathias had been so very kind in his offer and she wanted to take advantage of the opportunity, it being such a rare one. But no title, cover, or text had yet to catch her eye. None yet had called to her, so to speak. Not at first, anyway. No, not at first. But then, no more than two feet away, she saw it.

It sat on the shelf like a missing tooth. Grotesque in all its glory, bound in its eternal blackness, contained within the dimly cast old library, the book sat like a missing tooth in a mouth full of otherwise decaying teeth. At first, Priscilla could have sworn she was staring into an empty void, a place where a book ought to have been but was not, but as she stared, the void began to take form, and the longer she stared and the harder she stared, the more the form within the void seemed to be staring right back at her. Examining her. Analyzing her. Judging her. Priscilla's skin crawled at the idea, like an ant-hill.

Creepy, she thought as she raised the candle toward the void.

Alas, it was only a book. The blackest book in all creation maybe, but a book all the same. A bit of tarnished golden metal that held together the book's cover had been revealed by the flickering candle, otherwise Priscilla would never have seen it. Even with the candle as close to it as could be without burning down the library, the book was still hardly visible but for its hardware. Head turned sharply to the side, she eyed the book suspiciously out of one eye. It was so black. It was so soul-stealingly black. It was the kind of black that gods saw when they died, and Priscilla was entranced by it.

For nearly a minute, she attempted to absorb what she was seeing, gazing dumbly into the pitch as wax dripped onto the floorboards, but eventually, hesitantly, she reached out and she pulled the book from the shelf. It wasn't particularly large, maybe the size of an encyclopedia, but it was heavy and thick, and it looked extremely old. And it appeared to have been burnt. Priscilla turned the book over in her hands, and from what she could tell, there was no title printed anywhere on its charred leather cover. She undid the black leather cord wrapped around it, and she began to leaf through its pages but the candle had burned down to nearly nothing, so she tucked the book under her arm and made her way back to the fireplace where more candles still burned.

Priscilla settled down in front of the hearth with her back against the warm stone, Indian-style like they showed her in school. Joseph still snored from across the room, and she took comfort in that. She felt like she had been wandering the library for so long, and she was glad to know nothing had changed in her absence. As strange as her day had been, if she had returned to find Joseph an aged and greying old man, she would not have been altogether surprised. Nevertheless, she was thankful that she hadn't.

Priscilla rested the book in her lap and looked down at it. What a strange looking book it was. She hoped it wasn't written in a different language like a few of the books she had seen on the shelves, or, God forbid, blank, like the one she found. She really didn't want to have to go back into the stacks in search of a replacement, the fireplace being so exquisitely warm.

But as luck would have it, moments later, when Priscilla opened the book's blackened cover, there, written on its first soiled page, was a word that she not only recognized, but one that captured and enraptured every single piece of her curious teenage heart, a word that tickled the tail of her every girlish fancy, and a word that made her want to rush to the market at that very moment and buy a brand new broom.

And that word was…

WITCHCRAFT

Holy shit, holy shit, holy shit, how…neat. Priscilla immediately began leafing through the book's pages. It was filled with what appeared to be hundreds upon hundreds of handwritten spells and incantations. She saw headings like LOVE SPELLS, DEATH

SPELLS, INVISIBILITY SPELLS, DEMON CONJURING, ENCHANTMENTS, and a section titled PURGATIVES AND EMETICS, whatever that meant. There were handdrawn diagrams and pictures and all sorts of different symbols and shapes, and Priscilla, well, Priscilla was absolutely losing her shit with excitement.

Scanning through the book's many pages, she could not have been more satisfied with her literary selection. *Boy, oh boy,* Priscilla thought. *Me and Joseph are gonna be witches! Then ain't nobody gonna fuck with us.* Then she started thinking about all the spells and curses she could cast on Everett. She was so excited that she almost jumped up to wake Joseph, but then reconsidered and decided that it could wait until morning.

Truth be told, she was feeling a little sleepy herself. It had been an unusually long day. So instead of waking Joseph, she picked up the blankets from in front of the fireplace and made a bed on the floor right in front of the couch on which he slept. Although it was warmer by the fire, Priscilla felt safer and more comfortable next to her friend.

After carefully placing her new book in her backpack, Priscilla laid down on the floor beside Joseph and curled up under the blankets. She expected the covers to smell bad, but they didn't, they actually smelled sort of clean. Priscilla was surprised. And relieved. For what seemed like hours, she laid there thinking about nothing but witches and all the witchy fun she and Joseph were going to have. Not that she necessarily knew a whole lot about witches. In fact, she didn't know much about them at all, but in fairness, she knew about as much as anybody else in Clockmaker, West Virginia.

She knew that witches could fly on brooms and cast spells and concoct potions, that they could change their appearance and talk to animals, that they had cauldrons and pointy black hats, and that they tended to cackle when they laughed, essentially every-thing that she had seen on television or heard in the school yard. Priscilla knew from watching *Bewitched* with Maw Scill that witches could be sweet and charming, even pretty, but she also knew that some witches were green and had big noses with warts on them. Having a big green beak didn't necessarily sound appealing to Priscilla, but she had a feeling that it was only wicked witches who looked that way. Samantha from *Bewitched* sure wasn't green, and she was a good witch as far as Priscilla could tell, even if she was a little mischievous from time to time. After a lengthy consideration, Priscilla decided that she need not worry about it because of course she was going to be a good witch, and good witches didn't grow warts.

She'd been taught about the Salem Witch Trials in school, but, at the time, she had only felt a sort of pity for the poor women accused of witchery and consorting with the Devil. Priscilla always felt like they hadn't gotten a fair shake, and that their trials were obviously biased in favor of their accusers. She never once even considered being wrong, that the women had in fact aligned themselves with the Beast and taken his mark, that they were indeed, despite the faults of their accusers, witches of the most Satanic nature. If Priscilla had considered this then maybe, just maybe, she would have entered into the practice of witchcraft with a bit more caution and apprehension, but as it were, she had not, and so Priscilla was all set to dive in head first without even checking the depth of the water.

Eventually, just before the sun came up, Priscilla felt her eyes beginning to flutter shut and she attempted to say a prayer, but before she could get the words dear Jesus out of her mouth, she fell fast asleep.

————◆————

ONE FIVE FIVE

ChaPTer sEVEn

———◆———

"Psssst. Pssssst. Scilly, wake up. Scilly, Scilly…Scilly." Priscilla forced one eye open to the sun-filled library. She felt as though she'd been asleep for only minutes. Joseph was above her, still lying on the couch, but he was now awake. His eyes were wide and confused, but not frightened so much as excited. He was jabbing Priscilla on her shoulder and when he saw her eye wink open, he whispered again, "Scilly, wake up. We done died and gone to Chinese Heaven."

Just as those words left Joseph's mouth, Priscilla heard a floor-board creak behind her and, startled, she quickly rolled over to meet the source of the noise. Still in a bit of a daze herself, her hair matted to the side of her face, crust in her eyes, Priscilla stared up at several girls, nine to be specific, who were standing, expressionless, in a semi-circle around her and Joseph.

The girls each wore matching white sleeping gowns, thin to the point of transparent, and their hair was long and straight and black and cut off above their eyes. They possessed the same milky orbs as Mathias and Elias, but with a defined slant. They were each barefoot, and their skin was silky, and of an almond hue. They were as beautiful as anything Priscilla, or Joseph for that matter, had ever seen, and though they ranged in height, there was very little difference between them otherwise.

For several moments they stared back at each other, the angelic girls and the bewildered friends, without a word being spoken. But of course, Joseph broke the silence. "Well uh…good mornin', ladies, egh eghm, my name is Joseph Henry Smith and this here is uh, uh, my friend…uh, Scilly."

The girls did not respond. They only glared back at Joseph and Priscilla blindly, almost coyly. Then, with tension at its peak, all at once, they fell into a fit of giggles, all nine of them with a soft delicate hand over their mouths. Priscilla looked back at Joseph, as if to say *what in the actual fuck is goin' on*, but she could tell by the expression on his face that he was just as baffled as she, although obviously more intrigued. God, he's hopeless, she thought.

Just then, behind the girls, there was a click of the tongue, and Mathias's voice interrupted the playful tittering. "Now girls, I thought I told you to let these two sleep. You should be ashamed. Hoverin' and gawkin'. Now don't nobody like to be woke up that way."

"Hey, I don't mind," Joseph said quietly.

Mathias said, "Now come on, out. Get outside and warsh up fer lunch. Out. Out. You can smell 'em later. Move it."

The girls began filing out of the library and the giggling started again. Mathias kissed each of their foreheads as they passed by him out the door, and when they had all gone, he stood there smiling. "Mornin', Priscilla. Mornin', Joseph, or should I say afternoon," he said.

Joseph shot up off the couch. "Afternoon, shit," he said. "What time is it?"

"Close to one, I reckon, I can't read a clock," Mathias said.

"Shit fire, we done missed school," said Joseph. "My momma is gonna whip my ass."

"Yep she is," Priscilla confirmed, wiping the sleep from her eyes.

"Ah shit," Joseph said, as he plopped back down on the couch, already defeated. "I'm gonna have to lie, that's just all there is to it. Ain't no way around it."

Priscilla got up off the floor and sat down on the couch beside Joseph, as close as she could sit. "Yeah, yer goose is cooked," she said. Then to Mathias, clearly amused, she said, "Miss Lynette said if he misses one more day, she's gonna beat him till his ears bleed."

Joseph scooted away from Priscilla with mock indignation, saying, "Get off me."

From the doorway, Mathias said, "Oh, don't ye worry 'bout a thing. You just tell yer momma you was with me, and you tell her if she has a problem with it, she can come see her old buddy Mathias and I'll set her straight for ya. Now see, there ain't nothin' to worry 'bout."

Joseph looked at Mathias wearily. "Mathias, sir, er…what have you, my momma will not hesitate to beat the ever-lovin' shit outta me if I come home with a line like that."

"He ain't lyin'," Priscilla confirmed. "I seen her use a shoe on him once."

Joseph buried his head in his hands. "Oh my damn head aches."

Mathias said, "Well, you know what I always say, deal with trouble when it comes. Y'all take yer time, but you come on down to the kitchen when you get movin'. You 'member how to get there?"

"I do," said Priscilla.

"Alrighty, good. I'll get ye home after. Oh and don't worry' bout my girls, they ain't used to company, but they real friendly. Bright too, just like they momma."

Joseph raised a brow. "Them's yer daughters?!"

"All nine of 'em. Got two boys too. Elias, you met," said Mathias with obvious pride.

Priscilla knew what Joseph was getting at, and she prayed that he would let it go there, but she knew better, and she was right.

Joseph said, "Now I ain't the smartest kid in the world, and I hate to break it to ya, but… I think yer old lady mighta been runnin' around on you, old buddy. I mean I could be wrong, but I do believe yer daughters is Chinese."

Mortified: definition one - feeling or showing
strong shame or embarrassment.
Mortified: definition two - affected by gangrene
or necrosis.

Of the two definitions, Priscilla was a classic textbook example of the first. Although given Joseph's current line of inquiry, she would have welcomed Fournier's gangrene and sudden necrosis with open arms and a chocolate cake.

But, once again, Mathias surprised Priscilla. Instead of being offended or angry, like Priscilla expected, he only gave an amused laugh, and shook his head. Then he said, "Aw, my wife ain't run around, I kept her on a tight leash. And any damn way, they ain't Chinese, Joseph, they's Siamese, half-Siamese. My late wife was from Siam or Thailand, or whatever they call it these days. Elias, he's half-Siamese too, and so's his little brother. I'll teach ye how to spot the difference 'tween Orientals another time, Joseph. Now gather yerselves. Lunch is ready."

Mathias turned and left, but from the hall, loud enough for her to hear, he said, "Don't forget to find ye a book, Priscilla."

Holy shit, the book. How could she have forgotten? Priscilla hadn't thought of it even once since waking. When she turned to look at Joseph, her eyes were wild with excitement and she was smiling from ear to ear. "Wait till you see what I found," she said.

Joseph eyed her, curiously and somewhat suspiciously, as she retrieved the book from the pack. "Shit, I can't wait," he said. "You don't never get this excited."

But when Priscilla showed Joseph the book, his reaction, well, his reaction was a bit of a letdown. He didn't seem to possess one single shred of interest or enthusiasm for what she was showing him. Sure, he was feeling sick from the moonshine but she expected at least some interest, and he was offering her none. Even after attempting to show him some of the spells and pointing out how strange and old the book appeared, Joseph was not impressed. Then he vomited in his mouth and swallowed it. Finally, after a short debate on the subject, Joseph said, "Well I tell ya what, we'll give it a shot, and when it don't work, you can put that book up on the shelf next to yer Bible, sound good? Now get that thing away from me, I feel sick."

Priscilla looked at him bitterly. "Fine," she said, and she slammed the book shut. No matter what, she had a feeling about this book, and she wasn't going to let Joseph talk her out of it. For a moment they only stared at one another, but then a wicked little smile formed on Priscilla's face.

"What are you smilin' at?"

"Oh nuthin'… I was just thinkin' bout that whoopin' yer momma's gonna give you, that's all."

Joseph nodded with understanding. "I'm glad you think it's so funny. I hope she tans yer ass just for bein' with me." Then he stood up. "Let's go. We can talk about you flyin' over Boone County on a broom later, I'm feelin' worse by the minute. I need water."

◆

Lunch with the Elders was like nothing Priscilla or Joseph had ever experienced. There were so many of them, Elders that is. They were everywhere. Big ones, little ones, old ones, young ones, Siamese ones. Several of them even had red hair like Priscilla. All chatting and eating, and cooking and cleaning, they moved amongst one another with the ease of the seeing—fluidly, rhythmically, as though they were not hindered by their blindness in the least. And although she should have expected as much by the way Elias and Mathias got around, this seamless circus fascinated Priscilla to no end.

Once, the year prior, she and Joseph were flattening pennies on the railroad tracks and a massive constellation of Starlings materialized over their heads. For nearly ten minutes they stood there, just staring up at the incredible performance taking place in the sky above them. The mass of birds swooped this way and that, all in unison, and all in harmony, never colliding, never hesitating. Not once did they even so much as graze one another. Not a single ruffled feather as far as Priscilla could tell, and now, watching the Elders move about their kitchen, she was reminded of the Starlings.

Over lunch, which consisted of braised rabbit meat, and roasted carrots and turnip stew, Priscilla and Joseph met the entire clan, all thirty-four of them. Mathias's brother, Zacharias, made sure of that. He ushered Priscilla and Joseph around the massive kitchen and attached dining hall with apparent delight, introducing them to each of the many Elders with the same vigor as the first. It was dizzying. Disorienting, even. All the names and all the faces. All the eyes bereft of sight. Stories of her brother, stories of hunts, stories of drunkenness, stories of calamity and broken bones, and all stitched together with side-splitting wise cracks and defamatory jokes. Priscilla had never heard so much cursing. All of them, even the kids, cursed like sailors. By the light of day, the Elders and their place of inhabitance was far less sinister than Priscilla had perceived the night before. It was, in fact, rather serene.

Zacharias, like Mathias, was a charming man. Nehemias, she liked too. He had taken to calling her Scilly, like Joseph, and that made her blush for some reason. Their wives too, Priscilla cared for very much. Mathias's younger brothers had chosen two sisters from Tennessee to wed and they were both as chatty and as nice as any two woman could be. They also had the biggest butts that Priscilla had ever seen on the back of a person, like prize-winning peaches they were. Priscilla suspected that they were both probably very good mothers. Truth be told, Priscilla liked just about everyone she was introduced to that afternoon. They were all so pleasant and so welcoming, the way people in church ought to have been but weren't. They made Priscilla feel at home, right away.

Her favorites though, if she had to pick them, and she did not, but if she did, would have been Mathias's youngest son, Josias, the slow one, and Nehemias's daughter, Shoe String, who was affectionately called that because she was skinny as one. First of all, Josias was simply a riot. For being slow, and only four, he could not have been more comical. When introduced to Joseph, Josias spit something brown and coagulated in his hand then reached it out to Joseph to shake, and when Joseph hesitated, Josias said, "Don—, d'don—, don't be a pussy, J—, Jo—, Henry." Then when Joseph still didn't reach to shake his hand, Josias said, "Ah, heck," and wiped his hand on his chest, sat back down, and began eating again. At which point all in attendance fell into laughter.

Shoe String, on the other hand, Priscilla idolized. She looked to be only slightly older than Priscilla, and sure she was skinny, real skinny, but one thing was all too clear. Shoe String did not take shit from anyone, especially boys. Priscilla liked that a lot.

At one point, one of Shoe String's many male cousins—Priscilla couldn't remember which of Mathias's brothers he belonged to or his name—made a smart remark about Shoe String's big feet, and Shoe String, to no one's surprise but Priscilla's, then responded by punching the boy square in the chest, and after he had fallen, she mounted him and twisted his nipples until he screeched for forgiveness. When the shattered, shameful words "I'm sorry!" exited the boy's mouth, Priscilla had to refrain from rushing over to hug Shoe String and ask for her autograph.

Joseph's favorites were all too obvious. He had four of them, Kut, Samui, Samet, and Phuket, Mathias's teenage daughters. One was fifteen. One, sixteen. One, eighteen. And one, nineteen. And Joseph was on cloud one thousand. Oddly enough, it seemed to Priscilla that the four girls, in all their sensual yet somehow innocent blindness, were responding quite favorably to Joseph's charms. When Priscilla had first seen him chatting with them outside around the piano, she had worried that he was on the verge of doing or saying something foolish, but the next time she looked, all four of the girls were laughing, one was ruffling his hair, and another was patting him on his chest.

Thank goodness, Priscilla thought, *maybe I'm not the only one who likes Joseph after all*. And it is true, she did think that, but what she felt, on the other hand, was her very first tinge, or maybe tinge is too strong of a word, maybe what she felt was a whisper. That's it, a whisper. She felt her very first whisper of bitter, unjustifiable jealousy. Priscilla didn't take note of her feelings as such, but she did walk away from the kitchen window, liking the four Elder girls that much less and for reasons that she could not yet identify. Priscilla's least favorites, if she had to pick them, and she did not, but if she did, would have been them.

Eventually lunch came to an end and Priscilla and Joseph said their goodbyes. "Come on, Prince Charmin', they'll be here when ye come back," Mathias said, as he dragged Joseph away from his daughters.

The plan was for Mathias to walk Priscilla and Joseph back to Clockmaker, but Elias insisted on returning them himself. "Dang it, Daddy, now I got 'em up here and I can get 'em back," he said, and after some serious haggling, Mathias took the key from around his neck and handed it to Priscilla, and he sat down on a stump next to some of his family, all of them tongues-a-clickin', and 'watched' as they walked away.

"It was a damn fine pleasure to meet you both," Mathias said. "A damn fine pleasure." He also said, "Elias, you come straight home, boy, I got chores for ye," and finally, "Y'all come back and visit any old time, make sure to hang on to that key, and if either of ye ever need anything, don't ye hesitate," but it wasn't until they had been gone for some time that Mathias even thought to ask if Priscilla had remembered to take a book.

◆

It wasn't long before Joseph recognized his surroundings and sent Elias home, but not before Elias could remind Joseph about his mother's fondness for getting drunk and taking off her clothes. To which Joseph responded with something along the lines of "Eat shit and die, blind boy."

They actually hadn't been too far off track the night before. Joseph had simply gotten turned around in the dark. It could have happened to anyone, or so he said. Either way, he assured Priscilla that they would be home in no more than an hour.

By the time they reached Priscilla's backyard, where they started, the sun was nearly set. The days were getting shorter. Joseph opted to walk Priscilla home as opposed to taking the quicker route behind Maw Scill's house. He was in no hurry to cross paths with his mother, the school would have surely called by now. Besides, he intended on coming inside and attempting to talk Priscilla's mother out of something to eat, but when they spotted Everett's car in front of the house, it was decided that it would be best if he just went on home and faced the music, no matter how out of tune it sounded.

Before he left, Joseph promised that if Lucky hadn't come back by the following day, they would continue their search after school. "We can start where we found Everett's hand," Joseph said. "You want me to take the backpack?"

"No… I'll take it."

"Alright, well, bring it to school with ya. We'll need to restock at the hideout 'fore we go lookin' for Lucky…"

"Okay."

"Well, see ya tomorrow, ass-hat. Wish me luck," said Joseph. Then he walked off.

Priscilla wanted to shout something about Joseph's naked momma, just to get in one last uppercut before he left, but she decided not to. There would be time for that, but for now there were more pressing matters to consider. Priscilla had a decision to make… Go inside to tell her mother about Jeremiah, or head straight for Maw Scills?

Normally, Everett worked the afternoon shift at the mine. Priscilla assumed that he was home because of his recent disfigurement. It was going to be real hard to mine coal with one hand. She stood behind his shed, peering up at the lit kitchen window. She couldn't hear any hollering or screaming. That was a good sign.

How many times she had sat outside by that shed listening to Everett yell and curse, she could not remember. God, did she ever hate him. More in that moment than ever. Knowing that she was not his daughter was liberating in that way. It allowed her to loathe him more… freely. More passionately. More fully. But more precisely, it allowed her the pressure and heat necessary to begin the process of crystalizing her coal black hatred of Everett into a goddamned diamond, one that she would someday have cut, polished, and set into the center of a great golden crown.

Priscilla could hear Maw Scill's television blaring from on the hill, and she figured, screw it, she could tell her mother about Jeremiah tomorrow. Going inside could only make things worse. Everett was irritated by Priscilla's very presence, and no matter what she did, how she behaved, or how she spoke, he always found something to come down on her about. Then when Everett would start in on Priscilla, that's when her mother would come to her defense. It was a scenario Priscilla had seen played out a thousand different times, in a thousand different ways, but it always ended the same. The house quiet. Everett, in his chair in the dark living room, admiring his scars. Her mother, licking her wounds in the bathroom, trying not to cry, and Priscilla, sitting in silence in her bedroom feeling like somehow it was all her fault. Screw it.

On the short walk up the hill, Priscilla's mood lightened a little. She had been a party to an unusually eventful couple of days and she was more than ready for the warmth and comfort of her grandmother's house. She was ready to kick off her old stinky boots and curl up with a blanket, and for a bite of whatever leftovers Maw Scill was sure to have lying around. She was also pretty excited to tell her about meeting Mathias and his family, and about how Joseph's momma, Lynette, used to get drunk and run around naked and pee on herself. But more than anything, what Priscilla really wanted was time alone with the book.

"Aw, who cares, what's in a name anyhow, huh? In my day, no one went around callin' themselves Chicanos, Mexican Americans, Afro Americans, we was all Americans. After that if a guy was a jig or a spic, it was his own business," Archie Bunker was saying to his son-in-law when Priscilla switched off the television. BLIP.

Up to this point, Maw Scill had been fast asleep in her chair, but as soon as the screen went blank and silence filled the old house, she stirred awake.

"I was watchin' 'at," the old woman said.

Priscilla smiled. "Now Maw Maw, you was sleepin'."

"Horseshit," Maw Scill muttered. "I was just restin' my eyes."

Priscilla switched the television back on. BLIP. Archie's fat head filled the screen once again.

Maw Scill picked at the corner of her eye and adjusted her glasses, which had fallen while she slept. "Little girl, where in the hell have you been, the school done called, and oh…child…" Maw Scill paused, and to Priscilla she looked as though she was on the verge of either laughing or crying or perhaps both, but she did neither. Instead, all chicory and sugar, Maw Scill said, "You looked in the mirror today?"

"No mam," Priscilla said, feeling all of a sudden self-conscious of her appearance.

"You feel alright? Yer eyes is blacker than tar. And goodness gracious, yer hair. Girl, you look like you done slept in the woods. Get on in the kitchen where they's light so I can tend to you."

While Maw Scill bathed and fed Priscilla, Priscilla told Maw Scill all about her adventures, about finding the chunk of Everett's hand, about getting lost and meeting Mathias, about Jeremiah and California, and, of course, about Joseph's momma. She also brought up the story Mathias told her about he and Maw Scill stealing fireworks and the only thing Maw Scill had to say about that was, "I ain't sayin' I did it, and I ain't sayin' I didn't do it, but I will say this. Stealin' is bad. No matter how drunk ya are. And yer damn right we did it. Santa brought Maw Maw a two hundred dollar fur coat for Christmas that year too." But through all the scrubbing and washing, and all the meatloaf and mashed taters, Priscilla somehow, some way, failed to mention anything to her grandmother about the book.

In between bites of potatoes, Maw Scill told Priscilla that she was glad that she hadn't decided to stop and see her mother. That it wasn't the right time. Then she said, "Yer Momma come up here this afternoon lookin' for you after the school called, drunker than a skunk, all emotional, wearin' long sleeves."

"She worried?" asked Priscilla.

"Naw, well, she was, till I told her you left with Joseph and that settled her. She said Everett's been drunk since yesterday. Said she been waitin' fer him to blow all day… I reckon you better plan on stayin' up here for a little bit. Who knows how long that'll be…" Then she said, "I can't even believe y'all found the other half of that dickhead's hand."

"It was so gross, Maw Maw. Lucky took three whole fingers, and most of his palm." Priscilla had her nostrils flared and her eyes to the ground. She was clearly reliving the experience in her mind as she spoke.

Maw Scill grinned. "I imagine it was gross," she said, half-amused. Then she said, "I don't feel even a little bit bad for him, do you?"

Priscilla returned the grin and shook her head, and they both had a laugh at that.

"Serves the bastard right," Maw Scill said. "He deserves only the worst in life."

◆

Thirty-one minutes later, Priscilla was sitting on her grandmother's back porch, wrapped in a light brown quilt, looking up at the moon. Her belly was full and she was warm and content. She could smell the soap that Maw Scill had used in her hair, and feel the night breeze on her face. Maw Scill had been right though. Priscilla had looked in the mirror and her eyes were black as tar.

"Like a fuckin' raccoon," Joseph had said earlier in the day, and he had not been exaggerating. Nevertheless, her head no longer hurt and the floating spot had disappeared from her vision, and she felt a sense of comfort that she hadn't felt in days. Maybe weeks. But then she fucked around and opened the book.

Worn from use. Charred and burnt. Tarnished metal. No title. Black. Priscilla was not ready for it. Not in any way. Every single ounce of tranquility that she had been feeling was sucked from her the very moment she cracked the book's cover. Like a lead anchor tied around her soul, she felt an immense weight all about her. It seemed to be drawing her, even dragging her, into the book's soiled pages. She was entranced. Her heart was pulsating rapidly, one hundred and four beats per minute to be exact. Fear had entered her blood stream, and upon feeling the book's mammalian-like pull, Priscilla knew with cold hard certainty that the book was real. Joseph was wrong, and the book was real. As excited as Priscilla wanted to be about this realization, she still could not help but be frightened.

And she was right to be a little scared. This book was about to become Priscilla's whole world, her everything. Her life and her reason for living. It would carry her to places beyond her wildest dreams and it would pry open parts of her that she didn't know existed. It would keep her awake at night and drive her from bed in the morning, and when she looked in the mirror, she would see it. It would bend her. It would break her. It would become her. It would replace her prayers. But she didn't know that then, and so she kept reading.

As Priscilla read, a bright orange caterpillar watched her, contemptuously. The caterpillar, who for the sake of the story will be called Harold, was near death. The lower half of his abdomen had been smashed into the concrete, rendering him immobile, and his guts were splattered around him. When Priscilla came out onto the porch, she had stepped on him, unknowingly and unintentionally of course, but she had crushed him all the same. Harold, it seems, had been nearing the end of a long and arduous journey to a group of trees that he spotted in Maw Scill's backyard seven months prior. They would have been the perfect place for his transformation. He knew it the moment he saw them. Another week, tops, and Harold would have been there, hanging, cocooned, from a limb, cozy and content, digesting himself into soup. Three more weeks and he would have had wings.

But not now. Not ever. Harold was going to die and he knew it. And this made him furious. How dare this careless creature come along and bring an end to his life? Had it no idea what he was to become? How great? How perfect? This was not meant to be Harold's destiny. Oh, no. He was meant for great things, wonderful things, for perfect beauty, and yet there he laid, mangled and broken, warm yellow fluid oozing out from under his prothoracic shield. Now what was he worth?

And so, Harold lay there helpless upon the pavement, all six of his eyes set on Priscilla, watching her. He watched her sit down and get comfy, something Harold would never do again, then he watched her open a book and stare down at its first page. He watched her eyes go wide at what she was seeing. When she flipped to the next page, her gaze intensified and she read these pages for, what seemed to Harold, quite a long time. Finally, she flipped to the next page, and whatever was on those pages sent her into a deep contemplation, and for some time, she only stared out into the night.

Then Harold watched Priscilla suddenly stand up. She sat the book down and walked across the porch. When she returned, she was carrying a garden claw. The one Maw Scill used to dig weeds out of her rose bed. However, Priscilla did not return to her seat. Instead she knelt before the book with her knees on the concrete, the garden claw dangling at her side. With her free hand, she flipped to the third page. What Priscilla did next confused Harold, but it also brought him a miserable sort of satisfaction. She held out her free hand over the book and let it hang there. She seemed to hesitate. But only briefly. Then she lifted the garden claw high into the air and sunk it into the center of her palm.

Under the dim porch light, blood began flowing immediately. Priscilla retracted the claw and squeezed her bleeding hand into a fist. Harold watched the blood fall on the book, and he watched a hazy, lime-green smoke rise up from its pages. He heard the hiss of the chemical reaction. He smelled the sulfur in the air. The blood made him think of his own leaking thorax, and the internal pressures that were about to burst one of his eyes. To make matters worse, his hearing was beginning to fade. And just as soon as he became aware of that depressing fact, his vision began to fade just the same. Harold's gaze fell away from the creature that caused his death and he closed his eyes in surrender. *This is it… This is it. God fucking damnit, all I ever wanted was to fly*, were Harold the caterpillar's last thoughts before he died.

◆

The world is always changing. Always shifting. Constantly. The changes are small, though. Most people don't have the bandwidth to notice them, and yet, all things are in a perpetual state of motion or flux. Nothing is fixed. Nothing is ever the same. Even in Clockmaker, where the sun seems to set at a slower pace, and where watching fireflies dance in a field is considered too much excitement for a Saturday night, even here, all is amorphous and blurred by the speed of motion.

On this night, however, as Priscilla's type O-negative blood fell on to the book, the world and all of its moving parts stopped. For a single instant, time and matter were paralyzed, static and still. Nothing changed. Not one thing. But then there was a shudder as the wheels of fate began to turn once again, and just like that, the instant passed.

This glitch, as it were, went unnoticed by all but five—God, the Devil, a monk in Myanmar, and two men from Montana who were high on psilocybin. For those two men and the monk, that instant felt as though it lasted forever, and neither one of them was ever quite the same again. The monk later recovered and described the event by saying that he felt as though his physical form were being folded into a two-dimensional trapezoid. He had no words for what he saw. Beyond those five, however, no one noticed. The world simply stopped, then kept on spinning. Much the way it does when a loved one dies. Particularly close kin. Maw Scill had fallen back to sleep in front of the television, Lavinia was staring hard into the bathroom mirror, Everett was passed out in his chair, Joseph was lying in bed scratching at his arm, and Mathias was playing the piano. They were not kin to the deceased, so to speak, and did not notice any change. Priscilla, on the other hand, was gasping, and twitching, and convulsing violently, and her eyes were rolling back in her head.

She was kin, alright. Her soul had died, and this was part of the grieving process.

'The Crystal Ship' by The Doors plays

———◆———

Chapter EIGHt

'Get My Rocks Off'
by Dr Hook plays

Birds chirped, bees buzzed, a dog barked in the distance. Joseph woke up the following morning with one thing, and one thing only, on his mind. Pussy. Vaginas, not cats. He set up in bed and stretched his arms and yawned. Sunlight poured through the curtainless window, causing his daily morning erection to cast a shadow on his stomach. It was going to be a good day.

Mathias Elder's daughters. Good Lord Almighty, thine hath seen the light, Mathias Elder's daughters. Joseph was lust-struck, but he could not decide, for the life of him, which one he liked the most. Phuket, Kut, Samet, or uh… um. Joseph couldn't quite remember the fourth one's name. He was actually impressed with himself that he remembered the other three, being such strange names and all, but who the hell cared. Names weren't important, not to Joseph anyway. He remembered the important parts— their legs, their hips, their lips, and every slip of their nightgowns.

The hardest part in deciding was that he felt like he had an equal chance with all four of them. They each seemed to have been enamored with him, and Joseph just could not bring himself to break any of their hearts. How could he? Even the oldest one, Phuket, with her pouty lips and amazingly perky and pillow-like bosom, even she seemed to be more than interested in what Joseph had to offer. But then there was the tiny one, Samet. It would shame the Devil, the things Joseph would do to spend even three minutes exploring that girl's naked frame. Oh my my my, what he was to do, he did not know. Decisions, *dee-cisions*.

The one thing Joseph did know was that one way or another, he was going to have to find his way back up to Elder territory, and soon. Those girls were all he could think about, that and his damn itching arm. All through the night, it had prickled and tingled until it burned, and it had kept him awake most of the morning. If it hadn't been for thoughts of those sweet, sweet girls, he may have very well gone insane. He could have sworn that he had, at one point, been on the verge.

After rising and shining, Joseph kissed his mother on the cheek and was out the door. He wanted to leave early so he could check two of his traps on the way to school, although he hoped they would be empty. He didn't feel like dealing with death today. No, not today. As previously mentioned, he had only one thing on his mind.

Luckily, the trap in the barn loft and the one by the Pratts' pond were both empty. Joseph dusted his hands on his jeans, and he was off to school with a little more than a bounce in his step. The thought of what lay between the thighs of those four girls was with Joseph his entire walk to school, and by the time he reached his first period history class, his imagination was running wild with the many possibilities.

These possibilities were limited, however, by the fact that Joseph had next to no experience with girls. He had kissed his cousin once when he was nine, or rather his cousin had kissed him, ugly as she was, but that was basically it. He'd heard talk over the years, mostly from other boys who also had little to no experience in such matters, but when it came down to it, Joseph knew as much about getting pussy, or what to do with it after he got it, as a nun knows about autoerotic asphyxiation.

That didn't matter much to Joseph though. He had a basic enough idea. Or so he thought. He knew what went in what holes, but beyond that, well, he would just have to figure out the rest along the way. He wasn't about to let a little thing like details stand in between him and those sweet, blind Elder girls. And if their blindness was contagious? Well then, may crows peck out his eyes, he did not care. *Let 'em cloud over*, he thought. *Blind ain't so bad. I'll just learn the tongue clickin' trick. To fuckin' hell with sight.* His loins had been awakened, and now there would be no putting them back to sleep. Joseph was even beginning to wonder if he might just be in love, as crazy as that sounded.

He was so swept up in his fantasies, in fact, that it wasn't until he was sitting alone in the cafeteria during lunch that he realized that Priscilla had not shown up to school. Instantly, he felt a sense of worry. It wasn't like Priscilla to miss school, not to mention church, and given her reason for missing church the other day was that Everett had almost killed her with his chainsaw, Joseph couldn't help but feel justified in his concern. Priscilla was a tough girl, she had been dealing with Everett for years, but she was still just a girl. And Joseph had no doubt that, after losing half his hand, Everett was sure to only get meaner. Joseph didn't finish his lunch.

He was still picking peanut butter and jelly from his teeth when he hit the schoolhouse steps. His mother would be getting another call tonight. No doubt about it. She was surprisingly understanding the night before, but tonight would be different. A call from the school two days in a row, no matter the circumstances, would guarantee a belt across his bare ass. There were no two ways around it. But that didn't matter because Joseph had a feeling. A bad feeling. And he was going to act on it.

ONE SEVEN SEVEN

He decided to try Maw Scill's first. But there was one small problem. The fucking Mire Clan. Two of them. Kester, who Joseph knew all too well, and his oldest brother Merle, who Joseph had never met, but had heard about, and who had to be pushing at least thirty years old. The two of them were unloading bales of hay from the back of a pickup truck when Joseph came walking up around the bend. Kester noticed him first, and he motioned to his brother. Then they both climbed down out of the truck and walked toward the road to intercept him. "Ehhhh, fuck," Joseph said to himself. "Here we go."

"Well, look who we got here," said Merle, as he and Kester stepped into the road. They were both filthy with coal dust and dirt and grime and God knows what. Joseph was maybe ten feet away from them, but already he was sure he could smell them. His plan was to keep his mouth shut, and his head down, and just keep walking. It was a simple plan. He had more important things to worry about than these two clowns. So, no matter what they said or did, he would ignore them, and just keep on moving. He wasn't running away. He simply did not have time. There was a difference.

That plan went to shit pretty quickly though.

Merle stepped in front of Joseph, as Kester circled behind him. Joseph stopped walking. He looked up at Merle while keeping track of Kester in his peripherals. For a moment, they regarded one another, Merle with his smug sneer, and Joseph looking like Sisyphus watching the rock roll back down the hill, yet again. Then Merle said, "You don't look so tough to me."

"Tougher than he looks, bub, I'm tellin' ya," warned Kester.

Joseph didn't respond. He took a deep breath, lowered his head, and stepped around Merle, intending to continue on without a word. Just as planned. But that's when he felt a hand take hold of his shirt collar, and he was yanked backwards. He stumbled, tripped, and landed on his ass in the middle of the road, the Mire brothers standing over him. "Fuck you think yer goin', faggot? I was talkin' to you," Merle said.

Kester seemed to be keeping his distance, and his mouth shut, and by the look on his face, Joseph assumed the beating he gave him was still fresh on his mind. He hoped that was true. If it was, Joseph would only have to take out Merle, and Kester would surely back off.

But Joseph wanted to give talking one more shot first, so, as he stood up and dusted himself off, he said, "I don't want no trouble, fellas. I got things to do. I know y'all think I got one comin' to me, but let's save this one for another day. What do ya say?"

Merle looked from Joseph to his brother. He said, "I don't know, little brother, what do we say?"

Kester took a second to respond, but when he did, he said, "It's up to you."

"This little boy whips yer ass…has you cryin' out for our momma…but it's up to me…" Merle shook his head like he was disappointed. "Alright then."

The tension on Merle's face seemed to let up. *Maybe there wouldn't be a fight after all*, thought Joseph.

"He's the one that knocked Mary out too, chipped her tooth," said Kester.

Maybe not. Shit. Joseph sighed. Then he watched in real time as Merle's expression turned sour as antique milk. Standing more than a foot taller than Joseph, Merle reached out slowly and took ahold of his shirt collar in a fist, pulling Joseph an inch closer, and lifting a little so that Joseph had to raise his chin. Joseph did not resist or even flinch. He allowed it to happen.

"Oh yeah, cocksucker, you sure as hell do have one comin'," Merle said, and he drew back with his free hand and made a fist. "I'd say you got two."

It was that last line, "I'd say you got two," that sealed Merle's fate. He was far too confident that what he held in his hand was a soft, frightened kid, and just as the word 'two' left his lips, Joseph tucked his fist against his own chest, and spun with all of his might, sending his elbow square into Merle's jaw with a TINK. It happened fast. So fast that Joseph's momentum spun him around backwards, and when he turned back toward Merle, it was over. Lady Luck was in his favor.

Merle crumpled, all six feet five inches of him, in the middle of the road. Out cold. Literally snoring. Joseph was so stunned that a single blow to the chin did the trick that he almost forgot about Kester, but when he spun around to face him, postured for attack, Kester was already running back toward the truck.

Joseph shouted, "Hey asshole! You forgot yer fuckin' brother!"

Kester didn't look back or respond in any way. He jumped in the truck and smoked the tires. Kicking up rocks and dirt, hay bales falling off the back, Kester lit out of there like his house was on fire, and he left nothing behind him but a cloud of dirt and dust in the air and five or six bales of hay in the road.

Joseph looked down at Merle. He was starting to show signs of life. Which, on one hand, was a good thing. Joseph did not want to become a murderer. On the other hand, he was pretty sure that the clean elbow to the jaw was a fluke, and if he let Merle get up, Lady Luck might not be feeling so generous. So, like Kester, he got the hell out of there.

By the time he got to Maw Scill's house, Joseph was so out of breath that he had to pause on her front porch to gather himself before knocking. The tussle with the Mire brothers had taken his attention momentarily, but he still could not shake the feeling that something was wrong with Priscilla. However, when Maw Scill finally came to the door, Joseph's worry was relieved quite a bit.

Not only was Maw Scill's face not racked with any kind of distress or alarm, but she was actually wearing an awkward sort of smile, half-cocked and kind of loopy. The opposite of upset, she looked… drunk. Or sedated, or something. He wasn't sure what to make of it. But when she opened the door, Joseph could see a bottle of Jim Beam dangling at her side, and putting two and two together, he surmised the reason for the odd yet comforting look that was plastered on her plastered face. Maw Scill was fucking wasted.

"Hey Maw Maw," said Joseph, playfully.

"Well good afternoon, sugar, give me a huuug. Yeeeessss. How are you today, honey, you good?"

"I'm good, Maw Maw," said Joseph, mildly surprised. The old woman had never hugged him before. She was clearly in a good mood, drunk or not. Then right before she let him go, one of her hands slipped down, and she squeezed his butt cheek. Firmly. *What the fuck?!* Joseph went from surprised to dumbstruck in one second flat. But Maw Scill moved on, casual as pajamas.

"Well that's good, sugar, that's real good. Say, how's yer fine ass daddy doin'?"

Joseph raised a brow. A high, wide brow. "He's fine, I reckon… Say, uh, Maw Maw, you seen Priscilla up here today?"

Completely disregarding the question, Maw Scill said, "Good Lord, yer daddy sure is a fine-lookin' man. *Mmmhmm*, the things I would do if I was forty years younger would shame the Devil. So many muscles. One time I seen him up under his truck, workin' on it with his shirt off and I just about creamed my old panties and I—"

Joseph couldn't listen any longer. He had to cut her off. It was too much for him to handle. "Priscilla, Maw Maw. Yer granddaughter.

Have-you-seen-her?"

"Oh sure I have, sugar. She'll be stayin' here a while. That child is in the damnedest way too, I'll tell ya. Happier'n a pig in shit. She ate her breakfast and said she was skippin' school today. Said she had somethin' more important she wanted to do, and she was just all smiles about it so I told her to go on. I says, 'Go on, little girl.' Told her to take a hooky day, she deserved it. Then I got to thinkin', well hell, I reckon Maw Maw Scill deserves a hooky day too." And she lifted the bottle at her side and tilted it toward Joseph, giving him a sloppy, exaggerated wink.

Joseph smiled at her, shaking his head with absolute wonderment. What a rare sight, and a treat. Maw Scill did not believe in playing hooky as a matter of principle, and she had always made that clear. Though he had seen her on the bottle quite a few times, this was a side of the woman that he had yet to be acquainted with.

So, Joseph said, "Well, alright, Maw Maw. Good for you. She out back, or uh…?"

Maw Scill plopped down in her chair in front of the television. "Nope, she lit out after breakfast. Said to tell you she was at the hideout."

Joseph shot the shit with Maw Scill for a few more minutes and stole a biscuit from the kitchen, then he said goodbye and set out for the woods, scratching at his arm along the way. The goddamn itching and scratching was relentless.

When he arrived at the hideout, the ladder was down and he climbed the tree and lifted the hatch without hesitation. And immediately, he regretted it. Joseph wasn't sure what he expected to find inside the old tree fort, not at all, but he certainly did not expect to find what he found. As it turns out, he wasn't quite… prepared.

Dozens of strange symbols drawn in white chalk now covered

the old boards that composed the inner walls and ceiling of his beloved hideout. The windows had been blanketed, candles burned everywhere, all of the hideout's regular contents were shoved in one corner, and in the other corner, Priscilla was sitting motionless beside a tin bucket, reading a book. Like the walls, symbols were drawn on her face, but with something black. Not chalk. Coal dust?

Joseph started to ask her what in the actual fuck she was doing, but Priscilla raised her forefinger, silencing him, and she kept it raised for several seconds until, finally, she finished whatever she was reading. And then she looked up.

Right away, two things were notable about Priscilla's face, besides the hieroglyphics of course. The first was her eyes. They were bloodshot to shit, like the vessels had dilated to the point of bursting. Her left eye, in particular, was flooded. The other noticeable thing was her grin. It formed on her face as soon as her eyes met Joseph's, and it was the wickedest little grin that he had ever seen Priscilla wear in all the years that he'd known her.

"Yer right on time!" she said, cheerfully.

Looking around the hideout, Joseph said, "On time?"

Priscilla jumped up with the book in her arms, and started blowing out all the candles as Joseph pulled himself up into the fort. Then she snatched the blankets off the windows and sat down beside Joseph, her feet dangling through the open floor hatch. She was still beaming with excitement, but she looked like death. Joseph could only stare at her.

"Christ on a stick, Scilly…what the hell are you doin'? Are you alright?" Joseph was genuinely concerned. Priscilla's eyes looked bad, and all the shit drawn on her face made him think she might have gone insane.

Prisicilla looked at Joseph intently, still clutching the book to her chest, but she didn't answer him right away. She seemed to be savoring her next sentence. Then she said, "I gotta' tell you somethin'."

"Please do, Scilly. Please tell me somethin'."

Priscilla started to speak but then she stopped. She shuffled around a little bit, and pushed the smile from her face. Then she looked at Joseph, squarely. She still hesitated, however, but when she finally found the words, they came out soft and sweet, as always. "I know how this might sound," Priscilla began. "But… well, this here is a real witch book… And I'm gonna be a real witch… And yer gonna help me."

Joseph didn't respond, he only looked at her. He was completely unamused.

"Now Joseph, I see you lookin' at me like that. I ain't crazy. Don't give me that stare. I ain't bein' a kid about it neither. I know how it sounds, but I swear I'm bein' serious."

Still nothing from Joseph. Not at first. He was eyeing the walls now. The symbols Priscilla had drawn were giving him the creeps. Eventually he said, "Is that the book you got from Mathias?"

Priscilla nodded. 'Yep!'

Joseph thought for a moment then he said, "Alright, Scilly. I'll humor ya. So what makes you think this here's a real witch book?"

"Well, 'member when I told you about havin' my first organism?"

"Uh huuuh."

"Well, when it happened, I kept seein' this goat."

Joseph raised an eyebrow. "You kept seein' a goat…?"

"Mmmhmm, it was in my mind. I kept seein' his face, and smellin' him, with these big old curly horns, and well, I don't know exactly how it…but last night when I opened this book… there was a picture of the same goat."

Joseph started to interrupt and explain to her how easily that could have been a coincidence, but Priscilla kept on.

"Now I know that could just be happenstance but when I put my blood in the book last night, it started smokin'. Green smoke even, bright green, and…well." Priscilla stopped, seemingly considering her next words. Then she said, "Joseph, I got this feelin' in me…it was like electric. Like my whole body was vibratin', even my blood was vibratin', and I could hear it, the vibratin'. It was all around me. At first I had my eyes closed, for the feelin', but when I opened 'em, all I could see was the moon. I was so close to it. And it was so pretty…I just… Well, I never seen anything so pretty, and I looked at it for hours… Then I fell asleep."

"You fell asleep?"

"Well, I dunno exactly, but all I remember is the moon, then I woke up on Maw Maw's porch this mornin'."

"What the shit, what do you mean you put yer blood in the book?"

"I stabbed my hand," said Priscilla, sticking her hand out for Joseph to admire the wound. "See. And I let the blood leak on it."

"Christ, why?"

Priscilla shrugged. "That's what the book said to do."

"Let me see it," said Joseph, and Priscilla raised her hand again. "No, the book, dummy. I don't wanna see that infected thing. You better get some 'Curochrome on it, 'fore the doc has to cut it off."

As Joseph reached for the book Priscilla snatched it away. "You can't see it," she said.

"Well, why the hell not?"

"I don't know, but that's what it says in the book. Says I'm not supposed to let anyone else read it. Says it's real important. I gotta keep it with me at all times or keep it hidden so can't nobody find it."

"Ain't that about a crock of shit."

Priscilla smiled, and shook her head. "I knew you'd say that. It don't matter, though. That's just how it is. You in?"

Joseph considered his options. Option one. He could either take Priscilla seriously, which he felt inclined to do. After all, it was Priscilla. She never had much of an imagination and certainly no inclination to lie, but this was a lot to swallow, so to speak. *I mean, witches? Real witches? Come the fuck on.*

His second option, however, only made his first option look that much better. If he didn't want to go along with this whole witch business, then he could always hog-tie his best and only friend, drag her up to Chestnut Ridge, and let the quacks at the looney bin sort her out. Joseph had heard his father say something along those lines about one of his aunts years ago, but otherwise he had no idea if that was even a real possibility. They might not even accept little girls who think they're witches, maybe only real psychos, and, even still, who would Joseph pal around with after school if Priscilla was wrapped up in a strait jacket? He sighed. "What happened to yer eyes?"

"Maw Maw said my blood vessels burst from gettin' hit so hard, don't change the subject, fucker. You in or what? Now, come on. I need yer help. You can be my assistant. It says boys can be assistants." Priscilla said that last part assuringly and went on. "We need to collect a bunch of stuff, and I don't even know what half of it is, but I bet you do. All kinds of different plants, and dead animal parts. And we gotta build stuff. It's gonna be fun. And the best part is, think of all the spells we can cast on people if it works. Everett, the Mire fucks, we could turn 'em into damn…frogs! Oh and love potions! Maybe I could brew you up some love potions for the Layfield sisters, whatcha think about that?"

Love potions for the Layfield sisters. If Joseph wasn't on board before, which he was—she had him at dead animals—but if he hadn't been, he certainly was after the mention of love potions. Priscilla had him figured out just fine. He knew it, she knew it, he knew she knew it, and she knew that he knew she knew it. Joseph never had a chance. It wasn't the Layfield sisters, however, that were on Joseph's mind. They were old news. Joseph was saving all of his potion for four special young ladies, whose names he kept struggling to not forget. *Phukut, was it?*

Joseph shook his head at Priscilla. Defeated, and dry as a scab, he said, "You don't know me."

Priscilla's eyes lit up, and she hugged the book tight to her chest, smiling a wide and goofy smile at him. She was practically squirming with excitement. How could Joseph have possibly said no to something so insanely adorable and sweet as Priscilla was just then? He couldn't have. There was simply no way, scientifically speaking. Nothing with a heart and two eyes could have denied that girl in her current state, and it was at that very moment that Joseph realized why Maw Scill had let her skip school. It was the exuberant and sparkling look on Priscilla's otherwise battered face. Her eyes glittered behind the blood, and she couldn't seem to quit smiling, even when she was attempting to be serious. Joseph had never, ever seen her like this before. She was glowing.

"I don't gotta let you draw that shit all over my face, do I?" asked Joseph.

"Nope!"

Joseph shook his head at her, then he took a big deep breath and let it out. "Alright, well…let's get to witchin'. What do we gotta do?"

"Oh, no. Slow down, cowboy," said Priscilla. "I wanna know how bad yer momma whipped yer ass last night."

Joseph looked down through the hatch, past his dangling legs, at the ground below. This was always an issue between them, Priscilla's freedom. She had it made. Sort of. She could basically come and go as she pleased, she never had a bedtime, and she could even spend the night at Joseph's house without first asking her mother anytime she wanted. She could miss school without a phone call, she could miss church without being threatened with Hell, and she could mostly come and go as she pleased. Day or night. She had it made.

Joseph on the other hand was not granted permission to do any of those things under any circumstances for fear of immediate physical harm to his backside. The amount of times he'd felt the sting of the belt was uncountable. His innate longing for liberty saw to that personally. Fortunately, last night's events witnessed his mother take on an inexplicable change of heart. He had missed school, and his mother hadn't struck him, even once.

"You know, it's the darndest thing, Scilly," said Joseph. "When I came in, she was ragin'. She pinned me in the corner with her dough roller, I mean she was M.A.D mad. Then she asked me where I'd been all night and day and I couldn't think of nothin' else, so I just told her like Mathias said. I said me and you got lost lookin' for Lucky and Mathias Elder took us in for the night. And Scilly, I swear to you she went soft as a cloud, soon as I said his name. She asked me all kinda questions, how he looked, was he well, all about his kids and his wife. It was wild. Never seen my momma all dreamy like that. She said they was the best of friends when they was young."

"She tell ya about pissin' on hers—"

"No, she did not mention that, and I didn't neither. I was tryin' to steer clear of a beatin', remember?"

Priscilla laughed. Then Joseph laughed too.

Then he said, "Yeah, we laugh now. I ain't gonna be laughin' later when she finds out I left early today."

"From school? Why'd you leave early today?"

Joseph hesitated to tell her the real reason he left early, but then he did anyway. She was his friend, she could know that he cared about her, right? "Cause of you, dickhead," said Joseph.

"Me?"

"Yeah, you. I was worried when you didn't show up at school. That ain't like you, and what with Everett's hand gettin' bit off, well, I dunno. I figured he mighta been mad, and I wasn't sure if you stayed at home or up yer Maw Maw's or what and, and… Hell, I don't know, I was just worried is all."

Priscilla smiled at him genuinely. Then she said, "D' awwwwwe, Joseph, you was worried 'bout little old me?"

Joseph's cheeks went flush. "I wasn't worried about shit, forget it. Just forget it. Now, you wanna do some witchin' or not? Get yer damn book out." Joseph continued muttering under his breath as he stood up. "Man comes into his own hideout, and 'ere's damn stars and circles all over the damn walls…"

Priscilla let out a quick, sharp giggle, and it didn't not sound, altogether, like a pigeon. She was really on one. He couldn't even pretend to be mad at her. He liked this side of her. *She was all wild and frisky, and and and. . . spunky?* As was often a problem, Joseph couldn't find the right words to define the way he felt, or maybe he had, he couldn't be sure, but he was going with spunky, either way. *Fuck it.* Her damn bloody eyes made her look scary as shit, he knew that for sure. There was no denying that.

Still grinning up at Joseph, Priscilla said, "For the life of me, I just can't picture yer momma and Mathias Elder bein' friendly, can you?"

"Not in a million fuckin' years," said Joseph. He reached out and touched one of the symbols on the wall. Then he looked up at several symbols drawn above his head and studied them. "Green smoke, huh?"

Priscilla nodded repeatedly. "Yep."

"What about Lucky?"

"The book's gonna help me find him."

"The book…"

Priscilla nodded, practically geeking out.

"Well," said Joseph, "lay it on me. But if yer skin turns green, or you fall off the back of a broom stick, and break yer neck, I don't wanna hear shit about it."

Priscilla squeaked. Then she said, "First things first."

On a small table that Joseph had made out of stolen wood, she sat the book down and consulted its pages. "Okay," she said, "says here, 'If you are to be a witch's assistant, you must be sworn into the coven. To do that you must give an oath of blood, you must renounce faith in all but yerself, and you must dig yer own grave.'"

Joseph looked at her, slightly stunned. "Now, Scilly, you know more about it than I do, but ain't you worried about goin' to Hell for this? This sounds like some devil shit if I ever heard it."

Again, Joseph didn't know what he expected her to say, what with her face all scrawled on like it was, but he damn sure did not expect Priscilla Louise Carpenter, the girl who never missed church, who never took the Lord's name in vain, who never did anything fun without first questioning if it was a sin, to, without flinching or hesitation, look him square in the eyes and flat-out say, "No." But that's what she did. She flat-out said no. Joseph couldn't believe it, and Priscilla must have recognized the look on his face because she elaborated, but what she added only served to astonish her friend all the more.

She said, "I thought about it, and well, God ain't never worried about me, Joseph, and I ain't gonna worry 'bout God no more. It's just me and you, pal."

"Well… I can't really argue with that, can I?"

Priscilla picked up a knife, and said, "Nope, ya sure fuckin' can't. Now give me yer hand."

◆

COLLECTION

Collection was the first main chapter in the book, Priscilla explained as they climbed down out of the hideout. After Joseph completed his initiation, the first thing they would have to do is find and collect a long list of things, all of which would be used to not only prepare the witch's sanctuary, but also to prepare the witch. As well as ingredients for the creation of potions, and performance of spells and sacrifices, and the like. She assured Joseph this would be fun. He was skeptical.

She told him that she had already begun preparing the hideout by drawing protection symbols on the walls, but that the symbols on her face were part of her own initiation and that Joseph would have to remind her to wash them off before they went home.

"I promise," said Priscilla as she hopped from the ladder to the ground. "Yer gonna love it. Most of the stuff we need is dead animal stuff. And you love dead animals! We need eyeballs, and skulls, and worms, and Joseph, we even gotta build me a flyin' broom!" That last statement burst out of her like she'd been waiting to tell him for a year.

Joseph looked at her. He wasn't altogether unamused, but this whole ordeal was simply too much for him to wrap his head around, let alone get excited about. On top of that, he was positive that Priscilla had cut him too deep. His hand, despite being wrapped, still dripped blood, and he was trying not to complain. Up in the hideout, after she spit his blood into a bird's nest, Priscilla told him not to be such a pussy about it, and he kept quiet after that, but not because she called him a pussy. The word pussy had reminded him of Mathias Elder's daughters, and that occupied his mind all the way down the ladder.

"Yeah, yeah, yeah, brooms and eyeballs, let's just get this over with. I wanna get my hand fixed up better 'fore I bleed out. Then I'll get excited."

Priscilla consulted the book, then she closed it and flipped it over so that the back cover was facing up. Then she said, "Open yer eyes wide and don't blink. When you speak, make sure yer lookin' at the book. You can't look away from the book or blink as yer speakin'. It says this is real, real important. No matter what, you cannot—"

"I get it, I get it, don't look away or blink. Why'd we have to come outside for this?"

"Because the book says so, Joseph. It says you must be outside among the world, so that all in existence can hear yer words. Will you just trust me a little bit? I mean, fuck."

Joseph sighed. "Alright then, shit. What's next?"

Priscilla gave him a loving smile, then lifted the book up in front of his face, and she said, "Look at it."

Joseph obliged her, and in that moment, staring, wide-eyed and unblinking, at the abysmally black book, he realized what Priscilla already knew. This was not a game. The book was real, and this was not a game. The instant Priscilla sucked the blood from his hand up in the hideout, he should have known. The writing was on the wall, figuratively and literally, and yet somehow the gravity of their undertaking had escaped him. But not now. Now, eyes fixed on the unholy black book, there was no denying it. It was real.

"Repeat after me," said Priscilla.

Joseph pushed the book out from in front of his face so that he could see her. "Yer positive you wanna do this?"

Bordering on chipper, Priscilla said, "Course I am, why?"

"Well… I kinda got a funny feelin'."

"Funny how?"

"Funny like...like, I think you might be right. I think this might be real?"

Priscilla looked at him incredulously. "Yeah, dickhead, that's the point. I been tellin' you. You think I stayed up all night long readin' fairytales? Huh? Look at all the shit on my face. You think I'd slice yer damn hand open if I thought it wasn't real? Well, maybe that ain't the best example, but do you think I'd be drinkin' yer blood if it weren't? Of course it's real. I told you, I ain't crazy, and I ain't five years old. I know the difference 'tween reality and make-believe."

She had a point. Several in fact. Joseph couldn't argue with any of them. So, he said, "Okay, fuck it. Here we go. Eyes wide, let's do this."

"Alright," said Priscilla. "Repeat after me."

———◆———

A word from Joseph

You ever hear of Blackdamp? Most folks ain't never heard of it. But it's some wild shit, I promise ye that. It's a type of atmosphere. One where flames won't burn. Back in the day, coal miners used to carry domesticated canaries to detect the presence of Blackdamp in the mines. It was real simple, if the canary dies, get the fuck outta there. Now days they have electronic monitors, but back in the day, they used canaries. Pretty damn smart, if ya ask me.

The way Blackdamp works is carbon dioxide replaces oxygen to the extent that if you was to happen into one of these areas of Blackdamp, you'd just flat-out fuckin' die. Keel over. The thing is, it's not like goin' pearl divin' on a pool pump, where if you take a deep breath, you can just stay under water and ya know…hang out. If you take a deep breath and go into an area of Blackdamp, that shit will suck the oxygen right out of yer pores. Even if you pack yer lungs like a fuckin' free diver, Blackdamp'll suck the air right out of ya. Asphyxiate ya. Kill ya.

Well, that's what that book was like. Blackgoddamndamp. Except it didn't suck way our oxygen, it sucked away our boredom to the point it almost got us killed. I reckon what I'm tryin' to say is…it was pretty well on after that. Pedal to the metal. No turnin' back. She read aloud and I transcribed, and I'll tell ya right now, when that list was done, there was some sick fuckin' shit on it. Eyeballs, and intestines, and skulls, I can't even begin to tell you how many animals we killed that first month. Christ. Hundreds. That part of the collection process, as it were, I came to find, never stops. That and herbs. A witch always needs more herbs and more dead animals. Always. Damn near every spell she ever cast required some combination of the two.

It might sound funny, considering all the dead animals and what not, but those early days, when we was just tryin' to gather all the tools she was gonna need, they were the happiest of my youth. Priscilla's too, I would wager. You gotta understand, we grew up in *Clockmaker*. Not Los Angeles. Not Miami. Hell, not even Dayton. Clockmaker. We skipped rocks and shattered bottles against abandoned cars for fun prior to the whole witchcraft business. We had nothin', and the least of what we had was direction, but witchcraft, or, I reckon, the pursuit thereof, changed all that.

I mean, you just can't imagine the sense of purpose that kids like us felt, tryin' to hunt down the right wood to make a flyin' broom-stick. For the first time, our lives carried some sense of adventure. Some sense of significance. We had direction, and it was beautiful. Things went to shit pretty fast, don't get me wrong, but at first we may as well have been ridin' rafts with old Huck Finn.

Now, if memory serves me, it took us a little under a month to collect everything. We spent every day at it. Well, I spent almost every day at it, but Priscilla, she spent every single day. Ya see, I still had to go to school and church, and do chores and shit, but Priscilla, she just said, "Fuck it all." After Everett lost the better part of his hand, he never went back to work at the mine, and Priscilla, I don't believe, ever stayed another night in his house.

Not with him alive, anyway. She lived up at Maw Scill's or in the cave from there on out. And Maw Scill was an old woman, so she couldn't keep up with Priscilla, let alone control her, though she tried at first. So Priscilla just ran wild. Witchin' became her life.

And it's not that her momma didn't care about her. I don't think that's the case at all. Lookin' back on it now, I think Lavinia had it in her head that Priscilla would just be better off without her, away from Everett, and away from the fuckin'…nightmare that her life turned out to be. Lavinia had dug herself a hole two hundred feet deep, and I reckon she wanted to get Priscilla out before the walls came down. Then again, I'm just guessin'. But I never once got the feelin' that Lavinia didn't care about her daughter deeply. Never once. You could tell by the way she looked at her. She had nothin' but love for Priscilla.

Honest though…Lavinia had nothin' but love for everybody. She did. She was a good woman. She ain't care if ya had a hair lip, or dirty clothes, or if ya cursed a lot, or nothin'. She was a damn good woman. She just had a rough go at it, is all…

Anyway, enough with the mushy stuff. Like I was sayin', it took us about a month to find everything. Mind you, we needed plenty more than eyeballs. We had to find three different size mortar and pestles, crucibles, jars, and bowls, and bells, and all kinds of shit. We scavenged most of it. Stole some of it. Between my house and Maw Scill's house, and the church, which we cleaned completely out of candles, we made off with quite a bit actually. But I'll tell ya this. Under no circumstances did we steal from Everett. That was a line we did not dare cross.

Yes sir, no doubt about it. We pilfered, foraged, rummaged, and flat out shoplifted. Of course, we bought a few things when we could, but we didn't have much money. So we did what we had to. I trapped, shot, and killed squirrels, coons, frogs, opossums, deer, beavers, doves, pheasants, quail, grouse, turkey, rats, mice, fish, you fuckin' name it, and I killed it. I ran my traps day in and day out for the first four weeks straight.

Priscilla started helpin' me though. She even learned to use the rifle, and started guttin' 'em herself. Learned to skin 'em too, dead animals that is. You never seen a young girl so determined to do anything as Priscilla was to be a witch. I watched a piss sack burst in her face one time when she was cleanin' out her first deer, and she puked like the fuckin' Exorcist. Now, I laughed my ass off at her, but she retched for a few minutes, then she wiped off her chin and finished the job without sayin' a single goddamn word. You have any idea what the fuck I'm tryin' to say? You ever had a piss sack burst in yer face? It ain't easy to move forward after that.

Lookin' back on it, I don't think I have ever been as proud of a person as I was, that day, of Priscilla Carpenter. Hell, I can see her now. Clear as day. Covered in piss and puke and blood. She gagged the whole time, but she opened that son of a bitch up, and she got its guts out. Sure enough. And I was already proud of her for doin' just that. I was. But when she finished, she plucked the heart up out of the pile of entrails and held it up like an icon. Blood just drippin' from it. And before I could get the words *you ain't got the balls* out of my mouth, she bit into it like a peach. I couldn't fuckin' believe it. I mean, could not fuckin' believe it. She puked again, of course, and dry heaved for a few minutes. But the point had been made. Respect had been earned. She knew it too. She knew she was blowin' my fuckin' mind, and she loved it. That was Priscilla for ya, I reckon.

All and all, most of the things we needed were relatively easy to acquire. The only real issues we had were with the broom, the cauldron, and I guess some of the herbs and mushrooms. Well, the broom wasn't really an issue, but it took us a week to find the right wood to make it. Only the wood from one particular kind of tree would do. It had to be taken from a healthy, virgin hemlock grown from gypsum. It was real goddamn important. The book was very specific about that. Not that I ever read it, but that's what Priscilla told me. And I ain't ashamed to admit, I questioned her quite a bit in the beginnin' about what was in 'at book. It weren't easy for me to just take her word for it, but she was my friend, and even if I ain't trust her fully, I was goin' along with her anyway.

Yeah, I reckon the cauldron and the herbs were the only things we couldn't find without help. Now, between what me and Priscilla knew, and our mommas and grandmommas, we tracked down quite a few herbs and mushrooms, but Priscilla didn't want to tell anybody what we were up to, so we were kinda limited on the questions we could ask without too many questions in return. I couldn't just walk up and ask my momma where to find a cauldron, ya understand. That would have led to way too many questions, and I was a shit liar back then. Still am.

So what did we do? Well, we did the only thing we could think to do. We went to see my Uncle Bob, that's what. He was the only person we could think of at the time who would help us without givin' us any shit about it, or without askin' too many questions. Till the day he died, he was that way. I could ask that man for an unregistered pistol and a pair of handcuffs and he wouldn't flinch. He'd just hand me what I needed. He was as fine a man as there ever was.

I mean that with all my heart. My Uncle Bob, like my daddy, was a damn fine man, but even though he was surely my father's brother, them two could not have been more different. When they was growin' up, one of 'em left out the front door and the other out the back. That's what my granddaddy told me one time, anyway. I never knew if that was a figure of speech or if he was bein' literal, but, even as a kid, I knew what he was gettin' at. It was obvious, even back then.

For instance, my daddy was a family man. He hardly ever drank, didn't curse, and I can't remember him ever missin' a day of work. I'm sure he did, over the years, but it was rare enough that I can't remember the day. If you asked around Clockmaker back then, I reckon most folks would have said my daddy, old Jimmy Smith, was an honest man, maybe even a right nice feller. I figure you woulda been hard pressed to find someone to say otherwise.

This was not the case for my uncle, however. Not in the slightest. Uncle fuckin' Bob was a beer-gut havin', belly-shirt wearin', booze guzzlin', women chasin', smokin', cursin', fuckin', fightin', perpetually unemployed son of a bitch. He didn't go to church. He didn't vote. He didn't give a damn. He liked to drink and fish and fuck, and fuck and fish and drink, and he didn't care in which order, as long as at the end of the night, his belly was full of one or the other. He told me one time that a man can live off of pussy and liquor for eight days before he dies. He said, *Trust me, boy, I know from experience.* And I believed him. Still do.

Uncle Bob's Top Ten Words of Wisdom

1. **It's better to sleep alone than with an ugly woman.**
2. **Sobriety is a fuckin' bore.**
3. **Don't never let no bitch tell you what to do.**
4. **If she can't cook, she ain't worth a fuck.**
5. **Fishin' is better than religion on Sunday.**
6. **Never take no shit for growin' up poor.**
7. **Never hit a woman. Unless she's really askin' for it.**
8. **If you jerk off enough in the shower, you'll get a hard-on every time it rains.**

9. **It ain't litterin' if it's evidence.**
10. **Friends before money, and money before women.**

Yea, Uncle Bob was sure enough rough around the edges, but that ain't to say that he was lackin' in good nature. He was friendly, real friendly, overly at times, but he was ill-mannered and coarse to the extent that most folks thought him savage. My mother, in particular, never once conversed with her brother-in-law without the tip of her nose obstructin' her view. Not never. Lookin' back, I reckon she envied his freedom. She was like that, my momma.

None of that shit mattered to me, though. I couldn't have thought that crazy fucker was any cooler if he'd owned two tigers and a helicopter. I mean, I loved my daddy dearly, but when I was a teenager, Uncle Bob was my hero. Priscilla, on the other hand, liked Uncle Bob well enough, I reckon, but she was also, admittedly, a little scared of him. Couldn't blame her. He did almost kill her, once upon a time. 'Bout shot her.

Well, he shot at both Priscilla and me, and he didn't actually know it was us, but he still shot at us. Right through his fuckin' front door. Wacked out on speed or somethin', he was. The blast left a hole the size of a watermelon. If I hadn't heard the shotgun rack inside the house, we would have both been dead and likely headless. Good Lord, you know he didn't even apologize to us neither. Only thing he said was, *You'll holler out 'fore you step on this property next time, won't ya.* And he laughed. I was honestly surprised that Priscilla was so eager to go and see him. But that's what we did. Sure enough.

Anyhow, Uncle Bob's house weren't far, but it took about half an hour to walk there. I remember we was worried he'd be too drunk to help us. You had to catch him before five o'clock on most days or he was next to useless. So we were walkin' fast.

Luckily, when we got there he was sober, because he knew exactly how to help. We told him what we needed and I remember his response to this day. I says, We need a cauldron and a bunch of different herbs and mushrooms, and he says, *A cauldron, what the hell you wanna do, be a witch?* I told him, No. Priscilla wants to be a witch, I'm just helpin'. Then just like that, Unc says, *Well, there's an old claw foot tub out back. It's cast iron. Should do. It's heavier than the weight of regret, but if you can move it, you can have it. Then he says, Far as yer herbs go, I can't help ya with them, but I know just where to send ya.*

Now I always thought it was kinda funny, even as a kid, but Uncle Bob, uncivilized as everyone made him out to be, was the only person I knew back then who was friends with black folks. Everybody else stayed to their own, but Unc didn't have a care one about skin color. He even had a few black lady-friends over the years. Quite a few, actually. And wouldn't ya know, that is right where he sent us. He says, *You remember Sheree? That fine-lookin' thing with the big scar on her cheek?* And I says, Yes, and he says, *Welp, her momma's the one you wanna see. She got all the herbs and shit you could ever want.*

So the first thing we did was abandon The Hideout. A witch simply cannot be without a cauldron. They go hand-in-hand. And we found out pretty fuckin' quick, we weren't gonna be able to get that bathtub up in the trees, and even if we did, the floorboards would have never supported it. So we decided to move our operation. We needed some place easy enough to access but also hidden, but also kinda close to my uncle's too, 'cause we had to drag that heavy son of a bitch 'n' bathtub. So we did some thinkin' on the matter, and we decided Dead Kid Cave would be perfect.

I know what you're thinkin', so allow me to elaborate. Dead Kid Cave was this old limestone cave that Priscilla and me discovered a couple years before. Ya see, behind Uncle Bob's house was what my mother always called an ode to white trash. It was in fact a solid fuckin' acre of knee high weeds littered with everything from rusted out cars and stacks of tires to bathtubs, bed frames, motorcycle parts, cans, bottles, sinks, rakes, swing sets, and you name it. If you saw it and called it a junkyard, wouldn't nobody bat an eye. Anyhow, beyond the junkyard was some of the densest forest I ever seen, and about three quarters of a mile into that forest was Dead Kid Cave. We called it that because the first time me and Priscilla went inside it, we found the remains of a dead kid. Not a corpse, just the bones. They was still there when we come back draggin' that tub too. Priscilla eventually made him the centerpiece of her altar, the dead kid. Gave me the fuckin' willies at the time, but that's what she did.

To be or not to be? That was old Bill Shakespeare's question, or Hamlet's, I reckon. My question to you is this. How did two kids, by themselves, and one of 'em a frail little girl, mind you, manage to drag a four hundred pound bathtub three quarters of a fuckin' mile through the woods and into a cave? I'll tell ya how. It took ten hours with a rusty ass chain and come-along winch, and still, both of us had to pull back on the lever at the same time to budge it. We'd hook to a rock or a tree, then drag it ten yards. Hook to another tree, drag it ten yards. Hook to another tree, drag it ten yards. Finally, we hooked to stalagmites to get it into the cave. Damn near all day it took us. Haulin' and draggin'. We both liked to have died, we was so exhausted. And I bitched and cursed the whole time, but we got that bastard in there.

I'll tell ya this. Hard as it was draggin' that heavy fucker, I woulda dragged that tub ten more miles just to bide my time, if I woulda known what gettin' them herbs was gonna involve. The bathtub was easy. The herbs…they was some whole other shit.

Now, back in those days, black folks stayed in their own part of town when they wasn't workin'. To say the least, there weren't too much minglin' between the races. Where black folks lived, people called it, *The Knob. Nigger Knob*, actually. I think most folks called it that. I know I did. I don't call it that no more, mind you, and I ain't proud I ever did. But hell, back then even Uncle Bob called it that, and they was his friends. It was different times, for sure. And that ain't no excuse, but it is the truth. Folks just ain't know no better. They was ignorant. Simple as that. But anyway, that's where my Uncle Bob sent us. The Knob.

Now, The Knob was on the outskirts of town, and the house we were looking for, accordin' to my uncle, was the oldest, shittiest house on The Knob. So after we got the bathtub moved, we got us a list of herbs together, and a few days later, we went to find Sheree's momma, Gertrude.

But before I go into it, understand, segregation between races in America done come a long way by seventy-one, that's for damn sure. Rosa Parks was arrested in fifty-five. The Civil Rights Act, I believe, was in sixty four. And fair housin' was in sixty-eight, right after King was killed. So things had changed quite a bit across the country, but not so much in Clockmaker. Takes a little longer for legislation to make its way up the holler, so even though some laws changed, we was still operatin' on a simple understandin'. And the understandin' was this: Stick to yer own.

So, us goin' up there was kind of a big deal is what I'm gettin' at Anyhow, Uncle Bob warned us folks might look at us funny up on The Knob, but not to worry. *They's all good people*, he says. *Suspicious is all.* So we expected a few sideways glances, but we surely did not expect every single goddamn person we came across to stop what they was doin' and eye us like a passin' fuckin' plague. But that's just what happened. Sure as shit. Soon as we came up over the hill or the Knob rather, people just stopped and stared. Out windows, over coffee cups, under cows, there was eyes on us every step of the fuckin' way. I was shittin' in my damn pants. I remember askin' Priscilla, How bad you want these herbs? And you know, she ain't even look at me, all she said was, Bad, and kept on walkin'. Weren't an ounce of fear in her. That girl was determined to be a witch, come Hell or high water. Or both.

We found the house pretty easy, though. It was sure enough old and shitty. Hell, we stood in the road starin' up at it for damn near five minutes tryin' to figure out if it was abandoned or not. All the windows was boarded up. Roof was saggin'. Ivy'd done overtaken it. Nails stickin' out here and there. I will say, most of the houses up 'ere was pretty well kept though, all but that one. I remember bein' surprised by that. Growin' up, I'd always heard black folks lived dirty, and their houses weren't nice. Now, mind you, they were mostly tar paper shacks on the Knob, but they was looked after, cared for, and that was more than I could say for a lot of the white folk's houses I'd been to. I remember thinkin', I don't reckon most white folks know a goddamn thing about black folks. And I pretty well decided then and there to stop listenin' to any more racist bullshit from anybody.

But, I digress.

We was standin' there starin' up at this old rickety house when I felt somethin' on my shoulder, and when I looked, I saw a hand. Not just any hand neither. This hand was the biggest blackest hand I ever seen, and it was attached to the biggest blackest man I ever seen. And for a split second, I was sure I was gonna be eaten. Fee fi fo fum, I smell the blood of an Englishman. Ya understand me?

This big old boy looks right at me and says, real dry like, *Y'all lost?*

I thought, Fuck we're done for. The jig is up. Our bones are bread.

So I says, Uh uh um well uh see uh well, and Priscilla she just jumps right in and says, *We's here to see Gertrude Green. Bob Smith done sent us up here. Is this her place?*

And just like that, the mighty bastard turns soft and says, *Well why ain't ya say so, come on in.* Just like that, *Come on in.*

Next thing I know, we're standin' in this dusty old kitchen, surrounded by hundreds upon fuckin' hundreds of labeled jars and bags and baskets, starin' at thee one and only Gertrude Green. And let me tell ya, that bitch scared the daylights out of me. Just the sight of her. I hate to speak ill of the dead, bein' Tommy's mother and all, but good God, she was hard to look at. I bet the damn ugly stick was whittled down to a toothpick by the time it was done with her. God of fuck, I mean she had warts all over her damn face and hands. Moles, and hair, and I mean in all the wrong places. None of it on her head. And Christ, don't even get me started on that bitch's teeth, I'll fuckin' puke. They looked like she chewed on bricks. All the exposed nerves, and what not. Five hundred fuckin' pounds too, and stinkin'. She was misery to witness. True fuckin' misery.

Afterward, Uncle Bob thought that was funny as hell, sendin' us up there without warnin'. *I figured I'd let that old swamp donkey be a surprise*, he told us. God love him, he was a funny fucker like that.

Carryin' on. Gertrude didn't say a word when we walked in the house. She just sat there breathin' heavy, eyeballin' us, her one big old eye wanderin' around like it lost somethin'. Then to Big Tommy, that was the big fucker who walked us in, her son, she says, and I'll never forget it, she says, *Nigga, if theses little white devils ain't here to spend money, it's gonna be yo ass.*

Fuckin' Gertrude, she was mean as she was ugly.

So Big Tommy, he tells her, *I think they got money, Mommy, they says they here for herbs. They friends of Bobby Smith.*

And in response, do you know what that old bitch did? She just spit on the ground at me and Priscilla's feet, on the floor of her own damn house. Then she says, *Some nerve, droppin' that name 'round here.*

The whole time she's just lookin' us up and down. Up and down. Then she says, *Boy, go on outside and finish yo chores. I want that coal bin full by dark.* And soon as Big Tommy pulled that door shut behind him, she lit into us. *Looky, looky, looky, what do we have here,* she says. *Must be a cold day in Hell. Bobby Smith can send you two shits up here to Miss Gertrude, after my wears, but he can't send not one single word to my baby girl. That sounds 'bout right. Goddamn devils. Get what ya can, take what ya want, if I seen it one time, I seen it a thousand times. Take, take, take.*

It was somewhere right about there that Priscilla cut her off. Real calm, and real even like, Priscilla says, *Miss Green, Bobby Smith ain't send us up here. He only told us you'd have what we need and where to find you. Now we got fourteen dollars and eleven cents, and we aim to spend it all here, but if you wanna keep on about Bob Smith that way, we can take our money elsewhere, because I don't care to hear it.*

Whoo, that fat bitch didn't know what to say. You could see her gears turnin', tryin' and failin' to come up with somethin' smart. It was clear to see, she loathed bein' outdone by a little white girl with a pocket full of money, but she couldn't fight it neither. I bet she didn't make fourteen dollars in a month sellin' herbs.

So finally Gertrude, she says, *Fine, what the hell you want?*

And Priscilla, she just hands her the list, and Gertrude starts readin' it. And that's when shit changed. All of a sudden, Gertrude looks up at us real serious like and she just stares at us. With one eye, anyway. The other'n was all over the damn place. But she's just starin' at us real intense with the one eye, and she says, *Little girl, are you sure you want what's on this here list? I mean, real sure?*

I remember thinkin', Fuck she knows. She knows what we're up to. It was the way she asked the questions. How serious she was. How calm. She fuckin' knew.

But Priscilla ain't react. She thought for a moment, but she ain't react. She just looked at Gertrude, and says, *I'm sure I don't know why the hell it would matter to someone like you, but yes, I am sure. Real sure. Now, again, mam, if we could get on with this.*

I'm tellin' ya right now, that book made Priscilla damn near fearless. I mean she ran her mouth around other kids before then, but her talkin' like that to an adult was unheard of. Un-fuckin'-precedented. Most times she could hardly get her name out.

So at this point, Jabba the Hutt kinda smirks and starts noddin' her head, kinda like she knew Priscilla was goin' to say what she said. She looks at the list again, then back at Priscilla. Then at me. Then down at the list again. You could tell she was thinkin' cause her wonky eye was goin' squirrely. Then she asked Priscilla what her name was, and Priscilla tells her. Then the old blob says, *Alright then, Priscilla, bring me Solo and the wookie. They will all suffer for this outrage!*

Naw, I'm just messin', she ain't say that, she says, *Alright then Priscilla, I'll make you a deal. Miss Gertrude'll give you all the things you got on yer list here, but I don't want no money. I want you to make an old black woman a promise. A real promise. Can you do that?*

I almost spoke up and told her to shove her deals and promises up her smelly old ass, but Priscilla just gave her a little nod, and she kept on. Gertrude says, *Good, now I know what y'all is doin'. This ain't the first time I done seen a list like this. Same one came knockin' on my door 'bout twenty-five years ago… First white woman to ever set foot in this place. And you the second.*

Then she says, *So I'll get ya all that's on yo list, most of it anyhow, some of it gon' have to wait till spring, and I won't charge ya no money, but in return, I want you to make me a love potion. So whatever man's I gives it to gone fall deep, deep in love with Miss Gertrude.* Then she says, *Sound like a deal to you, white girl?*

And that was that. Priscilla agreed. She says, *Fine, I'm already makin' one for Don Juan here. I reckon I'll make one for you too.*

I remember thinkin', Holy shit, that is gonna have to be one king-hell powerful potion to make a man fall for this rancid old beast. But alas, that was the deal.

Then some crazy shit happened.

I must have been scratchin' at my arm, cause all of a sudden that fat fuckin' bitch lunged forward in her chair, snatched a hold of my wrist, and yanked me right up close to her. I damn near pulled out my buck knife and stuck her, she had me so scared, but as soon as I reached for it with my free hand, she bent my captured wrist up toward her good eye and says, *It's a worm.*

I says, *What the—? Fuck you!* It was just a fear response. The words just shot out. Like I said, she scared the ever-lovin' shit out of me. I thought she was gonna take a bite of me, I really did. It took me a second or two to figure out she was only inspectin' my arm, not tryin' to eat it. And her damn grip was strong too. Felt like she had me in a mechanical vice. It sure did, but I'll tell ya right now, it did not look that way. Her goddamn swollen, lumpy, fuckin' grimy, circus freak hands were made of flesh ungodly, and Christ, I think she only had four fingers on that hand. I couldn't be sure, they were so twisted up and fat.

So, anyhow, in response to me tellin' her fuck you, still latched on to my wrist, she says, *Ha, you couldn't handle this ass, little boy, now stay still.* Oh good lord, I couldn't imagine, the thought of that woman's nether regions, her wretched old hairy snatch, I bet the smell of it coulda knocked a buzzard off a shit wagon.

Then she says, *How long you been itchin',* and I told her a couple weeks, and she says, *You like playin' in cricks, don't ya,*

*boy? Yeah you do. Well, you got two options, wait six more weeks
and the worm will die on its own, yer body'll eat up the decay, or…
Miss Gertrude will snatch it out for you right now.*

I instantly tried to pull free of her grip. Weren't no way I
wanted that old fat hag workin' on me, but like I said, her grip
was strong, and she held tight, and she says, *No, I reckon you
don't have an option. That's okay, I've been there. You just go on
and close yer eyes. Miss Gertrude'll make it quick,* she says, and
she reaches down with her free hand and the bitch come up with
a big ol' fuckin' knife, 'bout twice the size of my own.

Priscilla moved to help me, but Gertrude, she points the knife
right at her, and if Priscilla wouldn't have stopped, she woulda
impaled herself. Gertrude says, *Easy, little witch, if I aimed to kill
yer boyfriend, he'd be dead. And you,* she says to me, she says, *you
quit bein' such a little wee-wee. Close yer eyes, I'll have it out in
two shakes of a lamb's tail. Besides, if'n I kill you, every pig with
a badge from here to Morgantown would be huntin' my black ass.*

Then real quick like, right over top of the little itchy spot, she
takes that knife and slices a shallow X in my arm. Quick, like fuckin'
Zorro, that woman was. *You greasy goddamn troll,* I screamed, or
somethin' to that affect, and that old bitch just snickered, and says,
Hard part's over, ya big chicken, now close yer beady fuckin' eyes.

And I told her no at first, but she insisted, and she had that
knife, so that's what I did. I closed my eyes. At knife point. With
Gertrude Green latched on to me, I surrendered out of pure fear.
I admit it. But by the power of her grip, it ain't seem like I had
a whole lot of choice in the matter either way. So like I said, I
closed my eyes.

Next fuckin' thing I know, I feel this circular pressure on my
arm. Then all these little prickles and somethin' warm and wet on
the inside of my wrist where the itchy bump was. Then I feel the
prickles kinda squeeze together, so I just had to open my eyes to

see what the hell was happenin' to me. And what did I see? I see the biggest scariest fuckin' leech you ever seen in yer goddamn motherfuckin' life rear back like a fuckin' Arrakian sandworm, and come mouth first down on my arm! It fuckin' screeched when it did, too! Or squealed! Fuck! Felt like a thousand fuckin' tiny teeth diggin' into me all at once, and suckin'! Goddamn, I could feel it suckin'. Fuck, I say!

I look over at Priscilla, she's frozen, fuckin' deer in the headlights, and Gertrude has firm hold on my wrist and she's got this quart jar upside down on my arm, and that fuckin' leech is just goin' to fuckin' town on me. I screamed. I admit it. Like a little bitch. I tried to pull free too, but old Jabba, she had me. Between that fat bitch and the leech, it was a near perfect portrait of Hell, from what I can remember.

I don't know how long it took. I fuckin' fainted. I was told it only took a couple minutes though. When I came to, she still had me by the arm, and she was screwin' the lid back on her leech jar, her crazy eye bouncin' all over the damn place. Then she reached down beside her chair, and come up with a bottle of iodine. She applied it, then she finally let go of my wrist.

I sat there on the floor a minute, inspectin' my arm, tryin' to get my wits about me. I remember her sayin' to Priscilla, *A worm for a worm, little witch, you remember that. A worm for a worm.*

Eventually I stood up and dusted myself off, and that swollen eyesore, she gives me this sly old lecherous wink, and when I turned to move away from her, she fuckin' smacked me firm on my ass and laughed about it. Fuckin' perverted old skank.

Lord, how I scrubbed and washed that night. I was sure I'd never get the smell of her and that leech off me, and honestly, I'm not sure I ever did. To say I felt violated by that whole situation would be an understatement, but I must admit, that goddamn spot on my arm never itched again after that. I never looked at worms the same again neither, but I suspect that's reasonable.

Post-surgery, she made me and Priscilla wait outside while she put together our order. You could hear her big old ass movin' around in there. The house yawnin' and tremblin'. Floor boards creakin', jars rattlin'. I was honestly surprised that rickety old shack could hold her. Hell, I was surprised her own two legs could hold her.

We sat outside there, oh, a couple hours anyways. Kickin' rocks and shit. Talkin' bout Gertrude. Bout witchin' and what not. Watchin' Gertrude's boy, Big Tommy, drag buckets of coal up from the riverbank to the house. Back then, a lot of folks still burned coal in their houses, 'fore gas and electric moved in. Dirty as it is, it weren't hard to replace. Hell, it blackens everything it touches.

Eventually though, Tommy come up the hill with his coal bucket full, and he dropped it behind the house, and when he come back, he had a big old tater sack slung over his shoulder. All the herbs and shit was inside, all labeled and taped up in newspaper.

Now, we could tell Big Tommy was a little slow. It was obvious the way he talked. But I coulda swore he was a grown man. Turned out he was seventeen. Just a kid like we was. Also, turned out Big Tommy was as fond of his momma as we were. When he handed us the sack, just as we was about to walk away, he looks at us real earnest like, and says, *Say, uh, I'm real sorry 'bout my mommy, but I was thinkin', well—y'all folks think it might be alright if I tag along with ya? I can help ya carry yo sack.*

So I says, Ain't you got no other friends? And he says, *Naw, they scared of me, 'cause of Mommy.* Then, like a sign from God, he adds, *Bein' honest, I just can't stand to look at that bitch no more today.* And just like that, we knew he was one of us.

The three of us busted our ass the next few days, collectin' all the loose odds and ends Priscilla was gonna need. She wanted to have everything collected and set up by Halloween. Accordin' to the book, Halloween was one of several nights throughout the year that were particularly ripe for witchin' purposes, and Priscilla wanted to take full advantage of it. Now, me and Tommy tried our best to convince her we had time to trick or treat, at least a few houses, but she wouldn't have it. She called it kids' stuff, and said we was too old for it. Even after we told her about our genius costume idea. I was gonna be Tom Sawyer, she was gonna be Huck Finn, and Big Tommy was gonna be, well, you know… Jim. We had a dead cat lined up for Priscilla to drag around and everything. Devil follow corpse, cat follow Devil, warts follow cat, ya feel me? And before you go gettin' all self-righteous, Big Tommy's the one who came up with the whole idea, not me. So, fuck yerselves.

Actually, Big Tommy turned out to be a right fine addition to our circle. Or our pentagram, if ya will. He helped Priscilla durin' the day, when I was at school, him not havin' to go to school neither. And slow, he mighta been, but I'll tell ya this, that boy was a whole heck of a lot smarter than most folks gave him credit for. Not only was he helpin' Priscilla with witch business, he was teachin' her all sorts of new and useful information. He knew way more than I knew, that's for sure. He knew everything about herbs, and plants, and mushrooms, especially where to find 'em, but he also knew basic economics and marketin' strategies too. It was wild the shit he knew. When it came down to it, the only slow thing about Tommy was how he talked.

We were honestly pretty surprised by how much he knew, but it made sense. There weren't no way Gertrude was walkin' her fat ass up and down mountains. She made Tommy collect, deliver, and transact everything she ever sold. So he knew a thing or two, and he was happy to teach us. But on top of all that, Tommy was just pleasant to have around. Good natured in every way. Like I said, a right fine addition to our circle. Well, anyhow, I could go on forever, but this ain't my story. Y'all likely don't give a damn what I think no ways.

But I do wanna tell ya one more thing. Since it weren't mentioned earlier. The words Priscilla had me repeat when I was sworn into her coven, my renunciation of God, you remember that? I do. I still got the scar on my hand to remind me. Now, I don't know why it was left out, God's will maybe, but I think you ought to know the words I spoke. Seems important somehow. I'm not sure exactly why. Maybe so you can learn from my mistakes, and not make the same one's yerself. Who could guess. Then again, maybe the Devil is workin' through me, and this is just another way for him to get his message out. I honestly don't know anymore. Either way, I feel compelled, so…here they are.

UPON THE SEED OF MILK AND SKY
MORNING RAIN SHALL SEE HER FLY

KNOW THE BEAST AND KNOW HIS EYE
OF KINGS GIVE BANISH TO ALL BUT I

SHED THE SKIN TO FEED THE LIE
OF GODS GIVE BANISH TO ALL BUT I

KNOW THE BEAST AND KNOW HIS LIE
OF KINGS GIVE BANISH TO ALL BUT I

MEND THE SKIN TO FEED THE EYE
OF GODS GIVE BANISH TO ALL BUT I

———— ◆ ————

CHAPTR NinE

———◆———

Man will never be free until the last king
is strangled with the entrails of the last priest.
—Denis Diderot

'Spirit' by Ghost plays

Sunday, October thirty-first, nineteen seventy-one. It is Halloween night. The moon is a waxing gibbous. Hendrix is dead. Janis is dead. The Lizard King is dead.

God is pacing. The Devil is doing what the Devil does. Richard Nixon is at his desk. His head is in his hands. It's all over. The Grateful Dead is at the Ohio Theater. Jerry is playing his blonde Stratocaster, and Keith is hiding behind his piano, smashed on acid. Charles Manson is bleeding from his forehead. He has been sentenced to death. Helter Skelter.

Jeremiah Carpenter is riding in the bed of a pickup truck. Mathias Elder is drinking and building a fire. Gertrude Green is pacing. She does not know where her son is. Maw Scill is handing out little chocolate candies to costumed trick-or-treaters. So is Uncle Bob, sort of, except he is high on mushrooms and keeps hiding when he gets a knock at the door. Joseph and Tommy are walking, and Lavinia is standing over Everett with a knife. Everett is sleeping.

Priscilla is alone in a cave. The skeleton of a dead child hangs before her. In front of her is a small wooden table. Upon the table rests skulls of varying species, two burning candles, a picture of her mother, a bundle of twigs, a mirror, some rose petals, and the book. Around the cave, protection symbols have been etched into the walls, the entrance has been sealed with raccoon blood, dozens of church candles burn, more skulls are impaled on stalagmites. In the center of the cavern is a cast iron bathtub, and underneath the bathtub is a hardwood fire. Inside the bathtub is a brew. The brew consists of Chickweed, Indian Pipe, Red Clover, honey, Sweet Everlasting, Coltsfoot, Mullein, Soap Wart, Satyr's beard, a lock of Priscilla's hair, several drops of her blood, her saliva, her urine, water, garlic, dirt, the head of a chicken, one white rabbit minus its eyes, two earthworms, a single fishbone, and four rose petals. Behind Priscilla, the brew is beginning to boil.

Priscilla stands at her altar. Her entire body is covered with protection symbols. They are drawn on with red lipstick. Her body is cloaked in dark wool cloth, fastened around the neck with a chord. She is nude underneath. Slung across her back is an old grey military pack that belonged to her grandfather. It is meant to hold the book. Her eyes are bloodshot. Her breathing is even.

Beside her altar is a cabinet with broken doors. Salvaged from Uncle Bob's backyard, it now contains dozens upon dozens of labeled jars and tins that hold the extent of Priscilla's plant, fungus, and biological collection. The cabinet, missing a leg, is now partially supported by Limestone. The cabinet does not wobble.

It was into this cabinet that Priscilla replaced the tube of lipstick. Then she quickly plucked it back out and applied a generous amount to her lips. *For good measure*, she thought.

She raised the mirror and gazed at her reflection. This was it. She was about to become a witch. A real live witch. Technically,

she was already a witch. Her blood was in the book. An oath was sworn. But to Priscilla, it didn't feel real. Until she could actually cast a spell, or fly a broom, or concoct a potion, or something of the like, logic would not allow her to believe it. Even when she was cutting the eyes from a rabbit to make the brew. Even then, she still couldn't completely accept it. She needed magic.

But tonight was the night. If all went as planned, she would soon be confronted by irrefutable proof of her witchhood. With her own two eyes, she would see, and she would know, and then there would no longer be any question. However, if all did not go as planned, if say, for instance, nothing were to happen, not even a puff of smoke, then, well, she was prepared for the worst. The worst being Joseph giving her shit about it until the day she died. It would be constant and endless, of this she was certain, but she was prepared for it.

That said, Priscilla was pretty *gosh darn* confident that this was going to work. Everything was ready. Her lair was ready, she was ready, the brew was almost ready, and the boys would be back any minute with cigarettes and booze. Tonight was just the beginning. She could feel it. And it tingled.

For Priscilla, it had been a long month, and not an easy one either. But it was an interesting month, no doubt. A lot had changed. She was now living at Maw Scill's house all the time, or at the cave. She hadn't slept at home since Lucky ran away with Everett's hand. Also, today would be the sixth Sunday that she missed church, and she had only seen her mother twice in that time. She couldn't believe it was possible, but according to her mother, Everett had gotten worse, meaner, drunker. Both times Priscilla saw her mother, she looked tired and old.

Priscilla also hadn't been going to school. Her plan was to start going back eventually, but she wanted to get a handle on the whole witchcraft situation first. When it came down to it, if she

was honest with herself, school just seemed trivial and rather…
meaningless, especially in comparison to the exemplary education
she was receiving in the woods. Between the book and Big
Tommy, she had learned more in the last few weeks in the forest
than she had in the last two years in the schoolhouse.

Speaking of big Tommy, he was another one of the changes
that had occurred recently. Priscilla loved having him around.
Joseph did too. After the day they got their herbs and Tommy
left with them, he never really went home again. Not to stay,
anyway. He would still check in on his mother, on an almost
daily basis, to bring her food and the like, and he still worked for
her, collecting and brokering her herbs, but he never slept in her
house again.

He started sleeping in the cave. With Priscilla's permission of
course. The truth was, she felt at ease around Big Tommy. She
recognized in him a type of kindred spirit, given that he was the
only kid she had ever come across who had it worse at home than
she did, and almost right away, a significant bond was formed
between them.

So after he asked to sleep in Priscilla's lair and explained why,
she felt almost obligated to take him in. Of course, Gertrude
had been nice enough when she met Priscilla, but according to
Tommy, it was all a ruse. He said that his mother only pretend-
ed to be even the slightest bit cordial in order to get what she
wanted. Which was a love potion. The only way she could ever
possibly find another man—magic. On any other day, at any other
moment, she was a bitter and abusive tyrant. The things she had
done to Tommy, beating him, locking him in closets, molesting
him, it made Priscilla sick to think about.

So on the very same day that she made his acquaintance, with
all the herbs still in the sack, Priscilla swore Big Tommy Green
into her coven. She drank his blood, and made him denounce

God and dig his own grave. And since then he had been nothing if not an absolute joy to have around. He was smart and sweet and helpful, and Priscilla could tell already that Tommy was one of them. Just this morning, for instance, he told Joseph to 'go fuck a chicken,' and if that was not a sign of compatibility then Priscilla didn't know what one was.

Then there was the book. The book was the quintessence of change, the paragon, the epitome. Not only did the book itself change, physically, but Priscilla had recently begun to notice that the book had a bit of a tendency to change the things it came in contact with as well, including people. Including herself.

First of all, the contents of the book changed. Words moved around. Pictures and diagrams appeared and disappeared. Reappeared. Bizarre things. The writing in the book seemed like it was evolving, but in no particular direction, at least not one that Priscilla could recognize. She was positive, however, that when she read the recipe for her brew, the night before, there had only been mention of a rabbit's foot, but this morning when she read it again, there it was. *One rabbit, eyeless.*

And then there were the other changes. The changes within herself. Priscilla, on one hand, felt better than ever. Just having it near her, the book instilled within her a confidence that she could have never imagined possible. A newfound sort of power seemed to surge inside her. It felt incredible. In each and every way. So far, the only negative aspect of the book was that her finger tips and palms had begun to turn black. She assumed from holding it. She tried scrubbing it off, at first, but nothing worked to remove it, not even gasoline, and since then it had only gotten worse. Darker. But that's it. No problems otherwise.

The boys, on the other hand, hadn't been so lucky with Priscilla's precious little witchin' book. That's what they had taken to calling it, the practice of witchcraft that is. 'Witchin'.'

Priscilla kind of liked it when they called it witchin'. It made it seem more fun than dark, but no matter how much light they made of the situation, neither Joseph nor Big Tommy could go within two feet of the book without complaining about a stench. Joseph compared it to the smell of a dead skunk he had once come across. Tommy compared it to his mother's feet. They were both accurate.

There was also the one time that Priscilla, without thinking, asked Joseph to hand her the book. He reached down to pick it up, and as soon as his hand touched it, he passed out cold. Limp. His lips even turned blue. Priscilla was sure he was dead, but all of a sudden, just as she was about to run for help, Joseph's back arched and he gasped. Air filled his lungs, and color bled back into his face. He was alive, thank goodness, but needless to say, Joseph hadn't gone near the book since. All he said after it was over was, "Whoa…I'm alive…the butt-sweat was an illusion."

Indeed, it had been a month of change, or evolution perhaps, depending on the lens through which it is viewed, but Priscilla was taking it in stride. Anytime things got hard, she closed her eyes and pictured herself flying. A broom beneath her, a pale yellow moon calling her, the night sky unfolding all around her. At times she could even feel the wind in her hair. It was her future, and in her darkest hours, it beckoned to her.

Just as Priscilla laid down the mirror and began adjusting the cord around her neck, Joseph and Tommy returned with the goods. Vodka and five factory rolled cigarettes.

"Perfect," said Priscilla.

Tonight was the night. She immediately sprang into action. She handed Joseph the bundle of twigs and the cigarettes, and to Tommy she handed the rose petals and vodka. Then she dunked a large cup into the brew, filling it to the top.

Joseph gagged. "Holy fuck, you ain't really gonna drink that shit, are you," he said.

"Yes…yes, I am, now shut yer face. Just stand there, and when I give you the signal, I want you to put the twigs and cigs in the tub. And Tommy, when I give you the signal, you toss in the rose petals and that vodka, not the whole bottle though, just pour it in, alright? Great. Now, are y'all ready? Okay, grand. Are you sure? Glorious. Like sure, sure? Okay, okay, fuck a duck, here we go."

Standing in front of the cauldron with her back to the altar, the cup grasped tightly with both hands, Priscilla closed her eyes. A moment passed, then she raised the cup high in the air. Here it is, she thought. The moment she had been waiting for.

Priscilla spoke. "Oh, Sweet Lucifer, to thee I drink, to thee we give thanks, and to thee we give sacrifice. Hear my incantation. Hear my call. Humble us with yer power. Fill me with yer void."

Barely loud enough to be heard, Joseph whispered, "Holy fuckin' fuck," and Priscilla downed the cup.

Big Tommy said, "Whoa."

The taste of the brew was intense. It hit the back of Priscilla's throat with the acidity of stomach bile, and nearly made her vomit. But she choked it down. Slowly. It was one of the most difficult things she had ever done. Nothing she had ever tasted before that day could have prepared her for the old cheese, foreskin, and cadaverine combination that she had just willingly dumped down her throat. But she did it. She got it down. Slowly.

Her mind and stomach swirling, she thought she could hear one of the boys asking her if she was alright, but the voice sounded far away and distorted, and though she thought she could hear it, she could not bring herself to reply. She was beginning to panic. Her heart was racing, and she could hear it growing faster and louder. She could feel the brew working inside her, but there was no way she was going to be able to keep the shit down. She could feel it rising in her throat, and to make matters worse, she could no longer see.

And just like that, it went away. Her mind was clear, and her stomach settled. Priscilla paused for a few seconds while doing an internal evaluation, but then she stood up straight and opened her eyes. Joseph and Tommy were watching her, clearly concerned.

"You okay," Big Tommy said. His voice was still slightly distorted, like vinyl played at half speed.

Priscilla nodded at him, and spit on the ground. She was fine, a little unnerved maybe, but fine. The show would go on. She pointed at Joseph and nodded at the cauldron. Joseph watched her carefully for another moment, then he kind of reluctantly nodded his head, and tossed his offering into the tub. Then Priscilla pointed at Big Tommy, and he tossed in the petals, and emptied the bottle.

Priscilla watched the offerings sink slowly into the heinous bubbling brew, the taste of it still lingering strong in her mouth. When the last cigarette finally sank, she turned to her altar and said these words aloud:

A rabbit's eye, a child's vein,
we call the beast to know his name!
A drop of blood, a bit of grain,
we call the beast to bring the rain!
Hail him, he who is legion.
Hail him, he who has many names.

One gentle blow through puckered lips and out went the candle on Priscilla's altar. For a moment, no one spoke or moved. They only waited. Listened. Each of them, their ears strained against the silence. A few moments passed, and Priscilla said, "Let's go outside."

But when they got outside, nothing had changed. Nothing happened. Crickets chirped. The wind blew. Everything was the same as before. The spell hadn't worked. All three of them searched the sky for some sign, but still, there was nothing. No change. Priscilla was devastated. Her fear had come true. She was a fake, a phony, a fraud. A charlatan. A dumb kid with a big imagination. *Oh, what was she thinking, how could she have been so stupid? Flying on a broom?! Making potions?! Oh, you bird-brain, you bonehead, you halfwit, you, you… you…ignoramus.*

Then it happened.

It began with a single brilliant bolt of lightning, one that lit up the night like the Devil's own lantern. Then at nine forty-five, post meridiem, on October thirty-first, nineteen seventy-one, in Clockmaker, West Virginia, a black thunder cloud burst open, and rabbit piss rained down from the sky.

'Meet Me at the Creek' by Billy Strings plays

◆

"Piss," said Sheriff White. "It's rainin' piss."

"You foolin'."

"I ain't."

"Well, that can't be."

"I'ma tellin' ya, it is."

Deputy Knotts eyed the Sheriff suspiciously. "You reckon you been gettin' enough sleep, Sheriff?"

"Now goddamnit, Deputy, I been rained on, and please believe, I done been pissed on, and I'm here to tell ya, it's rainin' fuckin' piss. Get on out here and check for yerself if you don't believe me."

Sheriff White was standing in front of his station, holding the door open, staring up at the sky, trying and failing to make sense of what was falling from it. Drenched from head to toe with what was, in fact, urine, he was having a difficult time rectifying the inconsistencies of his current reality. Having spent seventy-three years on this earth, forty-two of them in law enforcement, he thought he'd seen it all.

Deputy Knotts joined him outside, the day's newspaper held open over his head. Sheriff White stuck out a cupped hand, and when a puddle formed in it he gave it a sniff, then he held it up for his deputy to do the same.

"That ain't necessary, Sheriff. I smell it."

"See," said Sheriff White. He sniffed at the puddle again, then discarded it.

Before the deputy had a chance to respond, one of the phones started ringing inside the station.

Sheriff White let out a long sigh. Staring up at the night sky, he dumped the piss out of his hat, gave it a good shake, and put it back on his head. "Gonna be a long night, Deputy. Answer that phone, and start a fresh pot. Make it strong." Having pulled his revolver from its holster, he handed it to Deputy Knotts. "Here, clean this off too," he said. "Before it tarnishes."

"Ain't you comin' in, Sheriff?"

"I'll be in. I need to think a minute."

"But Sheriff, it's…."

"I know…" said Sheriff White. "It's just piss. It'll wash off."

◆

Kathleen Gibbons, in addition to playing piano at her church and teaching kindergarten, had quite a few other hobbies. She liked to bake, she liked to play solitaire, and she liked to knit, but she also liked to change into her nightgown without drawing her blinds, she liked to read erotic fiction, and on nights when it rained, she liked to strip off all of her clothes and frolic in the forest… She would stand nude among the trees and twirl with her arms out, letting the water fall on her face and skin. To Kathleen, it was a type of natural cleansing, not to mention a practice in exhibitionism, and so she always looked forward to an evening of rain. In fact, she got so excited when she heard the first drops hit her tin roof that she made it twenty feet from her back door before she even noticed that she was covered in piss. Unfortunately, her home, like most, did not have running water, so after covering her well with a sheet of tin, she dried off the best she could and went to bed. In the morning, she woke up sticky and confused. She was only twenty-two, so that happened to her from time to time.

◆

Maw Scill sat in her kitchen, listening to the rain. She wasn't aware that the rain was actually rabbit waste, so she was cursing the cats for the smell that had crept into her kitchen. The little sons of bitches, one of them must have done their business in her house. She was sure of it. She could hear them meowing and yowling outside on the back porch. They wanted in, or so she thought.

"Well tough titty little kitties, you wanna piss in Maw Maw's house, you'll stay outside till ye drown," she said, aloud.

She sat there a while longer but the sound of the crying cats began to irritate her, so she stood, walked to the television, and turned the volume all the way up. Then she changed the channel. An Alfred Hitchcock film was in progress. That would do. It wasn't *The Birds*, which was easily Hitchcock's best work as far as Maw Scill was concerned, but it would do. She stood watching the screen for several minutes, then she slowly made her way to her chair. She was ready to close her eyes. She felt particularly sleepy, besides *wouldn't nobody be trick or treatin' in this weather.*

The funny thing is, if Maw Scill hadn't cranked the volume on her television, she might have realized that a version of *The Birds* was taking place all around her. Much like in the movie, her house had been surrounded by countless small creatures, but instead of rabid, squawking birds, it was cats. Piss-soaked, whining cats. Nearly two hundred of them. Every living cat in Clockmaker, to be exact. They were amassing in a circle around the house, some of them pacing, some of them sitting. All of them clearly eager. And one of them was on the back porch giving birth.

◆

Superman hid underneath a delivery truck in front of Layfield's Market. Piss rain or liquid kryptonite beat down all around him. The red S on his white t-shirt was bleeding from the acidity. His eyes burned.

Three sopping wet ghosts covered in sheets ran crying down a dirt road, sloshing through puddles of bunny whiz. Their little sister, a princess, trailed them carrying a plastic jack-o-lantern. An assortment of candy floated inside it. The princess had swallowed some of the rain, and was feeling ill.

Batman and Spiderman sat eating chocolate and watching a movie about a kidnapping while their mother phoned the Sheriff about the unusual rain.

A Pirate and his older brother got stoned in the front seat of their parents' car with the windshield wipers on. Three Dog Night played softly on the radio. Both of them were glad they skipped trick-or-treating to get baked.

An astronaut, a clown, and a wizard walk into a bar covered in piss, and the bartender says, over the jukebox, "Hey Eddie, ain't them yer kids?"

◆

Everett Carpenter woke up in his chair. The house was dark. He sat there for some time, collecting himself and listening to the rain fall. He lit a cigarette and began smoking it, then he quickly stood up and felt the crotch and rear of his pants. He could smell piss. But it wasn't him. His pants were dry.

"Thank fuck," he said to himself.

Still quite drunk, he staggered over to the window, and stood, looking out at the rain for a while. He watched it drum on the hood of his car in the driveway. He loved that car. It was a classic. There wasn't a scratch on it. Pristine in every way, it turned all the young girl's heads when he drove it through town, and this rain was going to rinse it off real nice. He couldn't wait to see it sitting there the next morning. It would sparkle in the sunshine.

He found Lavinia sprawled out in their bed. He watched her sleep for a few minutes. He considered waking her up with his dick, but there was no point. All the pain pills the doctor had him on made it nearly impossible to get hard. "You got lucky, bitch," he said, softly. "If it weren't for the pills, come mornin' you wouldn't know whether to shit, come, or bleed."

In the kitchen, he snagged another beer and leaned against the sink. He could still smell piss. It had to be the septic tank. Maybe it was full. He hoped not. He didn't have the money to hire anybody to fix it, and he damn sure wasn't climbing in there himself. Besides, it was only three years old. He pitied the little bastard who installed it, if it was already fucked up.

As Everett was sitting back down in his chair, he glimpsed it. Briefly illuminated by a strike of lightning, on his coffee table beside the stack of Elvis coasters that he bought, two years prior, from the flea market, laid a thirteen inch wooden handle carving knife.

The knife had also come from the flea market. Not that it mattered, but it had. And there it was.

◆

"A one. A two. A one, two, three, four."

G A B C

C D E F

E F F# G

G G G F

"Goodness gracious, great balls of fire!" Mathias lit into it. His right hand took off like a bat out of Hell. Gliding effortlessly across the urine-soaked keys of his piano, droplets sprang up behind each and every note his fingertips played, and not a single note did he miss.

His left hand, on the other hand, it stumbled in awkward and late, but it was wearing a slick little boogie woogie, and by the time it caught back up, the lick was already cooking along. For as drunk as he was, and as hard as the rain was coming down on him, Mathias was sounding pretty goddamn good.

"Wooweeee!" he called out to the night. Cackling and laughing like he was, he could hardly keep up with the words of the song. He spit and sputtered and gagged on piss, and laughed and gagged some more. He was out of his mind with not only booze, but absolute and total fucking astonishment as well. It was the sheer absurdity of it all. It tickled something deep inside his heart. Here he was playing Jerry Lee Lewis under God's own divine piss storm, and he simply couldn't get over that fact.

◆

Priscilla, Joseph, and Big Tommy had spent the entirety of the storm just inside the mouth of the cave, where they could witness the spectacle and still stay dry. Aside from the initial victorious cheers when the first drops fell, they had all remained rather quiet. Watching piss fall from the sky after performing a Satanic witchcraft ritual would weigh on the minds of just about anyone, and these kids were no different. Even Big Tommy, simple as he was, had plenty to consider. A couple of times, Joseph attempted to make a joke, but neither of them landed.

The rain went on for two hours. Not all night, like Priscilla expected, but long enough to get most of the trick or treaters. So she could hardly be upset. Furthermore, she was a witch. A real live witch. Not a faker, not a phony, and not a charlatan. A real fucking witch. The thing was, if she was a witch and witchcraft was real, then that meant that the Devil was real, and she and her friends had pledged their allegiance to him.

It wasn't that she hadn't considered this before, but now that it was real, and the gravity of her decisions were real, she felt a little nervous. But she thought on the subject as the piss rain fell, and she decided that no matter what, as long as she remained a good witch, as long as she stayed away from any of the evil spells, that ultimately she would be alright, that God would understand.

As the weather was beginning to let up, Joseph put his hand on Priscilla's knee and said, "Well Scilly, I'll give it to ya. Yer a witch, alright. My mind is fuckin' blown."

Priscilla smiled at him. "Told ya…dickhead."

And with that, they all collapsed into laughter. The tension of the evening, like ice under the weight of Gertrude Green, finally broke. Priscilla was glad about it. They all were.

But then, just as the laughter came to an end, Priscilla's bowels turned. And they turned quick. Like, real quick. Like, so quick that Priscilla didn't have time to think, or move, or even turn her head. And just like that, the chicken head, piss, spit, blood and rabbit stew-brew emulsified in her stomach and came erupting out of her, and onto Joseph's open-mouthed, wide-eyed, terrified face.

Tommy, who had been sitting on a rock a few feet from Joseph, fell flat on his back, holding his stomach, and began howling with laughter.

Joseph very carefully wiped the foul, chunky vomit from his eyes, so that he could open them, and from around his mouth and nose. He looked horrified, and horrifying. Priscilla was just about to apologize to him, just about to say, "Oh my God, I am so, so so sorry," but just as she opened her mouth to speak, her bowels twisted again, and again she purged on Joseph's face.

Tommy couldn't speak. Tears rolled down his face. He wasn't even laughing anymore, he was just holding his stomach and making strange noises, almost like a bullfrog. It was the first time that Big Tommy had ever laughed that hard.

"I want…my goddamn love potion," said Joseph.

◆

ChaPer TEN

The following morning, Priscilla and Big Tommy woke up beside the cauldron. It was still warm from the night before. Joseph returned home shortly after Priscilla had defiled him, not only to clean the puke off, but also because he had school to attend. Priscilla and Tommy stayed in the cave and talked long into the night, and when they fell asleep, Priscilla's head was resting contently on Tommy's arm. Like Joseph, he made her feel safe.

After taking time to wake, they set about tidying the lair. They cleaned up all the vomit, the best they could, and emptied the contents of the cauldron into a bucket. It smelled terrible. Tommy offered to wash the giant tub with lye, but Priscilla told him that the cauldron must never be cleaned. According to the book, she told him, a witches' cauldron gets more powerful with every use. The energy of each brew is absorbed by the metal and must never be rinsed away or washed. "Just scoop out them brains or whatever that is 'ere, and that clump of hair, and that ought to do it," said Priscilla.

After snubbing out all but a few candles, and a long warm hug, something that neither Priscilla nor Tommy was accustomed to, they parted ways. Tommy had to tend to his mother, and Priscilla hadn't seen Maw Scill in days. How many, she wasn't real sure, but she was sure that Maw Scill was probably starting to worry about her and Priscilla felt guilty at the thought. And although she had no intention of claiming responsibility for it, she also couldn't wait to hear what Maw Scill had to say about the mysterious 'storm' in the night. Priscilla finished washing her face, changed back into her dress, and snubbed out the remaining candles.

CATS AND DRUGS

After so long in the dark, her eyes took a moment to adjust as she emerged from her lair. She could see that Tommy was standing at the mouth of the cave with his back to her, but she couldn't see what he was looking at. As she came up beside him, he said, "I reckon they's some folks gonna be reeeeal sore today."

As Priscilla scanned the forest surrounding the cave, her heart sank. The vast and budding foliage that had previously been so completely lush with reds and oranges was now yellow and crispy. All the plants, all the grass, all the trees, wilted and burnt from the acidity of the storm.

Well shit. This was certainly an unintended consequence. Priscilla and the boys had only wanted to ruin trick or treating. They had envisioned the Layfield girls running home drenched in piss, maybe falling face down in a puddle, but they hadn't considered this. "Go on home, Tommy," said Priscilla. "Let's meet back here when Joseph gets out of school."

As Priscilla made her way to Maw Scill's house, the consequences of her actions began piling up. Almost every bit of plant life that Priscilla passed, on her nearly hour long walk, had either turned yellow or been killed altogether. Luckily, most people had already harvested their gardens for the year, but that is also where most people's luck ran out. Paint ran down the sides of houses in streaks, and it puddled up and corroded on the hoods of cars. Several people along her walk were emptying buckets or pumping tainted water from their wells. Others were pulling down yellowed clothes off of lines and rewashing them.

When she passed over Pinch Creek, she looked down from the bridge. A few dead fish floated in an eddy, and a few more were dead on the bank. She didn't hear the singing of a single bird, and to top it all off, all of Clockmaker now smelled like an outhouse. Priscilla walked the rest of the way, with her head down, her pride melting away like piss-soaked paint. Just like the old saying goes, when it rains, it pours piss.

But there is another old saying. It goes, a woman being never at a loss, the Devil always sticks beside them. And that's right where the Devil was, right beside Priscilla. He walked beside her, down the dirt roads of Clockmaker, stroking her hair. Watching her. She couldn't see him of course, but he was there, and when he saw the downtrodden and dejected look on her sweet face, he smiled, knowing that all of her troubles would soon be forgotten. For he had left a little surprise for Priscilla on her grandmother's back porch.

Maw Scill was sitting at the kitchen table when Priscilla came through the door. She was smoking and working a crossword puzzle. "Well, holy shit, look what the cat dragged in," she said.

"Mornin', Maw Maw."

"Mornin', yer ass, girl. Where in hell you been?'"

" …I been with Joseph?"

"Well what the shit you been doin'? I ain't seen hide nor hair of you in damn near four days."

"…I'm sorry, Maw Maw. We just been in the woods. Me and Joseph and our new friend, we built another fort is all…"

"Well, you better be sorry. Makin' yer old Maw Maw worry like that." She took one last pull from her cigarette then mashed it into the ashtray. "Come on over here and sit down. You been down to see yer momma today?"

Priscilla pulled up a chair at the table and said, "No mam. I ain't."

"Well good, she was up here a'lookin' for you this mornin' and I ain't wanna tell her I ain't seen you for four damn days, so I lied and told her you was at the market for me. So that's where you was this mornin', the market. Got it?"

"I got it."

"She said to come on down and see her when ya got back. Dickhead won't be there. I reckon his precious fag wagon got messed up in the storm last night, and he's taken it up to Latrobe to get fixed. She said he'll be gone till tomorrow. I reckon he was next to tears, the way yer momma talked. Serves him right, don't it?"

"It sure does," said Priscilla with some relief. At least one good thing came from last night.

"Yeah, we both thought so too. We had a good laugh about it. Damn holler smells worse than the jake though."

"Momma laughed?"

"She sure did. A couple times. I was surprised as you."

In that moment, every bit of doubt or regret that Priscilla had concerning the success of her first spell was washed away. Her mother had laughed. It was such a rare thing, Priscilla was sorry that she wasn't around to witness it. And as far as regrets, well, forget those. Priscilla would have single-handedly poisoned and burned every living plant in the state of West Virginia if it was sure to get a smile out of her mother, let alone a laugh. Her efforts had been redeemed, if only in her own eyes, but either way, that would be enough.

Then Maw Scill said, "Oh shoot! I near forgot. Guess what I found in that old milk crate on the back porch when I woke up this mornin'."

Priscilla eyed her suspiciously.

Maw Scill began to tell her but then she paused and said, "Ya know, why don't you just go on back 'ere and take a look for yerself?"

So that's just what Priscilla did.

The next statement is true. The previous statement is false. Attempting to derive truth from either of those sentences leads to what is known as a paradox. The Raven Paradox states that the observation of a green apple increases the likelihood of all ravens being black. The Crocodile Paradox poses the question, if a crocodile steals a child and promises its return if the child's father can correctly predict the crocodile's exact intentions for the child, how should the crocodile respond in the case that the father predicts that the child will not be returned?

The Porcupine Paradox suggests that despite the best intentions, intimacy cannot occur without substantial human harm, or that porcupines, like humans, by their very nature, can never get too close to one another without suffering a prick. The Cat Paradox, put simply, is a paradox that discusses the possibility of the existence of multiple realities in which a cat placed inside a box, along with a vial of toxic acid, is, after a given amount of time, either alive or dead, or both.

A heartbreaking perversion of the Cat Paradox is the paradox with which Priscilla was presented when she pulled back the old blanket that covered the top of the milk crate on her grandmother's back porch. Super-positioning halted, wave-form collapsed, Priscilla stared down at six newborn kittens, five of them black with orange and white stripes, and one of them—the tiny one, the runt, the last born—was pure black, like coal in a dark mine.

The five with the black and orange stripes were all dead, and flies buzzed around them. Their bodies lay strung around the inside of the box, and each of their heads was missing. The black one had bright green eyes like Priscilla, and it sat in the corner of the crate casually grooming itself. Their mother was nowhere to be seen.

Priscilla watched on, stunned, for several moments, attempting to determine the cause of such a strange and terrible scene, but then, just like that, it hit her. Holy shit, this was the moment she had been waiting for. She couldn't have been more sure. She could feel it in her bones, like the opposite of withdrawal symptoms. Her Familiar had finally found her, and it had come in the form of a precious little, tiny little, shaggy little, black kitten! Priscilla gushed with excitement, box of gore be damned.

Without a second thought, she reached down into the crate and removed the runt. And it was a girl! A little, tiny, baby girl kitty! "Oh, how perfect, how perfect," Priscilla said, softly, and she held the cat up to her face, and kissed it.

The book had been clear. Priscilla must not, under any circumstance, attempt to seek out or coerce a Familiar Companion. When a witch was ready, her Familiar would find her, and not before. The book said to be patient, but to remain open and aware at all times. And she had, she had been patient and almost overly receptive. And now here she was, the little darling, black as night and splattered with blood.

Priscilla cradled the fragile beast in her arms and it immediately nestled itself into the folds of her dress, an expression of contentment settling over its small furry face. Priscilla gazed down at it. She could hear it softly purring.

'Too many puppies' by Primus plays

Out of nowhere came a foul stench that Priscilla immediately associated with the decaying glaring inside the crate, and her gaze shot to the makeshift kitten coffin at her feet, but almost right away she realized that the smell wasn't coming from below her. It seemed to be all around her. No matter how she turned her head, it was inescapable.

Then it came to her, the scent, she recognized it. It was the goat. The one she had envisioned. The one that had made her… well, ya know. It was him. She knew it. It had a savage odor like none other Priscilla had known. She had helped clean a horse stable once, and she had helped Joseph dispose of many a carcass over the last month, but nothing, not even the witch brew vomit that still clung to her nostrils, could even palely compare to the poison rot miasma of the goat. It reeked like decomposition and afterbirth, and it burnt Priscilla's nostrils.

But once again, as quick as it came, it was gone, leaving Priscilla scanning the tree line in search of some heinous bleating creature. She dared not close her eyes in its pursuit. After some time, a breeze picked up, and Priscilla looked back down at the kitten in her arms. It purred as it did before, seemingly oblivious to the presence of any potential threat.

Priscilla once again looked into the crate. The striped kittens remained headless. It was surely a sad sight, but she didn't feel much about it. For whatever reason, she understood that for the one to live, the five had to die. Fragments of remorse, smaller than the teeny tiny little kitty she cradled, coursed through her. Mostly she was excited, and she felt, well, sort of good. She'd definitely had worse days. So what the grass was yellow, she had a cat.

After inspecting the milk crate, the dead cats, and the alive one, Maw Scill deduced that the culprit was none other than the kitten's own mother, which explained the feline's absence. "Infanticide," she called it. She said she had seen it a few times over the years. "Granted," she said, she had never seen a dam eat off her own catlings' heads, but she reckoned stranger things had happened. And that was that. Maw Scill dropped the dead, headless kitties into an old potato sack, which she kept a cupboard full of, and sat the sack on the back porch, saying, "Tell yer buddy to deal with these."

Then she turned to Priscilla, who was still holding the lone survivor, and she said, "I don't suspect old nigger cat's comin' back for her young'n here, so we got two options, the way I see it. First option is, I kill it."

Priscilla clenched her fists at the words, *kill it*, and her back muscles tensed, but Maw Scill continued.

"I'd do it quick now, mind you. Wouldn't feel no pain…or we could have Joseph do it, I reck—."

Priscilla interrupted, "What's the other option, Maw Maw?"

For a moment, Maw Scill could only watch her, admiringly. Priscilla didn't understand the woman's stare, but it made her uneasy in a bashful sort of way.

Maw Scill went on, "Option two is, you care for that little baby like it's yer own."

Priscilla's eyes lit up. "Now don't get carried away, sugar," Maw Scill said. "I'll keep it some over the next month or so, if'n you need me to, but it'll be all yer responsibility after that. You'll have to bottle feed it ever' day, till it's ready to come off milk. And I'm gonna go ahead and say it. Even then, that little cat still might not make it without her momma."

Priscilla was already anxiously nodding her head before Maw Scill could finish laying out the prerequisites.

"You'll have to keep it here, till it gets bigger anyhow. And if the thing pisses in my house, it'll be yer hide, young lady, you understand me? Little Nigger Cat here's yer 'sponsibility."

"Her name is Lightnin', Maw Maw!" Priscilla corrected.

Maw Scill smiled with mock surprise, "My oh my, well, do forgive me, child, I take it then that, since you done named her, you decided on option two?"

Priscilla nodded eagerly.

"I'm shocked," said Maw Scill, with a hint of sarcasm. "Let me fetch ye a basket to keep her in. She likely needs fed."

Maw Scill retrieved an old wicker basket and several of her late husband's red paisley hankeys. She lined the basket with the hankeys and then showed Priscilla how to bottle feed the infant cat. With the bottle drained, two drops short of dry, Priscilla lowered Lightning into the basket, and the three of them sat down in front of the television.

Maw Scill was one of the few people that Priscilla knew who owned a television, being that so few people in Clockmaker had the funds for such a luxury. Maw Scill paid for hers with the insurance money from her late husband's death. She said she needed something to keep her company when the house got quiet and dark. Since she bought it, Priscilla had never seen it turned off. It stayed on twenty-four hours a day, and with the volume turned up so loud that Priscilla could sometimes hear it from her bedroom at her parents' house when she laid in bed at night, some forty yards away.

On nights when the wind was right, and the house was quiet, the far off sounds of *Bonanza*, *The Brady Bunch*, and *Bewitched* would float like ferries through Priscilla's open window. Maw Scill's favorite show was *All In the Family*. Priscilla's favorite was *The Andy Griffith Show*. The theme song in particular. So when Priscilla stayed with her grandmother, that's what they did together. They watched television. Occasionally, if Maw Scill was drinking, they would make cookies and listen to Elvis. Maw Scill loved Elvis. But mostly they watched television.

Priscilla ran the back of her finger along the furry ridge of

Lightning's spine. The cat was curled into a ball, sleeping serenely in the basket. Maw Scill was snoring in her chair. The television droned. As infatuated as she was with her new baby kitten, Priscilla could not wait to see her mother. So as quickly and as quietly as she could, cat-basket in hand, Priscilla slipped out the back, easing the screen door shut behind her.

For a second, one of Maw Scill's eyes opened, then it closed again.

◆

All Priscilla wanted in the whole wide world was a great big hug, and as soon as she walked in the front door, she began calling for her mother. But the house was quiet. It was odd not to see Everett in his chair, but she could smell him more clearly than ever. "I'll get ya," she whispered.

She called for her mother again as she came down the hallway. Still no answer. She called for her again. Nothing. Then, in the bathroom, she found her. She was face down on the tile. She was dead. No, not dead. For a split second, Priscilla would have sworn that she was, but then she noticed the overturned bottle of vodka beside the toilet, and the shallow rise and fall of her chest. She was dead, alright. Dead drunk.

For several minutes, Priscilla tried to wake her. "Momma. Mommaaa, wake up," she said, at times almost pleading. "Wake up!" She poked her and pushed her, peeled back her eye lids, and nothing. She lifted her arm, and it fell limp. Nothing.

Priscilla sat on the floor in the hall outside the bathroom watching her mother. A few hours went by, but the drunken heap on the floor never stirred. Before Priscilla left, she covered her mother with a blanket and put a pillow under her head. She combed back her hair and righted the bottle, then she kissed her mother on the cheek.

All she wanted was a hug, just one dumb hug, and maybe, just maybe, to see her mother smile. Was that too much to ask? Was it? On the way down to the house, in expectation of her mother's good mood, Priscilla had even been thinking up different jokes that would perhaps draw a laugh out of her. Once again though, she should have known better. A hug and a smile were hard to come by.

Lightning's basket in hand, Priscilla walked out of her childhood home, scoffing at the crocheted mat hanging beside the door that said HOME IS WHERE GOD AND FAMILY MEET, and as she stepped down into the yard she said to herself, "Knock knock, Momma?"

Then, because her mother wasn't there, she answered herself, "Who's there, little angel?"

And eventually, Priscilla said, "Nobody, Momma. Nobody."

◆

Lavinia woke up just as the sun was going down. Her head was throbbing like a heart valve before she could even open her eyes. *What day is it?* she wondered. She sat up with her back against the toilet, and realized for the first time that she was not in her bed. How had her bedding gotten in the bathroom? She held up her pillow and looked at it. For several minutes, she was earnestly confused. Then she saw the spilled vodka on the floor and the empty bottle sitting next to it. Beside the puddle was a small dirty shoe print, and though it was barely visible on the pale orange tile, it was clear enough for Lavinia to finally understand what happened. Priscilla had come home while she was passed out drunk.

Lavinia curled into a ball on the floor, and sobbed until long after dark, the throbbing in her head having descended to her heart.

Worlds. Levels. Dimensions. Realms. Realities. Universes. Planes of existence. Some alternate, some parallel, but all fragile and all subtle. They weave and spiral outward, flawlessly, ever expanding and accelerating in the eternal race to the Godhead, to the vertex of all vertices, to the culmination of all that is, and all that ever was, in this world or any other. The souls that inhabit these worlds run the same race.

Commonly enough, under certain circumstances, a soul can mentally inhabit multiple worlds, realms, or dimensions, simultaneously. Occasionally, a soul can transfer its physical form from one dimension to the next, but such abilities are generally reserved for the souls of gods and not teenage girls…generally.

The souls that inhabited the realm in which Priscilla dwelled, the people of Clockmaker, most of them anyway, had very little experience with any other realm but their own. To say the least, in Clockmaker, a conversation about time warps or lysergic acid was rarely overheard, and so, for Priscilla, the realization of these other realms came as a complete and total fucking surprise.

According to the book, but not verbatim, a novice witch cannot just go flying on brooms and brewing love potions, all willy nilly. Those are Level Two and Three Spells, and casting Level Two and Three Spells requires a bit more…preparation. A bit more… training.

For example, the piss rain was a Level One, General Spell, and there were only two Level One Spells to choose from. Along with the Piss-Rain Spell, there was the Cock-of-Fire Spell, which neither Joseph nor Tommy liked the sound of, especially in the case of some malfunction. So they went with the former. Leading up to Halloween, Priscilla had to ingest eleven flies and spend a day basically hyperventilating and then holding her breath in a pattern described by the book before she could even begin concocting the brew that she was to drink. Three hundred breaths and twenty holds in all, and eleven flies, one by one.

Which was easy enough, but love potions were Level Two Spells, and broom flying was Level Three, and in order to perform either of those spells, Priscilla had to jump through more than a few hoops, so to speak. She couldn't just fire up the old bathtub and get to cooking. Oh no. Under no circumstances was she to attempt a Level Two Spell without first performing one Level One Spell. And two, Level Two Spells were required before performing a Level Three Spell, and so on, all the way to Level Six, and even then, each level had its prerequisites. Like a kung fu master, she was going to have to earn her belts.

LEVEL ONE - TRIAL SPELLS
LEVEL TWO - SPELLS OF OTHERS
LEVEL THREE - SPELLS OF SELF
LEVEL FOUR - SPELLS OF EARTH
LEVEL FIVE - SPELLS OF DEATH
LEVEL SIX - SPELLS OF LIFE

Fortunately, Priscilla had already completed a level one spell, so now all that she had to do, in order to make the love potions for Joseph and Gertrude, was to, again, according to the book, and this time, verbatim, *Drink four cups of Death Tea—named for its flavor, and a thimbleful of the blood of menstruation.*

Which sounded easy enough, but Death Tea is a potent and intoxicating beverage. Its effects come on quick. Within ten to fifteen seconds. It contains a multitude of plants, many of them Tryptamine rich, and a small variety of fungi, including Amanita Muscaria, and Hericium Erinaceum. Many of these ingredients are highly psychedelic.

Try to remember, Priscilla had a plan, but so did the book. Priscilla wanted to become a witch, to cast spells and fly on a broom, real simple like, but the book wanted something more. The book wanted Priscilla to become, to grow and change, to develop and master. Priscilla wanted to be a witch, no doubt about it, but the book had not the patience for the frivolous wants of school girls. The book would make her earn her wants, work for her wants. Every single last one of them.

"I just love how every time you get to witchin', you gotta drink the nastiest fuckin' shit on the planet," said Joseph. He was hiding behind a stalagmite, far away from Priscilla, near the entrance to her lair. Candles burned all around.

Priscilla didn't say a word. She just stared down at the cup of thick black 'tea' in her hand. She was hesitating.

"Tommy, you better back on up, cousin, you seen what happened last time. Took me three days to get the stink off. Come on, chicken, drink that damn shit."

Tommy moved.

From under the hood of her cloak, Priscilla glared at Joseph. It was the putrid odor of the tea that gave her pause, not fear. It was the smell. *It was worse than the goddamn goat*, she thought.

Once again her expectations led her astray. Never did she imagine that being a witch was going to smell and taste so absolutely horrid, but here she was, and damnit, it was the smell that made her hesitate to drink it, not fear. She wasn't a chicken. And that was the truth, sure enough, but that's only because she didn't know any better. Had she known better, she would have been stricken with fear.

Priscilla raised a middle finger to Joseph, and she kept it raised until she finished the cup. When she finished, she slammed it down on her altar. Hail, Satan.

The book was wrong. Fuck fifteen seconds, she felt the tea al-

most instantly. Yes, it tasted bad, real bad. Bad as it smelled. Bad as death. It lived up to its name and then some, but, as luck would have it, Priscilla's taste buds, well, they rapidly disappeared. Then her hands disappeared. Then her arms. Then her whole damn body. She felt like an Alka-Seltzer dropped in water

The last words Priscilla heard, before she tore through the spacial fabric and became extricated from this realm completely, came from Big Tommy. He said, "dO yOu feEL anYthiNg yEt, SciLlyyyyYyYyYyYYYY?"

'A Cowboy's Work is Never Done' by Ray Coniff plays

From Joseph and Tommy's perspective, the only thing that Priscilla did was drink the cup, slam it down, gag a little, lower her middle finger, and fall to her knees, where she stayed, palms to the earth, like a Satanic Muslim in prayer…for three hours.

From Priscilla's perspective, bodyless, and yet somehow fully mentally intact, she was soaring, no, that's not right, she was blasting high, high into the sky. Clouds rushed by her at an alarming rate until finally she was thrust upward into a giant glass cathedral held together by metallic hardware studded with multicolored jewels. Inside the cathedral, surrounding her formless self, were amorphous shapes and fractal patterns, some resembling ancient hieroglyphics, all swirling and circling around her, inspecting and analyzing her. Never had a sixteen dimensional shade of purple ever, in all of her years, attempted to communicate with her, but that's what happened. The stranger part was that Priscilla seemed to understand what the shade of purple was trying to tell her. It was telling her, *Don't forget to wipe your feet on the mat,* and it was laughing at her. The shade of purple was laughing at her. And the damndest thing was, as far as Priscilla could tell, she didn't even have feet. It was all rather unsettling.

But before Priscilla had so much as a moment to orient herself to this new environment, a horned figure, like Al Mulock in the opening frame of *The Good The Bad and The Ugly*, rose up in front of her, so close that she could touch it, had she hands. The figure was all gold and seemed to be made of crumbling rock, like a three-eyed, androgynous stone statue come to life. Its eyes had many pupils and around each pupil was an iris that could have contained within it entire universes, for all Priscilla could discern. She tried to follow its horns to their tip but they only spiraled on forever, above them. The truth is, it all happened so quickly that she barely had time to evaluate any particularity of her situation.

The figure raised its hands and shrugged, then it inched so close that Priscilla couldn't see around its face, and it stuck out its tongue. The tongue was long and skinny and gold and at its end there was a fork, like a snake. The tongue flicked in and out of its golden mouth, smelling and tasting Priscilla, and she wondered if it was going to eat her, but it didn't. Instead, it began to dance. Playfully, but elegantly, as if it was showing off its talents. Dipping and spinning, its eyes never left her. They stayed fixed in space, and in their sockets, and its body moved around them. Then it was gone. Sucked away and obliterated by some unknown force. As was the glass cathedral, the golden horns, and the sky.

Now Priscilla was in the desert, three great pyramids stood before her, just like the ones she had read about in school. But everything was cast in red, like she was wearing rose-colored glasses. In the distance, beyond the pyramids, walked what looked like a camel.

Priscilla watched on as the camel came toward her, slow and steady, and with every step the camel took, the world around she and it changed. She watched on as time passed at a highly accelerated speed, countless civilizations were constructed and then destroyed and then replaced with other civilizations, only to be destroyed and replaced again. Bare earth, then green, then signs of life, then civilization, then fire and smoke or ice or water or locusts, it was moving so fast, it was hard for Priscilla to tell. Over and over, civilizations came and went, came and went, came and went, rapidly, as if looping or cycling. Seventy, maybe eighty times, it was impossible to count, Priscilla saw the Pyramids be erected and then destroyed, erected and destroyed, erected, destroyed, but in the midst of it all was the goddamn camel. He was walking right through the middle of it.

Unfazed and unimpressed by the passing time and the evolving world, the camel walked on. Its course clear and direct, it walked with purpose and complete indifference to the turbulence surrounding it. Over and over, all around it, civilizations came and went, but the camel was steadfast. When the camel was close enough, Priscilla could see that it too, like the golden horned dancer before, had three eyes, and it had three humps on its back, and on each hump was a crimson satin pillow, fringed along the edges.

Mere feet from Priscilla, the camel finally stopped, and for a moment they only stared at one another. The camel chewed lazily at the air. Close up, Priscilla could see that, although the camel's head was indeed that of a camel, it was also, at any given time, the head of a billion other creatures, as well. Constantly shifting and blurring, the faces formed then dissolved in a pattern that constituted the whole of the creature, and at one point, mingled indiscriminately among that of lions, lizards, and lambs, she was sure she saw her own face. Before the camel departed, it gave Priscilla a sly wink, and went on its way.

Then Priscilla noticed that her knees were beginning to ache, which was weird because she didn't even have knees, and as soon as that thought crossed her mind, it all cracked and popped and fizzled out, and she found herself, once again, on the limestone ground inside Dead Kid Cave.

Her knees were on fire, but not literally. After so long on the floor of the cave, they had atrophied, and Priscilla could not straighten them, so she rolled on to her side, hoping to release the pain. Tommy was standing over her. The effects of the tea still lingered, and covering Tommy's face, just below the skin, she could see a tribal sort of inner tattoo that pulsed with his breath. Past him, she could see Lightning peering out of her basket from atop the altar. The kitten's eyes were wide and changing colors like a kaleidoscope. Her fuzzy little ears were at attention, and the tribal pulsing was on her fuzzy little face too.

"Welp," said Joseph, "that was easy enough." He was still hiding behind the stalagmite. "Kinda borin', if ya ask me."

Tommy said, "Are you alright? Can you stand?"

Priscilla didn't respond. She couldn't. She was still very much discombobulated from the tea, but additionally, she was now experiencing an acute state of bewildered shock. What in the name of God had just happened to her? She didn't have the words to describe it. Had it been a vision? No, that wasn't right. The goat had been a vision. This was something more. She felt as though she had been sucked up a long tube and transported to another universe, one astoundingly and completely different from her own, and yet equally real in all aspects. She felt like she had come face to face with some kind of God. She felt…she felt…small. One thing was certain, she had not been ready for that shit. No, no, no, she had not been ready.

Then she vomited. This time, into a tin bucket that Tommy was holding.

"Oh, noooow she's got aim," said Joseph. "Ain't that fuckin' convenient."

Sometime later that night, Joseph and Big Tommy sat around a small fire that they had built just inside the mouth of Dead Kid

Cave. They looked out into the dark forest and up at the stars. The nights were getting colder, and they held their palms toward the flames. Priscilla was leaning against the inner wall of the cave, feeding Lightning milk from a bottle.

"Welp, that is some wild shit, I'll give ya that. I ain't never hearda nothin' like it before," said Joseph.

"Lord, I ain't neither," said Tommy.

"Well, that's the best I can tell ya, and that really ain't even half of it," said Priscilla. "It was more than I can explain. I reckon I just don't have the words. It's like, well, I dunno, it's like, you know the camel and the golden demon guy, well, with both of 'em, it was like bein' in the presence of a…of a god…" Priscilla trailed off, but then added. "Or somethin' like a god. Does that make sense?"

"Bout as much as shittin' in yer own shoe," said Joseph. He was looking for a laugh, but didn't get it.

Then, rather sheepishly, Tommy said, "I s'pose I understand. Kinda like, when you think too long 'bout dyin', and it makes you feel real real small…Is 'at right?"

"Damn, Big T, why the hell you thinkin' 'bout dyin' for," said Joseph.

Big T seemed to think a moment. Then he shrugged.

Priscilla said, "Yeah, Tommy, that's right. It was kinda like facin' death. Death with three eyes, and three humps, but death just the same, I reckon. It was every bit as scary as dyin', I know that much. And in hindsight, I'm not so sure that tea is named after its taste."

"Well hey, the good news is you only gotta drink three more cups, and I'll have me one of them Elder girls fallin' all over me," said Joseph.

Priscilla gave him her stankiest eye. Again the joke did not land. "Shouldn't you be goin' home, ain't you got school tomorrow?" she asked.

"Hell no, it's Friday," said Joseph.

"It ain't Friday," said Priscilla.

"Fuck it ain't. Has been all day, last I checked."

"He ain't lyin'," said Tommy.

"I coulda swore it was Tuesday."

"You sure you ain't hit yer head on that ride to Egypt you took? Do you remember yer name, mam? Who's the president? What year is it?"

Another cold, stank eye landed on Joseph, but this time Priscilla decided to respond, and she said each word very carefully, "Priscilla-Louise-Carpenter, Richard-Milhous-Nixon, nineteen-seventy-go fuck yerself-one."

"Wooooooo, boy," said Tommy, thoroughly amused. "Here she come, now!" He had a beautiful smile when he used it.

◆

Priscilla spent the next few weeks in and out of different states of consciousness. At some point in the blur of days, her womanly time of the month came, and she consumed the necessary amount of blood, but how long ago that had been, she wasn't certain. The Death Tea turned out to be more of a task than Priscilla had anticipated. Not only did the stuff taste miserable, but its affects seemed to linger for several days, and she was having trouble keeping track of time because of it. On top of all that, each time she drank was more intense, and thus, more terrifying than the last.

The reality was that after the first night with the camel and the golden demon it took her seven days to summon the courage to drink the second cup, and eleven more days to drink the third. The following day she had her period, and the fourth cup of Death Tea she drank to chase away the taste of her own menstruation. Each experience with the tea was stronger than the last, and each one was also more complex and confusing than the last. Or so it seemed, from Priscilla's tweeked out perspective.

Oh, the things she had seen… The things that she had attempted to make sense of… These experiences were beyond all reason, beyond anything comprehensible or identifiable. She could hardly make sense of any of it, but if the first cup had been a breeze, the last cup was a category five hurricane, with no eye or end.

Giant, robotic, demonic, shape-shifting chickens. Halls of living, animated, diamond-studded, corpse statues. The removal and reinsertion of her heart and lungs by lizards in black robes. Swirling white voids. Swirling white voids that beckoned and laughed at her fear. Royal Hell-raccoons bearing gifts of glowing orbs and trash. Screaming fractal monkeys made out of ruby. The list went on, and on and on, deeper and further, until even the slightest comprehension of her expriences was impossible. Let alone their description.

As for the camel, she never saw it again, but the three-eyed golden dancer was always there. Somewhere, in the corner of every moment spent under the influence of Death Tea, it was always lurking, watching, grinning, dancing. Sometimes she saw it, and other times she only felt it. Then eventually, inevitably, the tea's effects would begin to fade and she would find herself with Tommy in the cave, or alone in the woods, or playing with Lightning. Or walking down Main Street at three in the morning, but that only happened once because Tommy fell asleep.

These days passed slow, and uncertainly. Lightning grew at an alarming rate, ten times the rate of a normal cat, and she was no longer a defenseless little kitten. Priscilla had expected to bottle feed her for several weeks, but the cat's taste for mice and other critters of the woods was insatiable, and it wasn't but a week or two after the cat's birth before Priscilla started finding tiny dead animals at the foot of her altar.

Several other notable things happened during this time. Joseph had started growing a mustache, although it looked more like dirt on his upper lip. Tommy began spending all of his time with Priscilla, and the two of them rarely left the cave or the forest around it. Joseph brought supplies on a daily basis, food and water and such, but it was decided early on, based upon Priscilla's behavior when drinking Death Tea, that they could not let anyone else see her in such an intoxicated state. What would they say? How would they explain? Priscilla's inability to discern real life from the effects of the tea worried both Tommy and Joseph greatly, but they couldn't dissuade or deter her, no matter how hard they tried. At one point, Priscilla wrote a note for Maw Scill, and Joseph delivered it, leaving it tucked into her door frame, before he knocked and ran away.

Also, the mine had a small explosion, leaving four dead, including Tommy's cousin, Wilfred Green, and injuring eleven others. Attendance at Mt. Zion Methodist/Pentecostal church grew steadily under the serpent-centered leadership of Pastor Swann. Jeremiah Carpenter crossed the West Virginia state line. Lavinia Carpenter took her 'last' drink of liquor. She even dumped the bottle that she hid behind the pots and pans. Mathias Elder fell asleep with a lit cigarette and almost burned down the library. And on December second, Kester Mire and Merle Mire Jr. followed Joseph from the Layfield Market, along the ridgeline behind the school, and into the woods. Then from behind a fallen tree, the two brothers watched Joseph walk into a cave.

◆

I did what? Every alcoholic knows those words all too well. Likewise, every alcoholic also knows what it means to spend days or even weeks piecing together a pure and solid bender. They wake up one day, or one night, the fog has lifted, the dust has settled, and they don't know how they got home, or why their couch is in the yard. Then the phone rings. The voice on the other end of the line says a bunch of impossible sounding things, and the alcoholic replies…

"I did what?" said Priscilla. The tea had finally worn off, and she was beginning to feel somewhat normal again. Well, maybe not normal. She felt different, as a person, very different in fact, but at least now she could walk, and talk, and think properly. For a while she wasn't sure if she would ever regain control of her motor functions, but finally the fourth cup had worn off, and here she was. But now this shit…

Priscilla had just finished recanting her experiences from the fourth cup of tea. She and Joseph and Tommy sat around a fire, and she told them that in her mind she had been wandering through an infinite hall made of marble, and that she had bathed in a great marble tub surrounded by fire, but then Joseph cut in.

"Nah, you just shit yer pants and laid down in the crick over there for the rest of the night."

Priscilla's heart plummeted. "I did what?" she said.

"Yep," said, Joseph, a great smile now on his face. "You drank 'at tea and did yer prayin' thing for a while, then you shit yerself. Stripped off yer hood, walked on down there to the crick, and laid down in the shallow. Stayed there all night."

"Oh my God," said Priscilla, as blood filled her cheeks.

"Yer tellin' me," said Joseph. "At one point you was just sittin' in the water, bein all quiet, and all of a sudden, you just up and yelled out, Opie Taylooor!"

"What?" said Priscilla, mortified. Definition one.

"You did," said Tommy, laughing. And Joseph confirmed. "Yep, you sure did."

"And just what the hell were you two doin' the whole time?!"

"What the hell do you think we was doin," said Joseph. "We

was laughin' our damn asses off."

"We was keepin' an eye on ya though," said Tommy, affectionately. "We made sure you ain't drown."

Priscilla put her head in her hands, and a sound like a quick giggle or a speed fiend's chuckle squeaked out of her.

"See there," said Tommy, as earnestly as he could. "It ain't so bad, you already laughin' 'bout it."

"I wasn't laughin'," Priscilla said, like she'd been gutted. "That was the sound of my soul escapin' through my mouth."

⸻ ◆ ⸻

A word from Joseph

What did one Deadhead say to the other Deadhead when the acid wore off? This music sucks. Get it? How many Deadheads does it take to change a lightbulb? One to actually change it, four thousand to take pictures of it, and twenty thousand to follow it around 'til it burns out.

Life is full of jokes. Heck, it may even be one. Just a big fat joke, all of it. God got good and drunk one night at Heaven's own open-mic night. He was feelin' particularly confident—brave even—and decided to try and get a rise out of the room. So he stepped on stage and up to the microphone, and as soon as he opened his mouth, BAM! Just like that, all matter and energy and life spewed forth into existence.

I doubt it happened like 'at. If it did, I bet he bombed. God's timin' just ain't the best, that's plain to see. And in comedy, timin' is everything. Hell, he probably got booed off stage for this one. I mean, look around, what a lame fuckin' joke this all is… What a lame and poorly timed joke. I reckon it gets funnier the older ya get. You roll yer eyes at it in yer teens, but as you get older, as yer friends start to die off, as yer hair proceeds to thin, as yer mind begins to wander, you start to see the humor in it all.

You may never actually hold yer belly and laugh about it, even if you live to be a hundred, but if yer lucky, one day you'll be able to shake yer head at it, and maybe even give it a dry smile from time to time.

I apologize for bein' so woefully macabre, I ain't had the best week. My dog died. Fourteen years I had her. I woke up last night in a panic, thinkin' I forgot to feed her. Just for a second, then I remembered she was gone, and I bawled like a child. My bottom lip puffed up and my cheeks tensed, and I just sat there in bed and cried…

Been cryin' a lot, to tell the truth. Everything makes me think of her. I can't even see a ray of sunshine without picturin' her bathin' in it. I lose it. Her water bowl, fuck, I can't even glimpse it, let alone get rid of it. It's just been sittin' there on the kitchen floor, empty. Sticks, balls, bones, beef jerky, everything reminds me of her. Hell, even other dogs. You never realize how many dogs are in the world till every one you see makes you sob, uncontrollably. I loved that fuckin' dog… I still do. Rest in eternal peace, Doctor Barkenstein.

Anyhow, enough of that, I'll grieve on my own time, like I was sayin'… the Grateful Dead. It wasn't until my old buddy Dirty Dave, he's retired in Florida now, but it wasn't until he took me to Philly in June of seventy-six for a four night run that any of the shit that Priscilla went through with the Death Tea made any sense to me at all. For years I thought she was just drinkin' a bunch of plants and blood and shit, and havin' visions like people had in church, ya know, just pictures in her mind. I didn't realize that what she was doin', what we helped her do, was makin' and consumin' highly, and I do mean highly, potent, highly psyche-delic herbal narcotic cocktails.

For years I really had no idea what to make of all her tales of golden gods and camels and shit, but I stayed on tour for seven years after that first four-night run at the Tower Theater, and I seen Jerry play live, oh a hundred odd times before he died. The last time I saw him was in eighty-seven at Madison Square Garden. And I'll tell ya this right now, I danced and partied to a lot of real fine music in those years, it don't get much better than Jerry, but I also ate, smoked, sniffed, injected, and rectally inserted damn near every known drug on the planet, and I assure you, there is somethin' to say about all that as well.

I never went near as deep as Priscilla, mind you. I ain't sayin' that. She saw and experienced things I still can't imagine. But then again, I never mixed period blood and frog eyes with the drugs I was eatin'. Or stickin' up my ass, for that matter. There was some other shit goin' on there. Some real…well, some real Satanic shit.

I guess what I'm tryin' to say is that I know some things about drugs at this point in my life, a good many things, actually. But I'll never be able to fully wrap my head around the shit that Priscilla was eatin' and drinkin', but I think I got an idea.

I mean, to put it in perspective, I am a full grown man. I weigh one hundred and ninety-four pounds. I have consumed lots and lots of drugs for lots and lots of years. Lots of booze too. My brain ain't exactly virgin to chemicals, is what I'm gettin' at. And if I, today, wanted to get really twisted in the best way, I would only have to eat four to five grams of dried mushrooms.

Now, Priscilla on the other hand, at fifteen years old, never been drunk or high in her life, probably weighed a hundred pounds wet…and she's drinkin' Death Tea. So let's talk about Death Tea. I don't recollect all the ingredients, mind you, but I reckon I can recall enough to get my point across.

Okay, let's see.

You know the red mushrooms with the white spots, like in fairy tales? Those are…well, I forget what they're called, but those is some of the most high powered psychedelic mushrooms on God's green earth, but they can also be deadly poisonous if you don't know what yer doin', so most folks don't mess with 'em. Now, the book's measurements wasn't exact, it measured by pinches and handfuls, things like that, but I'll bet one cup of Death Tea had at least half an ounce of those fairy tale mushrooms in it. Half a fuckin' ounce. That's fourteen grams, for folks who ain't never sold drugs. Hell, I'd be scared to eat even three grams of those fuckers. You with me so far?

Now realize, there was also at least one other cow shit covered breed of psychedelic mushroom that I know of that was added into that same mix, at roughly the same amount, and a dozen other plants that did God only knows what. So, break it down, she was drinkin' a tea that had, by my guess, probably twenty to thirty grams of assorted, dry, hallucinogenic mushrooms brewed and steeped in it. Throw in some period blood or fuckin' bat blood, whatever, a dozen random plants, Canary Reed grass, shit like that…steep it all in water, and you got yerself some Death Tea. Fuckin' crazy shit, cousin. She was a fifteen-year-old little girl… I don't know how she did it…

Speakin' of Dirty Dave, man, he was a wild sonofabitch. I seen that motherfucker smoke an LSD crystal in a meth pipe one time. Another time he ate ninety-seven peach Xanax in one handful and washed it down with beer. He ain't die neither. He got head-butted on Friday, and pistol whipped on Saturday, but by Sunday he started comin' back around.

I'll never forget, we was workin' for the pipeline company, I was twenty at the time, he might have been forty, hard to say, and me and him is down in this hole all covered in shit and mud, and he looks at me and says, *Man, to hell with this job, what do you say we bail outta here and go see the Grateful Dead tomorrow night?*

And do you know what I told him? I says, What the fuck is the Grateful Dead? You believe that? I had no idea. But we spent that evenin' listenin' to the Workin'man's Dead album, and twenty-four hours later, we'd done quit our jobs, thumbed our way to Philly, and was sittin' on the pavement outside the Tower Theatre smokin' a joint in the middle of a drum circle. We brought Dave's little brother Charlie with us. He was only fifteen at the time, but he wouldn't take no for an answer. So we brought him along, but we lost him in the crowd on the second night, and neither me or Dirty Dave or anybody seen the little bastard since. I reckon Dirty Dave's mother never did forgive him, or me, for that one.

Lord, those were the days, weren't they. Free drugs, free love, everywhere ya went. What I would give for just one more quaalude, you hear me? Just one more. Boy, I'd chew that fucker up quick, pour me a margarita, put a little salt around the rim, and spend the rest of the day in a fuckin' hammock, watchin' squirrels crawl around in the trees. And don't even get me started on all the orgies. My dick still has a bend to it.

Yeah them was good old times, that's for certain. But then Jerry died in August of ninety-five and well…that was the end of an era for me. For a lot of us.

Well, I reckon that's all I got to say for now…I got a pile of wood that needs chopped and stacked. The winter's gonna be long. I can feel it. I just can't sit in this house lately… It's the quiet… It's been gettin' to me. Ya know, it's wild, I always thought I would get tougher as I got older, that I'd cry less and less, but that ain't the case. I cry more and more as the years go on. Hell, anymore, it just comes outta me, even over little things, happy things, sad things. You wouldn't believe how often I cry… eh, fuck…I miss my dog…

How do you know when you got a real hillbilly girlfriend?

When she can suck yer dick and chew tobacco, and know what to spit and what to swallow.

See? Ain't that a funny fuckin' joke?

———◆———

Chapter ELEVN

Having consumed four cups of Death Tea, and a thimble full of menstrual blood, Priscilla was now ready to cast Level Two Spells. Level Two Spells, or SPELLS OF OTHERS, were spells that could be used to manipulate the bodies, minds, and lives of people and even animals, but not the witch herself. SPELLS OF SELF, remember, are Level Three. Some Level Two Spells include Spells of Sleep, Spells of Madness, Spells of Wealth, Spells of Enslavement, Spells of Beauty, and of course, the ever popular Spells of Love.

From what Priscilla could tell, the book contained hundreds if not thousands of spells, hexes, and incantations. Under Spells of Madness, for example, were spells that could make a person see spiders, lose their ability to remember, or even want to kill themselves. Under spells of beauty, there were spells for thinner noses, plumper breasts, smaller feet, and hair removal, along with a hundred other specific body modification spells. There were sections on how to create potions and charms, how to enchant different objects or curse them. The book was very clear, however. None of these spells were to be performed on the witch herself, until Level Three. Any attempt by the witch to utilize these spells to affect her own person would be met with the harshest and most dire of consequences.

This concerned Priscilla very little. The book had rules and she intended to follow them without compromise. Having previously been a Christian and avid reader of the Bible, she had a certain predisposition to blindly following, for good or ill. Whether it be divine providence or good old-fashioned fate, just about everything that ever happened in Priscilla's life, from Everett, to meeting Big Tommy, to her baby teeth being knocked out, to her religious background, (hg) had been a sort of conspiracy in preparation of her witchhood. Although she was unaware of it, all the little moments of her life had been leading up to this. Maybe it was God, or the Devil, or maybe it was the vibratory energy of the universe, but something, something other-worldly, since long before her birth, had been grooming her for witchery. And now, acclimated and accustomed to religion, to solitude, to fear, to pain, loss, and confusion, Priscilla was tailor-made to be a witch.

Wednesday, December Eighth, Nineteen Seventy-One

In the name of Satan, and for the sake of Joseph and Gertrude Green, Priscilla fashioned two potions. One moonlit night, she and Joseph burglarized several dozen pieces of glassware from the science lab at the school, and now, another moonlit night, Priscilla was putting corks into the top of two of the lifted vials.

The potion inside one of the vials was a bubbly pink, the other, a bubbly blue. As described in the book, these were, in fact, the intended colors of the finished products. As far as Priscilla could tell, they were a success. However, there was no way to be certain without anyone actually drinking them.

Priscilla held both vials toward a candle and eyed them curiously, and with just a little more than a teeny, tiny, bit of self-satisfaction. *She had done it, by George!* But she hadn't exactly done what she was told. Call it woman's intuition, but it dawned on Priscilla that what Gertrude Green needed was not a love potion, but instead, a beauty potion.

After witnessing the unintended consequences of her first spell, with all the damaged property and flora, and what not, Priscilla began to consider her actions a little more carefully. For instance, what would life be like for the poor sap that unknowingly ingested Gertrude Green's love potion? Or still yet, what of the poor sap's family? They would have to gaze upon Gertrude's grotesque form at every family gathering, every Christmas, every wedding, every funeral. And who, in the midst of grieving, would want to catch old Gertrude in the corner of their eye? Not Priscilla, that was for sure.

And that is why Priscilla made Gertrude Green not the potion that she wanted but the potion that she needed. As far as Joseph was concerned, well, he wouldn't be so bad to fall helplessly in love with. Most girls should consider themselves lucky. And when it came down to it, he was her friend, and she owed him more than one. And if a love potion was what he wanted, then a love potion was what he was going to get.

Priscilla tilted the vials to the side and watched the gurgling potions creep toward the cork. For the first time that she could remember, she was certain of something. She was certain that her decision to become a witch had been the right one. She felt so… so different, so wonderful, so strong, so…so powerful. That was it, she felt powerful For the first time in her entire life, she felt like she had power, like she could do anything. And she really, really fucking liked it.

"Well," said Big Tommy, "Mommy sure is gonna be happy 'bout this. She been axin' 'bout it every time I see her. Where's my potion, where's my potion, you know how she is…always bitchin' about somethin'."

Priscilla turned to Tommy and handed him the blue potion. "You tell yer momma, I made this special just for her. Tell her to drink it on an empty stomach, before bed. Tell her when she wakes up the next mornin', that everywhere she goes, she'll have all the men fallin' all over her. She'll be able to have any man she wants. You got that? …Good."

To Joseph, Priscilla said, "Here, fuckface."

Joseph, who was cleaning dirt from under his nails with his knife, stood up, and strolled over to her with his handout, saying, "Don't mind if I do."

Priscilla gave Joseph the potion, but not without a warning. She said, "You be careful with this. Make sure whoever you give it to, you really want 'em to love you. The way the book talks, whoever drinks this is gonna fall eternally in love with you, and they stay that way till they die. Okay?"

"Jesus fuck," said Joseph, "till they die?! I'm only sixteen damn years old, Scilly, I'm just tryin' to get laid for the first time, you couldn't have made it last a little shorter than that?"

Priscilla grinned. "Just messin' with ya," she said. "It lasts for two weeks."

Joseph let out a relieved sigh, but then he said, "Well, what happens after two weeks?"

"Ya know," said Priscilla, considering the question for the first time. "I don't know exactly. I guess it wears off." The book hadn't mentioned anything about this, and she was, honestly, not sure.

Joseph cocked his head at her. "So what if I got my hand up her shirt when it wears off?"

Big Tommy let out a bashful laugh, and Priscilla grinned again. She said, "I don't know, Joseph. Maybe you should just go about it the old-fashioned way, ya know, like take a bath every once in a while, comb yer hair, shave that stupid fuckin' mustache. If you want a girl to have sex with you, maybe you should just, I dunno, ask her."

Joseph glared at her. "Don't you dare. Oh, no, don't you dare try to take this away from me. I see what yer doin', don't think I don't. You are not gonna ruin this for me, I'm not gonna let ya. I been lookin' forward to this for too damn long. I done sold my soul to the Devil for this here potion, and I'm gonna enjoy myself, even if it's only two weeks. So you can wipe that shit-eatin' grin right off yer stinkin' face. Matter of fact, we goin' up to see Mathias Elder and his sweet, beautiful daughters tomorrow. You hear me? Tomorrow."

Still grinning, Priscilla said, "Give me a couple days. I'm makin' somethin' for Mathias to thank him for the book. I can't give it back, not now. Maybe not ever, and I don't wanna go back up there empty handed. Come on, don't look at me like that. I'll stop messin' with ya. Just wait two days."

"Alright then, *Samantha*," said Joseph. "Get to wigglin' yer nose, you got two days."

◆

Thursday, December Ninth, Nineteen Seventy-One

Gertrude Green stares into a cracked and dirty mirror. A thick patch of black mold has overtaken the wall behind it. The black mold creeps up the wall and on to the ceiling. The light above the mirror flickers. In her reflection, Gertrude remains expressionless. She is lost somewhere in her mind.

Gertrude was born in Southern Alabama in nineteen ten. The daughter of Herbert and Bertha Green, Gertrude was born with a vestigial parasitic twin. Besides a single leg that grew out of her lower back, Gertrude's twin sister had formed completely inside of her. Somehow, in the womb, she had absorbed her sister, and become her host. At three years old, the spare leg was amputated, and for a while, in the beginning anyway, it seemed like little Gertrude would turn out just fine, but as the years went on, things changed.

By the age of eleven, Gertrude was six feet tall and weighed two hundred and three pounds, and her behavior had become increasingly violent, because, according to the young Gertrude, her twin sister, Gladys 'whispered evil to her.' Unfortunately, for Gertrude, her parents had grown to fear her, and the idea that their rapidly-growing daughter had an evil twin living inside her, speaking to her and convincing her to commit violence, was an idea that neither Herbert nor Bertha could even begin to comprehend in any meaningful way. So, unfortunately for Gertrude, she was handed over to the state of Alabama.

Diagnosed with Dementia Praecox, more commonly known as schizophrenia, no one, not her parents, not the doctors, not even the other mentally ill children she was housed with, took seriously Gertrude's rantings of a malevolent sibling claiming squatters' rights inside her. Gladys was an auditory hallucination, or so they told her. That is, until the day Gertrude, at twelve years old and four hundred and twenty-nine pounds, got her first period. A heavy one.

On that day, with Gertrude strapped to a bed by her wrists and ankles, her white hospital gown and the white sheets on the bed, drenched with blood, a doctor and two nurses watched Gertrude thrash about in agony. They watched the skin on her torso bulge and stretch, almost to the point of ripping, as what were obviously hands and feet and elbows and knees pushed and punched and kicked from within her, in what seemed an obvious attempt to escape. At one point a perfectly formed face, frozen in a scream, appeared just below Gertrude's right breast. The face pressed hard against the inner lining of her skin, like it was attempting to breach the surface of water for air, so hard that the doctor was sure that it was going to break through Gertrude's flesh, and come gasping and shrieking into existence.

And when it didn't, when the face seemed to eventually give up, or drown, or die, settling back into Gertrude's body to, he could only assume, be consumed, the doctor crossed himself. One of the nurses was crying and moaning. The other nurse was holding the crying nurse, and she was muttering, *Oh dear Jesus, oh dear Jesus*, over and over, and over. Gertrude, now calm, was watching them all. In her tired, blood-filled eyes was rage, and the words *I told you so* were written plainly in her smile. The blood between her legs had ceased its flow. Figuratively speaking, for Gertrude anyway, it was Independence Day.

After that, Gertrude no longer heard Gladys's voice. She hoped she would also no longer continue to gain weight, but she wasn't that lucky. And in another testament to her luck, or lack thereof, despite the fact that she didn't hear her sister's voice anymore, she was not released from the asylum. She was kept there for three more years. Neither the doctor nor the two nurses was able to admit what they had witnessed and Gertrude continued to be treated as a schizophrenic. Of the paranoid type, at that. When she was sixteen, the asylum lost funding and she, along with all of the other patients, was released. She was never vindicated.

Now, staring between the cracks on the dirty mirror, the mold on the wall undulating in her peripherals, the veins standing out on her forehead, Gertrude is thinking about her days in the asylum, about her Independence Day, and about Gladys. It was the taste of the blue potion that she had, only moments ago, consumed, that got her thinking. It reminded her of the taste she would get in the back of her throat after the nurses would inject her with sedatives. And sure, the taste of the potion sickened her, but at the same time, it carried with it a sort of morbid nostalgia, and before Gertrude turned out the light, still staring into the mirror, she said, "Goodnight, Gladys."

◆

FRIDAY, DECEMBER TENTH, NINETEEN SEVENTY-ONE

Big Tommy had spent the night at his mother's house. It was her behavior that concerned him. After handing her the potion and giving her Priscilla's instructions, she began acting strange. Strange even for her. It was true, his mother was an ugly and nasty human being in most every regard, that much was obvious even to Tommy, but, nevertheless, he still cared deeply for her, and when he saw her hands trembling like they were, the vile of potion threatening to wriggle free of her grasp, he gave pause. He took notice of her general behavior and after a short evaluation, he decided to stay with her. His mother was a lot of things, but nervous or shaky was not one of them. She was deliberate with her movements, steady, and so much sharper than anyone would ever expect.

So Tommy stuck around, and he sat up all night. He wanted to be there just in case something went wrong. Not that he didn't believe in Priscilla, he did, but she was new to the whole witch-craft business, and this was his mother, after all. As bad as she was, she was his mother, she had given him life, and he would never forgive himself if anything went wrong and he was not there to help her.

Just as the sun was coming up, Tommy began to fade. His eye-lids got heavy, and he was just on the edge of sleep when a blood-curdling scream erupted from his mother's room, and brought him up and out of his chair. For a moment he was confused, it didn't quite sound like his mother. He thought maybe he had dreamed the scream. Then it came again, another shriek, sharp and loud, and Tommy broke for the stairs.

By the time he got to the top of the staircase, she had stopped screaming, and he could hear her crying. As he approached her bedroom door, he slowed his pace. There was something else now, in addition to the crying… Was it… Was it… laughter he was hearing? His mind raced to make sense of it, and he hesitated in reaching for the doorknob, but with all the nervous worry that one great-big sweet boy could stomach, Tommy eased open the door to his mother's room.

A long slow creaking sound followed, and what Tommy saw standing in front of his mother's old broken vanity mirror nearly buckled his knees.

◆

Priscilla was alone in her lair. The hood of her cloak was up. Over the last few weeks, the cave had really started to feel like home, as had her cloak. The more time she spent in the cave, in her lair, wrapped in her cloak, toiling over her cauldron, the less time she spent worrying about the rest of the world and all the mundane and trivial problems that came along with it. Thoughts of Everett, thoughts of her mother, thoughts of Lucky, thoughts of living in an actual house, thoughts of electric lights, thoughts of school and teachers, thoughts of church, they all seemed to be dissipating into the ether of her mind. Even Maw Scill was a phantom in Priscilla's recollection.

As hard as it may be to believe, that dank, dark cave, with its spiders, and damp, drafty air, was the one place on earth Priscilla felt she could call her very own. And rarely, in those days, did she leave. In fact, she slept there alone for the first time the previous night, and she had been waiting for Big Tommy to show up all morning. She had only just finished dismembering a dead crow when he finally arrived. It was nearly noon.

Priscilla hadn't exactly been worried, but she had been pretty darn curious as to how Gertrude was going to react to her potion. Priscilla was a real-life, no bullshit, Satanic witch, she was sure of that much, but she was new to this, and she was also just a kid— her confidence level wavered constantly. So, despite her success thus far, she was more than mildly interested in the results of her latest experiment. To say the least, Gertrude's overall satisfaction weighed heavily on Priscilla. Health concerns and side-effects be damned. Was she satisfied, was the question Priscilla really wanted an answer to.

And she got that answer, the very moment Tommy came into sight. It was obvious by the bounce in his step, and the glow on his face. Had Gertrude woken up a boneless blob of skin, there was no way Tommy would be beaming like he was. "Another satisfied customer," Priscilla said to herself.

"She's beautiful, Scilly! I can't believe it. I mean she is knockdown, drag out, drop dead, slap me silly, gorgeous! I mean a stunner, a real stunner! I just can't believe it! It's like a miracle!" Big Tommy was clearly elated.

Priscilla attempted to calm him. "Easy, easy, Big Tom. Slow down. Whoa, heyyyyyy. Heyyy."

Tommy wasn't listening. He came right up to Priscilla, wrapped his big arms around her, and lifted her off her feet. "A miracle, it's a miracle," he said, as he spun her around in circles. "You'd never believe it! She's beautiful!"

After a few spins, Tommy sat Priscilla down. In the couple of months Priscilla had known Big Tommy, she had not seen him quite this happy, nor had she ever heard him speak above much more than a whisper, and so she was compelled to let him keep on, but her ego wasn't about to let God get credit for this one.

"Whoa, big fella. Two things," said Priscilla. "First, I'm glad yer momma's happy, but that weren't no miracle. It was witchcraft. I did that. Me. Priscilla. Got that. And second, oh my gosh, keep on goin', tell me everything. I want details."

Big Tommy smiled even bigger. "Well," he said, back to his normal, hushed tone, "she been sewin' a new dress all mornin'. Ain't none of her clothes fit her. She's tiny now, not much bigger'n you. She made me go down to Layfield's to buy her new makeup, red lipstick even, and smaller pads to soak up her monthlies… Oh, and her eyeball ain't even cocked no more."

"Really?! I set her eye straight?!"

"Mmmhmm, straight as can be! She said she still can't see out it, though. She said her heart still hurts her somethin' awful, too… And her breath still stinks like eggs, that ain't change a bit. But I tell ya, she's purtier than anything you ever seen."

"She ain't mad I switched potions on her?"

"Naw, she was too busy starin' in the mirror to be mad, and— say, Scilly, you might wanna grab Lightnin'."

Priscilla turned to find Lightning on top of her altar, casually gnawing on crow remains. "Bad kitty," said Priscilla, as she scooped her Familiar into her arms. "That crow is not for you."

According to the book, Priscilla should eventually be able to control Lightning as an extension of herself, but so far, this was not the case. Like every cat Priscilla had ever come across in her life, Lightning seemed to do only what Lightning wanted and nothing more.

"No," said Priscilla, five octaves higher than normal, as she stroked Lightning's fur. "That crow is not for you. That crow is for our friend Mathias. Yes it is, it's for Mathias. Do you hear me, little kitty? It's for our friend. Yes it is. Good little kitty."

◆

When the bell finally rang, Joseph nearly sprung from his desk. He'd been watching the clock above the chalk board, like an apathetic hawk, for the last hour. All he could think about was the weekend. It was Friday, and that meant no more rules, no more books, no more teachers' dirty fucking looks, but it also meant that he was less than twenty-four hours from being back in the arms of his four exotic loves, Phuket, Kut, Samet, and whatever the other one's name was.

He had it all planned out. After checking in with Priscilla and Tommy at the cave, he would go home, do his chores, and shave his mustache, because Priscilla and Tommy were right, it looked like dirt. Then he would trim his fingernails, bathe, watch some television, and go to sleep early. He wanted to be fresh and clean come morning. He knew the Elders had a keen sense of smell, and Joseph did not want to offend.

Dead bodies, beach balls, pirate ships, rubber ducks, they all drooled at the way Joseph went along with his feet two inches from the ground, floating as it were. His eyes glossed over like some kind of speed freak at a Sunday night drive-in, staring up at the screen all hollow-eyed like the rest of the world didn't exist. All the way down the front drive of the school, Joseph went about like this, oblivious, floating. Not literally, of course, no spells had been cast, but he was floating the way one does when one is swept up and driven by the prospect and possibilities of new love.

So needless to say, as Joseph made his merry way into the woods behind his uncle's house, he had no idea whatsoever that he was being followed.

◆

Merle Mire Junior was his father's first son. Kester was Merle's little brother. What bothered Merle the most was not the fact that Joseph Smith had attacked him, or his little brother, or knocked out his little sister, but that Joseph had made Kester squeal for his mother. The Mire kids had taken many beatings over the years, fighting and violence were common in their world, but it was the fact that Joseph had shamed Kester that really made Merle hot. And Merle Mire Junior just could not let that go. Upholding what was left of his family name, of his father's name, was a burden he accepted without much question. Besides, after the elbow Joseph planted on his chin, he wanted blood.

The original plan, after Merle and Kester followed Joseph to the cave the first time, was to beat him and strip him, to leave him tied up in that cave for a day or two, maybe piss on him or something, then set him free. But then they saw what Merle called 'the giant nigger' come out of the cave, and their plans changed quicker than rabbits fucking. For several days they laid in the brush, watching the mouth of the cave. From what they could tell it was only Joseph, his little cunt girlfriend, and the 'big coon' that ever came and went. What they were doing inside the cave, neither Merle nor Kester could determine.

The new plan was cattle prods. Thirty-six inch, eight thousand volt, cattle prods. Merle borrowed them from the man whose farm he shoveled shit on. "If they can drop a cow, they can drop that giant nigger," Merle had said. Kester agreed.

It all could have worked out, too. The Mire Clan could have had their revenge, their day of brutal vengeance. They could have taught that cocky little Smith boy a real lesson about respect. They could have restored honor to the Mire family name. Yes, they certainly could have. But there was one small problem. One small, furry black problem. And without either Merle or Kester's knowledge, that small, furry black problem was sitting in a tree, high above their heads, watching them, licking its furry little paws.

◆

It came to Priscilla with perfect clarity. A vision. Joseph had just showed up, and she and Tommy were in the process of cramming an undead crow into a small cage when, all of a sudden, out of nowhere, she was struck with a vision of tree limbs and branches and leaves. *What the fuck is goin' on?* The thought barely went through her head before it was dashed away by the force of the continuing vision. Beyond the limbs and leaves, she could see Kester Mire and another man crouched behind a fallen tree. With a quality of sight that far surpassed her own, she could hear them and she could see them talking, and she could see them watching and pointing at a cave.

But whoa, wait a second, Kester Mire and this other man, they weren't watching just any old cave. That was Dead Kid Cave. That was her cave. They were watching Priscilla's cave. Her lair. They were outside.

Then she saw the two men get up and move toward the cave—was it actually her cave? It looked like her cave. Yes, it was her cave. Priscilla was desperately trying to make sense of what she was visualizing. Then it hit her, what was happening. She was seeing through Lightning. And what she was seeing, the two men outside her cave, coming toward her cave, was happening now. What she was seeing was happening now. *Holy fuck, it's happening now.*

And just like that, she snapped out of it. Priscilla slammed shut the door to the crow cage, and as quickly and directly as she could, she spoke. "Kester Mire and another man are outside with cattle prods, they'll be in here in maybe fifteen seconds, blow out all the candles and grab some rocks. Quick, Joseph, goddamn it! Now!"

When Merle entered the mouth of the cave the sun was high in the sky. His blood was pumping clean, and between the cattle prod and the Old Grandad he felt as good and cocksure as any

Mire ever felt. But as soon as he rounded the first corner, and the cave turned dark, he knew he fucked up. And good.

The first rock that came out of the darkness hit Kester square in the face. It shattered his front teeth, likely broke his nose, and knocked him out cold. Merle ducked, instinctively, as another rock whizzed by his head, but then another rock, the size of a softball, hit him in the neck, and that one brought him to his knees. He gasped for air as a sharp pain coursed from his throat to his brain, and another rock tagged him above his ear. Then another rock. And another. He fell on to his back, clutching at his neck and head. The tables had turned. He was out of options. He lifted the cattle prod and pulled the trigger, zapping nothing but air. It was all there was left to do.

It was to no avail, however. As soon as the prod began to spark, it was snatched from his hand, and a giant black fist came crashing into his jaw, decimating his consciousness instantaneously.

The last thing Merle Junior saw, in that brief, static, flash of electric light from his raised prod, scared him more than he had ever been scared before, and he pissed himself. It was only a glimpse, stained in crackling blue-white light from the prod, but what he saw chilled his previously boiling blood, and made him want to cry out for his mother. Dozens of animal skulls and bones, a spinal column, candles, a jar of eyeballs, a crow in a cage, mushrooms, bloody pentagrams, an inverted cross, an altar, the skeleton of a child, a little girl in a cloak, a black cat, a bathtub. Then, a black fist. THUD! Lights out.

While unconscious, Merle had a dream. It was a good dream, too, but it didn't last long, and when he came to, at the end of a cattle prod, it didn't matter that he had forgotten what the dream was about because he was tied up and fucked. And when a man is tied up and fucked, his dreams matter very little. Even the good ones.

TWO SEVEN NINE

"Well," said Joseph. "That there is Kester Mire, and that there is his older brother. Merle, I think his name is."

Priscilla was relighting candles as Joseph and Tommy dragged the two comatose men closer to the bathtub. Although Kester had only been hit by one rock, it had been Big Tommy's rock, and Kester's face was pulverized. Merle Junior, in comparison, had gotten off easy. There was a wound on his head, but there wasn't a single drop of blood anywhere on him.

"Leave 'em propped against the cauldron," said Priscilla. "Tie their wrists and ankles. I know just what to do with these two fuckers."

Joseph dropped Kester's legs, and Kester hit the ground. "You reckon maybe you wanna fill me and Tommy in on this plan of yers, Scilly? I mean, I know yer a witch and all, and I don't know about you, Tommy, but I ain't tryin' to spend the rest of my damn life in jail for murder."

"I don't wanna go to jail," said Tommy.

"Murder!? What the shit makes you think I'm gonna murder somebody?" said Priscilla.

"Hell, I don't know, I just figured, well—what, with you bein' all dark and evil, now."

"I don't wanna go to jail," said Tommy, again.

"Goddamnit, ain't nobody goin' to jail, and I ain't about to do no murderin' on nobody, neither. Now finish tyin' them up 'fore they start to stir. Are you even sure Kester ain't already dead?"

"He ain't dead," said Joseph. "I can see him breathin', and hell, old Merle here, he's smilin'."

"Stupendous," said Priscilla. She picked up her book and began leafing through its pages. After finding what she was looking for, she sat the book on her altar and began mixing and mashing different things in a crucible. Finished with securing the Mire brothers, Joseph and Big Tommy stood back and watched Priscilla work. Her pace was feverish. Lightning watched, too, from the shadows.

After a few minutes, Joseph said, "So if you ain't fixin' to kill these fellers, Scilly, you mind tellin' us just what it is that you are fixin' to do, or is that like top secret witchin' shit?"

Priscilla spun on her heels to face him. She was still a rather innocent-looking little girl, but the grin on her face was as evil as anything ever conceived during the holocaust, and the twinkle in her eye was brighter than a morning star.

Calm as can be, she said, "Slaves, Joseph. I'm gonna make them our slaves. Sound good? Great. Now hit 'em with the fuckin' cattle prod. They have to be awake for this."

◆

Saturday, December Eleventh, Nineteen Seventy-One

"Sit, slaves," said Priscilla. She was standing in front of her altar.

Merle said, "Fuck you, you fuckin' bitch," but he sat, anyway. Kester sat too. They both seemed unnerved by their inability to not follow Priscilla's instructions. Joseph and Tommy stood over them with the cattle prods.

"Kester, punch yer brother in the face as hard as you can," said Priscilla.

Kester looked at his brother, and said, "I'm sorry," but just as the words came out of his mouth, his fist came from out of nowhere and blasted Merle square in the nose.

"Ah, what the fuck, brother," said Merle.

"Shit, I'm sorry, Merle, I'm out of control."

"Good slave," said Priscilla. "Now stand up. Both of you."

Merle Junior and Kester both stood up, and looked at one

another. Merle Junior's nose leaked blood, but it was dark blood, almost black.

"Now, bark like a dog," said Priscilla, and just like that, both Kester and Merle began to bark and whine like blood hounds. Kester even howled.

"Enough," said Priscilla, and the barking stopped.

"Enough is right, you little bitch," said Merle. "I don't know what the fuck you did to us, you no good nigger-lovin' mother-fucker, but I promise to God, I am gonna kill you for this."

Priscilla grinned. Tommy stepped toward Merle, and drew back his fist.

Priscilla halted him. She said, "Thank you, Tommy, but I'll take care of this."

Then she said, "Merle, let Kester kick you in the nuts. Kester, kick Merle in the nuts. Hard."

They did as they were told.

With one of her slaves on the ground holding his testicles and the other slave standing over him, Priscilla said, 'Listen to me, motherfuckers, and listen real good. You are mine now. I own you. I own yer mind. I own yer body. I am yer master. You will lick cat shit off my boot if I tell you to. You will chew off yer own arm, rip off yer own dick, or throw yerself in front of a speedin' fuckin' train, if that is what I want, and if I ever hear either of you ever say the word nigger again, I will castrate both of you, balls, dick, and all. And I will feed the pieces to Lightnin'. Actually, now that I'm thinkin' of it, I'll make you castrate yerselves. And again, I will feed the pieces to Lightnin'. Do you fuckin' understand?"

Priscilla could have simply told them both not to say the word nigger, and as her slaves, they would not have been able to do otherwise, but where was the fun in that?

Neither of the slaves spoke, but they surely understood. Priscilla looked down at the open black book in her arms and began reading aloud. "Yer orders are this. In the name of Satan, and as slaves of this coven, you shall never speak of this coven to any livin' soul outside of this coven. You shall never admit yer enslavement to this coven, or speak of any of the events surroundin' yer enslavement. As slaves of this coven, you shall do my biddin', and that of my brethren, Joseph Smith and Tommy Green, and of my Familiar, Lightnin'. As slaves of this coven, you shall die, if necessary, to protect yer master and all members of this coven, from harm or compromise, of any sort. In the name of Satan, the Lord of Flies, these are yer orders."

Priscilla closed the book and slipped it into her shoulder pack. Her slaves gazed vacantly at her, their mouths hanging open as if entranced by an Egyptian death jewel. Kester was standing, and Merle was still on the ground holding his crotch with one hand. Priscilla watched them for a moment, admiring her handy work. Then she took a deep breath and smiled, and in an all-of-a-sudden chipper voice, she said, "Now, Merle, Kester, it's a beautiful day today, and we got some things to do. So I want you two dipshits to stand guard, just inside the cave. Make sure you don't let no one in while we're gone, and don't you dare touch a fuckin' thing. There's clean water in that jug, and when we get back, I'll let you go home and see yer family. Kester, you can take care of yer teeth then."

Kester began to whimper. He hadn't spoken much all morning, and when he did, his voice was trembling. He said, "Th-th-thank you, Priscilla, and I'm…real sorry, Joseph."

Merle Junior said, "Jesus fuckin' Christ, would ya look who turned pussy, now. Yer a goddamn shame to our daddy's name, you know that? Ain't you got no pride?"

Priscilla shook her head with exasperation. "Merle," she said. "Punch yerself in the face. Twice. I wanna hear a bone break."

◆

On the walk to see Mathias, Priscilla felt like she was Dorothy in the Wizard of Oz, well, the Satanic hillbilly Wizard of Oz, anyway. Instead of a Toto, she had a Lightning. And Joseph, well, he was clearly the Tinman in search of a heart, or at the very least, a piece of ass. Tommy, the living embodiment of the Cowardly Lion, was in search of courage, obviously, and the crow, the one sitting calmly in the cage that Priscilla was carrying, well he, whether he knew it or not, was on a journey to find a new brain, or to align itself with one, at the very least. All that was missing, as far as Priscilla could tell, was a yellow brick road and a pair of ruby slippers that she could click together if the shit hit the fan.

Though it was indeed her home, it felt good to be out of the cave, and despite having to wear civilian clothing for the first time in a while, she was happy to be breathing in the cold December air, to feel it on her skin, and to be skipping along the path to see her unusual friend and benefactor, Mathias. *The wizard.*

In general, there was excitement in the air. Joseph was a little pissy because he stayed up all night helping Priscilla enslave people, and didn't have a chance to shave or bathe, but she covered him in jasmine oil, and that seemed to make him feel better. Tommy, ever positive, was just happy to be invited somewhere, and to meet new people, especially people that he had heard so many fascinating and wonderful things about. And Lightning, well, she was just mauling and thrashing chipmunks and mice, all along the way, so she was obviously enjoying herself. Even the crow seemed to be delighting in the journey.

All in all, Priscilla was having a right, pleasant day. She was a witch. She was a witch, and she had a gift for Mathias that she was sure he would love, a gift that she hoped would serve as payment for the book that she borrowed but intended to keep. And, to top it off, she even had two brand-new slaves waiting for her back at her lair. Yep, when it came down to it, it was a damn fine day to be a witch.

The looming cliff face with the iron framed door in the center, bearing the inscription one nine zero nine, looked different during the day. It looked less like the entrance to Hell and more like the home of an elderly, scholarly troll, sort of quaint and somewhat inviting. It had taken them nearly two hours to make it to that point, and now, standing before the ancient door, Priscilla had the feeling, once again, that she was in Oz.

Priscilla handed the crow cage to Big Tommy, and she retrieved the rusty old key from her shoulder pack. Lightning was sitting in front of the door, waiting. Priscilla stepped around her cat, and inserted the key in the lock. When the door opened, she expected to hear piano music, but there was none. The tunnel inside the rock was dark and quiet.

During the day, the outside of the rock looked much different, but the inside of the rock did not. As they walked along the tunnel, past the spiders and stone mastiffs, Priscilla couldn't help but remember how frightened she had been the first time she had come through there. It seemed like a lifetime ago, or like it hadn't even been her who had been there before. She was essentially a completely different person than the girl she was then, mentally anyway, and walking through the tunnel, that fact couldn't have been more clear to her.

To think that she had once been afraid of the dark, or the woods, or of strangers, even blind ones, was ridiculous. Just look at her now, leading the way through the tunnel, the boys trailing her. She simply couldn't be the same girl she once was. It was the same rock, and the same tunnel, no matter how they appeared in the day or night, that was evident enough, but she was certainly not the same girl.

The first Elder they ran into was Zacharias. He was walking up from the common house that was connected to the library and kitchen, toward the fire pit.

Priscilla hollered, "Hey Zacharias Elder, you old stinker!"

Zacharias stopped walking and turned toward them, clicking his tongue. Then he put one hand over his heart, and said, "Land sakes alive, if it ain't the one and only Priscilla Carpenter. Get over here and give yer cousin Zachy a hug. Good Lord, you smell like nine kinds of death…and what is that…sandalwood? What do I smell on you? It's uh… It's funky."

After a round of introductions, Zacharias said, "Y'all just wait here. I'll go fetch Thias, for ye. Just sit tight. I'll be right back." He said it so casually, like it was just another day. Then he scampered off toward the common house.

Within a few moments, Mathias appeared in the doorway and he walked out on to the porch, shouting, "Come on down, come on down."

The next five minutes of Priscilla's life went by in an ultra, slow-motion blur. First Mathias hugged her tight, then he shook Joseph's hand, and introduced himself to Big Tommy. Then after commenting on their collective stench, to Priscilla, Mathias said, "I gotta surprise for you," and he stomped his foot down hard, three times, causing the whole porch to vibrate.

Priscilla instantly heard a rumbling inside the house, followed by the sound of a dog's bark, and all of a sudden Lucky burst through the doorway on to the porch. Mathias said, "Looky who Elias found."

Lucky ran directly to Priscilla, and began licking her and jumping on her, whining and whimpering. He nearly knocked her over, but she didn't care. She was too happy. She couldn't believe it was him. He looked so healthy and alive. Even his coat seemed to have a shine to it. She had never seen him look that way before. At some point, Lucky noticed Lightning lurking behind Big Tommy, and Lucky attempted to introduce himself, but Lightning put an end to that idea quick. As soon as Lucky got within five feet of her, the cat began hissing and showing her claws, and Lucky backed away fast as he could. Lucky knew damn well better than to play with that fire. Even Big Tommy took a step back. Lightning was still a kitten, but she wasn't necessarily little anymore, and it was obvious just by looking at her that she was not a cat to be fucked with.

"Yeah," said Mathias, "Elias got one hell of a nose on him. He tracked Lucky down the day after you left. I been takin' real good care of him. He sleeps at the foot of my bed now. Comes to my foot stomp, feels the vibrations. He's a real sweet dog. We get on well, me blind and him deaf and all."

Then Mathias said, "But hey, I near forgot, I got one more surprise for ye," and he stuck two fingers in his mouth and gave a quick whistle.

And all of a sudden, there he was, like he had never been gone. He just appeared in the doorway, smiling. His hair was longer and bleached blonde by the sun, and he had a light beard, but Priscilla knew it was him the moment she saw him. And with that recognition, her heart began to swell.

Her brother had come home.

"Is that you, Priscilla Louise?" said Jeremiah Carpenter, just as charmingly as any man could.

Priscilla was up on the porch with her arms wrapped around him before she even had time to think. She squeezed him tight around his mid-section and pressed her face into his chest. He smelled just as she remembered, like river water and campfire smoke.

"Well I missed you too, little sis," said Jeremiah.

Priscilla squeezed him even tighter. "Momma thinks yer

dead," she said.

"Yeah," said Jeremiah, "I figured she might. I'm goin' to see her tonight. Now look up here at me, let me see that pretty little face of yers."

Reluctantly, Priscilla let go of him, and looked up.

"Girl, look at you. You have grown up. You must have gained a foot since last time I seen you. Done went and got pretty as hell, too. How old are you now, fifteen?"

"Yep, for two more months," said Priscilla, obviously blushing.

"Wow…," said Jeremiah. "Just, wow… You are a sight for sore eyes. No offense, Mathias."

"Ah, go fuck yourself," said Mathias.

Jeremiah grinned. "Man, it sure is good to be back," he said. Then he paused and squinted his eyes, and said, "Holy shit. If it isn't the one and only Joseph Smith." Jeremiah came down off the porch and gave Joseph a big hug and a wink, saying, "It's good to see ya, buddy. Long time. Glad to see my sister's still keepin' ya around."

Then, still hugging Joseph, Jeremiah said, "Alright, so are one of y'all gonna introduce me to this giant fella with the crow here, or what?"

◆

Roughly eleven minutes later, Priscilla, Tommy, Jeremiah, and Mathias were gathered around the bar in the library. Jeremiah was playing bartender. Joseph was off in search of Kut, Samui, Samet, and Phuket, who Mathias had said were washing clothes in the creek. Well, Mathias actually said *crick*, and he also said *warshing*, but the fact remains the same. Lightning was killing a mouse inside the Elders' barn. Priscilla knew what her Familiar was up to because she kept having sporadic visions of it, and truth be told, it was kind of freaking her out. Controlling her new ability to see through Lightning was something that she was definitely going to have to work on. *Poor little mouse.*

"First of all, why are yer hands so damn black? You get a job in the mines? Is yer soap broke?" Jeremiah asked the questions casually as he prepared drinks.

"... Can we talk about that later..." Priscilla replied.

"Alright... How's Momma?"

"Well," said Priscilla, shaking the image of a bloody mouse from her mind, "it's been a while since I seen her, but she's the same, I reckon. Still drinkin' a lot."

"What do you mean, it's been a while since you seen her?"

Priscilla was not sure exactly how to respond to this question. However, it seemed like her best option was to start from the beginning. Just coming right out and saying that she had spent most of the last two months shacked up in a cave with Big Tommy, practicing Satanic witchcraft seemed...abrupt, to say the least. It had to come up, eventually of course. She had brought the crow for Mathias, and that would have to be explained soon, but not just yet. No, not just yet. Besides, she also had to tell Jeremiah that Everett was not his father, and that was a whole other situation altogether. And so, this was all going to require a bit of tact.

"Well..." Priscilla said. "Well, Everett kicked Lucky, so Lucky bit off his hand, and—"

"Bit off his hand...his whole hand?"

"Well no, not the whole hand, but most of it. He really got him good. But then Everett hit me with his chainsaw, and—"

"Whoa, whoa, what the fuck, what do you mean he hit you with his chainsaw, like with the blade?"

"No, the engine... Knocked me out... Split my head. Look here." Priscilla leaned forward and parted her hair to show her scar.

"Jesus Christ," said Jeremiah. "Alright...go on."

Priscilla went on. "Well, after he knocked me out, Momma thought it'd be best if I stayed with Maw Maw. I think Momma's scared Everett's gettin' worse-meaner. I think he's been drinkin' more too…cause he ain't workin'…and that's part of it."

Mathias and Tommy sat quietly, listening, as Jeremiah buried his head in his hands. "Goddamnit," Jeremiah said, softly. "I don't know why I would have expected things to get any better while I was away…" After a moment he sort of shook his head, and said, "Well, how's Maw Maw, is she good at least?"

Oh boy, here we go. "She's…good," said Priscilla, "but uh…I ain't seen her in a while neither…"

Jeremiah was clearly confused. "Wait, what—what do you mean, where the hell you been stayin'? With Joseph?"

Priscilla let out a long sigh, and massaged her forehead. *Oh boy*, she thought. *Here we go.* "Okay, so I gotta lot to say, and I don't know how to say it, so I'm just gonna tell ya. And it's gonna sound crazy, and yer not gonna believe me, but that don't matter cause I'm gonna prove it to ya after. So, just listen to me, alright?"

Jeremiah, Mathias, and even Tommy all nodded in unison. Jeremiah said, "Take it easy, little sister. Take yer time. Tell us what you gotta tell us. Ain't no masks round here."

"Damn right," confirmed Mathias.

"Damn right," said Jeremiah, and he reached across the bar and clapped Mathias on the shoulder.

"Okay," said Priscilla, "here we go… So, alright… So, Mathias, you remember when me and Joseph first came up here, and you told me to borrow a book or two…?"

"I do," said Mathias.

"Well…I borrowed yer witchcraft book, and…now I'm a witch. And I been sorta…livin' in a cave the last couple months… with Big Tommy…he's my assistant…and friend, of course…and I bewitched this here crow to give you sight, Mathias… as a, well, as a thank you…for the book."

The room was silent. There was a whole lot of absorbing going on. Big Tommy's eyes were wide and nervous-looking. Finally, Jeremiah said, "Okay. My little sister done lost her mind. She's around the bend, who needs another drink?"

"See, I told ya. I knew you'd think I was crazy! Well, I ain't. I ain't crazy."

"Sis, I hear what you're sayin'," said Jeremiah, "but I just can't—"

Tommy spoke up. "She ain't lyin," he said, his voice like the low E on a standup bass. "She ain't crazy, neither. She's a real life witch… She turned my mommy beautiful. And she made it rain piss."

Mathias nearly choked on his liquor. He gagged and then sat up straight, his cloudy, opaque eyes shining with what appeared to be astonishment.

"Christ, what? You alright?" said Jeremiah.

Mathias settled back on to the barstool, and took a breath. Then he said, "It took me three days to get the smell outta my hair.'"

"What the fuck," said Jeremiah. "You mean piss? Yer cosignin' this shit? You mean it actually—"

"Yeah, I mean it actually rained piss. Warm, acidic piss,'" said Mathias. "On Halloween night. I thought the goddamn world was endin'.'"

"What in the name of fuck are you three talkin' about?" Jeremiah asked, earnestly.

"I'm a witch,' said Priscilla, 'and I made it rain piss on Halloween this year."

"She did," said Big Tommy. "Then she puked all over Joseph."

The room was once again quiet for a time. Then Jeremiah said, "Oh, we are havin' another drink," and he pulled all four glasses to the center of the bar and began pouring whiskey in them.

Mathias said, "So…let me see if I got this straight. You found a witchcraft book in my library, you used that book to become a witch, you made it rain piss from the sky, and you have a crow in a cage that's gonna give me back my sight. Do I have that straight?"

"Yes," said Priscilla. "Well mostly. See I wanted to cast a spell that would fix yer eyes, but for some reason, all the human Vision Restoration spells are all Level Four spells, and I've only made it to Level Two so far, and I can't skip steps, the book makes that real clear. So, I can't fix yer eyes, not yet, but this crow here, I got him hexed, and he can be yer eyes till I get to Level Four. I mean…if ya want…"

They all watched Mathias, waiting for his response. It didn't come quick, but when it came, it came with conviction. "You ain't lied to me once yet," he said. "I'd know if you did. So either yer bat shit fuckin' crazy, or yer a witch… And I don't reckon yer crazy. I've seen some weird and unexplainable shit in my day. Hell, I seen piss rain from the sky. Well, I ain't see it exactly, but I damn sure witnessed it. I know it happened. So…if you say you can make that crow be my eyes, well, I reckon I owe it to ya to believe it." Then he said, "So give me the gift of sight, kid."

"You want it?"

"I want it."

Stoned and in an extraordinary state of awe, Jeremiah said, "This is too far out."

"Alright," said Priscilla, "let's do it." Then she stood up and walked to the center of the library. She returned with the bird cage, and sat it in front of Mathias, on the bar.

"How does this work, exactly?" asked Mathias.

"Well, I don't…exactly know," said Priscilla. "I do know, all you have to do is open the cage, and let the crow out, for the spell to take hold. And once it's free, well, I think you ought to be able to see through his eyes."

Mathias paused for several moments, thinking, then he said, "Let's do it outside. If this works, the sky's the first thing I'd like to see… Is that alright?"

Priscilla considered the question, and she couldn't find any harm in it, so they all filled their glasses one more time and went outside. Priscilla's adrenalin was running so high that the alcohol had hardly even touched her. She could feel her heart beating in her chest, and she could hear it in her ears. *Please let this work,* she thought. Please let this work.

Mathias stood on the porch at the top of the steps. Priscilla, Big Tommy, Lucky, and Jeremiah were gathered behind him. Several Elders were scattered about the property, engaged in different activities, blind gardening, and blind wood gathering, and such. Several of the younger Elders seemed to be playing blind hide and go seek. Priscilla could see Joseph across the property, leaning against a tree, talking to one of Mathias's daughters while she swung back and forth on a tire swing, her hair flowing out behind her. Blind swinging.

In one hand, out in front of him, Mathias held the bird cage, and for several seconds he only stood there, staring up at the sky with his broken eyes. What he was thinking about, Priscilla could only imagine. She looked at Tommy, who was already watching her, and tried to smile. Tommy put his arm around her shoulders, and pulled her close. Then Mathias opened the cage.

At first the crow didn't move. It sat, perched, in the center of the cage. It flicked its head back and forth, and made several clicking noises, but it just stood there. It looked as though it was debating whether or not to attempt escape, searching for possible traps or obstacles.

Then it moved. It stepped from the center perch to the ledge of the cage's opening. Priscilla was waiting for it to take right off into the sky, wings flapping for dear life, and go squawking away into the now setting sun, never to be seen or heard from again. Any second now, it would leap into the air and fly away, and leave Priscilla earthbound to wallow in failure and self-pity. She could feel it coming.

And just as that thought crossed her mind, the crow took flight. It pushed off so hard that Mathias dropped the cage, and it went tumbling and banging down the steps, black feathers floating to the ground. The crow ascended high into the sky in front of them, and the higher it flew, the deeper Priscilla's heart sank. The crow was leaving. It was flying away. It was practically gone. Priscilla heard Jeremiah ask Mathias if he could see anything yet. Mathias shook his head.

Priscilla was all set to begin her apologies when suddenly the crow changed its course. It swooped right, and disappeared behind a massive oak. When it re-emerged on the other side of the tree, it was in full dive bomber mode, like a small black missile with feathers, and it was headed straight for them. But instead of blowing them all to smithereens, the missile transformed back into a bird, and when the crow was only a few feet away, it slammed hard on its bird brakes. It leaned back, and opened its wings, flapped them hard, three or four times, did a slight rotation, and landed gently as could be on Mathias's right shoulder.

Mathias, who had previously been facing the sky, turned his head instinctively to see what was gripping him, and when he did, the crow turned its gaze toward Mathias, and the two creatures' eyes met.

There was a moment of absolute and utter silence. Then Mathias said, "Hooooly shit, I look old." The crow squawked.

"It worked," said Priscilla, relieved. She looked up at Tommy, and he was smiling down at her.

"I never had a doubt," said Big Tommy, and he pulled her in a little tighter.

"Fuckin' hell," said Jeremiah, "can you see right now? Can you fuckin' see?" He was flabbergasted. His mouth hung open like a half-wit.

Mathias turned around to face them, the crow still calmly perched upon his shoulder. At first he said nothing. He looked toward Jeremiah, and as he did, the crow did too. Then Mathias looked Joseph up and down, and at the exact same time, so did the crow. Then Mathias looked to his right, first at Big Tommy, then down at Priscilla, and he lingered there for a moment, and once again, so did the crow. For one eternal moment, Mathias and the crow on his shoulder just stood there looking directly at Priscilla. Then, finally, Mathias answered the question that Jeremiah had asked.

Tears began running down his face. He turned back to Jeremiah and said, "Yer eyes are blue, and you need a fuckin' haircut, boy." The two men embraced one another.

"Can you fuckin' see?"

"I can, I can see."

"Yer shittin' me?"

"I ain't."

"You gotta be."

"I ain't, I can see." And so forth.

Then Mathias turned to Big Tommy, and he said, "And you, you are the biggest sonofabitch I ever seen. How old are you, son?"

"Seventeen."

"Seventeen... Jesus Christ, you ain't even full grown," said Mathias, and he clapped Tommy on the shoulder, affectionately. "How much you weigh, two twenty?"

"Two thirty-five," Big Tommy said, in an aw-shucks sort of way.

"Holy shit, two thirty-five at seventeen… What's yer last name, son?'

"Green, sir. Tommy Green's my name."

Mathias grinned, knowingly. "No shit," he said. "Tyrell Green ain't yer daddy, is it?"

"He is."

"Get the fuck outta here, yer kiddin' me?"

"No sir."

"Wow, just wow…the way stars align sometimes…makes you really question whether or not there's a God, don't it…Some co-incidences are just too much, ya know. Tyrell Green, yer daddy, was business partners with my daddy, and me too for quite a few years. Fuck, he was our Baltimore connection all through the twenties and thirties. Our Man In B-More. You have no idea, the good times I've had with yer daddy. Holy shit! He still got a thing for big-legged women?"

"Well, he's dead, but my mommy got the biggest legs you ever seen. Well, she used to…"

Mathias turned somber. "Dead? How long?"

"Oh ten, or…I guess, eleven years now."

Mathias shook his head at the words he was hearing. Then, without warning, he wrapped his arms around Big Tommy and hugged him long and hard. Tommy didn't accept the hug so much as allow it to happen. He stood stiff with his arms at his sides. "I'm real sorry to hear that, son," said Mathias. "I really am. He was a damn fine man. Gentle and good humored as they come. Maybe if we have some time, I'll tell ya some stories later." He squeezed Tommy again, and finally let him go

Then Mathias kind of hesitated, as though he were preparing himself, but after a second or two, he turned to Priscilla. And to her, Mathias said, "Damnation, girl…look at you…I never could have imagined how pretty you are. Priscilla, I—well, I…I'm never gonna be able to find a way to pay you back for this. I don't reckon a way exists." Then he threw his arms around her and squeezed. "I can see, sweetheart…I can see it all…Heaven on earth, I can see it all!" The crow on Mathias's shoulder let out a long, victorious SQUAAAAAAWWWWWWWK!

"Does that mean I can keep the book?" said Priscilla, her face up against Mathias's chest.

Mathias thought on it before he answered, then he said, "Of course you can. From now on, around here, you can have anything you want. Anything at all. What's mine is yers."

Eventually Mathias let go, and after giving Priscilla another long regard, he turned and walked down off the porch. For a while, he and his crow stood in the dying grass and stared up at the sky. The sun was nearly gone, and the clouds were smeared in shades of orange and purple. The night was cold, but it didn't seem to bother him. He was marveling at the first sunset he had seen in nearly two decades, and through the eyes of a crow, at that. He didn't even attempt to stop the tears of joy that ran down his cheeks. He just let them run.

Priscilla came up behind Jeremiah and took him by the hand. It was already so good to have him home. She loved him dearly. Maybe even more now than she ever had. She hoped, more than anything, that he was there to stay. She was getting used to not feeling so lonely, and she wanted it to last. And as she and her big brother stood there watching Mathias and his crow watch the sky, Priscilla just came out and said it. It was what needed to be said.

"Jeremiah…Everett ain't our real daddy."

Jeremiah turned his head and looked down at her. His eyes were narrowed with skepticism. "He's not?"

Priscilla, still watching Mathias, slowly shook her head.

"Well," said Jeremiah, as he put his arm around Priscilla, "son of a bitch. This day just keeps gettin' better by the minute, don't it."

"It sure does, big brother. It sure does," said Priscilla, a hopeful smile rising up on her face. Then she blinked, and when she did, she saw Lightning rip a mouse's head clean off.

They all spent the day lounging around the Elder estate. They sat bullshitting in the sun for a while. Talking, laughing, catching up. Mathias told Big Tommy a few stories about his dad, including one that started with a truck full of moonshine and two sisters named Tina and Trina, and ended with Tommy's dad and Mathias jumping naked out of a second story window, chased by the sisters' husbands, and the echo of shotguns.

At one point the topic was raised and the question was posed, what exactly had Jeremiah meant, before he left town the year prior, when he said, "Find a vein and fuckin' dig it, dig into the layers of existence, it's all chemicals and motion, don't you know anything?"

"Yeah, what the hell *did* you mean by that," asked Mathias. "Goddamn, I'm glad you remembered to ask, Priscilla."

Priscilla had considered that statement many times since Mathias first told her Jeremiah had said it. In the depths of Death Tea, the words *dig into the layers of existence, it's all chemicals and motion*, began resonating with her on a much higher level. The words began to make sense and take on a higher meaning. There was no way she was going to forget to ask about it.

However, Jeremiah's response did little to enlighten her. He said, "Did I say that?"

"Hell yeah you did, that's the last thing you said to me 'fore you left. You don't remember? You was leanin' out the window of the car…"

"Oh, Christ, I don't know. I was followin' the ECCO."

"Do what?"

"Drugs. I was high on drugs. I don't know what the fuck I was sayin'."

They talked and laughed, and laughed and talked, and the evening rolled on, and Mathias took them on a tour of the property. He showed them the old moonshine stills, the shipping container garages that held the cars, the rock he used to sit on as a kid that overlooked half of Clockmaker, the tree his mother and father were buried under, the small waterfall where he scattered his wife's ashes, the rock his brother Nehemias fell off of when they were kids, and his favorite place to hunt deer. All the places he cherished the most and hadn't actually seen in decades. For Priscilla, watching Mathias rediscover these places was a type of magic that was far beyond any held inside her precious book.

Afterward, Mathias played the piano for everyone, not just his guests, but the entire Elder clan. There was food and drink, lots of drink, and some smoking too. Everyone sat around as Mathias played, and his brothers built another fire at the bottom of a brush pile. As Priscilla watched the flames rising higher and higher into the air, surrounded by so many people she loved, she made a silent conscious wish that the moment would last forever.

◆

Since Joseph was off somewhere in the woods with Phuket, the walk back to Clockmaker was made without him. Lucky, too, was left behind, not because he couldn't be found, but because when it was time to go, the dog wouldn't leave Mathias's side. And so, it was mutually agreed upon by everyone involved that Lucky staying with the Elders was for the best. Especially Lightning, Lightning firmly agreed. Also, Mathias gave Priscilla another book to take with her, one he claimed to have picked especially for her. It was called *Frankenstein* or *The Modern Prometheus*.

When they reached the mine, Priscilla and Jeremiah parted ways with Big Tommy. He wanted to check in on his mother and make sure that she was still adjusting alright, and anyway, Priscilla and Jeremiah had an unavoidable fish to fry. After Tommy had gone, Jeremiah said, "They don't make 'em much nicer than that old boy, do they," and Priscilla told him, no, they really didn't. Then she said, "He'd kill people if I asked him to though."

They were on their way home for the first time in a long time, and Priscilla didn't know what to expect, especially out of Everett, but Jeremiah told her not to worry, that he was right beside her, and as long as he was beside her, everything would be alright. Nevertheless, she was uneasy. Even her newfound witch-confidence wavered at the thought of Everett. But now she had her big brother to keep her safe, and that would have to give her all of the courage necessary to face him. So home is where they went.

'Comin' Home' by Lynyrd Skynyrd plays

To Priscilla, home was dark and quiet. It was drafty in the winter and it smelled like smoke year round, coal smoke in the winter, and tobacco smoke the rest of the time. That was how she remembered it anyway, but what she and Jeremiah walked into was a house so different from the one in her memories that she had to consider whether or not new tenants had maybe moved in and remodeled, or perhaps she and Jeremiah had walked into the wrong house by accident.

As it turned out, they were not in the wrong house. Priscilla was just a little tipsy still. There had simply been a few changes while she had been away. First of all, Everett had taken a new night-maintenance job at the saw mill, and he wasn't at home, and secondly, their mother had apparently taken out a whole new lease on life and quit drinking. Or so she said.

Lavinia's plan was to get her teeth fixed, and get a job of some sort, and she wanted her own car. And, furthermore, she was tired of living in such a dreary house, so she had spent the last two weeks making the place more livable. She had even dug into her secret piggy-bank, the one she hid from Everett, to buy new curtains for the living room, end table lamps, and scented candles. It had caused a fight, but it was worth it.

All of this information was relayed, of course, after Lavinia finished bawling hysterically. She had been in the kitchen tending to a pot roast when Priscilla and Jeremiah first walked into the house, and as soon as they came into the kitchen, Lavinia dropped her wooden spoon, fell to her knees, and began to sob and cry. It took nearly half an hour to calm her down. All she could say was, "I'm just too happy." Priscilla finally got her hug, too. She got several of them actually, and she treasured each and every one.

The three of them were up until well after midnight, sitting around the kitchen table, catching up, eating pot roast. It was decided on the walk there that witchcraft was not to be mentioned. One thing at a time was the consensus. So neither beauty potions nor piss-rain came up in the conversation, nor did Priscilla's truancy, or her pact with the Devil, but she did tell her mother all about Big Tommy and about Joseph's dirt-stache, and about meeting Mathias, and about Lucky still being alive. And all of it, each and every story, made her mother smile. At one point she even told Priscilla to stop, because her cheeks hurt so much, and Priscilla got so carried away trying to keep her mother's face lit up and aching that she almost told her the story of how she showered Joseph with vomit. But she caught herself and held her tongue.

Luckily, Jeremiah picked up right where Priscilla left off, and they all spent the next hour talking, at length, about what he had been up to for the last year. To be more precise, Jeremiah did most of the talking. Priscilla and her mother mostly just listened, utterly fascinated. The places he had been, the people he had met, the things he had seen, all of it was like music to their untraveled ears. The Redwood Forest, Death Valley, Aspen, Boulder, Denver, Moab, the Great Salt Lakes, Hollywood, San Francisco, Las Vegas, Glacier National Park, Jeremiah took his mother and little sister on a verbal road trip through the western part of the United States, until finally they all hitchhiked their way back to Clockmaker.

And when his mother asked him where he got the money to do all of that traveling, Jeremiah looked her square in the eyes and said, "From smugglin' reefer, of course," and she just burst out laughing. It was the fourteenth time she had done so that night. Priscilla was keeping count.

Eventually, when the hours wound down, Jeremiah said that he was going to crash on Maw Scill's couch. Lavinia protested, but he explained that he didn't want Everett to come home and find him asleep in his house. He said he wanted to be awake the first time Everett saw him. Just in case. And when he put it like that, Lavinia couldn't help but to agree. "As sad as that makes me," she said. Then she said, "I swear to you, things are gonna get better around here. I promise they are. Now, give me a hug, both of you. I love you two so much, and son, I am so glad yer home."

◆

Outside on the porch, Jeremiah sparked up a joint. "It's weird bein' here…" he said.

"I can imagine," said Priscilla. "It's weird for me too." Then, after watching Jeremiah blow out yet another silver cloud, she said, "My name ain't skip, you gonna let me hit that shit or what?"

Jeremiah tilted his head to the side and grinned at her. "You ever tried it before?" he asked, as smoke billowed from his nostrils.

"Course I have," Priscilla snapped back, too quickly to sound believable.

Jeremiah's grin widened into a full on smile, and he passed her the joint. "For the record, I know yer lyin'," he said.

Priscilla flashed her classic wicked grin, and then took two small pulls on the joint. She exhaled casually, coughed twice, and handed the joint back to Jeremiah. "You gonna be around for a while?" she asked.

"Yeah, for a few weeks, then I'll be gone for a week, but I'll be back after. I'll likely be in and out over the next few months, makin' runs. I wanna stack up a million bucks by the end of next year and retire."

Priscilla nodded. In and out was better than nothing. Then she said, "Can I ask you a question?"

Jeremiah said, "Of course. No masks, remember."

"Right. No masks. Well then, do you think I'm gonna be alright? Messin' with the Devil and all?" It wasn't that Priscilla was worried exactly, but given what she was involved in, a little outside confirmation seemed like a wise thing to seek.

Jeremiah took his time pondering her question. She didn't know why, but she was sure that he was about to tell her that she had made a terrible mistake, that God would never forgive her, and she was destined for Hell, but of course he did not say that. He said, "Honestly, little sister, until today I never even thought God or the Devil existed. Never really gave it a second thought. Mathias neither. I know you got him thinkin' about everything different. You made him a different man today, one I never seen. He was like watchin' a little kid when he was showin' off them old stills. Ya know? And I know you saw him watchin' that caterpillar crawl along that branch? Like he was watchin' his first child bein' born. I mean, I don't know just what yer mixed up in, but whatever yer doin', well… what happened today was the most beautiful thing I have ever seen."

Priscilla considered her brother's words and said, "So, you think I should keep on doin' it?"

Jeremiah pulled at the joint, and rubbed wearily at his forehead as he exhaled. He was clearly taking time to search for the right and proper answer to her question. "Well," he said, finally, "I don't know. But best I can tell you is, no matter what happens, don't lose yer heart. Do yer best, and…and don't let fear ever stand in yer way. And if you fall, me or Momma or Maw Maw, one or all of us will be there to pick you up. That help at all?"

"Yeah…I reckon. Thanks," said Priscilla. "It does." She was telling the truth. Then she said, "Alright, well, I'll see ya tomorrow or somethin'."

"You really gonna go sleep in a cave?"

"Yeah…" she said. "I got slaves to tend to."

"You got slaves to—. You know what, never mind. I ain't even gonna ask. I'll see ya tomorrow, sis."

Halfway down the steps, Priscilla stopped and turned around, and said, "Jeremiah… I love you."

When he didn't respond, when all he did was sort of stare at her, she turned and continued down the steps. But just as she got to the end of the gravel drive, and was about to cross the road into the woods, she heard six words that she hadn't heard in a long, long time. Six simple words. Jeremiah shouted them, and they echoed through the hollow, and up into space. "I love you too, Priscilla Louise!"

'Mary Jane's Last Dance' by Tom Petty plays

◆

Priscilla made her way, rather slowly, to her lair. The winter wind was cool on her skin, and for once, the dark cloud that seemed to hang eternally over Clockmaker had lifted, and the stars were visible. Ever since her experiences with Death Tea, the stars had

become far more interesting to her, and when the night sky was clear, she couldn't help but wonder up at them.

Along the way she stopped in Uncle Bob's backyard and picked up a large piece of a broken bureau mirror that she had previously spotted. It was heavier than she thought it would be, but she still took it. She had a tiny mirror inside a makeup compact back in the cave, but tonight she had swiped black eyeliner from her mother's drawer in the bathroom, and she wanted to be able to see more than one eyeball at a time. Actually, she wanted to be able to see all of herself. All at once.

In general, Priscilla had never really cared for mirrors. She never particularly liked what she saw whenever she looked into them. Tonight however, after pocketing the eyeliner, she took notice of herself in the one above the bathroom sink, and for the first time in her life, she saw a hint of beauty in her own reflection. Maybe even more than a hint, if she was being honest.

Her body, so it seemed, like her mind and her life, was and had been changing at an unnatural and accelerated rate. Priscilla simply hadn't taken the time to notice. She'd been living in a cave, for Christ's sake. Brewing potions, having visions, hypnotizing slaves, worshiping Satan, it wasn't like she hadn't been busy. Besides, the lighting in the cave was terrible and she only had that compact mirror, so how was she to know?

Sure, she had, in fact, noticed that very morning, when she put on blue jeans for the first time in months, that her butt had gotten bigger, and also that her one and only bra could no longer be fastened, but until she saw herself in the mirror, it hadn't occurred to her just how much she had changed. It was significant. Her lips were fuller, her complexion was healthier, even her jawline, which had always been a little crooked because of Everett, appeared to have straightened out some. She couldn't believe it. The Level Three spells had been working.

THREE ZERO SIX

Priscilla didn't know what the long term effects of using Satanic magic to improve her looks would be, and at this point, she didn't really care. She was going along for the ride, either way.

All Priscilla knew was that things were changing, and that, for whatever reason, in addition to the stars, how she looked was beginning to matter, more and more. So after a brief deliberation between the teenage-girl and budding-witch parts of herself, she figured, what the heck, and she stopped by Uncle Bob's for the mirror. After all, just because she was a witch, it didn't mean she couldn't be pretty.

Priscilla froze in her tracks. She could see a fire in front of the entrance to her cave. She was maybe fifty yards away. Instantly, the thought of townspeople with pitchforks coming to burn her out flashed through her mind, but then she quickly remembered that she had recently enslaved two people and commanded them to guard her lair, and she relaxed and kept walking. What a relief. She wasn't in the mood for an angry mob. All she wanted was to get out of her jeans.

When she finally came upon the fire, lugging the broken mirror, she found Kester and Merle sitting beside it, poking at the embers with long sticks. They looked dejected.

"Why the long faces, fellas?" said Priscilla, with a touch of sarcasm.

"Fuck you," said Merle. "Can we go home now?"

"Why, of course you can."

"Great, 'bout goddamn time you showed up," Merle said, as he and Kester stood up and dusted themselves off.

Priscilla watched them for a moment. Then she said, "Kester, be back here at noon tomorrow, and Merle, you be here at daybreak."

Merle's mouth hung open. "What the fuck? Why do *I* gotta be here so early?"

Priscilla purposely let the question hang in the air for several seconds before she answered, simply because she could. It was a vulgar, albeit subtle, display of power, no doubt, but it was too easy, and it felt too good for her to resist. "Because it was yer idea to bring the cattle prods, fuckwad. And because you don't have a choice," she said, to a man more than twice her size, and nearly twice her age. "Because you *do not* have a choice." Then she said, "Now, go. Kick rocks. Before I feed you to the leeches."

◆

Everett arrived home from work just as the sun was coming up. It had been a long night, and he was ready to be out of the cold. At his front door, he sat down his lunch bucket and fished his keys out of his pocket. After disengaging the lock, he bent back down to pick up his lunch bucket, and when he did, he noticed a half smoked piece of something, not much larger than a match stick, stuck between the floor boards near the steps on his porch.

He walked over and picked it up. He held it up to his nose and he sniffed it. It was grass. He hated grass. In Everett's mind, only hippies and niggers smoked grass. He began to tremble. It was time to wake up Lavinia.

◆

Sunday, December Twelfth, Nineteen Seventy-One

Jeremiah woke up on Maw Scill's couch. Everett was standing over him. "Yer Momma told me you was home," he said, once Jeremiah's eyes had opened. Then he pulled the half-smoked joint out of his breast pocket and tossed it at Jeremiah. "Come on down and see me later, I just got off shift, I need sleep." At the door he stopped, and said, "And boy, if I catch you smokin' that shit at my house again, I'll beat the fuckin' brakes off ya…you hear me?"

Jeremiah said, "Yes sir," and Everett turned and left.

Big Tommy woke up to an empty house. His mother was already gone when he arrived the night before, and she still hadn't come home. It apparently hadn't taken her long to find what she was looking for, because she'd left a note beside the sink. It said, *I met a man. Wish me luck.*

Joseph woke up naked in a single bed, acutely aware that he was probably not going to make it to church. His and Phuket's clothes laid strewn around the room. Next to him, Phuket was still sleeping, and for a while, Joseph watched her. His first time, though it hadn't lasted long, was a success by every other measure. She didn't seem to mind that he hadn't showered, and when it was over, they held each other until they both fell asleep. The best part was that he hadn't even needed the potion. It was in the pocket of his pants, wherever they were, still full and uncorked. He started to get up and get dressed, but Phuket pulled him back down, and into her nude embrace. Yep, he was definitely going to miss church. His mother, and Jesus for that matter, would have to understand.

Gertrude woke up in a bed next to a man that she hardly knew. He was the second man she had ever slept with. She expected it to be more rewarding than it actually was. It felt more hollow than anything. She hadn't even been able to climax. As she quietly dressed, careful not to wake the man, she thought of killing him and harvesting his organs. She had a client in Charleston who was always in the market. But there was no time. She needed to get home. She had woken with a sharp pain just below her ribcage, and it was getting worse by the minute.

When Mathias woke up, he could still see. So he spent the morning playing his mahogany-stained piano with a black crow on his shoulder, staring up at the grey trees and the misty hills that surrounded his home. From time to time, he would look down and watch his aged fingers dance across black and white keys. And when Joseph came strolling out of his daughter's bedroom, with a little smirk on his face, Mathias saw that too.

When Priscilla woke up, Merle was already standing guard outside. He looked like shit. His cheeks appeared to be sagging off his skull. "You look terrible," Priscilla told him.

"To be honest, I ain't never felt better," Merle replied. He seemed sincere. When Tommy showed up a little later, Priscilla sent him and Merle off in search of birch twigs and three pounds of sugar.

When Maw Scill woke up, she fried several eggs and half a pound of bacon. She and Jeremiah sat in the kitchen for a while, eating and drinking coffee. Then Jeremiah talked his grandmother into finishing the rest of the roach Everett had thrown at him. "Good God almighty," Maw Scill said, as she co coughed and hacked over the kitchen sink. "I ain't smoked that shit in thirty years."

CHPTER TWlve

WHAT THE FUCK?! Aw, fuck me, what the FUCK?! MY EAR!!" Merle was in a state of bewildered horror. His ear had fallen off.

Kester let out a high pitched shriek and jumped away from it like it was a field mouse. The detached ear hit the ground beside Priscilla's altar, and came to rest at her feet. She stared at it. It was grey and hard looking, and the blood had already clotted along its severed edge. It was as if it had simply decayed off his head. This was beginning to become a problem.

Having slaves had been wonderful, no doubt. Especially now that Joseph was always shoved up Phuket's asshole, figuratively speaking, of course, Priscilla's slaves had become indispensable. The last few days, in particular, they had truly proven their worth. Big Tommy's mother, Gertrude, had fallen ill with what was, apparently, excruciating stomach pains, and Tommy was the only one that she would allow to tend to her. So, for days now, hard at work within the darkness of Dead Kid Cave, it had been only Priscilla and her slaves, the goddamn Mire brothers.

Which, as it turned out, wasn't so bad as she would have guessed. Granted, Kester and Merle both were dumb as two people could be, but with every passing day, they began to soften under Priscilla's thumb. More and more, they seemed to not merely obey her, but to follow her instead. That is to say, they quit constantly complaining when given commands, and they abandoned the idea of being set free, or at least, they no longer mentioned it. Kester in particular, with his bandaged up face, appeared to be oddly comfortable in his bondage.

There were only two problems. One, the two of them fought each other, constantly. They bickered and prodded and mocked each other, until, invariably, one of them would resort to physical violence, and then they would both wind up rolling around in the dirt, punching and kicking, and occasionally biting, until Priscilla told them to stop, which they would, immediately. Often, she felt as though she were in the possession of two extremely obedient yet fully grown toddlers, with the only real problem being that she could tell them what to do, but not who to be.

She had tried, and it hadn't worked. Her enslavement curse was obviously not without limitations, but the book was often vague in its description of spells and in the particularities of their casting, and so she was going into most of her pursuits relatively blind as to the results. Even with Joseph's love potion, the book only said, Whoever gives will receive questionless love from whoever drinks—Two weeks.

The other problem was that they were falling apart. Both of them, Kester and Merle. It had started almost right away. At first they just looked sick, emaciated. Then their hair began to fall out, in patches. Then the tip of Kester's nose fell off. And now this. Merle's ear. If it wasn't one thing, it was another. A witches' work is never ending.

She couldn't complain too much, however, because she could not remember ever being as happy as she had been recently. Not only had her first attempts at magic all been a success, but now

Jeremiah was home. He had moved in to Maw Scill's spare room, and Priscilla had gone to visit with them most every night. They would sit around and watch television until Maw Scill passed out in her chair, then Priscilla and Jeremiah would smoke pot and listen to a new band that Jeremiah was really into called Black Sabbath.

Jeremiah only had the one album. It was given to him by an ex-heroin addict named Ed the Limey, two days before Ed the Limey died of heart failure, according to Jeremiah. And Priscilla, she couldn't get enough of it. Maybe it was all the dope they were smoking, but never had she come across a music that spoke to her on such a deep level. The sound was so absolutely dark and crushing. She'd never listened to anything like it, and from the very first time she heard Ozzy belt the line *just like witches at black masses*, she was hooked. She felt as though the album had been made specifically for her. And who knows, maybe it had.

'War Pigs' by Black Sabbath plays

Craziest of all was how well things had been going with her mother and Everett. Not only did the two of them seem to be getting along better than ever, but Everett hadn't once been violent or even aggressive to any of them. Not that he had been nice or anything. He was still cold and distant, but having Jeremiah back around seemed to have softened Everett in the strangest of ways. If one didn't know any better, it might have been assumed that he had missed his son. To top it off, Lavinia was now sober, and so the mood around the Carpenter household shifted in a new and positive direction. Although no gifts and few niceties were exchanged, for the first time in years, they all spent Christmas Eve together.

So when it came down to it, Priscilla had very little to be bothered about, and the least of which were her two slowly decaying slaves, the two men who had once attempted to ambush her coven with cattle prods. Especially tonight. It was Christ's birthday, the sky was clear, and it was one hour to midnight. She had been waiting on this night for too long to be concerned with the loss of a single ear, or a nose, or a few patches of hair. No, not tonight. The witching hour was fast approaching, and she still had a few last finishing touches to see to.

"Quit bein' a little bitch," said Priscilla.

"Yeah," said Kester, "quit bein' a little bitch."

Merle looked at them both. One then the other. "I don't know what the fuck yer laughin' at," he said to Kester. "Look at yer fuckin' nose, you look like a fuckin' dead person."

Kester stopped laughing at once, and touched, self-consciously, at his face where his nose used to be.

"Ain't so funny now is it," muttered Merle, as he stooped to retrieve his ear. "Won't be laughin' when yer balls fall off…fuckin' numbskull."

Priscilla shook her head wearily. They would be sort of cute, if they weren't so damn annoying. "Both of you, go outside and wait. I need silence. I have to prepare."

"What about the rest of the sugar?" said Kester as he exited the cave.

"That should be enough, Kester, thank you. Now go. I have a fuck-ton of bat wings to count."

That's all it took to fly, bat wings and sugar. Lots of each. And a broom, of course. There were four more cups of Death Tea involved too, but those went down much easier this time. Having been previously acquainted with the tea, and its effects, Priscilla now drank with the knowledge that regardless of how crazy or confusing or intense it got, eventually it would end, and that no matter what, she was not going to die, even if it often felt that way.

But she also drank with the knowledge that with each cup, her power grew and expanded, and that was more than enough to get her through the hard times.

So, as far as *witchin'* goes, broom-flying was pretty simple. Priscilla and Joseph collected the wood for the handle months prior, which was admittedly a tad overzealous on her part, knowing full and well that she was not permitted to skip any steps in the book, but she wanted to be ready when the time came. She needed the wood to make a flying broom, for crying out loud. Who could blame her for getting a little excited?

The sugar, as it turned out, ended up being funded by Jeremiah. After Priscilla casually mentioned possibly having to steal forty pounds of it from the market in a nighttime burglary scenario, he insisted she let him pay for it, and eventually she gave in.

The bat wings, all one hundred of them, they were the doing of Kester, Merle, and Lightning. Lightning hunted bats the old fashioned feline way, which was a sweet gesture, but Priscilla needed more than one or two bats per day. So she put her slaves to the task, and low and behold, they excelled. In fact, after three days of hunting, they had trapped and killed well more than was needed in a retired mine shaft. Burlap sacks, that was the secret, according to Merle. "Smack a few around, get 'em woke up and swarmin', then bag 'em in midair." That was the ticket, he assured, and it would have been difficult for anyone to argue, given his results.

Priscilla finished counting out the bat wings and tossed each one into the bubbling clawfoot cauldron. Then she picked up her broom. She held it up before her with both hands, and studied it from left to right. It was perfect. The weight of it alone sent chills up her spine.

The handle was gnarled and twisted, and blackened with ash. At its end, bound to it with thin strips of willow, was a scraggly bouquet of birch twigs that added another two feet to its length, and another coffin nail to its wicked appearance. Priscilla struggled for the word to best describe it, but when it came to her, she knew it was the one. Badass, that was the word. Her witchin' broom was badass. She couldn't have felt more invincible, in that moment, had she held a razor sharp samurai sword.

At ten minutes to midnight, she stood in front of the mirror, adjusting her cloak. At nine minutes to midnight, she drank from the cauldron, three cups, back to back, of what was essentially bat wing Kool-Aid, being that it consisted solely of water, sugar, and bat wings. It was nothing compared to Death Tea, that was for sure, and she gulped each cup down with ease.

At seven minutes to midnight, she ate a spoonful of sugar. At six minutes to midnight, she recited the Devil's prayer. At four minutes to midnight, she vomited. At one minute to midnight, she walked outside into the cool winter air, and said, "Stand back, boys." Then she almost vomited again, but she swallowed it instead. And when she looked down at her grandfather's pilot watch and it struck twelve o'clock, on the tick, Priscilla didn't hesitate. She pulled down her grandfather's pilot goggles and said, "In the name of Satan, give me wings," and just like that, she took the fuck off.

'Highway to Hell' by ACDC plays

Ripping, tearing, streaking, soaring though the night sky. Higher and higher, and faster she went, up and over the trees, and then above the mountains, in a direct line toward the pale yellow moon. Her hair blowing out behind her, rippling in the wind. Her cheeks, rippling in the wind. She'd almost lost her grip and fallen off at about thirty-five feet, but now she was far above the forest's canopy, and she was sailing. She could feel the force

of the broom pulling her along as she went. It vibrated, no that's not right, it hummed, in her hands, like a clean, cool, combustion engine, and when she thought about turning sharp or dipping, the broom did exactly that. It turned on a frozen dime, and Priscilla didn't even have to do so much as lean. Simple hand gestures was all it took. Gentle nudges. The slightest tug. It felt as though the broom was now a part of her, and like her jaws or her hand, to make it function, all she had to do was think it so.

At first, she went high, high as she could handle, until the pressure in her head forced her to ease off and descend. When she came back down, she swooped along the top of the trees and aimed herself toward town, passing stars like they were standing still. Within minutes she'd flown over her school and her church and Main Street, and she had just passed over the drive-in theater when Jeremiah popped into her mind, and she changed course.

As luck would have it, he was on Maw Scill's back porch, smoking. Priscilla was circling the house at about eighty feet, and she could barely see the cherry glowing against her brother's sil-houette, but she knew it was him. Her plan was to come in quick and at the last second to hit the brakes, to suddenly appear in front of him, hovering, or floating, on her broom, maybe cackling for effect. That would freak him out real good. And Jeremiah was likely stoned, so she was about to really blow his mind.

She figured that all she had to do was wait until she was close, then pull back hard on the broom stick. Then she would steady it, so as to float, by pushing down on the front of the handle while pulling up in the center. It seemed obvious enough. After all, her broom was like her hand now. It would be just like cracking her knuckles.

What actually happened though…was not that. What hap-pened was when she got about twenty feet from the ground, and she pulled back, the tail end of her broom dropped hard, but she did not slow down. Not much, anyway. She hit the ground fast. Not hard, but fast. Fortunately, her angle hadn't been steep, but she still came in way too quick, and when she hit, she hit ass first, two feet in front of her brother. The broom came out of her hand, she skidded a few feet on her backside, began to roll, bowled over one of Maw Scill's cats, then through two tin trash cans, sending garbage flying, and cats running, and finally came to rest against the side of Maw Scill's house with a hard packing sound.

When Priscilla poked her head up from behind one of the thrashed trash cans, Jeremiah was staring at her, as were roughly fifteen cats. Jeremiah's eyes were wide, despite being baked, and a joint hung loosely between his lips. Priscilla was covered in something slimy that smelled like spoiled gravy. She could feel it dripping down her forehead. She had dirt in her mouth.

"Well, hey there, big brother," said Priscilla, flashing a smile and attempting to sound casual.

Jeremiah removed the joint from between his lips, and shook his head. Calmly, he said, "Did you uh…just come out of the sky on a broom?"

Priscilla nodded.

Jeremiah nodded in return, but slowly and methodically. Then he said, "You hurt?"

Priscilla, still barely visible behind the trash can, rotated her shoulders, then her arms and legs, then her fingers, toes, and neck. "Nope, I…think I'm good to go," she said, though her ass did ache.

Jeremiah nodded again, his gaze falling to the ground in front of him. "Alright," he said, and he tossed the joint in the grass. "That's enough of that for tonight. I'm goin' to bed. It's too cold out, and I am way too high for this shit. Nighty night, sis. Fly home safe…on yer… uh, broom." His voice began to trail as he walked into the house, but Priscilla could still hear him. He said, "Because that's what witches do, they…fly on…brooms…"

THREE ONE NINE

Good enough, Priscilla thought, as she watched the door shut behind him. Jeremiah may not have been impressed, but his mind was still surely blown. That would have to do until she could practice a little. No more showing off though until she could stick the landing, that was the lesson of the evening. There's no losing in life. You either win or you learn. That's something she heard Joseph's daddy say once. It seemed to fit.

Priscilla stood up, dusted herself off, and righted the trash cans. She wiped away the spoiled gravy from her face with a blanket that she found on Maw Scill's back porch. The blanket smelled like cat piss. She located her broom, and her goggles, which had also come off in the crash. Then she saddled the broom. What was the saying about falling off a horse? Something about getting back on. She couldn't quite remember, but she remembered the point it was trying to make.

Priscilla pulled her goggles down over her eyes, took a deep breath and said, "In the name of Satan, give me wings."

◆

'A.D.I.D.A.S' by Korn plays

The Wet Dream Telekinesis Theory states that because wet dreams are possible, telekinesis is possible. This theory assumes that modern physics and psychedelics are correct, and that all matter, on a subatomic level, is one and the same, a pure, condensed, vibratory energy. To put it another way—deep, deep down, a human being is no different than a rock, a lead pipe, or a tube of toothpaste. Or a beaver. And if that is true, if all things are made of the same primordial ooze, then the WDT Theory tends to hold weight, although it has yet to be accepted by the greater scientific community.

The basic idea, behind the theory, is as follows. An orgasm is something that normally requires direct, if not intensive, physical contact to achieve, much like lifting a large rock by hand. However, wet dreams subvert that fact, allowing orgasm to be achieved by mind power alone. And since all matter is the same, again assuming modern physics is indeed correct, the idea is that, with enough focus and concentration, with enough mind power, a person should be able to lift a large rock, the same way they bust a hands-free nut in their sleep, which is to say, without direct physical contact. So, once again, as previously stated, the WDT Theory claims that because wet dreams are possible, telekinesis is possible.

Priscilla had never heard of the Wet Dream Telekinesis Theory, it wouldn't be developed for many years to come, but she had been having wet dreams lately. The goat had returned. It had come to her, in her sleep, all smelly and warm, the last three nights in a row, and after each time it came, she had woken up confused and completely drenched in her own juices. And coincidentally enough, she had also been performing acts of telekinesis lately, which, to be clear, is a prime example of correlation not implying causation. This had nothing to do with physics. Both the dreams and her ability to lift objects with her mind were the direct, undeniable result of her allegiance with the Devil. Demonic Phenomenon. No theories or hypotheses necessary.

Speaking of telekinesis, Priscilla's eyes were rolled back in her head, and she had three lit candle sticks floating in mid-air around her when Joseph said, "Aw, shit, I can do that with my eyes closed."

"Fuck," Priscilla blurted, all three candles falling to the ground around her. "You scared the shit out of me."

Joseph chuckled and shook the snow off his jacket. Priscilla glared at him. Joseph said, "When'd you start paintin' yer eyes black like 'at?"

"Why," said Priscilla, batting her lashes. "You like it?"

"Yeah, looks real nice. Goes perfect with yer cape."

"It's a cloak, dick," said Priscilla, a bit too defensively. She'd had a rough morning, but after two hours spent removing splinters from her vagina, who could blame her. She had learned a valuable lesson however. Wear underwear when flying on a broom. Then she said, "How long you been standin' there, anyway?"

Joseph chuckled again, but with less enthusiasm. "Long enough to wonder if you done bought yerself a one-way ticket to Hell."

Priscilla continued to glare. Then she said, "I'm pretty sure floatin' candles ain't a damnable sin."

Joseph eyed her suspiciously. 'No…Scilly, yer probably right. I don't reckon that's damnable, but I was more so thinkin' about the two dead-lookin' bastards you got standin' guard out front in the snow. They ain't got no ears…Old Kester's missin' his nose. You don't see a problem with that?'

Priscilla raised her hand, her fingers splayed wide. She was staring directly at Joseph, unblinking. An X had been carved into the center of her blackened palm with a knife. The wound appeared purple and festering in the dimly lit cave, and Joseph grimaced at the sight. But just as he was about to say, *That shit looks infected*, one of the fallen candlesticks rose up off the floor of the cave, and slowly floated up toward Priscilla's outstretched hand. When the candle had ascended to the level of the X, she snatched it out of midair. Then she winked at Joseph and said, "Stifle yerself, Edith. Kester and Merle will be fine. I'm workin' on it. That's what's cookin' in the tub, right now."

Joseph looked toward the tub, then back at Priscilla. "Alright, alright, I admit, the candle trick was impressive. I mean…what the fuck, seriously, bravo, but all this shit yer doin'…it's all Satan this and Lucifer that. You don't think maybe—"

Priscilla cut him off, it wasn't like she hadn't already considered all of this. "What's done is done," she said. "My blood's in the book… If yer so scared, maybe you ought to start goin' to church more often. I reckon there's still time for you to repent for yer evil ways. Oh, that's right, you don't believe in such things, do you?"

"Yer hilarious," said Joseph, dryly.

"I know, and yer momma used to get drunk and run around naked," said Priscilla, as confidently as she had ever said anything. "What are you doin' here anyway, I ain't reckon we'd see you 'til the potion wore off, or 'til Mathias ran you off, whichever came first."

"Is that right… Well, I'll have you know, I ain't need yer stinkin' love potion. Puhket Elder likes me for me. We might even be in love."

"Buuullshit."

"Bullshit, nothin', I got it right here." Joseph pulled the glass vile from his pocket and held it up for Priscilla to see. "See there," he said. "She likes me for me."

"Ugh, yeah, cause she's blind as a box," said Priscilla. "If she could see that stupid dirt-stache…"

"I'll also have you know, Mathias Elder done gave me and Pooky his blessin'. He might kill me if I don't marry her but I reckon—."

"Pooky?"

"Phuket, Pooky. Don't you worry about it, that's what I call her. Anyhow, yer just jealous I got me a smokin' hot hottie who wants my body."

Just then, Big Tommy stumbled into the cave. He was panting and sweating, and looking altogether ragged. In between hoarse gasps, he said, "It's Mommy, come quick."

THREE TWO THREE

Joseph always carried his knife on his belt. Always. Even to school. It had a six-inch blade, blunt on one side, and partially serrated on the other. The blade and handle were both scarred and worn from years of use. From gutting animals to carving wood to picking at his toenails, Joseph felt naked without the blade on his side. His Uncle Bob gave it to him on his tenth birthday, and since then he carried it everywhere he went. Even to church.

For as long as Joseph could remember, his father had always said, *Real men carry knives.* This was not a way of condoning or encouraging violence, however. His father considered a knife to be not only a weapon, but a tool, one that was versatile to the extent of being a necessity for anyone who should endeavor to be prepared at all times. And so, real men carry knives, because real men are always prepared.

His father carried a small, company-issued folding knife in his pocket, but Joseph didn't have the self-confidence for that yet. Joseph's knife was big. Big and sharp. And as previously mentioned, it was partially serrated on one side. And tonight, maybe more than ever, he was thankful for his father's advice.

There was something inside Big Tommy's mother, and it was trying to get out. Or at least, that's what Big Tommy attempted to frantically explain to Joseph and Priscilla as they trudged through the snow. He told them how it all started with her stomach hurting, and how, a few days later, there was a bulge just below her ribcage, and the day after that, the bulge had a mouth and then teeth. Then a hand had formed, and it too began pressing against the inner lining of his mother's flesh. "Before I left to come find you," Tommy said, "it looked like a whole person was trapped inside her, tryin' to get out. It's real bad, we gotta hurry."

Before Tommy's very eyes, his mother had slowly transformed

back into her former gigantic, hideous self. Over the course of the last few days, her skin stretched and bubbled and popped as she widened and fattened, seemingly, to make room for whatever was growing inside her. "I never seen nothin' so scary, not even on the television," Tommy told them. "The funny thing is," he said, "she don't even act startled by it. She just keeps tellin' me, *You be still, boy.* She says, *I been waitin' on this my whole life. My whole life, she says. My whole life.*"

To say the least, Tommy's description of the events that led up to now had Joseph more than a little freaked out. As they trudged through the snow in the dark, Joseph considered the mess they were walking into, and for the life of him, he could not come up with a single way to rectify it, short of calling for the sheriff or a doctor, or from the way Tommy was talking, an exorcist. Maybe Priscilla had a plan. He sure hoped she did. She hadn't spoken a word the entire walk, so Joseph could only assume she was think-ing, devising some kind of genius way to handle all this. Maybe she had a magic spell that would fix everything. Maybe all they would have to do is brew up some sugar and blood in the old tub, and Gertrude would be right as rain. But if half of what Tommy said was true, then Joseph suspected that they might all be look-ing at a long night.

As can be imagined, Joseph had many expectations, as any person would when confronted with a situation so bizarre. But even the expectations formed by the wild imagination of a naive teenage boy, even a boy so heavily and acutely exposed to the paranormal such as Joseph, couldn't hold a flame to anything as twisted and distorted as the actual reality that he and his friends were fast approaching.

Inside the house, all was quiet and still, and cold. Floor boards creaked under their feet. A mouse's whisper could be heard. There was no wailing. There was no thrashing. There was no movement. A little bit of commotion was to be expected, but alas, there was none, and Joseph was on edge.

Priscilla still hadn't spoken a word. She just followed along quietly with the book clutched to her chest. Through the dark kitchen, Big Tommy led the way. Halfway up the steps, Joseph could smell blood in the air.

And there was blood. So much blood. In a glimpse, Gertrude was sprawled on the floor, naked, in the shadowy room. One side of her face looked as though it had been chewed off, and Joseph could see her teeth through her cheek. Her massive hairy breasts sagged across her. They too appeared to have been chewed on. One of her nipples was missing, completely. Just what could be seen from the hallway, before he'd even stepped into the room, had his mind threatening to come unhinged. And it only got worse once he was inside.

Gertrude's enormous gut was split wide open. Ribcage pried apart. Sternum shattered. It looked as though a quarter stick of dynamite had gone off inside her chest. Her heart, her lungs, her intestines, all matter of viscera, lay mangled and exposed. Blood and gore covered all. And even still, the worst was yet to come.

It wasn't obvious at first. It was camouflaged by the six hundred pounds of ravaged meat, skin, and bone that surrounded it, but as Joseph's eyes adjusted to the poorly lit room, it became more and more clear. It was some sort of creature, some sort of hideous, monstrous, humanoid creature. Malformed, veiny, and slick with blood, whatever the fuck it was lay face down and motionless on the floor beside Gertrude, with one of its bony disfigured arms doubled in half underneath it.

The bottom half of the creature was still inside Gertrude, and from what Joseph could tell, the creature appeared to be coming or growing out of her. Joseph's eyes tracked along its crooked spine, until the creature's back muscles fused with Gertrude's lungs and intestines. And once again, his mind malfunctioned. His brain simply could not, or would not, allow what his eyes were seeing to be reality. Gertrude was dead. The creature looked dead. Joseph couldn't help but think of a newborn chick poking out of its egg for the first time, covered in blood, little bits of shell still clinging to its head and beak. The similarities were unnerving.

Afterward, when Joseph would think back on it, what happened next was hard for him to remember. He could remember pieces of what happened, but he could never see the whole puzzle. His poor mind wouldn't let him. It wouldn't be until Joseph was thirty years old, after eating too many mushrooms at a stock car race in Louisville, that the memories would come flooding back to him, in multi-colored, vivid detail. In a veritable kaleidoscope of horror. It was one hell of a bummer trip, and Joseph spent the entire night on the verge of a complete mental breakdown. All alone, he stood with his face against the chain link fence, crying, tripping, watching the cars go round and round, until long after the race had finished and everyone else had gone home.

Big Tommy dropped to his knees beside his mother, seemingly unaware of the creature. Moaning and sobbing, he began stroking his dead mother's hair. He kept trying to look at her, but turning away and gagging. Joseph was paralyzed with fear. He looked at Priscilla. She was no better off. Still clutching her book, tears were running down her face, and she was shaking. When Big Tommy's moans turned into wails, and he started beating on the floor with his fist, Priscilla's tears ran harder. Agony, in its rawest form, overtook the room.

Then the creature growing out of Gertrude came alive. It moved quick. Joseph shouted, "Tommy, look out!" But it was too late. The thing reached up and seized Tommy by the shirt collar, pulling him down toward its maniacally snapping jaws. In one quick motion, the hairless, snarling creature pulled Tommy off balance and on to his side, and before Joseph could so much as think to react, it buried its teeth into the side of Tommy's neck. A thin misty arch of blood sprayed the air, and Tommy screamed.

Joseph lunged for Tommy. He grabbed him by the leg and began to pull, but Tommy was too big and too heavy, and the thing was latched onto Tommy's neck like a rabid dog. "Help me, Scilly!" Joseph pleaded, but Priscilla didn't move. Tommy spasmed, and kicked loose of Joseph's grip, and spasmed again.

Then, with his last bit of strength, Tommy attempted to twist free of the creature's bite, but as he turned, the creature remained latched on, and Tommy's neck tore open. A fountain of blood erupted. Tommy's legs began to kick and twitch, and then they stopped.

As the fountain poured from Tommy's throat, the thing, all purple and bloody, lifted its head, revealing a single cyclops eye, jagged broken teeth, and an empty cavity for a nose. It leaned into the spray of blood, allowing its face to be drenched, completely. Gasping, still attached to Gertrude at its waist, and still holding on to Tommy's collar, it pulled itself ever closer to the mortal wound, and to the blood that spewed forth from it. Rapture was the look on the creature's face. It too, it seemed, like Gertrude, had been waiting on this day for a long, long time.

It all happened in a matter of seconds, and Joseph, like Priscilla, was traumatized, but at the very moment that the blood stopped spraying from Tommy's neck, Joseph snapped out of his stupor and pulled his knife from his belt. He had only intended to cut the thing's throat, but instead, he leapt forward, slammed his boot down hard on the vile creature's back, and took hold of it, partially by the ear, and by a random patch of hair. And when he ran the serrated edge of his blade along the creature's neck, it cut through its soft bones like butter, and its head came off in Joseph's hand.

THREE TWO EIGHT

For a moment, he held it there, by its ear, out away from his body, until its single oozing eye stopped rolling around and its teeth stopped gnashing. Then, wearily, he dropped the head to the floor, and looked at Priscilla. She still hadn't moved, not an inch. Nor had she blinked, as far as Joseph could tell. Several drops of splattered blood now spotted her tear-stained face. She looked downright pitiful. And just as the words, "We gotta get out of here," came out of Joseph's mouth, she fainted and crumbled to the floor.

◆

The call came in on January fourth, nineteen seventy-two, at eight thirty-three in the evening. Sheriff White had just sat down at his desk with a cup of coffee and the day's newspaper. He was finishing an article about possible layoffs at the mine when the phone began to ring.

He didn't answer it right away, though. He let out a long sigh as he carefully refolded the newspaper and sat it down on his desk. Then he took a sip of coffee, then another, and then he picked the phone up off the receiver and put it to his ear, and said, "Sheriff White speakin'." Then, after a moment, he said, "Alright, slow down. Let me find somethin' to write with, hold on… I said hold on."

Sheriff White tucked the phone into his neck and held it with his shoulder so that he could take notes and sip his coffee at the same time. Then he said, "Alright start over, you seen—now slow down, you seen a white boy comin' outta the house, what time was that?…mhmm… mhmm, I understand…and the girl, over his shoulder, she was white too?…uh huh, yeah…anybody else see 'em?…alright, then what'd you do?…mmhmm…you ever been in 'at house before?…mhmm, oh I know Gertrude, I don't blame ya…uh huh…yeah…mhmm…Christ…Christ…what you—you say comin' out her stomach?…Jesus…alright, alright and you couldn't tell how many was dead?…uh huh…Christ almighty… alright, tell me yer name again?… Clive, what?…alright, you relation to Batina?…cousin. I figured, alright Clive Bevins, I want you to stay right there, and don't let nobody else in 'at house 'till I get there, you understand me, boy. I'm on my way… alright, just as fast as I can…alright."

Sheriff White sat the telephone back on its base, and leaned back in his chair, massaging his temples. "Christ," he said.

"What's goin' on, Sheriff?" asked the deputy.

Still rubbing his temples, Sheriff White said, "Nigger trouble, deputy… Got a massacre on the Knob… Call Junior and Stanley, tell 'em to turn on their radios and get up there. Gertrude Green's house. Stanley knows the place."

"You want me to come?"

"Nope. Hold down the fort. I'll radio if I need ya."

Sheriff White stood up, and gathered his things. Keys, revolver, and coat, and what not. His hat, he pulled from the hook by the door. Staring out at the falling snow, he said, "You know how my daddy lost his feet, Deputy?"

"Just a second, Junior," said the deputy. The deputy put his palm over the transmitting end of the telephone, and said, "One more time, Sheriff."

"My daddy," said Sheriff White, "I ever tell ya how he lost his feet?"

"…Well, no sir…I don't reckon ya have."

Still looking out at the snow, Sheriff White said, "Frostbite… old bastard got sloppy drunk one night, probably fell, and passed out in the snow between the shed and the house…had his steel-toed boots on…" Then he said, "Tell Junior to make sure he's got chains on his tires. He won't make it up 'ere without 'em." And he opened the door and walked out into the cold.

The deputy watched Sheriff White walk out to his squad car and get inside. He watched as the car backed up and pulled forward and disappeared into the snow-swept night. Then he watched the weather for a few seconds longer. It was coming down hard outside. "I'm back, Junior," said the deputy into the telephone. "Alright… yeah, Sheriff needs you and Stanley up on Nigger Knob…uh huh, yep, up at Gertrude Green's…yep… murder, well, a massacre's the way he put it…yep…yep, I'd bring one, you might need to flash it, you know how these animals get… yep, better to have it and not use it…mmhmm, yep…I couldn't agree more…alright…alright…alright… say, how's Dorothy and the kids?"

When Sheriff White arrived on the scene of the crime, Gertrude Green's house was dark. Clive Bevins, the man who'd phoned in the crime, was waiting beside a row of mailboxes. He looked cold. Sheriff White half expected an angry black mob to be gathered outside the place, hollering, crying, demanding justice, but there was none. There was only Clive, looking shifty and frightened, with his hands stuffed in his pockets. Sheriff White parked the cruiser in front of the house, Clive's eyes wide in the headlights. Sheriff White switched the heat on high and held his palms up to the vents. After a minute or so, he slipped on his department-issued gloves, opened the car door, and stepped into the chilly January air, leaving the cruiser running. The snow had let up some, but it was still frigid all the way to the bone.

Clive led Sheriff White to the side door of Gertrude's house. On the way he showed him footprints in the snow. They had already been mostly covered, and wouldn't be much help. At the door to the house, although Clive, frail and grey, was clearly his elder, Sheriff White said, "Wait out here, boy. When my backup arrives, you wave 'em down and send 'em in." Clive didn't argue.

Inside Gertrude's house, Sheriff White moved slowly. He

cleared each room on the ground level, checking in cupboards and closets. Department issued revolver in one hand, flashlight in the other, he moved room to room. Labeled jars and sacks cluttered every inch of space. Black mold grew on the walls. Dust and cobwebs clung to most everything. A stuffed and mounted deer bust hung crooked on the wall. By the looks of things, the house hadn't been cleaned or cared for in many years. It reminded Sheriff White of the Addams Family, had they been black and poor, and stupid. Finding many suspicious things, but nothing criminal, he ascended the decaying staircase, carefully, step by creaky step. On the second step, he began to smell blood. At the top of the steps, that was all he could smell.

Two dead, three dead, he didn't know how to radio it in. There were three heads, that was for sure, but the problem was that one of them, the one not attached to a body, the one laying in the corner of the room, only had one eye, and did not appear to be all the way human. And from what Sheriff White could tell, its decapitated body looked to have literally grown out of Gertrude Green's intestines. Viscera, blood, and gore covered most things in the bedroom, and it was dark, so it was hard to be absolutely positive, but it was also freezing cold in there, it was late, and Sheriff White did not have the time or patience to even begin to figure out the details of what actually happened.

The obvious facts were this. Gertrude Green was dead. Another person, a man, a black man, likely Gertrude's son, roughly seven foot tall, two hundred and forty pounds, was also dead. "Beyond that, who gives a good goddamn," the Sheriff muttered to himself. It was warm back inside his cruiser, and besides, he already knew that whatever happened in this house was pure *nigger mischief*, maybe even *Voodoo*, and Sheriff White damn sure did not have the energy for any *Hoodoo Voodoo nigger mischief* on a night this cold, or any other for that matter.

Creeping and sliding down off The Knob in his cruiser, Sheriff White passed his reinforcements, Junior and Stanley, in Junior's old Ford pickup. The Sheriff and Junior both rolled down their windows. "Evenin', Sheriff," said Junior.

"Evenin', fellers," Sheriff White responded. "How we doin' on this cold bitch of a night?"

"Oh…gettin' by," responded Junior. Stanley nodded from the passenger seat.

"I bet yer glad you put them chains on, ain't ya," said Sheriff White.

"Yes sir," said Junior. "We wouldn't made it up here without 'em. You called it, Sheriff."

"I always do," said Sheriff White.

"Yes sir, you do," said Junior, matter-of-factly. "Who's 'at in the back, the boy who did it?"

"Naw, his name is Clive Bevins. He's our uh…witness. He called it in. I'm takin' em down to the station so we can make sure he gets his statement straight."

Junior nodded his head, and wiped away some ice from around the window frame on his truck. "Yeeep, I hear ya," he said. "So you ain't need us no more or what?"

"Oh no, I still need ya. Y'all go on up there, it's 'at last house on the right, and bag the bodies. They all in the upstairs bedroom, you can't miss 'em. Bag all the guts and pieces too, and I mean all of it, every piece. I don't wanna see so much as a tooth left behind. If y'all need help gettin' Gertrude's big ass out of there, radio the station and I'll send Don up to help ya. Don't worry 'bout the blood. And listen good, not a single word about what you see up there to nobody, and I do mean nobody. You hear me over there, Stanley? Becky better not show up at the picnic runnin' her cocksucker about this one. We gonna handle this nice and quiet."

THREE THREE THREE

Junior and Stanley both nodded. Junior said, "You hear they layin' off thirty from the mine?"

"Be more like sixty from what I hear," Sheriff White countered.

"Yeeep, tough times is ahead," said Junior. "Welp, we'll get 'er cleaned up, Sheriff."

Sheriff White said, "See that it is, Junior. Y'all drive safe, it's a slick one out tonight. I'll see ya back at the station." Then he rolled up his window, and turned on his windshield wipers. Junior and Stanley pulled away. Sheriff White eased off the clutch and the cruiser inched forward. In the rearview mirror, he could see Clive Bevins in the back, huddled against the door, staring out the window. He looked sad. "You warm back 'ere, Bevins?" asked Sheriff White.

In Sheriff White's experience, the crime in Clockmaker was petty. Bar fights, theft, domestic issues, drunk and disorderly, nothing heinous. Rarely did he see murder, and when he did, it was most always black on black, or white on white, and at that, it was usually a family matter. Uncle kills nephew, brother kills brother, daughter kills mother, and so on. There wasn't much tension between black and white, as far as Sheriff White could tell. Not in Clockmaker anyway. While the people in the big cities were rioting and looting and going crazy over the last few years, worried about the Ku Klux Klan, Charlie Manson, and Martin King, the people in Sheriff White's town were working and taking care of their families. Folks simply didn't have time for those kind of shenanigans. That's the best Sheriff White could figure it, anyway. In fact, the only time he could remember there ever being an issue was back in sixty-two when he arrested a man named Andrew Gunther.

Gunther was a white man and foreman at the mine who was brought up on charges for the murder of a black man, a miner under his employment. While they were working underground,

Gunther shoved the man into a hole that, according to the other men who worked in the mine, had no bottom. After Gunther's arrest, with some prodding by the Sheriff, he confessed to the crime. He also confessed to shoving fifteen other black men down the same hole, over the course of the previous sixteen years.

Apparently one year he had gotten injured in a cave-in and spent eleven months on disability, but otherwise he killed steadily, once a year, as to not arouse suspicions. When asked for a motive, Gunther replied, "Well every time I pushed one down the hole, I thought to myself, that's one less nigger." He also said that every time he did it, he would wait and listen real close, but he never did hear one of them hit the bottom.

Sheriff White kept that confession hush-hush, however. Making the other fifteen murders public would have done nothing but start a race war, he was sure of it. He'd seen it happen to too many fine upstanding cities like Montgomery and Birmingham. So Andrew Gunther went to trial for the one murder only, the one he had been caught redhanded for. He got eight years in the state penitentiary, which Sheriff White thought was more than fair, and just as he had foresaw, race relations in Clockmaker continued to be a non-issue.

This was a matter of pride for Sheriff White, his handling of the Gunther case. It was a matter of pride back in sixty-two, and it still was a decade later. While everyone else was playing checkers, he was playing chess, always thinking three or four steps ahead, looking at the bigger picture, more than willing to give up a few pawns for the sake of a greater objective. It was merely his nature, instilled in him genetically. Just like his father, and his father before him, he came from a long line of men who possessed a wisdom far superior to that of their fellow man.

Sheriff White was thinking about all this, about Andrew Gunther, about racial tension, and superior genetics, and what not, as he pulled his cruiser up in front of an abandoned house that his sister used to live in before she died. Behind the house was a well. The well was made of stone and it was deep. Not bottomless, but deep. He knew how deep it was because he had helped his father dig it, forty years prior, when his sister, Ethel, first had the house built, but now she was dead, and the well was as abandoned as the house.

And it was to that stone well, on that cold January night, that Sheriff Earnest White led Clive Melvin Bevins, eighty-one years old, father of seven, grandfather of eleven. And it was deep down into that stone well that Sheriff White, sixty-three years old, father of none, threw Clive Bevins' body, after emptying the old man's pockets and shooting him, point blank, in the side of the head.

Back at the station, all was finally quiet. Junior and Stanley, as expected, requested help moving Gertrude Green's corpse, and Sheriff White sent his deputy to assist them. Junior and Stanley weren't the smartest men he knew, but they always came through in a pinch, and they were never hesitant to get their hands dirty. They were by no means Sheriff's Department material, but they had their uses, both of them. He knew that between them and Deputy Knotts, they would get the job done. And so, Sheriff White's mind was at ease. There wouldn't be any angry black mobs roaming around tonight, not in his town.

With his feet up on his desk, the pleasant, familiar aroma of freshly brewed coffee floating lazily in the air, Sheriff White finished reading the day's newspaper. It would be an hour or better before his men would be back with the corpses, and he was going to enjoy every minute of that hour, just as he had planned. To the quiet, empty station, Sheriff White said, "Checkmate."

———◆———

A word from Joseph

Death is psychedelic. Not for the dead necessarily, but for the people that the dead leave behind. You ever consider that? When someone you love dies, it's like the universe just stops on by, and slowly drags a sheet of blotter right through yer Kool-Aid. You know what I'm sayin'…? Life comes at you in tracers. Time distorts. Emotions spike. Pupils dilate. The rest of the world disappears, and all that is left is you. You and yer dead daddy, or yer dead sister, or whoever, and yer grief, but really it's just you. When that shit happens, when someone you really love dies, ain't nothin' else in the whole wide world that matters. Yer job, yer mortgage, yer car, yer vacation plans, it all just evaporates into the ether, and yer left sittin' alone in some room, rockin' back and forth in a chair that don't rock, starin' at the goddamn wall like the answer's written on it in Latin. Death is surely a tragic thing, but like I said, that shit is psychedelic. The closer you are to the deceased, the heavier the ride.

The way I figure it, the natural way for kids to become acquainted with death is when their granddaddys and grandmommas go. That's a gentle exposure, a nice slow drip. The unnatural way is when their friends go, when their pals go, the kids they skip rocks with… When that happens, well, a kid don't just exchange partin' glances with the basic processes of growin' old, the kid's life tends to take on a whole new color palette altogether, like a dose in the eye, so to speak, completely alterin' and magnifyin' the lens through which they view their own existence. It can have a damn powerful impact. Does that make sense at all?

Ya know what, forget it. I'm in over my head. My point is, when yer friends die when yer a kid, it can fuck you up quite a bit, but when yer friends die when yer a kid because you got bored and started fuckin' around with Satan, and gave his momma a potion that made a goddamn cyclops rip out of her stomach, and then tear yer friend's neck open, well, you can imagine how Priscilla had a hard time recoverin' from that shit.

Don't get me wrong, I was out of it for a couple weeks. In the short amount of time I knew Tommy Lee Green, he became a true, dear, and close friend, and his passin' hurt me for quite some time, but the sadness in Priscilla's eyes well…that was somethin' different. She took Tommy's death 'bout as hard as anyone could. Her and him was close. Closer than him and me, for sure. Tommy practically lived in that cave with her, and after he died, I don't reckon I seen her smile or laugh without at least some reserve ever again.

Ya know, when I think back on that night, now, it all feels like a dream, but what's funny is I can remember thinkin' the same thing back then. It all felt like a dream as it was happenin'. I re-member seein' Gertrude all busted open, and that thing comin' out of her, and thinkin' to myself, I must be dreamin'. Even when it latched 'hold of Tommy, and I seen its one big old red eye rol-lin' around, even then, I remember thinkin', This can't fuckin' be real. I mean, I know now that I was in shock. My adrenaline was spikin'. That's obvious enough, lookin' back, but back then I just thought, Well Joseph, yer fuckin' dreamin', pal. Any minute now, yer gonna wake up in yer bed. Snug as a bug in a rug. Momma's makin' bacon, you know what I mean? It wasn't until I accidentally cut that motherfucker's head off that I knew. But then I knew, alright. That head come off in my hand and reality came rushin' back to smack me clean off my barstool. And I knew then, it was real. Real as shit. Too real. The cyclops head was real. The blood was real. The guts was real. I was real. It was all real. And Big Tommy…well…he was really dead…

Poor Priscilla, she just collapsed. I didn't know what to do. I just remember bein' instantly overtaken by the idea that me and her both was goin' to fuckin' prison, and so maybe I did panic, but I just snatched her up off the floor, threw her over my shoulder, and I fuckin' ran. Ran for my damn life. For both our lives. Fast as I could with her on my back. Down the steps, out the side door, and into the woods below the house. I somehow had enough sense not to go runnin' with her down the road. Even in the chaos, I knew we'd be harder to track in the woods. I was operatin' off pure instinct, I reckon.

I thought for sure we was bein' follered by the law too, and it was snowin' like Hell, but I kept thinkin' I was hearin' hounds barkin' in the distance and men hollerin', like the Sheriff and his posse was hot on our trail. They wasn't, and I know that now, but I sure as shit thought they was back then, and so I just kept on trudgin' through the snow and the sticks, deeper and deeper into the hills, till I finally couldn't no more. So I sat her down and we laid there for a while, tucked up underneath a fallen hickory, until Priscilla came to. Then we laid there for a little while more. Not talkin' much. Mostly just cryin'… Bein' sad… When the snow let up, we made our way back to the cave.

Tommy got killed on the first of January, and that date will always hold significance with me for that reason. And though I never allowed his death to drag me down too far, understand that

I was never the same after that night, and I carry a little bit of Big Tommy Green with me everywhere I go. And it may sound kinda corny, but sometimes I feel like the only way I made it through all these years is 'cause Tommy's up in Heaven watchin' out for me, doin' favors, pullin' strings, rubbin' elbows with all the angels, scorin' blow for God, makin' sure I don't get run over by a truck, or shot by a stray bullet, or colon cancer…or herpes.

At the funeral, they buried Tommy and his momma at the same time, side by side. I cried my eyes out watchin' them two giant caskets get lowered into the ground. There weren't but a few people there, and I was the only white one, and the only one cryin'. Priscilla couldn't bring herself to attend. She was too ate up with grief and guilt. And there ain't no doubt she held some blame, but I don't reckon it was all her fault. She sure thought it was, though. And maybe it actually was, and that's what made it so hard on her. Lord knows I tried to help her, tried talkin' to her and what not, but hell, I was only sixteen years old my damn self, I didn't know what to say to console her. Even now, I'm not sure I'd know what to say in that situation. Would you? …I doubt it.

In the newspaper, Tommy and Gertrude's death was ruled a murder-suicide. The newspaper said that after an extensive investigation by Sheriff White, it was determined that some sort of squabble had ensued between the two, and that durin' this squabble, Gertude Green, accidentally or not, killed her son with a knife, and then turned the knife on herself. "It was obvious from the evidence, what happened," Sheriff White was quoted as sayin'. You believe that shit? From that day movin' forward, it's been pretty clear to me that cops are worth about as much as a stick in the fuckin' forest.

I'll never forget readin' that article. I read it over and over, and ya know, I was upset as can be, but I was relieved at the same time. Upset because the truth of the matter stayed hidden, and relieved that… well, the truth of the matter stayed hidden. Tommy would see no justice, but Priscilla and me wouldn't be seein' the electric chair neither, so there was that, and that would have to do. The article also said that at the funeral the caskets would be closed, due to the vi-o-lent and grisly nature of the crime. And they were, closed that is, and at the time, it hurt me to know I'd never get to see Tommy's face again, but truth be told, I'm glad for it now. I've seen quite a few people layin' dead in caskets since then, and that sight don't never leave ya. It sticks heavy in yer brain, and every time you try to recall that person, the image of their lifeless face is always right their waitin' to be remembered…

Anyhow, after, I don't know, a couple of weeks, I suppose, Priscilla all of a sudden came back around. I was sleepin' in bed one night, a few nights after Tommy's funeral, when I heard a tap tap tap on my bedroom window, not real hard but not real light. And my room was on the second floor, mind you. But I reckon, you might be able to guess what I saw when I rolled over. It was Priscilla, hoverin' on her goddamn broom outside my window. That was the first time I ever seen her fly on that thing. I ain't gonna lie, I screamed. Damn near came outta my bed. Bout knocked over my lamp. Yes sir, she scared the snot right out of me.

I remember listenin' for my parents, and when they didn't come runnin', I slipped outta bed and went on over to the window and slid it up. And when I did, the cold air came rushin' in, and she kinda inched back from the window, hoverin' as it were, and I could really see the whole of her. And good Lord, I'll never forget it neither. That long shaggy black cloak hangin' down into the night, her hood blown back and her hair all wild in the wind…snow fallin' all around her. She was sittin' way back on the broom, near the bristles, and she had hold of the handle with one hand, real casual like, the broomstick almost vertical, like she was poppin' a wheelie on a shovel-head. Her other arm, just hangin' limp at her side, like it was no big thing.

She even had her damn cat with her. You believe 'at? Well, I reckon you do, if you believe any of this shit, which ya should, but she did, she had her cat with her. I could see its eyes inside her cloak. Green and gold, with shimmers…

Matter of fact, that was also the first time I realized how god-damned gorgeous Priscilla had gotten. Don't get me wrong, she'd been goin' through some serious changes, and that didn't slip by me altogether at the time. I mean, yeah, I noticed her skin had all but cleared up, and I noticed her, well, her—well, I noticed her chest was gettin' bigger, and she was always goin' around naked under that cloak, showin' little bits of herself when she'd bend down and what not, but when yer close to somethin', it's hard to notice when it's changin'. It don't hit ya till the change is complete. It's like paintin' a masterpiece, sometimes ya gotta step away for a moment or two to really see what's yer lookin' at. Then it comes to ya. It hits ya all at once. And had it been a snake, it woulda bit ya.

That night though, I seen it. It hit me. Dead center, plain as day, clear as glass. My homely, awkward little friend, who talked kinda funny and kept her head down, who nervously tugged at her hair, whose eyes and ears were too big for her face, she'd changed. And she'd been replaced. What replaced her, well, that ain't easy to define but the best I can say is, she was replaced by the cutest little piece of Satanic ass you ever seen in yer mother-fuckin' life, cousin, holy shit! And that may be crude, I know, but I can't figure a better way to describe her. She wore her grief like a goddamn mini-skirt. I mean, if she didn't look like somethin' wrought from the Devil's own bitch factory then the Devil ain't have no bitch factory, you know what I'm sayin'?

Maybe it was the moonlight, maybe it was the black makeup,

but I remember thinkin', *Goddamn, Priscilla! You lookin' hotter than a greasy griddle in the middle of motherfuckin' July, girl.* But she was still in mournin', and rightfully so, so I just thought all that, and kept my trap shut.

When I got that window up, I stuck my head out, and I says, I whispers, What in the fuck are you doin'?

And she just says, and this here is a quote, I'll never forget it, she says, and floatin' in mid fuckin' air, mind you, wonderin' up at the winter moon, she says, *It's time to kick this shit up a notch, old buddy…My blood's in the book… The goat is me, and I am the goat. I am the star inside the circle.* Then she looks right at me and says, *I have four Level-Four Spells and five Level-Five Spells to cast before I can bring Tommy back to life. The slaves are already collectin' carcasses. You don't have to help if you don't wanna, but if you do, come to the cave in the mornin'.* Then she looks back up at the moon. It was cold as can be but she weren't even shiverin' a little, just floatin' there, I remember it. And when she finally looked back down at me, she says, *I know it sounds crazy, Joseph. I really do, but…* Then she pauses and kinda cocks her head, and says, *But did you ever think I'd be able to fly…?*

Did you ever think I'd be able to fly, that was her question to me, and at that, she gave me a weak little smile, pulled her broomstick in close to her chest, and flew away. In a flash, she was gone. Off into the night.

So what's yer craziest childhood memory? That's rhetorical. I look back on my youth sometimes, the way an infant looks at their own reflection in a puddle, with hazy familiarity coupled with astonishment. Like, hey, I think I know you, but say, how the fuck did you get over there? Or rather, how the fuck did I get here? How'd I make it to where I am today. Not that I'm anywhere special. Or anyone special… I'm just me… A point in space… A moment in time… A blip… A wink.

THREE FOUR THREE

But I am here today. As I live, and breathe, and shit, I am here today. And that's really more than any of us could ever hope for. Just to be alive. Don't ya think? Just to be here today? When yer dyin', the only thing you want is to live. You don't want a big house or a girlfriend, you don't care 'bout none of that shit. All you want is to be alive. To breathe one more day. If you were dyin', you'd trade anything for it. Just one more breath. Just one more sunset. Take my legs. Take my sight. Anything, just don't take my life. It all gets real simple at the end. When yer nothin' and you have nothin', happiness is just a breath away. It ain't till all this other shit comes into play that we start gettin' down on ourselves. So I reckon, when it comes down to it, all that really matters is bein' alive. That's it. Real simple. Everything else is fuckin' glitter.

And in light of that realization, I propose a toast. So raise yer glass if ya have one. If ya don't, well, stop readin' and get one. Do it just because ya can, not because the weed in Hell is filled with seeds, which it is, from what I hear, and not because booze goes great with a good book, which it does, but do it just because yer alive. You hear me? Just because yer alive. That's reason enough to celebrate. So raise yer glass. And raise that shit high.

Here's to Tommy Lee Green. May January first forever remain a day of remembrance for the ones who died too young.

— ◆ —

CHaPTER thirteeN

'Head Like a Hole'
by Nine Inch Nails plays

First, Priscilla summoned lightning—the electrostatic discharge that is normally created by thunderstorms—not the cat. For quite some time now, Priscilla had been able to simply close her eyes, and in her mind, she could speak her Familiar's name, and like clockwork, Lightning the cat would eventually, depending on distance, come sauntering into the cave, or wherever Priscilla was, with her tail tall and slowly swaying from side to side. But on the night of February first, nineteen seventy-two, Priscilla wasn't calling to her cat, she was making white-hot streaks of electric energy rain down from the sky with the point of her finger.

Standing with her back to the entrance of Dead Kid Cave, on a clear, cloudless night, with Joseph watching over her shoulder, and her slaves at her feet, Priscilla stood mighty and tall. Her unholy, black cloak flapping in the cold winter wind, she stood with one arm in the air and one finger outstretched toward the sky, like a satanic symphony conductor. She would point here and she would point there, and wherever she would point, a bold, beautiful, and brilliant streak of God's own electric would illuminate the sky. This went on for little more than an hour, and at the hour's end, with several small fires burning on the distant hills, Priscilla said, "Be back tomorrow at sundown, Joseph. We have work to do."

On February third, there was a blizzard, the deadliest in known history. It killed at least four thousand people. Fortunately, for everyone in Clockmaker, it happened in the country of Iran. It was an anomaly of sorts, understand. Due to a misalignment of Priscilla's pentagram relative to the moon, the cosmic energy of her blizzard spell collided with that of an Islamic, talismanic jaaduugar's poorly mixed prosperity spell, and the rest is, well… history. Temperatures dropped to negative thirteen degrees Fahrenheit and over the course of a week, nearly twenty-six feet of snow covered the southern region of Iran. Priscilla thought the spell a failure, having no knowledge of the happenings on the other side of the world, so the following day, to make up for it, she caused a small earthquake that shattered nearly every window on Main Street.

On February ninth, as the last of the snow was falling over Iran, Priscilla made it ultra-hail for seven hours straight. Chunks of ice, not snow, ice the size of baseballs rained from the sky, breaking glass and leaving dents and craters all over Clockmaker. It caused thousands of dollars in damage to property, and killed two people, which, of course, did not go unnoticed by most, particularly by local law enforcement. Between the lightning and the hail and the earthquake, most people didn't know what to even begin to expect out of the weather, or out of insurance companies, for that matter, but then on February tenth, Priscilla brought the fog, and people fucking lost it.

For four days straight, as Priscilla sat motionless inside her lair, a fog so dense and so thick that several people went missing in it came to rest over the tired little town of Clockmaker, and for four days straight, commerce and community and life in general came to a screeching halt. It was hard enough for people to walk from the house to the clothesline without getting lost, let alone trying to navigate an automobile in such density. Nevertheless, it took three coal trucks crashing before the mine shut down operations altogether, and that was on day one.

On day two of the fog, unable to leave their homes, marooned without obvious options or recourse, beset on all sides by some ominous, mysterious mist, some people were simply walking out on their front porches and shouting, screaming into a thick white abyss, desperate for some reply, some sign of life. Others wept uncontrollably. In less than twenty-four hours, many of the residents of Clockmaker had begun a slow isolated descent into madness. By six o'clock that evening there were so many calls coming into the Sheriff's station that Sheriff White literally said, "Ah, fuck it," gave up, took the phone off the hook, crawled under his desk, and went to sleep.

On day three, there was the first suicide in Clockmaker in over a decade. On day four, there was another suicide and a murder. One of the suicides was Davey Baker, whose older brother had also killed himself. The murder was of Mary Elkins. She was killed by her sister. Priscilla and Joseph went to church with both Davey and Mary, and the next day, after the fog had lifted, or rather, after Priscilla had allowed the fog to lift, Joseph came to Dead Kid Cave and told Priscilla of the two deaths. And what was her response?

"That's sad…do you know how to extract snake venom?"

◆

On Valentine's Day, the day before Priscilla's sixteenth birthday, Joseph took Priscilla to visit Pastor Swann. Apparently, Joseph and Pastor Swann had become quite close in recent months. Joseph's interest in snakes and snake-handling had led to many long, post-church conversations between the two, and so, when Priscilla needed a coral snake, Joseph knew just the man to turn to.

He was at his kitchen table drinking hot tea and reading the Bible when they arrived. They could see him through the window as Joseph knocked on the door.

"Well, good morning, young Smith, to what do I owe the pleasure?" said Pastor Swann, standing in the doorway.

"Mornin', Pastor, we ain't come at a bad time, did we?"

"Why, heavens no, Joseph. You're welcome here anytime, I've told you that. Say, who's your pretty young friend you've got back there?"

"Where's my manners?" said Joseph. "Pastor Swann, this here is my best pal Priscilla Louise Carpenter, and Priscilla, this here's Pastor Douglas Swann, the Snake Charmer."

Priscilla stuck out her hand for the pastor to shake it, and he did. "You can call me Pastor Swann, Priscilla," he said. Then he said, "And it's nice to finally put a face to the name I've heard so much about."

Priscilla's guard went up immediately. And carefully she withdrew her hand. She did not know this man. What could he have possibly heard about her? So much, at that. Who even would be talking about her? It had to have been Joseph. It had to be. And it had been quite some time since Priscilla had done anything that was acceptable to discuss with anybody, let alone a member of the clergy. So, what gives? Priscilla narrowed her eyes on them both.

"Don't look at me," said Joseph.

Pastor Swan smiled, and said, "Oh it wasn't this one that's been on about you, little lady. 'Twas your momma, Miss Lavinia, she speaks of you ever often in my company. She prays for the salvation of your soul on Sundays."

"Does she?" asked Priscilla.

"She does."

"Well, isn't that sweet of her," Priscilla said, clearly unamused.

Thankfully, Joseph interrupted before she could go on. He said, "Hey, so, Pastor Swann we was wonderin', can we take a look at all yer snakes you was tellin' me about?"

"Why, sure we can, young Smith. You wait here while I fetch my boots."

Pastor Swann led them around the side of the house, to a large shed with doors that opened on wheels. He unlocked the padlock, rolled the doors open, and the three of them went inside. Compared to the foot of snow outside, the shed was like a jungle, dark and warm. There was also the slight smell of rot in the air. Pulling on a string connected to a bare forty-watt bulb, and laughing at himself, Pastor Swann said, "Let there be light!" Neither Priscilla or Joseph gave him the laugh he was looking for, or even one at all.

The shed was maybe twenty feet long by ten feet wide, and it was filled with dozens of glass tanks, all differing in size, and each of them held one or more snakes, most of them venomous. With the lights on, Priscilla and Joseph began examining the Pastor's collection. Each serpent that their eyes stopped on, the Pastor spoke aloud its species. "Rattler," he said. "Copperhead," he said. "Gaboon Viper," he said. "Boomslang," he said. "Those are black snakes," he said. Then Priscilla crouched down low and said, "What's this one," and Pastor Swann said, "Coral."

Joseph crouched beside her and said, "Red on yellow?"

"Yep," said Priscilla. "Red on yellow. Work yer magic, Magic Man."

Joseph sighed, and outloud, but to himself, he said, "Alright, here goes nothin'." Then he stood up and turned to Pastor Swann and as casually as he could, but in an abnormally high pitch, he said, "So, uh, you think 'ere's anyway we can uh…get some of that there snake's venom? A thimbleful…to be exact?"

Pastor Swann grew stern and began eyeing both of them suspiciously. Then he said, "Why…would you want venom, Joseph?"

"Well, see…It's uh, for a science project, for uh, for…science…class."

Pastor Swann cocked his head to the side.

"Alright, listen, I'll be honest," said Joseph. "It's Scilly's birthday tomorrow, and uh…and…aw shit, I give up."

Pastor Swann's face cycled through expressions like a slot machine, mirroring the inner workings of his mind. Confusion, concern, intrigue, disbelief, understanding, and finally confidence, but then he sidestepped the question and said, "Priscilla, why do you no longer attend church? Your mother tells me you used to love church, but it no longer seems to interest you. I want to know why? Why have you forsaken God?"

Priscilla stood from her previously crouched position, slowly. She was contemplating how best to respond. If only the pastor had any idea what a silly question that was. He had deemed her a heretic merely for missing church. If he was even half aware of the truth, that question wouldn't have bothered to leave his lips, but telling him that she had sold her soul to the Devil in the name of Satanic witchcraft was too…on the nose. So instead, she massaged the creases out of a dress she hadn't worn in months, then she looked the pastor right in the eye and said, "Well, Pastor Swann, I found a new God… It's me. I'm God. That's why I don't come to yer church no more. I make ice and piss fall from the sky. Now, can we have a thimbleful of fuckin' venom or not?"

The Pastor was incredulous, in emotion and countenance, but he remained calm. His mouth opened to speak, but his voice caught in his throat, so instead of talking, he moved. He ripped the lid from atop one of the tanks, reached inside, and snatched up a small brown snake with a triangular head. It coiled around his hand and arm, and the pastor watched it carefully as he brought it up to his lips and gave it a gentle kiss on the nose. Then, with his eyes still on the snake mere inches from his face, to Priscilla he said, "This is Agkistrodon piscivorus, pit viper, cottonmouth…she's deadly as they come. And I handle her every day. But she never kills me… And do you know why she never kills me? Because my God protects me… So I'm going to throw this snake to you, Priscilla, and if you believe in your new God like I do mine, then you'll catch it, and if your new God loves you as does mine, then you won't die… Are you ready?"

Without hesitation, Priscilla said, "Bring it, fucker," and Pastor Swann did just that. He curled his upper lip, and tossed the snake right at her. And Priscilla caught it, but not with her hands. She caught it with her mind. Curling and coiling around some invisible matter, the snake remained otherwise frozen in midair between the two of them, held in suspended animation by Priscilla's raised black hand. Pastor Swann watched on in disbelief as the snake floated before him, backing slowly away, mumbling some prayer beneath his breath.

Then Priscilla lifted her stained black pointer finger, as if to say, one moment please, and she held it there for several lingering moments. Then she brought her finger down into a black fist and dropped it like a hammer, and when she did, the snake fell fast, and splatted on the ground, dead.

Priscilla turned her head toward Joseph and said, "I told you he wouldn't care about my birthday."

'Come Undone' by Duran Duran plays

"Dear sweet Jesus, girl, what are you?" Pastor Swann pleaded. "What have you done? How'd you—what in the—do not grieve for the Lord is your strength, do not fear for I am with you, do not be dismayed for I am—"

Priscilla raised her black fist in the air once again, and Pastor Swann stopped his rambling prayer.

In a soft, rhythmic tone, Priscilla began speaking, "Raise thy fist, and break thy wrist, and raise thy fist, and break thy wrist, and raise thy fist, and break thy wrist, and raise thy fist, and break thy wrist." Then her fist came open, fingers splayed, her flat black palm, outstretched toward Pastor Swan, X carved in the center. She began moving her hand in a circle, as though she were waxing an invisible Cadillac, and she continued, "Bend thy will, and break thy mind, burn thy clocks for sands of time. Gnash thy teeth, and bury thy dead, for ye will bake his earthly bread. Gnash thy teeth, and bury thy dead, for sleep will come at the foot of his bed… The Devil is now in you, Douglas. I am in you. Hail Satan."

With those words, Pastor Swann went limp. His arms dangled at his sides. His jaw sagged. His head hung on his neck. But his empty gaze remained fixed on Priscilla's black circling palm.

"What the fuck did you do?" asked Joseph.

"What I shoulda done from the start. I entranced him."

"A trance?! Like the one you put on Kester and Merle?!"

"Stifle yerself, ya goddamn wee-wee. No. I enslaved Kester and Merle. I took a little piece of each of their souls and locked them away in the two chunks of coal sittin' on my altar. Which, lookin' back, that was a mistake, I think…but no, this is just a trance."

"Alright, fine…just a trance. So, now what?"

"Well, now, old pal, unless you wanna try yer hand at coral snake venom extraction, I'm gonna order the pastor, here, to get busy on that. And once he's finished, I'm gonna tell him to put the snake back in this tank right here, then I'm gonna tell him to go sit down at his kitchen table, to pick up his stupid Bible, and to forget any of this ever happened. And when we leave, within a couple hours or so, the trance will fade, and for him this will all seem like a two-week-old dream. Sound good?"

"…*Stupid* Bible?"

"You heard me, fucker. Now go find yer slant-eyed sweetheart, before she dumps yer sorry ass. I can handle this. And pick her some flowers on yer way. Girls deserve flowers on Valentine's Day."

◆

February Fifteenth, Nineteen Seventy-Two

SWEET SIXTEEN

Priscilla was having a discussion with Merle and Kester about whether or not they wanted her to kill them. She apologized for what she had done, but that was all she could do. She had tried every beautification and revitalization spell in the book on them, and none of them worked or even had an effect. She couldn't bring herself to admit it to them, but she suspected that the reason none of her potions or spells would work on them is because they were in fact dead. Literal walking corpses. Sure, she could maybe set them free, though she hadn't tried. She was concerned they would drop dead the moment her spell was lifted, but even if she could unbind them from her, they couldn't possibly return to their family or anywhere in civilization. They were far too hideous to exist in the real world.

So after apologizing, she offered to kill them. Gently. Kester scratched at his chin with the one finger he had left on his right hand. Merle only stared at her, his yellow eyes bloodshot and bulging, threatening to fall from their sockets. Neither of them were quick to sign their own death warrant. Instead, to Priscilla's surprise, when Merle finally spoke up, through his partially unhinged jaw, he said, "Naw, musch as it pains ush to admit, we dhone decthided to shtay the coursthe. Bein' guhh, honesht, thish ish tshe mosht exthitin' thingk we efver got ourshelves intew, an… if ith's all tshe thame to you, we'll jusht shtay on. I guhh, know we look bhad, but we feel betther than ever, bofth of ush, I shwear it. Anywhay, we whannah sthee how thish thshit all endsh."

"Alright, then," said Priscilla. "You'll let me know if you change yer mind." Then she said, "Do what you want the rest of the day. Even God took a day to rest. But tomorrow we start early. We have to make lye." And with that, she left them to their devices.

A little later, as Priscilla was applying her makeup, Joseph walked in carrying a box wrapped in old newspaper. "Damn, you got this place lookin' good," he said. "I like 'em rock walls you got built out front."

"The credit goes to Merle and Kester. What's in the box?" asked Priscilla.

"Got ya a present," Joseph said.

"What is it?"

"Open it and find out, why don' ya."

Priscilla sat down the jar of black ash that she had been using to color her lips, and Joseph handed her the box. She sat it on her altar and carefully unwrapped it. She was not accustomed to receiving gifts, and it showed.

"I know it ain't much, but—"

"It's perfect."

"You like it?"

"I love it. Who made it?"

"I went up to see Pooky yesterday, and Mathias gave it to me for you. He made it. Now that he can see, I reckon he took up drawin' again. Me and Pooky built the frame for it this mornin'. So, happy birthday."

Priscilla removed the picture from the box, and admired it. Tears welled in her eyes but she did not let them fall. "Looks just like him." she said.

◆

FLASH FORWARD

Fourteen or so odd years later, Joseph came back to Dead Kid Cave. He had returned to Clockmaker to bury his mother, and on the night of her funeral, after getting skunk drunk with his father and uncle, Joseph walked out his uncle's back door and made his way through the woods. It would mark the first time he'd ever been in the witch's lair without the witch.

Even by the light of a single match, the spray paint scribbled all over the cave walls was obvious. Broken glass, empty beer cans and bottles, a pair of soiled women's underwear, burnt tinfoil, used condoms, cigarette butts—Joseph took in the extent of the damage. Vandals and degenerates of all kind, likely the socially unencumbered youth of Clockmaker, had obviously made this place their own. What was once a place of great mystery, magic, and evil, was now a debauched den of ignorance and boredom. Anything with value had been looted, and everything else had been smashed or pissed on, or both. Even the remains of the dead kid, himself, had been taken. Joseph felt like a maggot milling around inside of a decaying skull.

Two things remained, however. It was full of trash, and the word whore was crudely spraypainted in pink on one side, but the cast iron bathtub was right where they'd left it. It had likely been too heavy and worth too little to steal, which made sense, but that wasn't the only thing left. Also still hanging on the back wall from a rusty railroad spike was a smiling portrait of Big Tommy Green, hand drawn by Mathias Elder for Priscilla's sixteenth birthday, unmarked. Not a single drop of spray paint or piss or semen had touched it. For whatever reason, it had been spared. Why it had been spared, Joseph could not fathom. He stared up at the picture for a while, remembering his youth, remembering Big Tommy, and after a while ended, he left.

◆

'Priscilla Louise Carpenter,
High Witch of the Black Teeth Coven,
before you are hung by the neck,
do you have any final words?'
"If any of you have a message for the Devil,
tell me now, for I shall soon be in his company."

Surprisingly, unlike wet dreams, nightmares had never been a part of Priscilla's life, but they came to her regularly after Big Tommy died. In some of them, she was being chased by an angry mob carrying torches. In others, she was being hung by the neck. In one particular dream, she was wandering in a grave yard where she happened upon a tomb stone that had her own name etched into it. The date of death was nineteen seventy-two. The one similarity each nightmare had was that Tommy was in all of them. Sometimes he would be leading the mob, and sometimes he was a shadowy face in the back, or sometimes he was her hangman, tightening the noose around her neck, asking her if she has any final words. In the graveyard, when she found her own tombstone, Tommy was in the distance, standing over another grave with his back to her. Priscilla kept calling out to him, but he wouldn't turn around to face her, no matter how loud she called.

Oh, how Priscilla did miss Big Tommy. Like Joseph, Big Tommy had been her friend and protector, but with Tommy things were quite different. Tommy seemed to care for her more deeply or at least in a way that allowed him to show it more plainly. As where Joseph would make fun of her or punch her in the arm, Tommy would hold her hand and give her hugs. Once, he even kissed her on the forehead when he thought she had fallen asleep. He was gentle where Joseph was coarse, and he was warm where Joseph was cold. So as tight as Priscilla and Joseph surely were, she couldn't help but feel like when Tommy died, she had lost something that she would never find again. And there was no one to blame but herself.

And she did blame herself. In fact, she held herself solely responsible. For several days after Tommy's death, Priscilla did nothing but cry. She didn't eat. She didn't bathe, and when she slept, she had nightmares. All she seemed to be able to do was think about Tommy and weep.

On the day of his burial, however, the tears came to a sudden and permanent end. As she watched the casket being lowered into the ground through the eyes of her Familiar, perched high in a tree overlooking the cemetery, Priscilla had the realization that all of her sobbing and moaning was going to solve absolutely nothing. Maybe it was the feline-acute sound of the dirt being shoveled on to the casket, maybe it was watching Joseph cry uncontrollably for the first time since knowing him, but it came to her in an instant, and something inside her, naive yet intuitive, spoke loud and clear. It said, *You are not dead, you can fix this.*

And that was that. Priscilla took those ominous words straight to her heart, and when the final shovel full of dirt covered Tommy's grave, Priscilla zapped back into her body, dusted off the old broomstick, and took to the sky, in a manner of speaking, that is. What she should have done was dusted off the old copy of Frankenstein that Mathias had given her, and set about reading it, absorbing it, and implementing its lessons into her life, but she didn't. She went straight back to the Devil, straight back to the only source of strength she'd ever known. However, she did take a single evening to visit Maw Scill and her brother, but beyond that, it was all business. All witchin'. She attempted to visit her mother after leaving Maw Scill's, but from the road, Priscilla could hear Everett inside the house, screaming at the top of his lungs, and in that moment, the mean old son of a bitch finally sealed his own fate.

Since Jeremiah had returned, Everett seemed to have been attempting to turn over a new leaf, a less violent and sadistic leaf, anyway, and Priscilla had foolishly allowed herself to believe that maybe, just maybe, he was going to change, but as she stood outside in the snow, listening to him rage at her dear fragile mother, Priscilla decided then and there that old Everett would sooner rather than later be serving as a sacrificial lamb. Priscilla spit on the ground, and walked away. She was glad she never poisoned Everett, or dropped a block of ice on his head from fifty thousand feet in the air, though she had considered it, heavily, but there always seemed to be something holding her back. She never understood her hesitation, but now she was glad for it. His death was going to mean so much more than just her mother's happiness.

Priscilla put her slaves to work immediately, finding and gathering the necessary ingredients for her latest devilish pursuits.

Although Joseph had been mostly absent from anything witchcraft related since Tommy was killed, after a quick late-night fly-by he too began returning to Dead Kid Cave to assist in whatever way was necessary. Truth be told, his return was something more than a relief to Priscilla. She would, of course, continue her current path, with or without Joseph. She would certainly understand if he decided to back out completely, things had obviously gotten a bit sticky, but she was surely relieved when he didn't. Relieved to the extent that she almost burst into tears when he showed up the following evening carrying two dead raccoons. He just kind of walked in all nonchalant, and said, "Figured we'd need these," and when he did that, Priscilla's heart filled up all the way to top and nearly came pouring out of her eyes.

For what was to come had Priscilla on edge. Maybe even nervous, if she was being honest with herself. The book, for as frustratingly vague as it had previously been, with its *sprinkles of this and handfuls* of that, was adament and direct in warning about moving on to Level Five Spells, Spells of Death, too quickly or frivolously. According to the book, Spells of Death were the most difficult spells to cast. Difficult in that one of the prerequisites required Priscilla to smoke snake venom, or the Venom of the Gods, which the book described *as a mind-altering experience that has left many a witch unable to continue living.* Additionally, if performed incorrectly, Spells of Death, which were particularly complicated, often led to the death of the witch herself.

Furthermore, the book described, in great detail, the story of the first witch who attempted a Spell of Death. The short version of that story is as follows. *The witch thought the moon was waxing when it was actually waning and upon speaking Satan's name, she choked to death on her own tongue.* The end.

Needless to say, Priscilla was slightly intimidated, maybe even nervous. And if all of that wasn't enough, after smoking the venom, she was going to have to kill Everett. She was going to kill Everett and sacrifice him to Satan, in order to bring back Tommy. She would kill Everett with a Spell of Death, along with four other animals, and she would revive Tommy with a Spell of Life. And because Spells of Life required a human sacrifice, the head of a human, cut off at the collarbone to be specific, Priscilla would use Everett's severed head for that very purpose. Everett's death would serve not only as a blooming flower for her mother but as a seed of rebirth for her friend. And so it was written, and hermetically sealed.

Sure, she dealt with the fog like a professional, like a fucking doctor, and summoning lightning and ice came to her as naturally as picking apples. The motions to perform either of those tasks is actually quite similar. Whether picking apples or summoning lightning, it's all in the wrist. She could also now pick up, throw, and catch small objects with her mind. She could even pick herself up off the ground a couple of inches. Which was also rather simple, actually.

As the book explained, after the final cup of Death Tea, a witch should be able to access the realm of death without having to drink the tea. And the book was correct. So now, all Priscilla had to do was hold her breath, that's it. And if she chose to, she could, using visualization techniques, access the realm of death, and utilize it to manipulate the critical energetic fibers that bind all realms, and thus circumvent the natural order and mechanics of quantum and molecular physics, thereby achieving telekinetic abilities bestowed by the metaphysical plane.

So, sure, she could do some pretty incredible things, and the list even went on. She could also concoct poisons and potions that accomplished all sorts of things. She could fly on a broomstick. She could destroy entire crops with sky-born urine. She'd proved as much. But could she purposefully kill another human, and was she ready to die? Those were the questions that, in addition to the nightmares, had been keeping her from sleeping.

But the questions wouldn't last forever. Soon enough, the twenty-sixth would be upon her. The moon would be in its appropriate phase, she would have already had her period, and she would have not eaten meat for fourteen days, two days longer than necessary. The twenty-sixth would be the day and whether or not she was ready, it would come. Sure as death, it would come.

And on that day, as the sun is rising, with Joseph by her side, drawing deeply into her lungs, she would smoke the Venom of the Gods.

◆

The recipe that Priscilla used to concoct the Venom of the Gods is as follows. It has been revised by the author and a prominent (at least in some circles) chemist for clarity.

Step one, grind Reed Canary grass, which can be found along most any stream in West Virginia, or in the field beside Joseph's house, into a fine powder. Then mix the powder with lye made from the white ash of a hardwood fire, hickory was recommended by the book, and rain water. Stir and save mixture.

Step two, make a solvent from distilled coal tar, scavenged from the number nine mine. Using a basic moonshine still, distill the coal tar. (Note: Do not borrow a blind friend's still, and promise to return it. This process will destroy the still after the first run.) Unlike alcohol distillation, however, in which the immediate collection residue, or 'first run-off,' is discarded because it metabolizes in the human body

as formaldehyde and formic acid, which can lead to
serious illness, blindness, and even death, with coal tar
distillation the first run off is what you save.

Step three, this runoff is then added to the mixture of
lye and reed canary grass. After thoroughly shaking the
mixture, pour off the top layer of clear liquid and save.
The clear liquid is the solvent, and it is rich with the
Molecule of the Gods.

Step four, repeat the above steps, adding additional
solvent to the original mixture, at least three times,
in order to purify. Finally, mix all saved clear liquid
or solvents together. This will be the final solution.
Let the final solution evaporate. Crystals will remain.
Collect and save the crystals. A thimble's worth is
needed. (Note, to the reader—the above portion of the
recipe is also an accurate recipe for dimethyltryptamine
extraction.)

Step five, grind fox glove, procured from the late
Gertrude Green, into a fine powder, and save.
Four thimbles' worth are needed.

Step six, extract and save the venom of either the
mamba, cobra, or coral snake. A thimble's worth is
needed.

Step seven, in a copper container, mix the crystals
with the venom, and stir. Side note—smoking at this
stage of the recipe will lead to cardiac arrest within
seconds.

The final step is to add fox glove to the mixture of crystals and venom, and stir until the venom has been completely absorbed. Fox glove will prevent cardiac arrest. Allow this mixture to harden and dry completely before smoking. In order to achieve the desired effect, it is necessary to continue smoking until motor functions give out completely.

Amateur witches and civilians should not attempt to smoke the Venom of the Gods. Intense and permanent psychosis followed by death will result.

◆

FEBRUARY TWENTY-SIXTH, NINETEEN SEVENTY-TWO
FOUR PAST SEVEN ANTE MERIDIEM

'Il buono, il brutto, il cattivo' by Ennio Morricone plays

If she could light her mother's cigarette on a windy day then she could smoke snake venom in the goddamn rain. That very thought actually made a brief appearance in Priscilla's brain. Besides, what were a few measly drops of water to a witch as powerful as she, especially when she had her best pal there to hold a pink umbrella over her head. "Let it rain," Priscilla said to herself. "Let it rain." Holding a modified soda can to her face, she waited for the wind to subside and tried the lighter one more time. This time it worked and she inhaled.

At first, she felt a tingling sensation in her extremities. Toes, nose, fingertips, lips. It came on quick, almost instantly, and it only took two hits, two long, metallic hits. Then there was the sound of a hum or maybe a buzz, or a vibration, but whatever it was, it started in her ears and it grew, and as it grew it worked its way into her blood and began to course through her body. Like a wave of sound and feeling, cresting high above her head and crashing on her soul, the Venom of the Gods washed over her completely. She closed her eyes, exhaled a blue smoke, and leaned back against a tree. She was prepared for the worst. She could feel it coming.

Then it went away, the buzzing and the tingling, they both disappeared. Her legs stopped wobbling. Her heartbeat slowed. Her vision was no longer wonky. Just like that, she felt…sober. Normal. She took a few deep breaths and swallowed. Everything felt intact. She looked up at Joseph. The half of him not under the pink umbrella was soaked, but he didn't seem to notice. He was watching her intently. *I don't think it worked*, was what Priscilla was about to say, but then she blacked out.

When she woke up, she was in the hospital. Charleston Memorial Hospital in Charleston, West Virginia. Eight months had passed, but when her eyes eventually opened, her mother was there with her. She was sleeping in a chair in the corner of the room. Priscilla tried to move her legs but couldn't. She tried to move her arms, but they too were unresponsive. Her head, her fingers, her toes, nothing worked. Only her eyes seemed to be functioning properly.

In the days that followed, the doctors could not only not find any cause for her illness, but they were continuously stumped and perplexed by the diverse, novel, and alarming array of abnormalities they kept finding in her biochemistry. Not to mention her coal black hands. The doctors had no idea what to make of those. They couldn't identify it, and they could not scrub it off. The black that is. Not even with bleach or gasoline, which they tried. The only thing the doctors were certain of was that Priscilla was paralyzed. Other than that, they were lost.

Though it wasn't just her body that was damaged, her mind too seemed fuzzy. And her thoughts were erratic to the extent that she couldn't comprehend many of the things that her mother and the doctors would say to her. Her thoughts, much like people's words, were all twisted and reversed. But even still, she managed to make a few connections. She knew sort of what was going on, about one third of the time. The rest of the time was paralytic distorted psychosis. Neuroparalytic mania.

At one point, Priscilla attempted to use her telekinetic abilities to turn on an old radio that she had watched sit silent on her window sill for a week. She accidentally set off the sprinkler system instead. For two months Priscilla lived like this, trapped in her own body, a slave to the selfish and undisciplined nature of the hospital staff, lost in the chaos of her own misfiring synapses, and certain, when her mind allowed, that this was all punishment for her association with the Devil.

But eventually her thinking cleared. After ten months in the hospital, two of them conscious, she began to finally think straight. She could remember all the details of her life, who she was, where she was from, and she could remember the reason she was paralyzed in the first place, the goddamn God-venom. She still could not embody or call her Familiar, but fortunately her telekinetic abilities had begun to slowly return, and she immediately started using them to pester, confuse, and sometimes terrify a few members of the hospital staff whom she had grown to loathe while under their care.

Once Priscilla made a particular nurse get up and change the television seventeen times before the nurse screamed, 'WHAT THE FUCK!' and just switched it off. The nurse would change it back to the local news, and Priscilla would change it back to *Sanford and Son*. Over and over. Then when the nurse finally got fed up and turned the television off, Priscilla waited until she had gotten all the way sat back down before turning it back on again.

In that time, her mother never left her side, except to use the bathroom. All day she would sit in the corner of the hospital room, smoking and staring out the window, and at night she slept in that same chair with her feet up on the sill, next to the radio. Maw Scill and Jeremiah made the trip several times, and they brought Joseph along with them on a few occasions. Everett never bothered to come by.

But then one day, as Priscilla was telekinetically stealing the car keys from Nurse Cuntface's jacket pocket, she had an idea, a revelation even. Just as she was thinking, *That'll teach her to take the time to properly wipe my ass*, it came to Priscilla that maybe, just maybe, she could try to use her mind power to animate her limbs. So she tried it. And it worked. It took a few months but it worked.

At first, each action was solitary. She could stand, she could sit, she could walk and she could clap her hands, stomp her feet, and wave, but none of that could she do simultaneously, or gracefully. She could talk, but it came out sounding forced and slurred. Nevertheless, after a few more months of slow, clumsy telekinetic movement combined with physical therapy, Priscilla was quite nearly back to normal.

On April fifth, nineteen seventy-three, Priscilla was finally released into her mother's care. And what a glorious day it was. But then something unexpected happened. A few days after Priscilla was sent home, just when things were starting to look up, her mother and Everett were killed in a car accident. A coal truck's brakes went out, coming down Swisher hill, and plowed into them, shoving them off the road and over a seventy-foot embankment. Everett was killed instantly. Lavinia bled out, trapped upside down in the wreckage, beside the railroad tracks.

Being hospitalized had been a setback. It was difficult enough for Priscilla to get out of bed or to speak, let alone to ride a broom or bring her friend back from the dead. Needless to say, witchcraft had taken a backseat to the basic necessities of living, but when her mother was killed, well, that made witchcraft disappear. It also made Tommy disappear. It made Maw Scill and Jeremiah disappear. It made Lightning disappear. It even made Joseph disappear. To be painfully clear, Lavinia's sudden death made her daughter's entire world disappear.

Priscilla never went back to school, or church, or her lair. During which time her hands lost their blackness. She didn't go anywhere, in fact. She spent most of her time alone. Not even Joseph could get through to her, and no matter how Jeremiah or Maw Scill tried, they could not succeed in separating Priscilla from her grief. She seemed to be locked into it, and unable or unwilling to free herself. She would sit in silence and stare out windows or at walls, and she would go months at a time without speaking. Not even getting high and listening to Sabbath appealed to her, anymore.

Joseph and Phuket were married in seventy-six. Maw Scill died in her sleep the same year. It was this event that finally brought Priscilla out of her years' long trance. On her death bed, Maw Scill made Priscilla promise, pinky promise even, that she would find a reason to be happy again. And reluctantly, Priscilla stuck out her little finger. Maw Scill died that night. Jeremiah arranged the funeral, and damn near half of Clockmaker showed up to see the old woman off. Even Mathias showed up with Joseph and Phuket. Not a single person questioned him about the crow on his shoulder.

The following year, Priscilla met a man named John Perk. He sort of just showed up out of the blue, one day, as often the most significant people do. Priscilla was hanging clothes on the line, and suddenly, there he was. He had gotten lost looking for the road out of Clockmaker, or at least that's what he told Priscilla.

He had seen her hanging clothes on the line as he was driving by, so he stopped to ask for directions. If he hadn't been so handsome, Priscilla might have been concerned by his sudden appearance, but she was far too busy examining his chiseled exterior to worry about much of anything. He was about as handsome a man as Priscilla had ever seen, and as luck would have it, John Perk felt the same way about her.

Within the year, despite Jeremiah's disapproval, Priscilla moved to Boston with John. Sure, he was nothing like Jeremiah, but John was a good man, Priscilla was sure of it. So what he wore a tie and jacket on most days, and sure, he didn't like to smoke weed, and he didn't listen to Sabbath, or know how to tie on a fishing hook, but he was smart in other ways, and most importantly, he was kind to Priscilla. And when he told her that he loved her, he always looked her in the eye.

In the spring of seventy-nine, they were married in a Greek Orthodox church. Priscilla was twenty-three years old. John was thirty-one. At the ceremony, Jeremiah was the only person on the bride's side. He showed up late, but he was there when she came walking down the aisle. "Wouldn't have missed it for the world," he told her as she passed by.

Priscilla was twenty-four years old when she had her first child, a little girl she named Sarah. After Sarah came Daniel then Olivia. Jeremiah was at the hospital for all three births, and he always showed up with cigars. Joseph still wasn't around in those years. He had divorced Phuket and left Clockmaker, but beyond that, no one had any idea where he'd disappeared to.

At one point, Jeremiah sent Priscilla a newspaper clipping from the *Clockmaker Times*. "What are believed to be the remains of Merle and Kester Mire, two young men who disappeared in nineteen seventy-one, were found in the woods by hunters yesterday morning," the article said. The article went on to say that

"Despite the discovery of the remains, there were still no leads regarding their demise."

Then John made a small fortune on the stock market. It was nothing particularly extravagant, but land was purchased, a house was built, a nanny was hired, and Priscilla was able to return to school. She passed her high school equivalency exam, and began college at Suffolk University in nineteen eighty-six. She graduated six years later in nineteen ninety-three with a Master's Degree in Theoretical Physics. She was the first person in her family to have attended or graduated a university of higher learning. In nineteen ninety, Priscilla began developing the Thomas Green Foundation of Science and Mathematics. She wouldn't be reanimating Big Tommy's corpse, but at least his memory would go on.

In nineteen ninety-four, at the age of thirty-eight, Priscilla found a lump on her breast. By the time the tumor was discovered, cancer had spread throughout her body. She was given a month, maybe two, to live. That same evening, Priscilla went up into her attic, and from behind a stack of photo albums and a box of Christmas decorations, she retrieved an old wooden crate. She slid the crate from the shadows and removed the padlock that held it shut. From within the crate, she removed the book.

The following evening, for the first time since she was a little girl, Priscilla sought the power of Black Magic to kill the cancer inside her. Though she never mentioned that part of her past to him, the day John proposed to her, she made a silent promise to leave witchcraft behind her. There would be no room for evil, or the Devil, in the new life that she and John intended to create. Children, love, and laughter, those were their common goals, and witchin' no longer served a purpose.

Once again, the doctors could not explain Priscilla's recovery. "It surely had to be a miracle from God," one nurse said. Priscilla found her confidence rather comical. The nurse was wrong, of course, but either way, the cancer was in fact gone, and Priscilla would live. Once again, witchcraft…Satan…had saved her.

The cancer was gone, the book was locked in the crate, and the crate was slid back into the shadows. The only casualties were two neighborhood cats, whose corpses supplied the blood and bones that the book always required. They were a small price to pay, as far as Priscilla was concerned. Truth be told, she would have killed, deboned, and drained the blood of a thousand cats if it meant she would be alive to watch her children grow. Fortunately, the spell only required two animals. The cats were just convenient, as was the abandoned house at the end of the block. It served as a fine, one-time lair.

But despite her recent success, once again, Priscilla swore to herself the book would stay locked away in the attic this time. If the Grim Reaper came for her again, and he was bent on taking her, then she would go. She would walk next to the pale horse, and at the end of their journey, she would feed him an apple, or perhaps some oats. Until then, she had a foundation to run, and she wasn't going to be using any magic spells to make it happen.

Then came the grandchildren, Mark, then Chris, then the twins, Matthew and Lydia. Priscilla had never been happier, not even while flying on a broom. She loved being referred to as Nanny Scilla more than she could have ever imagined. It was her true calling in life. It was what she was born for, her purpose for existing. Not witchcraft. She was created to have children so that they too could have children, and the more time Priscilla spent watching them run and play in her backyard, the more certain of that she became. And all the while, through all those years, the book remained locked away in the attic.

A week after Priscilla's sixtieth birthday, she and John were sitting in their den beside the fireplace. John was reading a newspaper, drinking wine. Priscilla was watching Matthew and Lydia through the window as they attempted to build a snowman in the backyard. By the looks of the morning sky, it was going to be a beautiful day, which was rare for February in Boston. Then Priscilla heard a noise, like a brief static hiss, like a mechanical snake, and she looked around her, listening for the sound to re-occur. John was still reading the paper. He clearly hadn't heard anything, but then again, he hadn't been able to hear much of anything for some time. Nor could he see that well either. Old age had certainly taken its toll on him, but even as she watched him read the paper, oblivious to whatever strange sound she had just heard, Priscilla couldn't help but take note of just how endlessly in love with him she still was, after so many years.

Only a few seconds had passed, but when she looked back out the window, Matthew and Lydia were gone. Priscilla stood up and walked to the window. Maybe they had decided to play by the flower garden. Looking side to side, she could see the entirety of the backyard, which had an eight foot privacy fence surrounding it, and neither of the children were anywhere to be seen. Priscilla's heart sank. Something was wrong, she could feel it. Then she heard the noise again, a quick crack of static, like a whip, and she spun around. John was gone too.

Before Priscilla had even a moment to try to make sense of what was happening, the static and hissing came back, and this time it didn't go away. It started to pop and fizzle and get louder and louder until it was all that she could hear. Frantically, she began screaming her husband's name, and crying out for help, but the sound was so loud that she couldn't hear her own voice. She fell back against the windowsill, and covered her ears with her hands, but it was of no use. The racket was in her head too. There was something terribly wrong. Priscilla had no idea what was happening, but whatever it was, was not good.

Without her knowing, Priscilla had slid down the wall. She

could feel pressure on her ass, as though she were sitting, but in her mind she was standing. The dimensions and contents of the den began to distort and bend and multiply, as though her optic nerves had been replaced by funhouse mirrors. It was this same distortion that found its way into her body. It started with her toes and worked its way up, pulling, stretching and twisting. She could feel it move through her legs and along her back. There was no pain, only pressure. If she hadn't been so frightened, she might have actually enjoyed it.

And just when Priscilla thought she might be dying, just to really show her who was the boss, reality went ahead and split wide open. As though her life were a major motion picture being shown in a crowded theater, and a pipe bomb had just gone off in her projection room, killing the projectionist and destroying the film, Priscilla watched everything around her, including the air, melt and burn away into blackness. The source of the hissing, now combined with popping and cracking, was painfully clear. Reality was on fire. The tapestry of existence was burning. She closed her eyes. The sound was making her skull rattle, and she could no longer bear witness to the crumbling of the known. If this was it, if this was her time, then so be it, but she didn't have to watch it. Just a few moments after her eyes closed, however, silence fell around her, and a cold breeze began to blow.

Priscilla didn't feel dead, but she couldn't be sure, having never been dead before. She could feel the wind on her cheeks. She could hear a dog barking in the distance. Those were positive signs. Hesitantly, but not hesitantly enough, she opened her eyes, and when she did, a dense, mind-crushing, soul-retching, paradigm-shattering confusion overwhelmed her. Reality, by any definition of the word, had been skullfucked into oblivion, and Priscilla was standing on the precipice of its remains. Pink fucking umbrella.

She was no longer in her den. The fireplace and bookshelves, the chess table, the photos of her family, her husband, her grand-children, all the things that she expected and hoped would be there, had vanished. They had vanished, and had been replaced by rocks and snow and sticks. She was outside. In the woods. Her back was against a tree. A light rain was falling around her, and a young, teenage, dirt-stache clad Joseph Henry Smith was standing over her, watching her with rotten curiosity. Above him was a pink umbrella. He said, "You good, pal?"

Priscilla's blood went cold, ice cold, colder than the sickles that hung malevolently from the rocks around her, colder than the white snowflakes that clung to her black cloak, colder than the hand of a corpse cradling a witch's tit. Had she time traveled?

Was this an extremely vivid acid flashback? Was she dead, and this was Purgatory? Or Hell? Or God forbid, Heaven? The questions raced through her mind, and they would have continued to race had she not taken notice of her hands, but she had, and that stopped the questions in their tracks.

Her hands were the hands of a child, and her hands were black. The wrinkles were gone. The dark protruding veins were gone. The scar on the back of her wrist from when she had fallen down the steps, just after making fun of John for doing the same, it was gone too. This was not a time slip. It was not purgatory. The reality of her situation was too painfully clear to even consider denying. Priscilla was sixteen years old again. Her life, her family, her children, her grandchildren, they were all an illusion. In that very moment, another significant crack formed on Priscilla's heart, never to be mended.

Priscilla said, "What day is it, Joseph?" She nearly vomited out the words. It was the sound of her voice. Not only did it sound as young as her hands looked, but the Appalachian accent that she spent so many years trying to tame was now back like it had never left.

Joseph thought for a second. "I don't know, Saturday I reckon."

"Oh, Jesus Christ, what year is it?"

"What *year* is it? Holy Hell, you ain't hit that shit but twice, and you done lost the year? That must be some good shit."

"Joseph!" Priscilla cut him off. She was trembling, and she was beginning to cry. "Goddamnit, is it nineteen seventy-two? Is it, Joseph? Oh God, is it seventy-two? Is it…? Is it…? Is it nineteen seventy fuckin' two? Is it?" The words were coming out of her as though she were pleading for something that she didn't want but must have, as though her acquisition of knowledge was being forced upon her at knifepoint.

Joseph didn't answer her right away. Through tears, Priscilla watched his face go from bewildered and mildly alarmed to focused then relaxed, but finally, sincere and gentle as he could, Joseph nodded, and he said, "Yeah…Priscilla, it's nineteen seventy-two…I believe it's the twenty-sixth…of February. I'm not real sure, though." Joseph looked down at his watch, "It's ten to eight, in the mornin'…that means you been out about forty-five minutes, I reckon. You smoked God's Venom, you remember?"

Priscilla didn't respond. On the outside, in appearance, she was stupefied and lost. She was sitting on a rock in the middle of the woods, staring blankly up at Joseph, but in her mind, on the inside, she was staring through Joseph, and she was sitting in her living room in Boston, replaying old memories of her children on Christmas morning. She was cycling through the years and watching them grow older and older, until they started arriving with children of their own. She was watching her husband sit in the corner of the same living room in his Santa hat. His big, silly smile, and his Santa hat.

She loved to watch him watch his children open presents. His was a perfect expression of pure joy.

"Here, Scilly, just hang on to me. Let's get ya back to the cave, you look like hell. Come on, kitty, follow us." Before Priscilla knew what was happening, Joseph had hoisted her up like he was about to carry her over their marital threshold. She did not protest. She needed to be held, even if it was by a sixteen-year-old boy. As he carried her through the forest, Priscilla could only think about the last fifty odd years of her life, and how even if they had been nothing more than a drug-induced fantasy, a chemical mirage, she still loved and longed for her family all the same. It was as if they had all died.

Without John, who would keep her warm at night? Who would she cook for, clean for, work for…live for? Whose hand would she hold during scary movies? She was no longer somebody's wife, no longer a mother, or a grandmother. She was a child, a fucking child…and dear God, she was aligned with the Devil. Back in her sixteen-year-old body, the memories of her childhood were as vague as if she had lived them five decades prior, and all she could think about was Christmas with her children and the man that she married. Resurrecting Tommy Green was a distant, nearly forgotten idea.

One thing Priscilla remembered clearly was the book's short description of the Venom of the Gods: *'a mind-altering experience that has left many a witch unable to continue living.'* She had carried it with her all of those years, all through her false life, and she finally understood. One life was plenty. After living one, the thought of living another was enough to make most anyone yearn for a noose. And in that instant, being carried through the woods, in the rain, by a teenage Joseph Smith, she realized for the very first time that becoming a witch had been a terrible, unredeemable mistake, that no amount of magic would fix any of what she'd destroyed, and that she was unable, like so many venom-smoking witches before her, to go on living. As soon as she had a chance, as soon as she was alone, she would find a way to kill herself. There was no way around it. She would not go on like this.

Joseph hadn't carried Priscilla more than twenty yards from where he picked her up off the ground when the sound of a solitary horn began echoing over the mountains around them. At first Priscilla thought it was in her head, but when Joseph looked down at her, the alarm on his face said otherwise. The sound reverberated around them, and in its very essence, Priscilla could detect a clear subliminal element of menace or perhaps even evil. It was a long sour note that rang out like the marching commencement of some demonic legion, a note that could have only been born in the hollowed out antler of some long-extinct beast with six heads and twice as many gnarled spikes twisting up from under thorned crowns, a beast that roamed the earth when it was still dark and without stars. It was that kind of note.

The horn's unholy song only lasted a few seconds, six to be exact, but when it came to an end, it left a silence in the woods that would have made the crypts under Paris long for a little peace and quiet. Joseph didn't move. He stood there, in the now still forest, squinting for the snow and scanning the sky through the trees. Priscilla could see that his face had changed. Cradled in his arms, looking up at him, she could see that his face was now a reflection of his mind, and his mind was somewhere else. The confident grin that she had awoken to had been replaced by a distant, listless leer. Softly, Priscilla asked him, "What are you thinkin' about?"

Joseph didn't answer right away. He watched the sky a while longer without acknowledging her, but then he responded to her question with a question of his own. He said, "I ever tell you 'bout the time I heard my momma and daddy havin' sex?"

A sad, half-smile formed on Priscilla's face. "No," she said, "I don't believe you have."

"Well…they come home drunk from my daddy's Christmas

party one year. It was late, and I was only six or seven years old, so I reckon they figured I was out like a light…but I wasn't. Anyway, they went at it, damn near all night, and all night long, I couldn't sleep. All I could do was listen…and I could hear it all too…every little squish and splat…I ain't think I'd ever be able to look either one of 'em in the face ever again…'"

"Joseph…why are you tellin' me this?"

"Well," said Joseph, without any humor in his voice. "I used to think that was worst sound I ever heard in my life, till just now. Now I ain't so sure…"

'I Put a Spell on You' by Screamin' Jay Hawkins plays

◆

FEBRUARY TWENTY SIXTH, NINETEEN SEVENTY-TWO
FOUR PAST EIGHT, ANTE MERIDIEM

In defense of themselves, the Pittson Coal Company referred to the flood as an 'act of God'. After all, it was their dam that broke. Most everyone else said it was the fault of the mine owners and managers, the fault of men. After all, it was their dam that broke. The truth, however, was quite the opposite. Quite the exact opposite. The truth was, the dam broke because of the Devil and a sixteen-year-old girl. They alone were the cause. God and Man were merely accomplices.

Regardless of who caused it, with the godless sounding of Hell's Golden Horn, the coal slurry impoundment dam at the Pittson Coal Company Mine, at the head of Buffalo Creek Valley, burst wide open, thus unleashing one hundred and thirty-two million gallons of water that created a dense black coal-sludge wave, thirty foot high, and more than five hundred feet across.

The town of Saunders, located directly below the dam, was first to get hit. Then Pardee, Lorado, Lundale, Stowe, Crites, Latrobe, and so on. As the black water raged down the valley, it picked up trees, cars, houses, rocks, random debris, and most everything in its path, giving the wave a sort of charge and making it that much more destructive and lethal as it advanced.

Towering over telephone poles, and crashing down on chimneys, more than a hundred people were dead within three hours. Hundreds of homes were destroyed. Kids orphaned. Wives widowed. Being that it was a cold, snowy Saturday morning in February, many people were still in bed when the wave hit. Entire families were washed away in their sleep. The water swept away everything in its path, gouging out the land and gouging out life with the same indifference. At seven feet per second, it twisted up people right along with the rail lines and bridges. Fifteen towns along the Buffalo Creek Valley were destroyed.

Death, destruction, chaos. Blackness. A child impaled and torn apart by a stop sign, houses being ripped from their foundations, mobile homes being ridden like surf boards. A man from Stowe named Alvid Davis was working outside his home when he looked up and saw the flood waters coming down the valley. Alvid managed to rescue two of his sons. His oldest daughter Molly was pulled from the water two miles away, black and greasy and barely alive. Alvid's youngest son and daughter and his wife were never found. Later, in the hospital, Molly told her father that she was listening to her mother pray in her bedroom when the waters hit the house.

And so it went, death, coal sludge, and tears. Whichever God-fearing man was the first to say *'Come Hell or high water'* likely never imagined the two would arrive together, but in this instance they had, and in the aftermath of the flood, dead bodies were found hanging upside down in the trees.

THREE SEVEN EIGHT

Four hours and eighteen miles later, the last sludgy black suds, remnants of the flood, washed up on the boots of Sheriff White. He'd been expecting as much. Sheriff Merkin from Robinette had phoned an hour prior, just after his town was destroyed. He wanted to warn Sheriff White to what was coming down the valley in his direction. Merkin was ranting on about how some coal mine was going to be buying him a new squad car when Sheriff White hung up the phone. Merkin had always talked too much, as far as Sheriff White was concerned.

The endless blathering wasn't the only reason Sheriff White hung up the phone though. He simply was not concerned. As soon as Merkin mentioned the height of the water, Sheriff White knew it would never make it to Clockmaker. Even though Clockmaker sat at the foot of the Buffalo Creek Valley, by Sheriff White's calculations, he was pretty certain the hills would suck up whatever wave Merkin was going on about before it ever crashed down on his shores. So now, the black water barely messing Sheriff White's polished boots was yet another confirmation of his superior cunning and wisdom.

And if there was another thing that he would have put money on, had he known the proper bookie, it was that all the strange shit happening in his town recently, the piss rain, the lightning, the fog, the hail, the earthquake, the mess at Gertrude Green's place, and the black shit on his boots, it was all connected. It all had the same feel. There were no facts or clues that led him to this conclusion of course, it was all intuition and instinct. Nevertheless, he maintained the confidence of a man who was in possession of the murder weapon and a taped confession.

Standing in a creek bed that marked the town boundary, the Sheriff of Clockmaker, unincorporated, adjusted the revolver on his hip, and let a thin, syrupy line of tobacco juice leak from his lips. Where the Sheriff stood, if he had been wrong about the flood, about the amount of water moving in his direction, he would have been the first person in his town to be washed from the earth. This was not a coincidence. He had specifically chosen the Millfall creek bottoms, to wait for whatever flood might be coming his way. Sheriff White had a deep, deep faith in himself, in his intuition, and in his instinct, and from time to time he liked to test them. Besides, he once had a vision of his own death, and smashed into a creek bed with his lungs full of black water wasn't it..

If it weren't for all the bullshit that would be arriving by nightfall, he might have felt good about the day. After all, as he suspected, Clockmaker had been spared the destruction of the flood, not a single life was lost, and all was well, relatively. He should have felt, at the very least, satisfied, triumphant even, but he felt nothing of the sort. Watching the eddies of Millfall Creek turn black like squid ink, Sheriff White felt only bitter frustration. Politicians, reporters, inspectors, missionaries, city rats and outsiders of all kinds would soon be descending upon his quiet little town. They would start showing up tonight, and by morning there would be chaos. *Lights and cameras, questions and investigations, reports and phone calls, Jews and niggers, bullshit and more bullshit.* He could see it now. *Jesus Christ. It's comin'*, he thought. *It's comin'…*

LUCIFER

*'(Don't Worry) If There's a Hell Below, We're All Going to Go'
by Curtis Mayfield plays*

They arrived in droves. Religious missionaries, Army and National Guard personnel, state and county and town officials, the Red Cross, newspaper reporters, television reporters, mine inspectors, health and safety advisors, concerned locals and so on, all flocked to the Buffalo Creek Valley. Richard Nixon, however, could not make it. He was in Beijing when word of the flood reached his desk, so he sent the corrupt, charismatic Governor of West Virginia, Arch Moore, in his stead. Arch, having recently polished his shoes, chose to tour the afflicted area by helicopter and later described the 'awesome destruction' that he witnessed, as though he, himself, had been knee deep in the mud and blood. But all the same, along with the droves, even the Governor made his way into the valley.

The bulk of the population influx was felt by the town of Man, it being the closest inhabitable town to the disaster. The military and Red Cross constructed their bases there, and a temporary morgue was set up at an elementary school. The overflow, however, mostly the newly homeless, missionaries, and a few reporters found their way to Clockmaker, and before noon, Main Street was swarming with strange faces. Blockades were erected to direct the flow of traffic, churches were repurposed as shelters,

and Sheriff White had a man on every corner, five of whom were emergency-deputized in the middle of the night. Crowds were gathered here and there, some mobilizing to take action, some gossiping, and some staring dumbly at the commotion. A few people wore the hollow look of grief and took notice of nothing around them.

With everything going on, with all the disorder and confusion, with the circling helicopters, and the shouting missionaries, a smooth, unremarkable entrance into Clockmaker should have been quite easy, but when the Devil rolled into town, every person on Main Street, and even God, stopped to take notice. God noticed because, as he was bathing in the eternal fountain, something sent a jagged ripple through the cosmos. The people on Main Street noticed because, in a landscape marked heavily by shades of brown and grey, from the brooding sky to the leafless trees, the Devil arrived in the backseat of a metallic purple Rolls Royce Silver Wraith, with a metallic golden grill, golden trim and golden Spirit of Rapture hood ornament. Creeping slow. Engine rumbling. Windows dark.

Discussions, labor, commerce, even loitering seemed to come to a hault, as all eyes turned toward the low rumbling engine of the Wraith. A farmer lifted the hat from his head, missionaries crossed themselves, many of the women held a hand over their mouths, and a little boy in a flannel shirt scratched his head with curiosity, but all stopped and watched as the dazzling purple car crept along Main Street. No one in Clockmaker, not even the reporters from Charleston, with their suits and ties, had ever seen a machine quite like it. Not even Sheriff White.

The Wraith came to a stop in front of Layfield Market, and a small crowd began to gather around. Not too close though. Sheriff White casually pushed his way to the front and stood with his hands on his hips, lifting his chin in an attempt to see through the cars darkened windows. The Wraith sat idling, trembling, ominous, a cloud of exhaust coming up from its rear. But no one stepped out. Nor did the windows come down. After half a minute or so, Sheriff White stepped toward the car. A car worth more than he would make in his entire lifetime.

For a moment, the Sheriff stood just outside the driver's door, waiting. Then, just as he raised a crooked finger to tap on the glass, the door came ajar. Sheriff White took a few steps back.

All at once, three of four doors came open, and three men stepped from the vehicle, closing their doors behind them. The rear passenger side door did not open. Sheriff White's hand instinctively, but casually, found and came to rest on his revolver.

Maybe it was because the car was so clean, or so obviously expensive and luxurious, but the three men that stepped from the Wraith were the last type of men that Sheriff White or anyone gathered there expected them to be. They were black men. And not only were they black, but each of them was large, barrel-chested, and particularly striking, and they were, each of them, wearing matching black, tailor-made suits and black Porkpie hats. Black leather shoes, thin black ties, black shirts, black skin, black hair, from head to toe they were black on black. All but their eyes, which were bloodshot. And of course, their smiles, but they weren't allowing those to show. They stood solitary and grim outside the still idling automobile.

"Mornin', boys" said Sheriff White, in a way that made a statement, asked a question, and demeaned all at once.

The three men surveyed the scene around them, their faces stern and unflinching, but neither of them responded or even acknowledged the Sheriff's quasi-greeting.

Sheriff White gave more than enough time for a response, then he repeated himself, which he hated to do. Anyone who knew him knew that. This time, firming his grip on his revolver, and much more slowly, he said, "I said, *Mornin', boys.*"

Again there was no response. Only tension. But this time, the driver of the Wraith turned his head slightly and met the Sheriff's eyes. There was a brief stare-down, a sizing-up as it were. Then the driver reached up quick, and Sheriff White flinched, but the man only adjusted the toothpick in the corner of his mouth. The driver grinned. Sheriff White's nostrils flared, making his anger apparent. Without warning, the driver turned, walked around to the other side of the car, and opened the rear door.

Cooler than a polar bear's paw prints. Badder than Louisiana Lightning. Flyer than Sly Stone on a seven forty seven jumbo jet. When the Devil stepped out of the back of the Wraith, he did so with deliberate confidence. One foot, or rather, one black alligator boot, then the other. He stood up straight and tall, flexing his back against the long ride, stretching his arms for show. His dress was the same as the other men, except for a long black and white chinchilla fur coat that he wore over his suit, and in his hat was a black porcupine quill. The other men, they had no quills.

The Devil closed his eyes, and with his hands on his chest, he took in a long deep breath through his nose, and he let it out with a dramatic, "Ahhhh…moun-tain air…"

Then he casually turned to face the Sheriff. And with a tiger's gold-plated smile, and the cool, jazzy voice of a Brooklyn street thief, the Devil said, 'Good morning to you, Sheriff.' With more than a little flare, he tipped his hat to the aging lawman, and the gold on his fingers glistened, even though the sun was hiding that day.

"What in the mother fuck are you?" asked Sheriff White, sounding genuinely puzzled. If the Devil had showed up in his true form, four thousand feet tall, with scales and fangs and wings that spanned the entire state of West Virginia, he might have been easier for the Sheriff to comprehend. But he hadn't.

Immediately, the Devil's face lit up, showing a mouth full of gold once again. The question had clearly tickled something in his fancy. "Rest easy there, Sheriff. We mean you fine folk no trouble. Quite the opposite," he said. "My name is Black Lavender Luci (pronounced loose-ee). Perhaps you've heard of me?"

"Perhaps I've heard of you…well, Mister Black Luci, you'll have to forgive me, I don't subscribe to *Jungle Bunny Weekly*," said Sheriff White. "Please, do enlighten me."

"That's Black *Lavender* Luci, Sheriff. No need for the Mister. But you can call me Luci. All my friends do."

Sheriff White spit tobacco juice in the snow. He did not respond otherwise.

"As I said, we do not want any trouble, Sheriff. A nigga knows his place," said the Devil, his demeanor cool as ever.

The driver of the car, who was still standing beside him, said, "That's right."

"I am but a mere benefactor—" continued the Devil, elevating his voice loud enough for all to hear.

But he was interrupted by Sheriff White. "A bene-what?"

"A bene—a man of wealth and generosity, and I might add, taste. Do try to keep up, Sheriff. I was sent here personally by your governor, Archie Moore, to help all the fine and fair folk devastated by yesterday's tragic…tragic flood."

Sheriff White did not respond right away. He was nodding, almost compulsively. Veins were showing in his forehead. "Well, I'd love to help ya, I really would," he finally said, "but ya see, we ain't got no rooms left to board you boys. Whole town's booked up. You might wanna check in Man, I hear the Red Cross has tents set up. And if 'at don't work, well…I reckon you can take to the trees like yer ancestors."

The Devil smiled real wide this time. "Now don't you worry your pretty little head, Sheriff. We are not the type of niggas that rent, are we, Smiley?"

"Nope," said the driver, his face expressionless, his stare deadpan.

"No, we are not," the Devil confirmed. "We purchased a property on our way into town. Cash. We only came to Main Street for a few necessities. Sugar and such."

"The hell you say," said Sheriff White, incredulously.

"Oh yes, Sheriff, the deed was signed over to me, not an hour ago, by a lovely woman named…" The Devil reached into his coat and retrieved a piece of paper. He carefully unfolded it, examined it, and said, "White, Elmira White. Maybe you know the place, it's an old one story with a stone well in the backyard."

"Over my goddamn dead body, let me see that deed." Sheriff White was in motion before he could finish his sentence. He stormed around the car and snatched the deed from the Devil's hand. He was visibly shaking as he read.

"Easy lemon-squeezy," said the Devil, with a grin. "I just had these gators shined yesterday."

Sheriff White paid no attention. His concentration was on the deed.

The Devil said, "You do know, Sheriff, there is a difference between an out-of-focus photograph and a snapshot of clouds and fogbanks, right? Schrodinger? You feel me?" He was prodding the Sheriff.

Sheriff White stopped reading the deed, and looked up at the Devil. Rage and confusion smeared like lipstick on his face. "This is my sister's property," he said, ignoring the questions and provocations.

Light and playful as could be, the Devil said, "Well, I'll be a monkey's uncle, how about that. It sure is a small world, isn't it, Sheriff? You know, now that you mention it, Elmira did say that her son was a law man."

THREE EIGHT SEVEN

"Did she?" Sheriff White's words came out just above a whisper. His face was flushed with anger.

The Devil lowered his voice to match the Sheriff's and said, "She did." Then he said, "Would you like to know what else she said?"

Sheriff White nodded gravely.

"She said…that her son would not be happy about our little transaction, but for that amount of money both him and Ethel could kiss her lily-white ass…" The Devil grinned, and added, "For her age, your mother sure does have quite a bit of spunk left in her, doesn't she, Sheriff? By the way, who is Ethel? Your sister?"

Sheriff White looked as though he would either pounce or collapse at any moment. His fists were tightening into hammers at his side, one of them crushing the deed to his deceased sister's house. But then, all at once, he stuffed the crumpled piece of paper back into the Devil's outstretched palm and stormed off toward his patrol car, shouting, "Junior, Stanley, keep an eye on traffic. Deputy, man the station… I'm goin' to have a word with my fuckin' mother." At his car, he stopped, and turned back to the Devil, and the crowd of spectators, and said, "And you…slick, if you gave my mother one cent under seven grand, you and yer boys'll be hangin' by a tree 'fore sundown. You hear me? I'll set that fuckin' circus car on fire, and kill all of ya."

Calmly, the Devil raised a hand with four fingers extended, and said, "Fourteen, Sheriff. I paid her fourteen. Cash…of course. As I said, Sheriff, I am here to help."

Sheriff White started to speak, and faltered. His fists unclenched. He was caught in the position of a man who had just been fed way too much free acid. Thank you, but fuck you. He made to speak again, waved it away, and then just said, "Eh, god of fuck," and got into his car.

The Devil and his men, Junior, Stanley, and a few others watched the Sheriff pull out of view. A light snow had begun to fall. The Devil took hold of his lapels and pulled the chinchilla fur closed over his chest. From his pocket, he removed a thin, crudely-rolled cigar and a golden lighter. He put the cigar in his mouth, clicked open the lighter, and set fire to the green end, exhaling a large plume of skunky-smelling smoke. "When the law is away, a nigga will play," said the Devil, and he pulled hard on the cigar. Then, to his men, with smoke floating lazily from his lips, he said, "Alright, now let's have some fun. Y'all niggas grab Courvoisier and cigarettes…and grape soda. I'm finna' make it rain hundred dolla bills on all these poor white mothafuckas." The Devil walked around the car, and stepped up on a bench in front of the market, and real loud, so everyone on Main Street could hear, he shouted, "Good people of Clockmaker! For the next five minutes, Black Lavender Luci will be giving away hundred dollar bills to every man, woman, and child! Line up to receive yours!"

Then, as the line began forming, the Devil took in another lungful of sweet sticky dank. Exhaling, he looked down at Junior and Stanley who were standing idly by, with disturbed looks on their faces, and he said, "Y'all niggas wanna hit this?"

'Nobody Speak' by DJ Shadow and Run The Jewels plays

━━━━◆━━━━

CHaPTeR fourteEn

Priscilla tightened the noose around her neck. There was no point in saying goodbye to anyone. Unaware of the flood, she and Joseph had spent the previous day and night in Dead Kid Cave, trying to make sense of it all, and it hadn't helped. All night long they sat awake as Priscilla tried to make Joseph understand and appreciate what exactly happened to her after she smoked the venom. She tried to explain that she was a sixty-four-year-old woman, that she had lived an entire life, and in that life she had created a family that she loved and now missed so deeply that her heart ached, and without them, it was hard for her to imagine going on living. Joseph couldn't grasp it, though he did try. But he was just a kid.

So what was the point? She'd already said goodbye to her mother and Maw Scill many years ago. She had lost them, mourned them, and stood over their graves in her other life. Even Joseph was a relative stranger after so much time estranged. Besides, it wouldn't be Priscilla that was saying goodbye. Priscilla was gone. Who she was now was someone else. The little girl whose body she now inhabited had the wear of someone else's work boots or a rope around the neck. The fact of the matter was she was not a little girl. She was an old woman. An old woman with a family, with children, with grandchildren. She had arthritis in her knees, a bad back, scars, grey hair, and wrinkles. This body had none of those things. This body was a foreign entity. When it came down to it, she felt like she was about to hang a ghost.

To make matters worse, she wasn't even positive that killing herself was going to work. Since she'd been back, Priscilla had the unrelenting suspicion that she was still trapped in the illusion of the venom, that at any moment reality would break down again and she would find herself back under the pink umbrella. So if the illusion were real, then maybe even death wouldn't end things. Maybe death would only take her back, back to the pink umbrella, again and again and again.

She had chosen a tree that no one would find or happen across, deep in the woods, and even deeper into a briar thicket. Priscilla wanted to die, but she didn't want to be found. When it came to her thoughts, she was as detached as any one person could be from their own mind, but she did have sense enough to know that anybody who discovered a little girl hanging dead in a tree was going to have their day ruined, or worse. So she chose a tree that nobody would find, and that wouldn't break under her weight. Just because she was on her way out, it didn't give her the right to be inconsiderate of others. She made her bed alone, and she would lay in it alone, and the creatures of the forest would take care of her corpse. Whatever the bears and birds left behind, the flys and maggots would finish.

It had been little more than a day since she'd been back in Clockmaker, back in her teenage body, back in time, and her want of death had only intensified. She was so wrapped up in the loss of her previous life that she couldn't even begin to recognize the unusual opportunity with which she had been presented. Yes, she had lost her family, and her old life, and that was a terrible thing, a one-of-a-kind tragedy, but she was young again, and not only was she young again, but the wisdom of her past life was still with her, even if it had already begun to fade like a dream. Most people would give limbs for such an opportunity, to know then what they know now, or in this case to know now what she knew then, but Priscilla simply couldn't see it yet. All she could see were the faces of her children. Christmas mornings. Bedtime stories.

Truth be told, it would have only taken a few more days and Priscilla would have realized just how fortunate she was to be alive, to see her mother and Maw Scill again, to see Joseph again, to do cartwheels again, to start over. Unfortunately, her mind was in the process of recondensing, and or re-integrating back into her old brain, in an old dimension, and it was having quite a bit of trouble getting things dialed in. If Priscilla had only given time to adjust, time to heal, she wouldn't be sitting on a tree limb, twenty feet off the ground, with a noose around her neck. But she didn't, and she was. Grief and trans-dimensional mind-melt had her brain twisted past the point of normal operation, and killing herself seemed the only escape.

Priscilla stared down at the ground, her legs dangling below her. This was it. She'd kissed her cat. The book was buried. Her broom had been burned. Kester and Merle were free. They had wanted to watch Priscilla hang herself, but she told them they would have to take her word for it. She told them they were free to do as they pleased otherwise, then she walked off, dragging a rope behind her. With her meager affairs and estate in order, sitting on a limb, dawning her dirty black cloak, now was the time. The ground was twenty feet below. The rope was around her neck. Her last thought, before she let go of the tree, was, *Please give me death.* Then she let go.

Life is boredom masked by decay. Boredom is laziness masked by indifference. Laziness is apathy masked by nihilism. Apathy is fear masked by comfort. And fear is the unknown masked by death. We grow bored in life, not because we lack entertainment or because time passes too slowly, but because death, in its possibility, is ever present and ever pressing, and it casts its shadow over life, forever maintaining the potential to corrupt any moment left uncherished. And Death, Death is merely an illusion, albeit a persistent one. It wears no mask because it is the mask. It is the truth. Death is the truth. Death is.

How many times had Priscilla questioned if she was dead? How many times? The number was too many to keep count. She tried. She lost count with the third time she drank Death Tea. But if she was attempting to count then she couldn't be dead… right? Of course not. The dead don't count. At least, not that she was aware of.

Besides, not only did she still feel alive, she felt…well, she felt cozy. But wait, maybe she was in Heaven. Maybe she was actually dead and she had gone to Heaven. That was possible, although not likely, given her ties to the Beast and all, but maybe. Or maybe she was back in Boston, at home, in bed, in her other life, and at any moment her husband, she couldn't remember his name, would roll over and lightly kiss her forehead, as he did every morning. Or maybe this was still part of the first cup of Death Tea. Or maybe Hell was just more comfortable than she imagined. It was hard to say, not knowing.

Either way, she was not in a hurry to open her eyes and find out. The last thing she could remember was climbing the tree with the rope. So she had to be dead. The tree limb was sturdy. The hangman's knot was proper. She'd made sure of it. So… she was dead. Fuck. But she had just been counting…and she was su-premely cozy…so fuck again. *Here we go…Here we go.* Priscilla forced open one of her eyes. Then she raised her head and looked around.

Plush, purple, luxurious, satin sheets, and soft, fur blankets. Oak. Marble. Stained glass. Heavy drapes. Sybaritic soil. The room was mostly dark, but it was still light outside and some light shown between the curtains. Priscilla lifted her head off the pil-low for a better look. In the center of the room was a large opulent tub with ornate golden fixtures and marble steps surrounding it. On the back wall was a massive lighted fish tank. Inside it swam dozens of multicolored, exotic-looking fish. On the floor, a large black dog was curled into a ball, presumably sleeping. Tall candles burned on the mantle. A fire crackled below. A bizarre painting of some lactating animal with a bird's eye view hung above. All things considered, Priscilla still had no idea where, when, why or how she was. She still might be dead, for all she knew.

She examined her hands. They were still without wrinkles, spots, or blue veins. They were small and blackened around her fingertips, and that narrowed it down some. She was still a kid, which meant she was no longer being deceived by the venom. On the other hand, she was no longer wearing her cloak, and she was lost as to what that meant. What she was wearing now was…a shift. A silky, sexy, black shift. Cut low and lacy around the bosom, it felt like God's tongue on her skin. It was like some-thing women wore in the movies. Never, in her entire life or lives, either of them, had she ever worn anything quite so soft and fit-ting. Unfortunately, a mysterious wardrobe change did nothing to lessen her confusion. Maybe she would just curl back up under the covers and pray that her entire life was actually a dream.

Then the dog stood up, and Priscilla froze, one hand in the pro-cess of brushing back her hair. The massive black beast stretched long and hard, not noticing her at first. It yawned, and sat down to scratch behind one ear. But then, for whatever reason, it turned toward her and instantly it began to growl. Of course this is what she would wake up to, a dog mauling. Priscilla's shoulders slumped at the thought of being mauled, and her words came out just under a murmur. "Oh, for fuck's sake."

To be clear, this dog was no ordinary dog. It was more like a big-ass wolf. It was solid black, with black eyes like empty caverns, and on all fours, it stood nearly as tall as Priscilla. As far as its teeth, well, let's just say that it would have only taken one bite, no matter the bone. There was no doubt, the animal was anything but a killer. And if Priscilla wasn't already dead, it was looking like she was about to be.

The dog tensed and just as its growl deepened, just when Priscilla was sure it was about to lunge, about to pounce on top of her, ripping off one of her arms or perhaps her head and dragging her intestines out all over the bed, absolutely destroying the beautiful sheets and furs in which she was so recently snuggled, just as her life, or lives, were about to flash before her eyes, the bedroom door opened and the dog quickly stopped growling. It turned toward the door and began wagging its tail. Priscilla exhaled.

Standing in the doorway, naked from the waist up, casually picking out his afro, was a man that Priscilla had never seen before. He said, "Well, look who's finally awake. I apologize for Cupcake's behavior, but trust me when I say his bark is much worse than his bite. Ain't that right, Cupcake?" The man snapped his fingers, and as the dog sauntered over to him, to Priscilla, he said, "I trust you're feeling better?"

Priscilla nodded, automatically, without consideration. Then she asked, "Am I dead?"

Though the strange man was barely visible in the dim light, she could see that her question made him smile. "No, you're not

dead…you're in my home. In Clockmaker."

Priscilla considered for a moment, then she asked, "How'd I get here?"

Again, with the smile, and still picking at his hair, the man said, "Save your questions for dinner, it should be ready in an hour. I hope you like duck. And please, take some time to freshen up, the closet is full of clothes, you'll find they all fit you, and there's makeup on the vanity. Oh, and the shower is behind that door, there. I suggest you use it. You've been out a few days. I'll take Cupcake with me." Then, before Priscilla could get out another word, he turned and left, pulling the door closed behind him.

"Well shit," said Priscilla, to no one but herself.

◆

Joseph tracked Priscilla for three days before he found her. He started at Dead Kid Cave, where he ran into Kester and Merle, who were still standing guard, despite their recent emancipation. "Guuuhhain't nothshin' bether to do," they told Joseph. "Beshides, we ugh tried to go hhhome, but our erghmomma tsook one lookk at ush and went shcreamin' outt the houshe." Joseph understood their mother's reaction, he wanted to vomit at the sight of them, but as always, Priscilla's undead ex-slaves proved useful. They showed Joseph the direction in which Priscilla had walked off carrying a rope, and Joseph set out from there.

After smoking the venom, Priscilla was behaving abnormally, even for her. Even for the new her, the witch her. Joseph tried to convince her to let him carry her to Maw Scill's, or even his own house, but she made him take her to the cave, on the pretense that she had felt worse before and merely needed a day to rest, and if she wasn't better by the following day she would go home. So Joseph stayed with her in the cave all that day, watching after her, talking to her, making sure she didn't die.

Most of the time she just sat, hugging her knees to her chest, staring off into oblivion, but occasionally she would attempt to explain to him what was wrong. She would go on about having a whole other life, and a whole other family, and about how much she would miss them now that they were gone. She told him about her husband, a man named John, and about her first born daughter, about Boston, and about how her hands were too young to be her own. She told him about Christmas Mornings, about her kids opening their presents.

None of it made any sense to Joseph. To him, she sounded like she was losing her ever-loving mind. That wasn't the troublesome part, however. He was used to Priscilla sounding like a mental patient from time to time, but it was her sadness that had him really concerned. She was so so sad, and, believe it or not, given everything that had transpired thus far, that had Joseph more freaked out than anything. Even after Tommy died, she didn't come off half as upset as she was after smoking the venom.

Joseph was only gone for a few hours, but it was an hour longer than he anticipated. The next morning after smoking the venom, Priscilla claimed to feel better, and Joseph left, promising to return with cheese burgers and sodas but when he got into town, he found out about the flood. He talked to a few old men at the gas station for several minutes. They explained what happened, and why so many new faces were walking around. They also told him the school was being used to shelter the homeless for the foreseeable future, but all Joseph heard was VACATION. Then he spent nearly an hour waiting in line for burgers and soda. By the time Joseph checked in with his mother, and got back to the cave, Priscilla was gone.

So for three days, Joseph tracked her. It had been raining and snowing recently, and Priscilla didn't weigh much, so she wasn't the easiest to follow, but after two days, he found the briar thicket and the place where Priscilla crawled into it. Twenty or so yards deep into the thicket, Joseph found the tree, and still hanging from it was a noose, but Priscilla was nowhere to be found. Joseph lowered his head, feeling a certain amount of defeat, but then, just below him, he spied a new sets of prints. This should have given him a reasonable amount of hope, but for some reason, it made him worry even more. Staring back up at the empty noose, he said, "What the fuck is goin' on?"

It was starting to get late so he made his way back to civilization. He hardly slept that night, he was so worried, and the next morning, at first light, he crawled back into the briar thicket to start his search again. He started under the noose and began following the shoe prints. They were definitely not Priscilla's. Not only had she walked to her gallows barefoot, but this print was more than twice the size, and it was created by someone who weighed no less than three hundred pounds, or, thought Joseph, maybe by someone who was carrying someone else.

Joseph checked his supplies, the unholy sound of that horn echoing through the mountains, fresh in his mind. He'd come prepared, and he inventoried aloud. 'Apache dynamite, check. Rifle, check. Ammo, check. Big knife, check. Little knife, check. Flashlight—*that fuckin' works*—check. Compass—*that fuckin' works*—check. *Dry* matches, check. Canteen, check. Alright, Joseph…ain't no chickenin' out now.'

◆

"What in the holy fuck are you two gigglin' about?" said Sheriff White, to Junior and Stanley, as he walked through the front door of the station. Both men straightened themselves and attempted to look serious, but neither of them responded. Their eyes were noticeably red, and Junior had what looked like cake icing on his face.

FOUR ZERO ZERO

"Jesus fuckin' Christ," Sheriff White muttered. Then to Junior and Stanley, he said, "You two get out there and show that simple bastard in the bow tie and glasses from the school board how to get up to the school. Try not to fuck it up." Then he said, "When yer done with that, go up to the inn. Goddamn missionaries got the shitter backed up, and it's runnin' into the street. Deal with it."

The telephone rang. It had been ringing non-stop since the flood. Sheriff White sat down at his desk and picked up the hand-set, but only an inch. Then without saying a word, he sat it back down, and unplugged the cord from the back of the receiver.

"Probably another call about the fancy pants nigger," said Deputy Knotts.

Sheriff White buried his head in his hands. "Can't blame 'em," he said. "Most folks 'round here ain't never seen one like him. Hell, I ain't even."

"You know he was givin' out hundred dollar bills after you left earlier?"

Sheriff White eyed his deputy, disbelieving. "Yer shittin' me," he said.

"I ain't."

Sheriff White didn't respond. He just scratched at his head. He looked like he hadn't slept in days, and in fact, he hadn't.

"How'd things go with yer momma?" Deputy Knotts asked.

Sheriff White lifted his head. "I ain't got no momma no more. She's dead to me. I don't care how much that nigger gave her, he's a nigger. She ain't should have sold it to him."

"Honest, I can't believe she did… She must be hard up. Elmira hates spooks more than you do."

"Well, the way she was goin' on about that gold tooth monkey, you'd think she was ready to jump in his bed."

"Now I know yer shittin' me," said Deputy Knotts, looking seriously offended .

"I wish I was," said Sheriff White. "It don't make a whole lotta sense, does it?"

"No it don't…not at all, not the Elmira White I know," Deputy Knotts confirmed. Then after a few seconds, he asked, "So what you wanna do about it?"

"Well, I been thinkin' on that. And as much as I'd like to go over there right now and put bullets in all four of 'em, I think it's best we wait a few days. Let 'em get settled in. Let the commotion die down. Then we'll go over their and string 'em up like Christmas ornaments."

Nodding in approval, Deputy Knotts said, "We takin' Junior and Stanley?"

"Maybe. They ain't actin' right…like they doped up. You notice?"

"I have…"

"Yeah…well, anyhow, I don't see no reason me and you can't take care of this one on our own. Even if all four of 'em have guns, you know these city niggers can't never shoot straight."

Deputy Knotts flashed an arrogant grin. "No sir, they never can't," he said.

"No sir, they can't…" Sheriff White leaned back in his chair and put his feet up on his desk, a look of hollow concentration on his tired old face. "Yeah…" he went on, "we'll give 'em a few days, deputy…let 'em get settled in and comfortable…let 'em put their feet up on my sister's table, sleep in her bed, drink on that rotten old well water… Then me and you, we'll string 'em up, burn 'em, and throw what's left down the well. It'll be just like old times…"

◆

The house, if it could be called that, was like nothing Priscilla had ever seen. At no point in her life had she set foot in a mansion, but she could only surmise that she was in one now. Long, dimly lit halls, countless rooms, towering ceilings, gorgeous spiral staircases, the lavish grandiosity of the place made her once again consider if she may actually be dead. The place was too nice for earth. It was damn sure too nice for Clockmaker. And making her feel all the more deceased was the fact that most every room was empty. Empty of life, empty of furniture, empty of decor. Empty.

And so, all things considered, it seemed that still the most likely explanation was…dead. Priscilla was dead. She wasn't scared at the idea anymore though. At this point, she was mostly just curious. She wanted answers.

After nearly ten minutes of wandering the seemingly endless corridors, she finally found him. He was alone in a large sort of living room, the first furnished room she had seen yet besides the one she woke up in. A strange music was playing, and for a moment Priscilla stood there listening and observing. There was no way he could have heard her over the music, but nevertheless…

"Good evening," said the man, without looking up. "Make yourself comfortable, dinner will be ready momentarily." He was hovering tall over a chess table, still shirtless. He had one hand on his hip and the other was stroking his chin.

Priscilla did the opposite of making herself comfortable. She continued to stand in awkward silence at the threshold of the room. The issue she was having stemmed from her now unobstructed view of the stranger's toned and muscular backside. From where Priscilla stood, he looked like he was carved out of granite and chocolate. And Priscilla loved the taste of chocolate. *Only one way to get to the center.* She licked her lips. Uh-one, uh-two, uh-thr—. *Jesus Christ, you gotta get it together. Ain't no time to be thinkin' about* THAT *at a time like* THIS. Just as she finished the thought, the man moved his Knight, and said, "Checkmate." Then he turned to face her.

"Um…hi," said Priscilla. It was a pathetic response, even for her. In addition to the fluttering in her stomach, and perhaps because of it, she couldn't help but to take notice of how much she felt like a kid again. She was skittish, uncertain…horny, much more like her old self. It felt good. And also pathetic.

Clearly amused, the man said, "I see you chose not to bathe, or change out of that ratty old hood."

It was true, Priscilla had decided against bathing or changing into one of the many beautiful dresses that hung in the massive walk-in closet. Even though she tried on several and they did all, in fact, fit her. There were even three fur coats. They also fit her, perfectly. She couldn't help but to try some things on. It was her dream closet, after all, but the idea of actually wearing something other than her cloak, or bathing, or even using the makeup seemed like some sort of trap. Just the idea made her feel vulnerable, and so after taking time to ponder, she decided against freshening up altogether. And now, face to face with the most brutally handsome man she had ever seen, she intensely regretted that decision.

"I couldn't figure out how to work the shower and well, I ain't wanna put on clean clothes, and I…" Priscilla fumbled with her words.

His grin faded into a genuine smile and the man said, "It's okay, try to relax. You've been through a lot. Let me make you a drink. Here, please sit down."

Priscilla sat down on the edge of a long leather sofa, and watched him prepare drinks behind a bar at the far end of the room. Still she couldn't help but ogle. There was something about him. Sure, he had dark creamy skin, and he was tone and tight in all the right places, and sure, he had perfect teeth, and sharp sideburns, and the dreamiest eyes, but there was something else she couldn't quite put her finger on.

It wasn't until he was walking back with the drinks that she realized what it was. He looked just like Big Tommy, in the face anyway, but with different hair and different color eyes and older. They could have easily been brothers, though.

"What is this?" asked Priscilla.

"That, my sweet, is a gingerbread martini. I've never met a girl who can refuse them. Cheers, prepare to be amazed."

"Not the drink, I mean, who are you? Where am I? Ya know? What's the score, here?" Priscilla's words came out calm but confused.

"Ah yes, I see. Well, drink up," he said, as he sat down next to her on the couch. "Trust me, you're going to need it if you want an answer to those questions."

"I think I'd rather have the answers first, thank you," Priscilla said, as she sat the martini on the table in front of them. The table, by the way, was a large ovular piece of glass, held by a glossy black ceramic woman, nude and spread eagle.

The man nodded thoughtfully and said, "You're sure you wouldn't rather wait until after dinner for this? You must be ravenous."

"I'm sure." Priscilla answered without the slightest hesitation, although she was growing less sure by the second. A stark sense of dread had been swelling inside her because somewhere deep down, she knew exactly who she was talking to.

"I knew I liked you…no fucking around, no distractions…just what it takes to make a good little…witchy witch." There was nothing of harshness or malevolence in his response. He spoke with smooth, charming eloquence. "I think you already know who I am, but allow me to formally introduce myself. My name is Lucifer, King Devil of Hell, and your master, but you can call me Luci. It's a pleasure to finally meet you, Priscilla Louise."

Oh fuck. The canary keeled over. The boat's takin' on water. I'm dead. Now Priscilla was sure she was dead. Slowly, with her lips barely parted, and her eyes dewy and wide, Priscilla looked to her left, then to her right, then up and across the ceiling, then down at her own hands, which she turned over to thoroughly inspect her palms.

"You're not dead, if that's what you're so concerned about," said the Devil.

Priscilla looked up from her hands. "I'm not?"

"Oh no, you're very much alive, thanks to me. I pulled you from the noose just in time. You are alive and in Clockmaker, as I told you. Now…how about that drink?"

Priscilla didn't argue this time. She lifted the martini off the table and downed it. As though she needed it. Which she did. Then, sweet as she could be, she said, "Mmm, that's good. Can I have another?"

As the Devil mixed Priscilla another Gingerbread Martini, and himself some unknown concoction, the two of them conversed. The Devil lit a cannabis cigar, and it was hanging from the corner of his mouth, a pick with a black fist was stuck, casually, in his hair. Priscilla had moved from the couch, and sat down on one of the four stools at the bar, her feet dangling several inches from the floor. For some reason, she felt surprisingly confident, and oddly enough, frisky. Maybe it was the martini. It was certainly delicious. Or maybe, it was the half-naked fallen angel in front of her. Or perhaps, after a girl lives through killing herself, the weight of life simply hangs less heavy. Maybe it was a combination of all of the aforementioned.

"Is that grass?" Priscilla asked.

"It is."

"Can I try it?"

"Of course you can. Be easy though. That ain't the brick shit these hillbillys around here smoke. An incubi in the seventh circle of Hell grows that."

"Whoa, really?"

"Nah, I'm playin', a nigga named Francois in Amsterdam hooks me up. But it will get you high as a Georgia pine, believe that."

"Well…I been around," Priscilla said, and she took a long fat hit on the cigar. Then another, and she handed it back. "So yer really the Devil, huh?"

"I am."

"Like really, really?"

The Devil smirked. "What, don't believe me? It's because I'm black, isn't it?"

Priscilla almost spit out her drink. "That's not what I meant."

"Oh that's quite alright. Even black people expect me to be white. But being black is way too much fun."

"So then you really are the Devil…"

"I think you know I am," he said. Then in a much more serious tone, he said, "But unlike God, I don't mind proving it." As soon as the words left his mouth, his eyes went black. He raised one hand toward Priscilla, and when it was in her direct line of sight, he snapped his fingers. SNAP. And just like that, the mansion was gone.

Dressed in long, flowing, fringed beige silks, with only her hands and eyes exposed to the sun, Priscilla now stood high on a hill, overlooking a rocky desert landscape. The Devil, in similar attire, stood beside her. He was holding her hand. Where Priscilla was now, she wasn't sure, but she was goddamn positive she was no longer in West Virginia. There were Dogwood trees and sand and rock all around her, and in the distance, on top of a hill, some two hundred yards away, a crowd of men and several camels were gathered around three wooden crosses, from which three naked men were crucified.

Unable to hide the awe in her voice, Priscilla asked, "Where are we?"

"Golgotha," said the Devil. "You probably know it as Calvary. The year is thirty-three A D. That's the Son of God in the middle."

"You mean—"

"That's right. He'll be dead within the hour if you care to stay and watch."

"Can we stay for the resurrection?"

"The resurrection was a hoax. Christ's body was taken by grave robbers."

"Yer shittin' me?"

"It's true. His eyes went to market for a single piece of silver."

Priscilla stared at him for a moment trying to determine if he was being genuine. It seemed he was. "Well," she said, "that's okay then… We can go."

Still gazing at the crucifixion, the Devil said, "Good decision. I've seen this show before, it's not that interesting," and he snapped his fingers again. SNAP.

From Golgotha, he took Priscilla forward in time, to nineteen forty-seven, Paris, for dinner and wine at a charming little restaurant named Le Petite Chaise. And after another SNAP, to Bolivia to meet Eduardo for cocaine. The best in the world, according to the Devil. "Organic," he told her. Then the two of them, Priscilla and Satan, spent the evening back in Clockmaker, present day, getting high, talking, and listening to music from the future.

"So let me get this straight, yer sayin' you and God was best buds, but he got jealous of you over a girl angel, named, uh, Ariel, and that's why he banished you from Heaven?"

"Correct, of course he would never admit as much."

"Really?"

"You and your reallys. Yes, really. Are you that surprised? Anytime two men cease to be friends, it's almost always because of a woman. Gods aren't so different."

"Wow…he banished his best friend to Hell over a girl…"

"Well, not exactly. He banished me from Heaven. I chose to reign in Hell."

"Why?"

"After spending a few decades on earth, and several more in the electric head, I grew bored. You have to understand, back then earth wasn't nearly as interesting as it is today, there was no liquor, no herb, no cocaine, no bowling, no music, women still looked more like monkeys than angels. Even masturbation was a drag back then. Ruling over Hell gave me something to do."

Priscilla was mystified. She and the Devil had been talking for what seemed like hours, and the more he spoke, the more intriguing she found him to be. He was witty and insightful, and even though he clearly possessed an intelligence far greater than her own, he never once made Priscilla feel stupid for asking questions or not understanding one of his points. "So, what's it like in Hell?" asked Priscilla. "I really like this song by the way, what's it called?"

"Purple Rain. It was, or rather, it will be written by an artist called Prince in a decade or so. He's a loyal follower of mine. Dedicated. His guitar playing is proof of that."

"Well, I'll be. It's a real pretty song. You mind if I have some more of that?"

"Of course. Help yourself. Eduardo's only a snap away."

"You got the bill?"

The Devil picked up a hundred dollar bill up off the table, unrolled it, rerolled it tighter, and handed it to Priscilla. "I told you, you would like it," he said.

"Do I ever. I feel like a million bucks. Maybe more," said Priscilla as she cleared another white line from the mirror.

"I meant the music."

"Oh. I like that too."

"But to answer your question, what it's like in Hell… Hell is an ethereal, extravagant kingdom. A miraculous, golden spiral composed of elysian circles, bound not by dimension or time. It is exquisite beyond measure. It's certainly not what most humans think it is. All fire, lakes, and torture. Its essence is surpassed only by the heavenly planes…and it's actually quite cold in some parts."

"So wait, it's not where bad folks go when they die, or…? I'm confused."

"I can imagine, but I'll explain. Hell exists in sixteen circles. Sixteen being at the top. The bottom six circles are alone reserved for the punishment of evil sinners. It is those six circles that resemble the Hell you are familiar with. Fire, torture, the screams of the damned, blood, pain, etcetera. The next nine circles are for the righteous sinners, and the sixteenth circle I share with the holy sinners. And those top ten circles are as beautiful as any circle of Heaven."

"What are holy and righteous sinners?"

"I apologize, sometimes I forget those are foreign concepts here. A righteous sinner is a person who, intentionally or not, breaks the laws of God, but is not, by the laws of nature, evil. You see, in Hell, unlike Heaven, intentions are everything. When a person steals and then dies without repenting, it won't matter why they stole when they get to Heaven. Even if they only stole to feed their starving child, because they were left with no other choice, it won't matter to God. He will send them to me, to Hell. No matter how much they beg, and trust me they do beg, he sends them to me."

"However," the Devil went on, "in Hell, we do discriminate. To me, intentions are crucial to understanding. *Why* the person stole is everything, and that same person who stole to feed their starving child, who, as I, was cast unjustly from Heaven, would be labeled a righteous sinner in Hell."

Lucifer paused his explanation, and sniffed a line of Eduardo's snow. Then he lit another green cigar, puffed it a few times until the cherry was glowing hot, and continued in a more casual tone.

"Some people, Priscilla, are cruel and stupid. They are truly evil sinners, and they do true harm in the world. They kill. They rape. They envy. They hurt other people actively, and cause disharmony in the vibratory planes of existence, and in turn, well, they burn in Hell. Just like in the stories. Agony, suffering, those words don't come close to describing the eternity of evil sinners. But those who are wicked only in imagination, those who simply choose to follow other gods, those who allow others to live their lives as they see fit, those who only want true freedom, freedom of life, freedom of death, freedom to be, these people, these heathens, these free thinkers, these masturbaters, these people of independent virtue, they die the honorable many-headed death of the unholy hydra, they lick at the lips of all things black and delicious, and survey the fires of Hell from a privileged position, above. There is no torture, no anguish, no despair, for those who are righteous sinners. Oh no. For their bravery in life, they are awarded in Hell."

"Far out…" Priscilla said. She was truly impressed.

As the Devil continued puffing on his cigar, Priscilla asked, "So what's a holy sinner?"

"That's you, Priscilla. You are a holy sinner. You are a righteous sinner who has pledged their allegiance to me in blood."

There was a moment of pause and reflection, and then… "Fuck. I'm goin' to Hell," Priscilla said. She didn't know why it hit her so hard. She had expected for some time that she was probably headed for the sulfur pits, given the whole *witch thing*, but there was something about Lucifer himself confirming her suspicions, outright, that left her feeling like someone took a piss in her gingerbread martini. Although it could have been the blow that made her so suddenly anxious, but having never sniffed it before, Priscilla had no way of knowing or even suspecting the white powder caked around her nose could be a possible culprit .

"Of course you are, my love," said Satan.

"Fuck," Priscilla said. "There ain't no way around it?"

"I'm afraid not."

Priscilla didn't ask permission this time. She reached for the bill, rolled it tight, and sucked up one of the larger lines left on the mirror. Then she leaned back on the couch, and massaging her jaw muscles, she said, "Is there music in Hell, at least?"

"Oh yes," said the Devil. "Lots. Prince is there. Your favorite, Black Sabbath, is there. Most of the greatest musicians and artists are there for one reason or another."

"Well at least there's that," said Priscilla, perking up a little bit. "But why is Black Sabbath in Hell? Did they die? And I thought Prince was from the future?"

"Hell is eternal, my dear. They are in Hell because they have always been in Hell, and they always will be. In a way, you too are already in Hell. As are all who are destined for the black gates. If that doesn't make sense to you, have no worries. It shouldn't. Consciousness without time is incomprehensible to the human mind. But rest assured, me, you, Joseph, we are all in Hell right now, at this very moment, having a grand old time. Always have been, always will be."

"I think it's time for another drink."

"Oh, don't worry your pretty little head," said the Devil. "I'll take care of you."

"Gee, thanks." Priscilla did another line.

"Well what did you expect. You put your blood in my book. Of course you're going to Hell. Accept that, even if you can't understand it. The sixteenth circle awaits you."

Priscilla fanned herself with her hand. "Is it getting hot in here or is it just me?"

"It's you."

"Can I ask you a question? Why are you here? I mean, with me, takin' me all over the place, tellin' me all this…why?"

"Well," said the Devil, "I'm here for two reasons. To help with flood relief and—."

"What flood?"

"The one I caused. You were busy hanging yourself. Clockmaker is in chaos."

"Why'd you cause a flood?"

"I wanted a reason to interact with the fine, good people of West Virginia. That's how I get my kicks. Fucking with white boys."

"Why else?"

"Excuse me?"

"Why else are you here? You said two reasons. What's the second?"

"Isn't it obvious? You, my dear. I'm here for you."

Priscilla sat up straight, looking suddenly alarmed. "Yer not takin' me to Hell now are ya?"

"Of course not. I want get to know you is all, maybe help you be a better witch."

"Oh," said Priscilla, a look of relief on her face. "Thank God. Or…whoever."

"After my witches smoke the venom, they often need a bit of support. As you can understand quite well, I'm sure."

Priscilla nodded. She understood exactly what he meant. The God-venom was one hell of a trick alright. One hell of a lesson. But though she still felt within herself many of the intuitions only held by old women, the memories of her other life had nearly faded altogether.

As if to read her mind, the Devil said, "I realize the venom is difficult but I would bet that by now it seems more like a dream than anything…am I right?"

"Yeah," said Priscilla. "You are." She was being honest. She couldn't even remember the names of her grandchildren. Not one of them.

"You'll never forget the sadness of that loss though. Losing children is like no other loss, and that loss will stay with you and help to guide your choices. Giving and taking life is a serious matter. It must be understood thoroughly. That's why smoking the venom is necessary before performing spells of life or death. And in your case, that does include resurrection spells."

Finally, things were beginning to make sense. For once. Priscilla said, "So you do this for all witches?"

"No, not at all. I've only done this once before. Thousands of years ago. Most witches are not worthy of my concern. The witch before you, for instance. She was only in possession of the book for three weeks before she broke the rules and got herself killed. The temptation was too much. Trust me when I say that you are special and—"

Priscilla interrupted. "Who was the witch before me?"

"Her name was Opal Elder. You know her son, Mathias."

"Mathias's momma?"

"Indeed. Opal Engrid Elder, formally Opal Engrid Morgan. She was a brilliant woman, but she didn't have the stomach for Death Tea. She's the reason that whole family is blind."

"Wait, what? I thought it was moonshine that made 'em blind."

"Oh no, it was Opal. She tried to use the book to heal her husband's brain tumor, and when he died, she became careless, and started skipping steps. And you know what the book says about skipping steps."

Priscilla nodded gravely. "I do," she said. Then she said, "So then why did Tommy have to die like that? And his momma? What did I do wrong? I ain't skip steps. She was supposed to be beautiful." Priscilla could feel herself getting emotional, so she took a deep breath, and again, she said, "She was supposed to be beautiful."

The Devil laid his hand upon her shoulder. "Dear sweet girl, is that what you think? That you did something wrong? Oh, no no no, that wasn't your fault. Here, here do another line, that was not your fault. That entire mess was Gertrude Green's naive doing. Well, she and Gladys. But it was most certainly not your fault."

"Gladys…?"

"The thing that killed Tommy, that was Gladys. Gertrude, you see, had an evil twin sister who lived inside her, a bit of God's work there. Her name was Gladys. It's a long sordid tale, but what it comes down to is that the potion you created was not meant for two people to drink. And there were side effects… I am sorry for the death of your friend, Thomas Green, for your sake. He was a decent human. But his death was most certainly not your fault. Nor were the Persians."

"The Persians?"

"Never mind that. Thomas Green's death was not your fault. Do you hear me?"

"I do."

"Do you believe me?"

Hearing those words was like a lead weight had been lifted from around Priscilla's neck, and the guilt she'd been carrying around for Tommy and Gertrude began to ease. Priscilla nodded.

"He's well taken care of in Hell, though. I assure you," said the Devil. "Gertrude, on the other hand…well…"

"Tommy's in Hell too?"

"He is," the Devil said tenderly, "and one day you will be reacquainted. So cheer up, kid, Hell is really not a bad place to spend eternity. The food is great, the water is warm, and all the best musicians are there. Trust me on that. Would you like another drink?"

"Make it a whiskey this time," Priscilla said, holding out her empty glass.

The Devil accepted her glass but he sat it to the side. "I have a better idea, why don't you take a shower, get out of that filthy cloak, and after, we can snuggle up on the couch and listen to *Dark Side of the Moon* on vinyl. Sound appealing?"

Snuggle up?!

Side-bar. How does a shy, country girl from West Virginia respond when the one and only Lucifer, The Morning Star, The Little Horn, The Adversary, He Who Has Many Names, the Devil asks her to *snuggle*? After whisking her back and forth through time and around the world in a single night, after explaining the true nature of creation, after imbibing her with powers normally reserved for gods, after taking the form of the most mouth-watering and beautiful man she had ever laid eyes on, how should she, Priscilla Carpenter, a shy, coked-out country witch destined to spend eternity in Hell, respond to the Devil's invitation to…*snuggle up*? Anybody? Anybody? Nothing? Figures. This is how she responded. The same way anyone in her position would respond. She sidestepped the question, and said, "What's *Dark Side of the Moon*?"

"It's an album by some British niggas called Pink Floyd."

Snuggle up?! "Is it from the future too?"

"It is. It comes out next year, actually. It will be… groundbreaking."

"Wow… So if you know the future then we could like…bet on baseball games and horse races, and win like millions of dollars, huh?"

"Priscilla, my dear… I can make literally anything you could possibly think of or want materialize before your eyes with the snap of my fingers. The last thing you and I need is money. Now go get your sweet little ass in the shower."

"Can we smoke another one of them cigars first?"

Luci shook his head, amused. "Of course we can."

"And another line too?"

"Mercy mercy mercy," Luci muttered. "I've created a monster. You are never allowed to smoke this shit, by the way."

"Really? Why?"

"Because you will hate yourself for all the time you wasted snorting it. Stick to reefer, trust me." Then he added, "But yes… we can do one more. You feeling like a kitten or a tiger?"

Priscilla, feeling the answer was obvious, said, "Nigga… whadda you think?"

◆

Apache dynamite, prepped. Rifle, locked and loaded. Extra ammo, left jacket pocket. Big knife, right hip. Little knife, right sock. Flashlight, operational. Compass, operational, and in pack. Matches, in pack. Canteen, in pack. Joseph was crouched in the bushes outside an old house, and he had gone over his inventory for the last time. He had devised a plan, and now it was time to execute that plan, for good or ill.

He had spent nearly all day following the shoe prints through the woods. With no apparent aim, the prints meandered through the forest, up hills, down hills, around rocks, as if whoever left them was attempting to make tracking more difficult, but eventually they began moving in an obvious direction, and just before dark, they led Joseph down out of the woods to an old house.

Set back from the road, along route eight, he had been past the house a thousand times in his life, and he had always assumed it was abandoned. Tonight, however, there was a strange purple car parked outside. And even though the grass around the house was a foot tall, the shutters were barely hanging on, and no light shone from within, he had a gut feeling he was in the right place. So, crouched in the bushes, like a nervous lion stalking his prey, he waited.

He watched the house from the treeline as the sun disappeared behind the mountains. In that time, no one came or went. In fact, there were no signs of life whatsoever. The house, the woods, the air, they were all dead, and Joseph felt as though he were inside some kind of open-air tomb. Then he heard a noise behind him, but it turned out to be nothing, a fallen limb probably, and he continued to wait.

Eventually, after watching and waiting for nearly two hours, Joseph decided to take a closer look, but after circling the house and peering through all the windows, it still seemed as though no one was home. But then he saw Lightning, Priscilla's loyal Familiar. Camouflaged against the night sky, she was barely visible, but she was sitting high up in a tree, watching him. And when Joseph saw her, he knew then he was in the right place.

Back in the woods, he loaded his rifle, and checked his supplies once again. He had spent the last two hours trying to anticipate and prepare for all the possible scenarios that he could be walking into, and the worst of them was going to require fire power, and quite possibly dynamite. And least of all, *a goddamn workin' flashlight*. Because, by the looks of things, if Priscilla was in that house, she was likely in the cellar.

Joseph took a deep breath, then he set out across the backyard, rifle in one hand, flashlight in the other. Beside the car he paused, knelt, unsheathed the big knife, and sunk it into the fancy car's tire like a professional. "Just in case," he whispered aloud, as air hissed from the punctured rubber.

At the back door to the house, he planted the dynamite. Again, just in case. Then he checked the doorknob. It was locked. Shit. He moved around the house, checking all the windows and doors, but they were locked up like a nun's cunt. Damn-shit. Joseph stood looking up at the house, scratching his chin. He was really hoping for a stealthy, backdoor, secret agent type of entrance, but it was looking like that would not be possible. He was reluctant to admit it, but Plan B would have to do. It was the only option he had left.

Plan B : *Kick the fuckin' backdoor in, guns blazin', ready to die. Real wild west shit.*

Fortunately, just as Joseph was about to roundhouse the backdoor clean off its hinges, it opened up all on its own, and standing in the doorway, partially concealed by shadows, was the finest, most well-endowed woman Joseph had ever laid his two pitiful pubescent peepers on. She was tall, and firm, with bite-your-fucking-fist hips, and wet-your-lips skin, and over her head, concealing her face, was a black bag that appeared to be made of silk. But most notably, however, for Joseph anyway, was the fact that this woman was naked. Naked as a goddamned jaybird.

So the first thing he took notice of was not necessarily the woman's facial concealment. What he noticed was…her big, perfect tits. Like celestial orbs in the moonlight, like two fleshy crystal balls in which he yearned to see his future, or as Shakespeare put it, like ivory globes circled with blue, a pair of maiden worlds unconquered, her tits were manifested from a chimerical dream. They were a thing of great and magnificent beauty, and Joseph, no matter how he tried, no matter how he blushed, could not look away from them.

Had the woman not been wearing the bag over her head, Joseph would have surely recognized her straight away. Then again, it's hard to say one way or the other, whether or not he even possessed the strength to raise his gaze that high above her bust, bag or no. But surely, in the absence of the bag, he would have known her for who she was. Surely. Then again, maybe not. Maybe he wouldn't have recognized her unless he was in church and she was playing the piano in the prudish, brown dress she wore every Sunday. Either way, whether he knew it or not, Joseph was a fly stuck in a web of sorts, and the web was crawling with spiders. Sexy spiders. Sexy, big titty spiders. "God help me," Joseph said under his breath.

"Won't you come in," said Kathleen Gibbons. "We've been expecting you."

◆

Priscilla let the warm water stream over her face. The Devil, kind as he was, had offered to clean her, and she thought for a moment that he meant to join her in the bath, but he quickly clarified his offer, leaving Priscilla a little disappointed but mostly relieved. What he meant was that he would use his magic to change her appearance, just as he had in Golgotha and Paris, but Priscilla wanted, no, she needed a few minutes alone. She needed time to reflect, to absorb, to comprehend the mind-fuck that had become her life. And to come down off the goddamn cocaine. Jesus Christ, that stuff was powerful. Her poor little heart was going a mile a minute. She *needed* a shower.

Speaking of showers, it was the first time Priscilla had ever used one. She loved it. Even after Luci—Priscilla didn't like thinking of him as the Devil—had come into the bathroom to show her how to work the pesky shower knobs, he left before she began to undress. This caught Priscilla off guard. She expected him to be more like the boys at school, always lingering, always looking, always trying, not with her of course, but with the popular girls. Luci wasn't like the boys at school, though. Not at all. He was casual, even gentlemanly, in his affection for her.

In many ways, besides his face, Luci reminded her of Big Tommy. He was calm, gentle, attentive, he even held her hand like Tommy, but where Tommy was shy and awkward, Luci was charming and confident, and where Tommy was soft and doughy, Luci was all muscle, lean and cut…*and his lips, Luci had the most lucious lips she had ever—*. Once again, Priscilla found her mind wandering in unfamiliar and uncomfortable territory. The idea of actually having sex, doing IT, was not one that had really ever crossed her mind before, at least not in any serious fashion, and certainly not with any specific person, not even Big Tommy, but now it seemed nearly inescapable.

Anyway, she must have been crazy if she thought for a single second that Lucifer of all people, or angels, or whatever he was, would have any desire whatsoever to do the same things with her. He was a king, an angel, an immortal, able to leap through time and space with little to no effort. And he could certainly seduce any girl that he wanted, from Patsy Cline to Cleopatra, so why would he ever take the time with her?

Priscilla took a deep breath and tried to relax. She was getting ahead of herself, she was almost sure of it, but then she remembered what the Devil said about gods not being all that different from men. and she applied that to what her mother had once told her about all men being the same. 'They only want one thing," her mother told her, and now, standing in the shower, Priscilla couldn't help but to fill in the blanks.

Priscilla nudged the shower knob one way, and when the water got cold she quickly turned it back the other direction, over-correcting and scaulding her skin, but finally she found the sweet spot and leaned her head against the tile wall. What had she gotten herself into? *Witchcraft? Lucifer? Cocaine?!* She was going to Hell, and she had taken Joseph and Tommy with her. Was it too late to pray? Too late for forgiveness? Luci sure enough seemed to think it was. All Priscilla ever wanted was a little excitement and now look at her. She sure wasn't bored anymore, was she, bathing and contemplating her life in Satan's shower. Her mother would be so proud. "Oh for fuck's sake," Priscilla said aloud.

Then, from within the house, she heard what was unmistakably the sound of a gunshot. KERBLAM!

◆

Soaking wet, with a towel wrapped carelessly around her, Priscilla came out of the shower, slipped, and almost broke her neck on the tile floor, but instead crashed into the wall with an audible thud. Nevertheless, she made it back to the room where she and Luci had spent the evening getting high so quickly that debris was still falling from the hole in the ceiling above Joseph's head, and smoke was still billowing from the barrel of his rifle.

Joseph said, "Alright, you weird son of a bitch, I won't ask you again. Where's Priscilla?" His voice was quavering, not a lot, but enough to notice.

"Calm down," Luci said, casually, as though Joseph were a small child with a temper instead of a scared, angry teenager brandishing a lethal weapon.

"Motherfucker, I am calm! Don't tell me! I'll put a hole through you and yer little honeypot whore! Yeah, that's right, bitch. I seen From Russia with Love. This ain't my first trip around the bend. I will admit…you had me distracted for a minute. I said don't fuckin' move!"

Priscilla stood in the doorway, but she was behind Joseph, so he hadn't noticed her yet. She would have interjected earlier but the scene she walked into was one that required more than a little contemplation, digestion even. Not only had Joseph somehow managed to find his way into Luci's mansion, but he was now aiming a loaded rifle directly at him, at Luci, at the Devil himself.

Furthermore, in between them, Joseph and Luci, on the floor, there was a naked woman, down on all fours, with a bag over her head, and Luci, relaxing on the couch, had his feet up on the woman's back. The icing on the cake was Cupcake. The massive dog sat in front of the fireplace on a bearskin rug, insatiably licking his balls, oblivious to the drama unfolding around him. Alright, scene set. And action!

What in the actual shitfuckchrist is goin' on here, was the resounding question that penetrated Priscilla's every thought, but finally, she managed to choke out, "It's okay, Joseph. Just put the fuckin' gun down."

Joseph spun to face her, accidentally bringing his rifle with him, and Priscilla ducked, almost falling in an attempt to dodge his aim. She almost lost her towel too, but she recovered it at the last second, and tightened it up around her as she stood back up. Until now, Priscilla hadn't been able to see Joseph's face, but now that she could, one thing was clear. He was scared. He lowered his gun, and said, "Priscilla! Are you alright, what the fuck is goin' on here, are you alright? Are you?" Then he must have remembered he was holding someone at gunpoint, because suddenly he turned his sights and his weapon back on Luci, who was now grinning.

"I'm fine, Joseph, I'm alright, just put the gun down. Joseph! Put the gun down." Priscilla was speaking as calmly as she could. The last thing she wanted was for Joseph to pull the trigger. God only knows what the consequences for shooting Satan would be.

Keeping his gun on Luci, Joseph turned his head to look back over his shoulder at Priscilla, attempting to gauge the sanity of her words by the look on her face. Then he looked back at Luci, then back at Priscilla, and back to Luci again. Keeping his focus on Luci, Joseph said, "Priscilla, what in the fuck is goin' on here? This ain't alright. Not even close. This ain't the same house on the outside as it is on the inside, it keeps changin', and this mother-fucker here tried to honeypot me with this bag-head bitch."

"Joseph, I know. But put the gun down."

"You know? What the fuck you mean, you know?!"

"Joseph, put the goddamn fuckin' gun down, trust me. I'll explain everything."

Joseph did not put the gun down. He kept it trained on Luci. The vibe in the room was a strange kind of negative. Neo-tense. After a moment, to Priscilla, Joseph said, "Are you sure? Are you real sure? I'm tellin' ya, there's some weird fuckin' shit goin' on around here."

"You two niggas sure do curse a lot, don't you," interjected Luci.

"Fuck d'you call us? I will fuckin' shoot you, asshole. Say another fuckin' word. Say another mother fuckin' word," Joseph snapped back, heavily enunciating each word of the last sentence.

"Joseph! Put it down," Priscilla shouted. Then, much more calmly, she added, "He's…he's the Devil, Joseph. You hear me, he's the Devil."

Again Joseph looked back over his shoulder, weapon still raised, the look on his face now baffled. He seemed to consider, then he turned back to Luci. Joseph held his stare, held the Devil's stare, which was impressive even though Joseph wasn't quite convinced he was the Devil at the time. And truth be told, he held it for longer than most men had ever in the history of the world had the nerve to even attempt, but finally, after what was way too long for Priscilla, Joseph, exhausted, and defeated, lowered his weapon, saying, "Goddamn it, Scilly… Oh, goddamn it…"

"Goddamn it, indeed," said Luci. Then he laughed. HA HA HAHAHA!

Cupcake just kept licking his balls. Kathleen Gibbons remained an anonymous footstool.

Once, when Joseph was but a young lad, maybe five years old, a traveling Bible salesman came knocking. At the time, Joseph's father was at work, which was lucky for the salesman, otherwise he would have never made it through the door. Joseph's father hated salesmen of all ilk and kind, and he often said as much. Joseph's mother, however, was a bit of a pushover when it came to the tricks and charms of even the novice hustler, and in the hands of a professional she was made of straw and soft clay.

So for nearly two hours Joseph sat in the corner of the living room, keeping a skeptical eye on the Bible pusher as he slowly wrapped his pious tentacles around Joseph's sweet, naive mother. Maybe it was unencumbered intuition, maybe it was his father's influence, but even at such a young age, Joseph knew in his gut that the Bible salesman was a no good dirty swindler. A rogue and cheat of the worst kind. The kind that would take full advantage of his mother's generous nature.

From the look in the balding man's beady eyes, to the sweat stains under his flabby arms, to the plastic watch around his wrist, the Bible salesman reeked of snake oil and last night's liquor. But it was more than that. It was his nature. His very being. Joseph was too young to pick apart the salesman by his behavior, let alone his choice of time-keeping device, but what he did perceive came from the salesman's all too eager and out-right shifty energetic field. It was his aura that Joseph was absorbing. It was nasty, and he could not ignore it.

In the end, Joseph's mother did, in fact, go on to purchase a Bible from that salesman, and his father didn't speak to her for a week after, but that isn't the point. The point is that sitting across from the Devil, Joseph had an uncomfortably similar feeling to the one that he did on that day, so many years ago. Like the Bible pusher, something just wasn't right about 'Luci.' Besides obviously the whole Devil thing, of course. And even though Joseph couldn't quite put his finger on what it was, it would have been difficult for anyone to convince him otherwise.

Sure, sure, he seemed nice enough, and he was certainly hospitable, having offered Joseph grass and cocaine immediately upon meeting him, but there was something about him that Joseph simply did not like. Maybe it was the way he looked at Priscilla, or the way he too frequently grinned, or perhaps it was the way he licked his lips before each time he said something of significance. Or maybe it was the fact that he had a fully nude woman with a silky black bag over her head, roaming about his house, answering doors, and serving as a place for him to rest his feet. Maybe it was all those things.

But what was Joseph to do? Shoot him? Drive a stake through his heart? Throw Priscilla over his shoulder and run? Phone up Pastor Swann? *Cry for his momma?* Of course not. None of those options would work. So he did what anyone would do in such a situation. He took the son of a bitch up on his offer and they smoked some weed.

Joseph sat smoking across from the Devil at a long wooden table, one the Devil claimed to be an artifact of the Last Supper. Close to the table, Priscilla sat Indian-style on an antique-looking lounge chair. Her hair was still wet, but she was now clothed and wrapped in a fur blanket, because girls are always cold. Cupcake, who had by now warmed up to Priscilla, was also on the lounge chair, sprawled out with his head in Priscilla's lap. Priscilla was petting him absently. The naked woman was gone. Dismissed by the Devil, she, without speaking or gesturing in any way, stood up and left the room, her arms dangling at her sides, the bag still on her head. Where she went exactly, Joseph was sure the Devil only knew.

FOUR TWO SIX

The one bit of humor Joseph found in the whole mess was that despite the utter strangeness and relative severity of the situation, he could not manage for the life of him to stifle the half erection he'd been sporting since he walked in the house, or mansion, or trap, or whatever it was. In his defense, he'd never seen such a beautiful woman naked before. It had an impact.

So, after pretending to need to use the bathroom in order to do some snooping around, during which he found and read a nightstand copy of the original Holy Bible, Joseph found himself in a large parlor area, seated at the table from the Last Supper. Both Priscilla and the Devil were attempting to explain the situation he had wandered into, but Joseph's mind was all mush. He felt like a salty slug trying to solve an algebraic equation. He couldn't think. And he didn't really want to. But then the Devil said something that snapped Joseph back to reality.

"I'm sorry if Kathleen scared you. I thought you would like her," said the Devil. Joseph refused to think of him as Luci.

Joseph went blank in the face. "You thought I would like some honeypot demon bitch with a bag over her head?"

"Demon? You think that fine-ass thing is a demon?"

"Well…" said Joseph, stirring in his seat a little, and adjusting the crotch of his pants. "I reckon when you put it like that…it don't make as much sense…"

"Come now, Joseph. I wouldn't do you like that. We friends. Honeypot maybe, but demon, no. Demons aren't fit to greet guests. A demon would have eaten your dick right off at the doorstep. No, Kathleen is a living, breathing human, just like yourself. A local gal even."

"Local?"

"Oh yes, she was born and raised right here in Clockmaker. And I believe she plays piano in the church that you and Priscilla attend. Or used to attend, I suppose."

"Kathleen Gibbons?!" Priscilla and Joseph responded simultaneously, Joseph almost coming out of his seat.

"That's right," said the Devil matter-of-factly.

"You gotta be shittin' me? That was Kathleen Gibbons?" Joseph was incredulous.

"I assure you, that was her."

"But why's there a bag over her head," asked Priscilla.

"You wouldn't understand, my love."

"Try me," Priscilla came back quick.

The Devil nodded, shrugged, and said, "It gets me off."

"It gets you off?"

"Yes, sexually."

Priscilla eyed the Devil like he was dumb. "You're right, I don't understand.'"

"I think I understand," said Joseph, again adjusting his pants.

"I assumed as much," said the Devil.

There was a brief moment of uncomfortable silence, but it didn't last long. Joseph broke it. He said, "So what in the hell is Miss Gibbons doin' runnin' around here ass naked? Is she like… yer slave? Like Kester and Merle? It's like she's under some kind of spell."

The Devil's grin widened into a smile. "I hate to break it to you two, but your dear Kathleen Gibbons is a fucking freak of the highest order. A full-blown Satanist with a nature and discipline kink. And she happens to *love* black dudes."

"Aw, come the fuck on," said Joseph. "Now I know yer playin'."

"Nigga…do I look like the type of mothafucka who plays?"

"Alright, you got a point there, but hold on, why you keep callin' me that," asked Joseph. "I ain't callin' you no nigger."

The Devil's grin broadened as he said, "Nigga, Joseph. Not *nigger*. Nigga. Nigga is a…term of endearment."

"A term of what?"

"Endearment. It's like saying…my friend. You see, black people in this country have reclaimed and repurposed the word nigger from its former derogatory usage so that it has a more… positive sort of connotation. In the future, *nigga* is a word of much controversy and debate, but as a lover of language, I am quite fond of it. So please take no offense, young Joseph."

"Yeah, well…" said Joseph. And he left it at that. He understood what the Devil was getting at. He just wasn't sure how he felt about being the Devil's 'nigga.'

"Anyway," said the Devil. "What say we have a little fun?"

"I can't do any more coke, my jaw feels like a tombstone," said Priscilla.

The Devil chuckled. "No, no more of that shit. I was thinking more along the lines of a field trip."

"Like Golgotha," asked Priscilla, a chipper tone to her voice. "Cause that was pretty cool."

"Well," said the Devil, "similar actually. I was thinking of having Smiley drive the three of us down to the Lazy J for a drink and a game of pool. You kids ever rode in a Rolls Royce?"

"No, never," said Priscilla, with a curious and dreamy quality to her voice.

Joseph was not nearly as mystified by the suggestion. He said, "The lazy J? Mister Devil, I don't know what kinda fun yer lookin' for but the Lazy J ain't no place to be messin' around. That's a coal miner bar. My own daddy won't even drink at the J. And from what I hear, they don't take too kindly to uh…yer kind in particular."

The Devil said, "My kind? You mean, fallen angels? Omnipotent beings?"

"Omni—what? Hell no. I mean blacks, my nigga. Black bein's."

"Oh," said the Devil, as if he were only considering this fact for the first time, but then he said, "I'm only kidding. I'm more than aware of the goings on at the Lazy J, thank you though Joseph for your concern, but that is precisely why it's going to be so much fun. Nothing like a warm shot of liquor and a good bar fight to get the human blood flowing, right? So what do you say, you with me? Priscilla?"

Joseph and Priscilla looked at one another. He was expecting her to decline taking part in such a clearly foolish enterprise. But as it would turn out, maybe the only thing foolish about any of it was Joseph, for thinking that he could even attempt to guess what Priscilla Louise Carpenter was going to do, think, or say at any given moment. She was still Joseph's best friend, but anymore, who she was from day to day, he had no idea. Priscilla shrugged, saying, "I'm in. I love playin' pool, but can we not tell folks yer the Devil? They're already gonna flip shit yer black."

The Devil dropped a triumphant fist down on the table. "That's the spirit," he said. "I can always count on my witches." Priscilla blushed. Then he said, "Joseph, what do you say…my nigga? You in?"

Joseph shook his head wearily. But what he said was, "Alright, fine. Fuck." He wasn't about to let Priscilla go alone. But then he thought of something his father often said when referring to his only son, "One foot in the grave and the other on a banana peel," and Joseph put his mental foot down, saying, "You know what, no. No, I don't wanna go out drinkin' with the goddamned Devil at a goddamned coal miner bar. And Priscilla, I don't think you oughta go neither. It ain't safe… and I…I won't let ya. I'm puttin' my foot down." That last line he took from his father as well.

"Fair enough," the Devil conceded, an impressed look on his face. "You're right, Joseph, you're right. Sometimes I forget who I'm dealing with. What I find joy in, most humans do not, and for good reason…too much at stake. I apologize."

Joseph lowered his head a little. Maybe he had overreacted.

But then the Devil spoke again, "How about we burn down a few churches instead?"

"What?"

"I'm kidding. Of course," said the Devil. Then he said, "How about something sexual?"

"Sexual?" Joseph and Priscilla spoke in shocked unison. The Devil grinned wider.

"Sure," said the Devil, speaking mostly to Joseph. "I could call Kathleen back in, and we could all get drunk and naked…maybe break out the ether, some amyl nitrite, let our nether regions do the thinking for us, that's always fun, right?"

Joseph stared at him in dumb disbelief. The mere thought of bag-headed Kathleen Gibbons climbing on top of him naked sent a shiver up his spine and made his pants twitch. Having only ever been with one girl, one time, Joseph was more than a little intimidated by the idea of sex with a grown woman, unnerved even. Then, on top of everything, there was the thought of Priscilla, naked, and him, naked, and the Devil, naked, and, and, and, and…

"Maybe we should go to the J, that'd be alright, I could actually use a drink," said Joseph. "They probably won't even notice yer black. Maybe you could say yer Italian."

Ignoring Joseph, Priscilla said, "You mean, like…all four of us…have sex?"

Joseph couldn't believe it. Priscilla was actually considering the proposition. He could tell by the look on her face. He'd seen it before. She was intrigued.

The Devil nodded, clearly amused. "Sure, but…not exactly. I was thinking more along the lines of fun, like…playing spin the bottle, but instead of kissing lips, we kiss…the fun parts. Or we could all climb in bed, turn out the lights and play "Whose hand is that?"… Or perhaps some consensual waterboarding. Maybe break out the Ketamine, and handcuffs. A little baby oil. From there, the possibilities are nearly endless."

Priscilla was silent. Joseph was appalled. And mortified. Definition one. "Well, you can just go right ahead and count me out there, Luci-fer. I ain't into no fairy business. That's where I draw the line. I seen plenty dicks in gym class and I don't want no part of 'em."

"Oh come on, Joseph, we can turn out the lights. Pleasure is pleasure in the dark. We don't have to guess whose hands are whose, we can all stay quiet and pretend."

Priscilla giggled. Joseph grew suddenly serious and stood up, knocking over a drink in the process. Several grams of cocaine were ruined. Joseph didn't know how to feel. He was embarrassed, disgusted, and horny, and out of his element, a combination that mixed like vinegar and breast milk. He stepped back from the table and said, "Okay, Luci-fer, I really appreciate the history lesson, and you savin' Scilly from the noose, and takin' her to see Jesus get strung up and all, and it's been real interestin' gettin' to know ya, but I think we'll be off. It's gettin' late, and I reckon our parents is gettin' real worried about us. Scilly, you got all yer uh…stuff, yer cloak and stuff, uh…you ready?"

Priscilla's answer didn't come quickly, and when it finally came, it was not at all the one that Joseph was waiting for. Maybe he had seen a bit of intrigue in her eyes, but never, ever, in a million years, did he expect her to want to stay. She was surely just as repulsed by this asshole's perverted musings as he was. He was sure of it.

But he was wrong. Priscilla didn't get up, or even move. Her gaze fell in her lap. The Devil was silent. Joseph said, "Scilly? You uh…comin' or?"

Priscilla looked up at Joseph, and said, "I…think I'm gonna stay a while longer."

Joseph's shoulders slumped, "But Scilly, you—."

"It's okay, Joseph."

Joseph looked from Priscilla to the Devil. The Devil was already watching him, intently, and when Joseph looked in his direction, he turned up his palms and shrugged, one eyebrow raised, as if to say, *Sorry about your fucking luck, pal.*

Joseph looked back at Priscilla, attempting to remain calm. He felt like he was going to cry. He had spent so much time being worried and trying to save her, and from what? The Devil? A goddamn orgy? She wanted to be there. She wanted all of this. Good God, what had his life become? What he would give for the simpler days of skipping rocks, and breaking bottles on cars. Catching lightning bugs in jars. This witch shit was too much.

But those days were gone.

He tried one last time. Joseph walked over to the chair where Priscilla was sitting, and standing over her, he spoke softly, so the Devil couldn't hear. He said, "Are you sure you know what yer doin'? He ain't got you under no spell, does he?"

Priscilla smiled, reassuringly, and shook her head.

Joseph had no argument for the way he felt that wasn't obvious. Priscilla knew she was in the company of Satan. She knew what he wanted. What was there for Joseph to say? Not much. So, he said what he could. He said, "Alright, well…I'll pray for ya." And he actually meant it.

Joseph turned, tipped his hat to the Devil, and with a hard stare said, "I guess I'll see ya around…friend."

"No doubt about it," responded the Devil. "And Joseph, don't forget your explosives."

Joseph walked out of the Devil's swanky, infinity square foot mansion and onto the back porch of a decaying, single story, two room house. From the outside, it looked like any other abandoned piece of property that he'd ever seen. He squatted and retrieved the dynamite from under the porch. This had not gone as Joseph expected it might, not in any way, shape, or form. Not only were the guns, and knives, and dynamite unnecessary, but so was all of his nervous anticipation, and all of his concern and worry. Most of it, anyway.

Joseph shouldered his pack and rifle. Then he lit a cigar that the Devil had given him and he walked home in the dark, alone. One set of foot prints in the snow. A solitary figure moving stoned and slow in the moonlight.

◆

Mark Layfield opened Layfield's Market in sixty-two, and for the last ten years, he'd gone through the same closing process every single night: restock, mop the floors, count the register, turn out the lights, lock all the locks, double check all the locks. And tonight was no different. After closing down, he climbed in his truck and made his way home. En route, he stopped and asked Jim Smith's boy, Joseph, who was walking along the road, if he needed a ride. The boy declined, telling Mark that he needed the time to think. Mark wondered if the rifle on the boy's back had anything to do with it, but he drove on anyway.

The Smith boy got Mark to thinking about his own children, and how lucky he was to be blessed with three of the most charming, beautiful, and kind-hearted daughters that a man could have. They were truly a blessing from God, and he counted his lucky stars that he would never have to worry about finding one of them walking the road at this hour. Not that the Smith boy had ever given him any trouble, he hadn't, but the look Mark had just now seen in the boy's eyes made him wonder. He looked stoned.

When Mark pulled up in front of his house it was dark. This caused no concern however because it was late. The house should have been dark, it was after midnight. The girls would have gone to bed hours ago, and Linda was likely studying her Bible by candlelight, waiting for her husband to return home, as was her usual. Even as Mark sat for an hour watching television and eating a bologna sandwich in his underwear before going to bed, as was his usual, he never once considered something was amiss. But then he went upstairs.

When he found that Violet, his oldest daughter, was not in her room, he wasn't immediately worried. Maybe she had stayed over at a friend's, though it was a school night, which made the possibility unlikely, but not unheard of. He closed her bedroom door, careful not to wake the rest of the house. At the time, a mild curiosity occupied his mind, that and the thought of his head on a pillow. But then he opened Lilly and Daisy's bedroom door, and when they too were nowhere to be found, he began to panic. Mark dashed to his own bedroom, yelling for his wife as he went.

The candle beside the bed was burning, and the family Bible laid open on the night stand. Mark sat down on the edge of his bed. Outside the window, he could see his truck parked next to Linda's car in front of the house. But Linda was gone. They were all gone. Still in his underwear, Mark got up and searched the house. "Linda! Daisy! Violet! Lilly!" When he found no one, he sat on the couch for a while. He searched the house again, calling out their names as he went. Then he picked up the phone and called the Sheriff.

◆

Priscilla lies naked on a tiger skin rug in front of a fireplace. Kathleen Gibbons lays beside her. She too is nude, save the black silk bag still covering her head. Kathleen, propped up by one elbow, lightly drags the tip of her finger over Priscilla's breast and along her stomach. Kathleen's nails, painted pink, appear orange in the firelight. Cupcake is asleep in the corner of the room, his back to the fireplace, and the goings on for which it is was lit.

Priscilla is on her back. Her legs are in the air. Luci is between them, on his knees. His hands have a firm hold on her ankles. In Luci's eyes, Priscilla sees worlds, galaxies unfolding and overlapping. She sees time, in its physical form, spinning on its axis. She sees the lightning quick recoil of a viper. She sees all her youthful curiosities dissolving in the eyes of a fallen angel, the eyes of an emperor, a God-King of Hell.

'Rev. 22:20' by Puscifer plays

Priscilla gasped. Kathleen's touch had evolved. With the bag now rolled up over her nose, Kathleen was breathing hot on Priscilla's neck, allowing her lips to touch here and there, and sending chills down Priscilla's spine. But Priscilla couldn't begin to take her eyes off Luci. Never in six million and sixty-six thousand years would she have guessed that dabbling in witchcraft would have led to this. She was without words. Moans and whimpers, however, had not escaped her.

Luci lowered himself between Priscilla's thighs, letting her legs fall onto his back. Above the ginger patch of fuzz, she could now see only his eyes. She squirmed in his embrace. All the feels, all the touches, tastes, and smells, sensations, all the virgin territory being covered, was all but a fountain under which Priscilla was being bathed. Anticipation was twisting her into a knot of pure, unbridled ecstasy, and everything inside her begged to be untied. Let loose. Released. Satisfied.

Finally Priscilla remembered how words worked, though she wasn't sure why she felt the need to speak them. Maybe it was nervousness. Softly, half-seriously, she said, "I thought you came here to teach me how to be a better witch."

Luci paused and lifted his head, but only slightly. She could still feel the heat of his breath on her. Instead of answering her question, however, he posed one of his own, rhetorical and leading. He asked, "You know how I convinced Eve to eat the apple, don't you?" He licked his lips and grinned. Then he licked his lips again, but this time, just before his tongue slipped back inside his mouth, it changed. Right before Priscilla's eyes, all at once, Luci's tongue thinned and stretched, and forked at the end, then it disappeared back into his mouth in time for him to answer his own question. As his lips pressed against the mouth of Priscilla's eager womb, he said, "Snakes are the best at eating pussy."

———◆———

A WORD FROM JOSEPH

I told ya so. I fuckin' told ya so. I told ya in the beginnin' I met the Devil and you ain't believe me. Am I right? Don't even answer that question, I know I am. But that's alright, I wouldn't have believed me neither. But I fuckin' told ya, didn't I. Yes sir, I did. I fuckin' told ya.

Lookin' back on it now, honestly, it seems like a fever dream. *An itinerant carnival, a migratory tent show whose ultimate destination after many a pitch in many a mudded field is unspeakable and calamitous beyond reckoning,* as McCarthy put it. Over the years, I've considered it often, and sometimes it makes sense, but mostly it don't. And just when I think I got it all figured out, something else comes to me. As a matter of fact, only now does it even occur to me that my experience in meetin' the Devil was tainted by the fact that the Devil lives inside all of us, just as God does. Which means that any human bein' who meets the Devil is meetin' a part of themselves. How big that part is depends on the person, but everybody, includin' me, includin' you, has a little of old Luci in 'em. And I reckon, I don't know, but I reckon the Devil knows that too, and he uses that upper hand to manipulate folks as he sees fit.

Yeah, old Satan was playin' me like a fiddle that night, and I ain't even know it. He had me right where he wanted me, confused and uncomfortable and scared about the size of my pecker. I reckon it seems obvious, from the outside lookin' in, but it's different when it's you. And it's different when yer only sixteen years old. Hell, I didn't know what to do with one girl at the time, let alone two and Satan. But he knew that, and now, I reckon, I know that. I guess that's the power of fiction for ya. You could learn a lesson a dozen times, the hard way even, but there's somethin' about readin' it in a story that gives it clarification.

It seems to me, in that way, the power of fiction is unparalleled. It ain't the same as tellin' you somethin' or teachin' you somethin' outright, as far as understandin' goes. And in that way, the story is a mighty and powerful tool. For instance, right now, at this point in the story, if I still have yer attention, then I'm in yer head. In yer imagination. In yer fuckin' psyche. I'm buildin' from within, you understand? Right now, yer not just hearin' me, yer listenin'. Yer not just sittin' there waitin' for yer chance to talk, yer actually absorbin' what I'm sayin', takin' it in, processin' it, visualizin' it, mappin' it out. If yer still readin', this far along in the story, then I'd bet, right about now, I have yer complete and undivided attention.

You understand what I'm gettin' at? You catchin' what I'm droppin'? You feel me knockin'? Yeah, you feel me. Hell, you probably even think you know what I look like. You probably got a whole image of me fabricated in yer mind. I'd wager to say, you can probably even hear what my voice sounds like, can't ya? All rough, and hillbilly soundin'. Yeah, you think you got me figured out. I can tell by the way yer starin' at the page. I got a grip on ye, don't I?

You can picture me when I was a boy, sittin in church diggin' at my wrist, right now. You can see me gettin' sprayed with puke, guttin' a coon, walkin' in the snow all by my lonesome, huffin' gas, kickin' rocks. I'll bet you can even see me smokin' a cigarette at this very moment. As I write these words. Bet you can see it hangin' from my lips, the ash fallin' from it, the smoke risin' up off the cherry, all grey and lazy. Can you see it? Can you see the nicotine stains on my fingers as I punch away at these keys? Can you see the wrinkles around my lips? The ashes on the typewriter? You can, can't ya?

What it comes down to is this. Fiction has power. No doubt about it. And too many of us take stories for granted. We treat 'em as frivolous, harmless little things, things to be unconcerned with, things to gather dust on a shelf, but they're a whole lot more than that.

The things is, some stories ain't just stories. Some stories is somethin' more. Somethin' greater. Somethin' powerful. I don't know if this'n is. I reckon that's up to you to decide. But some stories, they get inside yer head. They get inside yer head and they change you. All the way down to yer core. They reshape the way you think, how you feel, and what ye believe. Between book covers, you become the characters and you live their experiences. You learn from their mistakes. You learn as if you made the mistakes yerself, and in turn suffered the consequences. So, at the end of a good story, yer forever changed, just like you lived it instead of read it. So as I said, in a way, a good story, a real good story, ain't just a story. It's somethin' more.

But it's deeper than that, ain't it? Darker, even. Sure, a good story can help you to learn, and to grow, and what-not, but a good story can also destroy the fuckin' world. A good story can confuse and deceive, and make folks behave in all sorts of negative and interestin' ways. Fortunately or unavoidably, I ain't sure which, most of the great writers and artists in general have also been decent humans, so not much darkness has prevailed in the way of literature, but then again, it only takes one good book to fuck things up.

Which, I reckon, brings us back around to the Bible, once again. Not the real Bible, not the thin one. I'm talkin' 'bout the big thick fucker. You ever consider why the rulebook for non-fictional life is written in story form? Likely not. Most folks who ever lived never considered it. But I have, and I'm here to tell ya—King James, or Moses Junior, or whoever added in all the drama, knew what the fuck they was doin'. If you want people to listen, to obey, you don't whip 'em, you don't starve 'em, you give 'em a good story, a real good story. Then they'll pay attention. Then you'll be in their head.

Hey maybe not, though. Maybe I'm full of shit and yer just readin' all this, thinkin' bout what's for supper. Maybe I'm not in yer head at all. Maybe none of what I've been sayin' is gettin' through to you, in the least. Maybe the Bible's narrative struc-ture is completely coincidental. Who the fuck knows. Maybe I'm batshit crazy. Maybe I accidentally inhaled some fumes off the God Venom, and I'm trapped in another life, waitin' to get sucked back to nineteen seventy-two. Maybe I'm dead and Clockmaker is some sort of Purgatory. It surely ain't Heaven, and I'm pretty sure it ain't Hell cause I ain't seen Priscilla. So who really knows?

Life is full of maybes, ain't it? I carry around a truck load of 'em, myself. Maybes that is. Even now, at my ripe, cantankerous old age, I still think in maybes. Maybes and what ifs. I know it's futile. But I still to do it anyway, out of habit mostly. Like, maybe if God would have paid just a little more attention to Priscilla, none of this shit would have happened in the first place. It wasn't like she didn't pray. Hell, before she got ahold of that goddamn book, she was prayin' on the regular. I know she did. I made fun of her for it, on the regular. Ya know, of all the maybes I have, I reckon that's the one I cling to most. Maybe it wasn't our fault, after all. Maybe it was God's.

Then again, maybe it was predestination. Maybe it wasn't God's fault, but rather his plan. Maybe it was all supposed to happen. Maybe God is movin' us around like hand-carved chess pieces. We see the loss of a pawn, the capturin' of a knight, but we don't see the greater plan. Maybe what we need to do, you and I, is to just sit back, relax, fire up a fatty, and trust that God, in all his grand mysteriousness, has a plan. Wouldn't that be nice, let Jesus take the wheel 'cause I'm way too fucked up to drive. All gas, no brakes, till yer dead and in Heaven. Sounds like an awful fuckin' big maybe to me, but who knows.

As much as I know of God, which is more than most, I'm still riddled with questions. That ain't changed. Like I said, lots of maybes. But there's one thing I do know for certain. It's what I thought about while I walked home that night in the snow, after meetin' the Devil for the first time. And it's what I've been tryin' to tell you from the very beginnin' of this story. God exists. If Lucifer exists, God exists. So, ya better start actin' right, fuckers. Judgement day is comin'. Quicker than you think too.

I'll leave ya with this. From Revelations twenty eleven.

Then I saw a great white throne and him who was seated on it. From his presence, earth and sky done fled away, and no place was found for them. And I saw the dead, great and small, standin' before the throne, and books were opened. Then another book was opened, which is the book of life. And the dead were judged by what was written in the books, accordin' to what they had done. And the sea gave up the dead who were in it, Death and Hell gave up the dead who were in them, and they were judged, each one of 'em, accordin' to what they had done. Then Death and Hell were thrown into the lake of fire. This is the second death, the lake of fire. And if anyone's name was not found written in the book of life…he was thrown into the goddamn lake of fire.

━━━━◆━━━━

DEICIDE

"Now," Luci said softly, "I want you to close your eyes... Keep your breathing steady... Do you feel the pinch in the back of your brain...? ...Good, that pinch is your link to the pineapple. Hold on to it, don't allow it to fall away... Keep it spinning... Now, try to envision three circles... Three circles made of an unbreakable metal. The image doesn't have to be sharp or in color. Try to envision them in their most rudimentary form... Can you see them...?"

Priscilla and Luci were laying next to one another in bed, Priscilla on her back, and Luci on his side, his head propped in his hand, watching her. Kathleen was in the kitchen attending to breakfast. The smell of fried pork, Priscilla's favorite, filled the air. At the foot of the bed was a large silver tray with chunks of strawberries and bananas on it, and several other exotic fruits Priscilla had never tried until the previous night. In the center was a pineapple, and it was spinning like a top. Priscilla nodded in response to Luci's question, but just barely. She was concentrating with all of her will.

"Good, now, draw a standing star inside those circles, and when they are fully formed, rotate them counter clockwise until they are inverted… Good, yes, you feel it, don't you? I can see it on your face. Perfect... Yes, okay now, breathe…steady…steady.'

The instant Priscilla inverted the stars in her mind, she felt a sort of release, like a lock being disengaged, followed by the sound of a steadily growing hum, high-pitched, but not quite a ring in her ears. Her vision of the three pentagrams floating in the blackness of her mind was suddenly infiltrated by glowing red dots, thousands of them fizzing up and overwhelming her mind's eye.

"Alright, Priscilla, keep it spinning…hold the pinch. Now… how do you feel about peaches, do you like the taste of a good peach?"

Priscilla nodded her head, almost imperceptibly, but she did not speak.

"Me too," said Luci. "Me too. Have you tasted a peach lately?'

Priscilla shook her head. "Perfect," Luci continued. "When the red spots are all that you can see, when all the dark turns completely red, I want you to say the word *peach*, and then snap your fingers."

Right away, Priscilla said, "Peach," and snapped her fingers. For a second, she thought it hadn't worked, but then she felt Luci move even closer to her than he already was. "Now open your eyes," he whispered in her ear.

When Priscilla opened her eyes, the pineapple was gone, and in its place now was something small and blurry, but it was hard to make out clearly because it was spinning so fast. Luci leaned forward, and with one quick motion, he snatched the spinning blur off the the tray, inspected it, tossed it in the air, caught it, and held it out to Priscilla, saying, "And that, my little sugar pussy, is how your Lord and Savior turned water into wine."

Priscilla sat up to take hold of the peach that used to be a pineapple. "Well, that was easy," she said, as she rotated the soft fruit around in her hand.

"Taste it," said Luci.

Priscilla took a bite of the peach, and her eyes lit up. Then with a mouth full of peach mush, she said, "So Jesus was a witch? I thought only girls could be witches?"

"Only girls can be Satanic witches," Luci corrected. "There are many types of witch. Many forms of magic. My own particular blend of hocus pocus requires a vagina, but many do not. Jesus was a Heavenic witch. As is God. As am I."

"Can I be a Heavenic witch?"

"Unfortunately, no. Heavenic magic is reserved for those who were born in Heaven. But that is exactly why I made the book. For the people."

"Why only women?"

Luci scoffed, "Because men can't handle this kind of power. They'd fuck everything up. God didn't build them equipped with the necessary tools to handle Black Magic. As I've told you, most women can't handle being a witch, let alone a man."

"Why's it so hard? It came to me pretty easy."

"Well," said Luci, relaxing back against the bed's headboard, "that is a good question. And I am not sure. I don't think it's a lack of ambition. Maybe it's the tea."

"Death Tea?"

"What else? To be honest, half of what makes you the bad bitch witch you are is your cast iron stomach and your unbreakable mind. Most aspiring witches *cannot* handle the Tea. And they never even get close to smoking the Venom."

At just the mention of Death Tea, Priscilla could taste it in the back of her throat, but she was preoccupied. She said, "You think I'm a…bad bitch witch?"

Luci grinned. "I do, indeed."

Priscilla's heart filled up, and almost came pouring out her ears. She'd never been given such a compliment, especially by anyone so, so…all-knowing. It was all she could do to contain herself. Invisible butterflies bounced around in her stomach. Then the breakfast bell rang, and Luci's eyes and smile got real big, and he said, "Hope you're hungry."

Priscilla watched him as he made his way to the kitchen. He hopped out of the bed, his dick swinging to and fro, his tight, caramel ass swaying, singing, "I wish I was an apple, hangin' from a tree, and every time my baby passed by she'd take a big bite of me."

Priscilla, not nearly as comfortable with her own nudity as Luci, chose to get dressed before breakfast. She went into the magnificent closet where everything was just her size and she first chose something comfy, but exchanged it for something sexy, a silky red gown with lace around her breasts. *Get along home, Cindy, Cindy.*

It amazed her how differently she'd been thinking recently. Her mind seemed to be operating on a new level, one highly revolving around and motivated by the idea of sexuality. After last night with Luci and Kathleen, Priscilla felt as though she had been once again liberated. Just as she had been by the book that led her here. She had been made to orgasm over and over and over again, until she was breathless, weak-limbed, and covered with sweat, until her legs spasmed and shook. Until she thought she would cry from pleasure. *Oh Cindy got religion. She had it once before but when she heard my ole banjo play, she was the first one on the floor.*

For hours she was licked, and sucked, and made to lose herself time after time. Hands and mouths, nails and teeth, and fistfuls of hair, both Luci and Kathleen made Priscilla come her brains out until the sun came up, and afterward they laid in bed for several hours eating and talking about different fruits. Kathleen didn't actually speak, she only ate strawberries and listened. When Priscilla asked Luci why neither he nor Kathleen would allow her to help them organism, Luci laughed, corrected her word usage, and told her very simply that last night was all about her and that next time he would most certainly be finding time for himself. Priscilla had blushed at this comment, she wasn't used to such kindness.

She also asked him why Kathleen had to keep the bag over her head, and why she never spoke, and he only told her that he preferred it that way. He preferred the mystery. Which was still odd, but then again, he was the Devil. He was bound to have a few eccentricities. Priscilla supposed she was lucky it was something as benign as a bag over the head and a little peace and quiet. He could have been into necrophilia. So it could have been worse. And she had to admit, when it came down to it, strange as it sounded, the Devil was pretty darn dreamy. And forget the things he could do with his forked tongue… Priscilla nearly melted at the thought.

She finished in the closet, and fixed her hair in the mirror. She even applied some eyeliner, which she hadn't been doing much since Tommy died. But now that she knew that she wasn't at fault for his death, it felt like the weight of the universe had been lifted off her shoulders, and as she drew black around her eyes, she wondered how she could have ever considered killing herself. How foolish that would have been. Thank God the Devil saved her. What if she had died without ever having multiple orgasms? After last night, she couldn't imagine. Surely it would have been a wasted life.

FOUR FOUR NINE

Priscilla strolled into the kitchen confidently, a bounce in her step, and a smile on her face, but it was short lived. There were new guests. Luci, still nude, had a folded Clockmaker Times newspaper in one hand, and a fork with a bite of something on the end, in the other. Kathleen, also still nude, save her bag and a white chef's apron, was washing dishes, silently. The problem was that next to Kathleen, there was now another woman. An additional one. Also nude with a bag over her head, but visibly much older and less in proportion, this other woman was drying the dishes as Kathleen handed them to her.

Additionally, there were three other women, two of whom looked more like girls Priscilla's own age, and one who was a little older, judging by the development of their bodies. These three too wore nothing but the black bag masks. They stood at the far end of the kitchen, at the opposite end of the table from Luci, motionless, silent, and single file, like erotic soldiers with limp necks and loose wrists. Luci seemed to be paying them no mind as he read his paper.

Priscilla stood motionless and awkward for several moments, trying to absorb what was happening. The bottoms of her feet felt cold on the tile floor. Then from the adjacent hall, in walked another woman nude with a bag over her head. Her ancient breasts sagged and swung. She had blue veins spiderwebbing along soft legs, and liver spots on her hands and neck. Fine grey curls fell out from underneath the black bag. Without a word, the woman entered the kitchen, kneeled down on the floor in front of Luci, and began rubbing his feet.

Just then, Luci noticed Priscilla lurking in the hallway, and he turned his head toward her, smiling and saying, "Damn the pines, you are even finer in the morning light. And I love that color red on you. Come sit down, eat, before it gets cold. Linda, be a doll and make Priscilla a plate would you."

Linda, the woman helping Kathleen do the dishes, sat down the drying towel, picked up a clean plate, turned to the stove and did as she was told. "Come sit. Don't be bashful," said Luci, to Priscilla. "They won't bite."

Priscilla, having previously felt sexy in the red gown, now felt only…silly, as she sat down at the table. For an excruciatingly long second, the hairy ass crack of the old woman rubbing Luci's feet stared up at Priscilla, menacingly, and she couldn't help but return the grimace. That is, until Luci said, "Don't stare too long, it'll ruin your appetite."

Priscilla looked up at him. He was grinning, as was his usual. Linda sat down a heaping plate in front of Priscilla, then went back to the dishes. "Eat up," said Luci. "It's a new day."

Priscilla half smiled, but she only stared at the food.

"What's the matter, little lamb," asked Luci.

Priscilla bit at the inside of her cheek, nervously, but finally she took a deep breath and said, "Who…are all these women?"

"Ah, of course. Don't you worry about them. They are of no threat to you. This happens every time I set foot on this planet. Bitches flock to me like moths to a flame."

"All…bitches?" asked Priscilla, thinking of her own mother… and grandmother.

Luci's grin widened, knowingly. "You don't have to worry about Maw Maw, Priscilla, or your mother. Only wicked women are drawn to my light. Hence my treatment of them. It's the reason I can never stay too long in any one place. They begin to pile up. It becomes… troublesome."

Priscilla let out her breath. At least she wouldn't have to worry about her mother winding up a footstool. Still though, the whole scene had her good and freaked out. But then Luci said, "Thank you, Linda," as Linda sat two glasses of cold milk on the table. And with those words, Priscilla's mind switched gears. She only knew one Linda, Linda Layfield, but there was no way it could be her. No way. Not preachy, judgey Linda Layfield. It couldn't be. But then, *holy fuckin' shit…* How many girls did she see when she came in the kitchen? Priscilla turned in her chair to face the three girls behind her, and her mouth drop open wide in stunned realization. "No fuckin' way," she whispered to herself.

Then she turned back to Luci, and when she did, he said, "Jesus, what is it?" Her face must have given her away.

Priscilla put both her hands on the edge of the table and leaned down over her plate, conspiratorially, her eyes wide, and said, several octaves higher than normal, "Is that the fuckin' Layfield sisters?"

Luci cocked his head to the side and said, "Impressive, how'd you know?"

Priscilla's mind was blown, bombed, nuked. Scorched fucking earth. She looked back again at the three girls, and sure enough, there was blonde hair coming from under each of their bags. There was Lilly, on the left, Priscilla could tell by her massive breasts. Daisy was in the middle, she was in the same grade as Priscilla in school, but much shorter than Priscilla. And on the right was Violet, tall and flat-chested. How many times had Priscilla been ridiculed and laughed at by those three, she couldn't count. And to see them now, stripped of all clothing and dignity, with bags over their fucking heads, all she wanted to do was laugh. So, she did. Hysterically. Wildly. She even slapped her knee, and when she finally regained her composure, she looked at Luci and said, "I can't fuckin' wait to tell Joseph about this, he's gonna die."

"He's probably going to wish he stayed," Luci responded. Priscilla agreed. Then she had an idea. She gestured over her shoulder, and said, "So uh, you can make them do whatever you want…right?"

"Does the Pope wear a funny hat?" said Luci. Priscilla could tell by the look on his face that he knew what she was getting at.

And so, Priscilla spent the next thirty odd minutes of her life eating breakfast with her feet propped up on Violet Layfield's bare back, with her shoulders being massaged by Lilly Layfield, and her feet being massaged by Daisy Layfield, that is of course, after she had them all bray like donkeys and pick each other's noses. The massages were Luci's idea. Priscilla had to admit, it was all pretty damn sweet. Pretty damn sweet indeed.

Post-breakfast, Priscilla spent an hour in the tub. Grandly constructed, and filled with bubbles, the tub was big enough for ten people, and her head was but an island in the center among the suds. As can be imagined, between breakfast, the massages, the bathtub, and the orgasms, Priscilla was feeling particularly good. And she had to admit, she could get used to this kind of living.

Luci, who, while Priscilla was being massaged by the Layfield sisters, excused himself so that he could handle what he referred to as 'Devil Business,' had returned, and was now sitting beside the tub. 'Children of the Grave' was playing softly on the stereo. Like Priscilla, Luci too was a fan of Black Sabbath. Just as Priscilla was blowing into a handful of bubbles, he said, "So I was thinking…we should have dinner with your parents this evening."

Priscilla stopped blowing. "Um…what? Why?"

"Well," Luci said, "I think it is about high time, and I'm sure you will agree, that Everett Carpenter get what's coming to him. Also… I want to meet your mother."

"Well, shit," said Priscilla. "I mean…are you sure?"

"Quite sure."

Priscilla, on the other hand, was not sure. She was not at all sure how she felt about the idea of dining with Luci—Lucifer— and her mother and Everett. But she also wasn't sure she had much say in the situation. Luci didn't seem like the arguing type.

Besides, he was right. It was high time that Everett got what was coming to him. High time indeed. "What are you gonna do to him?" Priscilla asked.

"Well… I was going to leave that up to you."

"Oh…okay."

"Fantastic," said Luci, standing up, and adjusting his collar. He was now clothed. "I will meet you back here at five."

"Are you goin' somewhere?"

"I have official business to attend to, actually. The state and local government are holding a townhall meeting in Man to discuss the flood relief effort. I have hands to shake and white people to make uncomfortable. Plus, quite a few of them niggas are on my naughty list and I have souls to collect."

"Alright," said Priscilla.

Luci walked up to the tub, reached out, and gently tilted Priscilla's chin upward, then he bent down and kissed her, soft, slow, and sweet. When he finally pulled away, still touching her chin, he said, "Stay as long as you like, or come and go as you please. Whichever. Also feel free to order these bitches about. They've been told to obey you. Oh, and don't be alarmed when more of them show up, as they no doubt will." Another kiss, this time on the forehead, and he walked away.

Priscilla said, "Before you go, I've been meanin' to ask you, why ain't I been able to summon Lightnin'? Ever since I woke up here, I ain't been able to use her eyes or nothin'."

Luci, looking back over his shoulder, said, "Oh, that's nothing to worry over. Cats hate me. Cats and Christians… Also this house exists in another dimension. She's probably waiting for you outside." Then, just before he left the room he said, "See you at five, gorgeous."

Gorgeous. *What the fuck is life?* Priscilla slowly lowered herself into the bubbles until her head was completely underwater.

Sheriff White slammed the handset down on the receiver. That was the third call about a missing woman in the last twelve hours. It all started late last night, when Mark Layfield called him at home, and told him that his wife and daughters were missing. At the time, Sheriff White assumed Mark was being either overzealous or naive. Linda had probably left him for another man and taken the girls with her. Simple as that. But now, after yet another call, Sheriff White was beginning to think that when he told Mark Layfield to calm down, and that everything would be alright, he'd lied.

There was a knock at the door. "It's open," said Sheriff White.

"Sorry to bother ya, Sheriff," said Deputy Knotts, peeking his head through the door. "But uh, there's a feller uh, Sam Gibbons, out here who wants to see ya."

"'Bout what?"

"Well, he says his sister is missin'. Says she ain't showed up to work the last two days."

Sheriff White let out a long sigh, and said, "Deputy, come on in here and shut the door." Then, after a few seconds, he said, "Go on, have a seat."

"What's up, Sheriff?"

"You trust me, don't ya, Don?"

"Course I do, Sheriff."

"Well, Deputy, I have a hunch. No evidence, mind you, but a hunch. And my hunch is that all the weird shit that's been happenin' around here, includin' these women disappearin', and our fancy nigger is all connected. 'Tween you and me, that is. And if'n I'm right—"

"You always are," Deputy Knotts interjected.

"Well, then I reckon we ought to not delay in dealin' with our little problem any longer. Does 'at sound fine by you, Deputy?"

Deputy Knotts nodded, and as he stood, he said, "Sounds fine by me, Sheriff."

"Alright, well, I reckon we'll need Junior and Stanley after all then. Tell 'em to be here around dark, and tell 'em to be sober. I ain't in the mood for no kinda shit out of them."

"Roger that, Sheriff. You ready for some more coffee? There's a fresh pot out here," Deputy Knotts said, moving toward the door.

"No. I reckon I've had enough. Send in the Gibbons feller on yer way out. And Knotts…keep an eye on yer old lady. There's fuckery afoot."

◆

Satan sits disrobed on a throne of whores in a small West Virginia town. Lucifer moves through a crowd in Times Square. Luci confronts Governor Moore in the corner of a crowded auditorium and whispers in his ear. The Morning Star deals Blackjack at a Vegas casino in the year nineteen eighty-six. The King of Hell walks along the lake of fire. The Lord of Flies stares out over the mountains of Switzerland. The Dark Star defiles a nun inside the Sistine Chapel . The Adversary is in a bathtub mainlining the venom of the gods. The Goat grazes in a meadow.

———◆———

Chapter Sixteen

When life gets hard, when it gets confusing and out of control, when a girl doesn't know what to do or how she's going to do it, when the failures of Heaven come crashing down all around, there is only one place to go. Just one.

Grandma's house.

And after everything that Priscilla had gone through lately, a little time with Maw Scill was just what she needed.

So, after bathing, she got dressed and set off to see her Maw Maw. And just as Luci had suspected, Lightning was waiting for her when she walked outside. Poised, tail swaying, a black spot in all the white, the cat sat in the snow along the road, seemingly impervious to the elements, as if she'd been sitting and waiting for centuries. As if she'd continue to sit and wait for centuries if necessary. Priscilla was so happy to see the little fur ball that she scooped her up and carried her tucked inside her coat the entire walk.

Along the walk, Priscilla thought about how much things had changed, and how differently she now felt about her life. She marveled at how, only mere months ago, she had been leery to even walk along the road, worried she might run into one of the

Mire kids, or someone from her church or school. And now look at her, kickin' up snow while the coal trucks rumble past, not giving a fuck. To think that she had been scared to sleep in that old abandoned cabin with Joseph the night they met Mathias and Elias was a trip. And now, most days, she either slept alone in a cave or more recently had slumber parties at Satan's house. *Who would have thought?*

When Priscilla came out of Owl Farm Holler, and crossed over Main Street, she got her first taste of the flood's effect on Clockmaker. Never had she seen so many strange new faces. She had to look for a landmark to make sure she hadn't accidentally wandered into the wrong town. Luckily, Layfield's Market stood where it always had, giving Priscilla grounding. It also gave her a sly little smirk because it made her think of Violet Layfield, the queen bitch, hee-hawing like a jackass with a bag over her head. One odd thing Priscilla noticed was that she seemed to be attracting stares, mostly from men, but she wasn't sure why. She honestly didn't think too much about it.

Coming up the hill to Maw Scill's house, Lightning leapt from Priscilla's arms and made her way to the woodline, likely in pursuit of game twice her size. That cat, more than anything, loved to kill. As Priscilla kicked snow off of her boots on the porch steps, Maw Scill opened the front door. "Good God, little girl, where in hell'd ya find that coat? Forget them boots, get yer ass inside. It's cold to the bone out here. Where you been? You just missed Jeremiah. He's off to Texas on one of his runs. Jesus God, what a coat, that's real fox, girl. D'you rob a furrier? Woowee, look at that thing. You eat today? I got stew on. Here, let me take this coat. Lord, it's heavy. You might have to let Maw Maw borrow this for her bingo night. You want some stew?"

Sometimes Maw Scill's endless questioning and pestering bothered Priscilla, but not today. Today it gave her nothing but comfort. After spending what seemed like a decade with Luci, it felt nice to finally be in possession of more answers than questions, and it felt even better to have a conversation about something as simple as what she wanted to eat, or how her day had been. The constant back and forth over the finer points of known existence—sex, God, drugs, and witchcraft included—had left Priscilla feeling mentally and emotionally exhausted. And a good, old fashioned, *Hey, how are ya?*, felt like an encouraging pat on the back.

Priscilla stuffed her face like she hadn't eaten in days. After two large bowls of beef stew and four pieces of rye bread with butter, she was a brand new woman. Kicked back at the kitchen table with remnants of the stew still glistening on her cheek, Priscilla finally just came right out and said it. She said, "Maw Maw, I gotta tell ya somethin'…"

Then she told her everything. From finding the book in Mathias's library, to Gertrude's unfortunate demise, to sniffing cocaine with Satan and everything in between, she laid it all out. She told her about flying on a broom and about the splinters that it left in her crotch, about Death Tea, about showering Joseph with vomit, about God, gutting animals, the real Bible, how Hell really works, and how if catered to appropriately, girls can achieve countless multiple orgasms in a single night. She told her about how much she still missed Big Tommy, and she told her about the Devil's plan to have dinner with Everett and her mother, and when Priscilla finished, all Maw Scill said was, "Well, I'll be…I always knew Linda Layfield was a slut."

Then after several moments of contemplation, Maw Scill said, 'I'll tell ya the same thing I been tellin' Joseph for months. The Devil ain't nothin' to mess with, but what's done is d—'

Priscilla cut her off. 'Joseph? You been talkin' to Joseph about me?'

"Well, 'course I have. I'm yer Maw Maw."

"That son of a bitch," said Priscilla.

"Oh don't curse him. He ain't have no choice. He tried to hold out, but Maw Maw's persuasive."

"Oh I bet," said Priscilla, crossing her arms over her chest. "He probably sang for a hot supper."

"No," Maw Scill said matter of factly, a small grin on her face. "I held his head down by the litter box and told him if he didn't start fessin' up quick, he'd be eatin' cat turds."

"You didn't."

"I did so. And he still wouldn't tell me, till I started diggin' my knuckle in his ribs." She held up a fist with the knuckle of the middle finger raised slightly, and winked at Priscilla.

"Maw Maw! You are terrible."

"Well," said Maw Scill, as if to say, *What do you expect?* "You think I was just gonna let you run wild without keepin' tabs on ya? If you did, yer wrong."

Priscilla smiled. Words couldn't describe how she loved this woman. "And you believed him when he told you?"

"Course not. I shoved his face a little closer to the cat shit."

"Maw Maw!"

"Well, I did," Maw Scill said with pride, and they both had a good laugh at that. Then Maw Scill said, "No, I thought Joseph was puttin' me on for a while. Then one night I was layin' in bed and I heard one hell of a loud bang…"

Priscilla had a feeling that she knew where Maw Scill was going with this.

"…and I got up and pulled on my nightgown, and walked over to the window, and just a few minutes later, you took off into the sky on a broom. And I still ain't believe it. Thought my mind was goin' on me, or I was dreamin', but then I threatened yer brother with the cat shit and a knuckle after he came back inside all stoned, and he confessed about the same thing Joseph did. So, I been believin' since then."

Priscilla sat thoughtfully for a few seconds. Then she said, "Why didn't you say nothin' to me?"

Maw Scill took some time to consider the question, then she kind of tilted her head, shrugged, and said, "When I was yer age, there weren't no tellin' me nothin'. And I mean nothin'. Yer momma, she was the same way. In one ear and out the other. And you, well, you know as well as I do, you ain't never gone no way but yer own. So, I reckoned if and when the time come you needed me, you'd be right where you are now." Then Maw Scill paused, and for a second Priscilla could see just how old she really was. As if something important had just crossed the little old woman's mind, she said, "I'll tell you one thing though, Priscilla, and I want ya to listen to me good. No matter what happens tonight with Everett, or any other night, I'm yer grandmomma and I'll love you no matter what. You understand me?"

Priscilla nodded. "I love you too, Maw Maw."

"I love you more. Now, before we discuss this whole dinner with the Devil situation, impress yer Maw Maw. I wanna see you use yer magic witch powers to turn down the sound on that box so I don't have to get up. My damn legs is killin' me today."

As the large dial on the television magically began spinning and the volume descended, Maw Scill said, "Hole…lee…shit."

◆

"Dear God… It's me, Joseph…Smith…again. I know yer real busy, and all, but I thought of a few other things I need to ask forgiveness for. I hope ya don't mind I got so much catchin' up to do, but stuff just keeps comin' to me. Like when I was eleven, I stole three cigarettes out of my momma's purse, and I lied about it, and when I was thirteen, I wrote Mrs. Laymen likes horse wiener on the chalkboard at school, and that same year, I climbed a tree outside Maryanne Lauver's house, and watched her change out of her cheerleadin' uniform…and, well, for all that, dear God, I ask yer forgiveness. And God, I can't say I'm sorry enough for the whole witchcraft thing, please forgive me and allow my ever-lastin' soul to enter the pearly gates…oh, and God, again, please take it easy on Priscilla too, she's doin' her best, and with yer guidance, I know she can be led right on back to the light… She ain't too far off, I promise. She's a good person… Alright, well… Amen."

Joseph opened his eyes and raised his head. He looked haggard. He barely slept all night long. All he could think about was if he had forgotten to ask forgiveness for some long ago sin, and if maybe anyone did baptisms on a Saturday. What it came down to was this. Now that the Devil was real, that meant God was real, which meant that it was well past time that Joseph got his act together when it came to Jesus. All night and all morning, he either read the Bible or prayed, most of his prayers sounding quite like the one above. He even skipped breakfast, preferring the solitude of his newfound faith to whatever his mother had cooking in the kitchen.

Around lunchtime, his mother called up the stairs to, once again, come and eat, but again, despite hunger pains, Joseph declined. His father however was not having it. He shouted up the stairs, "Boy, get yer skinny ass down here and eat, you keep playin' with that thing, you'll be blind 'fore supper."

◆

Dave Scofield's wife was making lunch when she disappeared. Dave was sitting in front of the television with his two boys when he smelled smoke. He walked into the kitchen and found his wife's clothes in a pile on the floor and a grease fire on the stove top. The back door hung wide open, and just before Dave's wife disappeared into the woods, he caught a glimpse of her. She was stark naked, and she was more than a hundred yards away so it was hard to be certain, but it looked like she was pulling a black bag over her head.

Jerome Jenkins came home just in time to find his oldest daughter walking across the front lawn without any clothes on, a silky black bag wadded up in her hand. She was stuck in some kind of trance. She wouldn't speak and she tried several times to leave, but Jerome tied her down to her bed, covered her with a quilt, and locked her door behind him. He sat down at the foot of the steps leading up to his front porch with a Bible and a shotgun, and waited. Then he realized he hadn't seen his youngest daughter all day long.

Junior and Stanley Jones were loading guns into the back of Junior's truck, when their sister, Brenda, fat as can be, started stripping off her clothes and making her way to the woodline. The brothers were so dumbfounded and disgusted at the sight, they didn't even think to stop her until she was long gone. They reluctantly searched for an hour, and after they found nothing, they phoned the Sheriff. "Sheriff, it's Junior. Say, I hate to bother ya but Big Brenda just took off into the woods in her birthday suit and we searched all over but we can't find her nowhere." Silence on the other end of the line, and then Sheriff White said, "Knotts has been trying to get ahold of you for an hour. You and Stanley get over here. We got a job to do."

◆

"Dear God…it's me again. Joseph. Forget everything else I asked for. Please just watch out for Priscilla… Amen."

———•◆•———

FOUR SIX THREE

CHPTER seveNTEEN

Warm cans of beer, instant mashed potatoes, canned beans, pork chops. Everett and Lavinia had just sat down at the kitchen table for dinner when there was a knock at the door. They both paused, and looked toward the sound, then back at one another. Visitors were rare.

Everett, shirtless, fork in his mutilated hand, knife in the other, wore the scowl of a man who loathed to be interrupted while eating. Another knock at the door. "You expectin' company?" he asked Lavinia. She shook her head. Everett sat down his knife and fork, placing them on the table, and he stared at Lavinia until she eventually got up to see who was knocking. He shook his head at her, as she went. Just before she opened the door, Everett said, with dull frustration, mostly to himself, "Never a goddamn moment of peace."

From the kitchen, the sound of the door opening could be heard. Then some muffled discussion, mostly Lavinia's side of it, followed by silence. "Who the fuck is it?" yelled Everett. When there was no immediate response, he yelled again. "Lavinia, who the fuck is it?" He could have easily turned around in his chair to look for himself, but lifting a single muscle seemed too much effort to put forth for another human being.

"It's Priscilla, Everett. It's Priscilla…" came Lavinia's voice, absently, from behind him, as she reentered the kitchen. She walked past Everett who was still eyeballing his mashed potatoes, and sat down opposite of him at the other end of the table. Everett looked up at her. She looked nervous. She said, "She brought a friend."

'The Next Episode' by Dr. Dre plays

As Everett cocked his head at his wife's comment, behind him Priscilla emerged from the living room with Luci at her side. Her eyes were painted black around the edges, but smudged and messy, as if she'd been crying and rubbing at them. She hadn't been of course, she did her makeup that way on purpose. She liked the way it looked. As did Luci. He told her as much. He said it made her look strung out and edible, so she left it streaking down her cheeks in places. Her lips were red, also at Luci's suggestion, and her hair fell in wind swept swaths about a shiny, floor-length, sky-grey fur coat. She had on a short black dress underneath, and black leather boots up to her knees. Luci in his finest black suit, also draped in fur, gold shining in his grin, gator shoes, pearl handle switchblade in his breast pocket, had decided that they should both dress appropriately for the occasion, and now there they both stood, quietly, gravely.

When Everett finally turned to face them, the blood drained from his face. In the aging, dusty little house, Priscilla and Luci stood out like goth-punk royalty at a barn raising, like thirty pieces of silver at the last supper, like someone smiling in Auschwitz. So obviously foreign in the small kitchen, at first it appeared as though Everett couldn't understand what he was seeing when he looked at them. He was angry, that much was clear, but he was also highly confused, and his face struggled with that expression.

Priscilla, with mock cheer said, "I hope you don't mind I brought company. Momma, Everett, this is my friend, Black Lavender Luci. Short for Lucifer. He's the Devil. Boy, it sure smells good in here. What you got cookin', Momma?"

Lavinia moved as though she didn't know whether to stand up, sit down, serve another plate, or jump out the window. She said, "Oh, well, um, I, well, I, yes, okay, you two have a seat, there's one more porkchop, where's my manners, I'll split it for you two, here have a seat, okay, can I get y'all somethin' to drink, Priscilla, uh, um Black, uh, Luci was it?"

Luci, removed his hat and said, "Miss Lavinia, you can call me Luci, and it is my absolute pleasure to finally make your acquaintance. I've heard so much about you, and yes… I would love a drink. Whiskey, if you have it?"

"Whiskey sounds fine for me too, Momma," said Priscilla as she sat down at the table.

Everett was staring hard at her, a look of disgust resting smugly on his face. He said, "Oh you drink whiskey now, do you?"

"Sometimes," said Priscilla, unapologetically.

"Is 'at right? My little girl's a whiskey drinker…ain't that somethin'. She's all grown up…all grown up…drinkin' whiskey and got her a nigger boyfriend. Ain't that special."

"Everett," said Lavinia, several cubes of ice slid from her hand and hit the floor. "That is no way to talk."

Everett shot her a hard stare. "Oh, so you tell me how to talk now?"

There was a pause, a consideration. "You know I ain't mean it like that."

"I damn well know you ain't."

Luci pulled out the chair opposite Priscilla, and sat down facing Everett. He said, "Talk to me how you like, as far as I'm concerned."

FOUR SIX SEVEN

Everett nodded his head repeatedly, in a ramping up sort of way, and said, "Well, I sure am glad you feel that way, mister *nigger*, I sure am. Say, Lavinia, darlin', why don't you go ahead and break out the fine china for this *nigger* here, he sure is agreeable."

Lavinia paled. Priscilla grinned. Luci grinned. "No need, I've eaten," said Luci, sarcastically, in regard to the china.

Lavinia walked back over to the table and sat down a glass of whiskey in front of Luci, and a glass of milk in front of Priscilla. "Really, Momma?" said Priscilla. "Milk?"

Everett cut in. "Yeah, what gives, Lavinia? Yer daughter comes home dressed like some flashy, big city whore with a godforsaken shit monkey on her arm, and you think she wants milk? Hell, I bet straight shine wouldn't get the taste of this nigger out her mouth, let alone milk."

"Everett please," said Lavinia. She looked to be on the verge of tears.

Priscilla, no longer grinning, stood up, stepped around the chair, and hugged her mother. She said, "Don't be sad, Momma. Luci's gonna take care of this."

"Oh is he now?" said Everett, his voice growing more aggressive with each word. "You gonna take care of me, boy?" Everett suddenly stood up and snatched a steak knife off the table with his good hand. Luci stayed seated. He didn't so much as flinch. Everett aimed the knife at him.

"Everett, stop. Just stop," pleaded Lavinia

"It's okay, Momma."

"Yeah, it's okay," said Luci.

Everett didn't budge, the steak knife stayed ready. He said, "Quiet, Lavinia. This nigger wants to try me. I can see it in his eyes." Then to Luci. "Don't ya, boy? You wanna try me, don't ya? Don't ya?"

Luci didn't respond right away. His eyes were locked on

Everett's. The room was quiet. Everyone was watching him, waiting for his next move. Just the way he liked it. Finally, he said, "Nigga, sit your stupid ass down before I tell everyone how you used to jerk your little dick to pictures of your own mother in a bathing suit."

Everett's position tensed dramatically, like he'd been hit with a low voltage cattle prod. The look on his face was an ever-evolving matrix of confusion and hatred. The steak knife trembled in his hand. He was clearly not prepared for those particular words to come out of Luci's mouth.

It took him time to find the ability to speak, and when he finally did, his voice came out weak and shaky. Everett said, "Nigger… you are gonna get up and walk out of this house right fuckin' now…or I am gonna cut yer big…monkey…lips…off… and drag you out dead."

The next words came to Priscilla with a fierceness. Repressed deep inside her for years, the words bubbled to the surface and popped out of her mouth with conviction and ease. They were words she had been savoring and sharpening on the edge of a grinding wheel since she was old enough to speak, and they tasted like hard tack candy when they left her lips. "Shut the *fuck* up, Everett," said Priscilla. "Just shut. The fuck. Up."

Everett, who had previously been swaying left and right, all tense and ready to kill, sort of softened. He turned, and aiming the knife at Priscilla, he said, "After his lips…I'm cuttin' out yer tongue… You hear me, little girl? Yer tongue… You been away from home…too long…"

"You'll do no such thing," Lavinia said, and stepped between him and Priscilla. Luci was still sitting calmly on the other side of the table, sucking at his teeth.

Everett shook his head with some sort of ironic or mock disappointment, and said, "You still ain't learned, have you, cunt?'

Then he started nodding and said, 'You will tonight.'

That's when Luci said, "I've had enough. Smiley, restrain this little bitch."

As Everett looked to Luci, trying to decipher what his last statement meant, Smiley emerged like a specter from the shadows of the living room behind him, and before Everett even thought to defend against a rear attack, the giant unsmiling black man was on him. He wrapped his massive arms around Everett's biceps and chest like a lasso, and squeezed until Everett's wrists went limp against his stomach. The steak knife fell from his grip and went clattering across the floor. Everett kicked and bucked and knocked over a chair, but he was no match for Smiley's Grizzly Bear hug. He screamed and hollered, "Let me fuckin' go, you motherfuckin' son of a bitch motherfucker, let me fuckin' go, nigger, nigger, let me go, motherfucker nigger."

Luci and Priscilla both grinned. So far, all was going as planned. Lavinia watched helplessly. Still standing between Everett and Priscilla, she said to herself, "God help me." Then she turned to face her daughter and said, "Priscilla Louise, this is not the way. You put an end to this. Violence don't solve nothin'. You know better. I know I've wished him dead too, but this ain't the way."

Priscilla looked her mother directly in the eyes, and leaning in close so that only she could hear, she whispered, "It's okay, Momma. Don't be scared. Me and Maw Maw came up with a plan."

Lavinia whispered back, clearly surprised, "Yer Maw Maw knows about this?"

Priscilla nodded eagerly. Lavinia looked at her daughter for a moment, stern at first, concerned, but quickly she softened, and said, "It's so good to see you. Yer gettin' big. Prettier every day."

Priscilla smiled, and turned red. "Momma, stop."

Everett had finally grown tired of struggling. Smiley had him pinned to the floor, straddling him, holding his wrists down above his head, playground style, as if he were going to test the strength of his saliva over Everett's face before slurping it back in. Luci stood over them, using a small white cloth to polish his switchblade, whistling softly. He said, "Ladies, I hate to interrupt your little sewing circle, but Priscilla this is your show."

"Comin'," said Priscilla, pleasantly. Then to her mother, smiling and in a whisper, "Don't worry 'bout Luci's knife, he just wants to scare him a little."

As Priscilla approached, Luci knelt beside Everett's head, still polishing his knife. Everett was no longer thrashing or cursing. He was trembling and panting. When he noticed Priscilla coming toward him and Lavinia maintaining distance, he erupted once more. "You bitch! You bitch, yer just gonna let this happen, I'll fuckin' kill you, you fu—"

Luci open-hand smacked Everett hard across the face, ending his tirade. "Easy, old man," he said.

Priscilla walked up slow, with a bit of flair (she'd been spending too much time with Lucifer) and stood over Everett, staring down at him for several moments, allowing room for the suspense to blossom. Then she knelt beside Luci, close to Everett's head, and said, "Ya know, Everett, all my life…I wished you dead…"

"And you found a couple niggers to do the job for ya, look at you. Big tough little girl, with yer make-up on…" Everett spit in Priscilla's face. "You'll burn in Hell for killin' yer own daddy, cunt." He bucked under Smiley's weight, but it was futile. "Burn in Hell, you fuckin' hear me? In fuckin' Hell!"

Priscilla didn't react to the spit. She breathed in slow, and she breathed out slower. She reached into Luci's breast pocket, removed the purple square, and wiped the saliva from her cheek. Then she leaned in close, so that she and Everett's faces were barely a foot apart, and said, "Old man…I am Hell. And you ain't my daddy."

"Cold," said Smiley, speaking for the second time since setting foot on earth.

Luci said, "Woo! Goddamn! You've been spending too much time with me, little lamb."

Priscilla stood up and walked across the living room. Beside the coal stove, she kneeled, loosened a floor board, and set the floor board aside. She then reached down into the floor and came out with a small jar. Inside it were three teeth. She stood up, jar in hand, and examined its contents. "You remember when I was real little…I spilled milk on the couch, and you hit me in the face with Red?"

Everett squirmed under Smiley's grip, but he didn't speak.

"These is the teeth you knocked out…baby teeth… You hear me, you miserable fuck? Baby teeth…" Priscilla's voice trailed off, and there was silence. Then she said, "I remember bein' so scared…I snuck outta my little bed…and found em…and put em in this jar… but I never really knew why I did….until now."

Everett, again attempted to buck Smiley off of him, but he may as well have been a child under his weight.

"All day long," Priscilla said, staring into the past, and walking in a slow circle around Everett. "I've been trying to find the strength to do this. Worried if I was doin' the right thing… But these." She held up the jar. "These have been sittin' under the floor of this house, collectin' dust for ten years…for ten years, sittin' and waitin' just to remind me what an evil fuckin' asshole you really are…" Priscilla stopped pacing and looked down at Everett squarely, and said, "And now, Ever-ett, it's judgment day."

Luci waved his switchblade in Everett's face, grinning from ear to ear. "You hear that," he whispered. "Judgment day, nigga."

"S-s-s-so that's it," Everett said. "You just gonna kill me. Alright…okay, you go on then. You go on, you'll regret it. Mark my words, whore. This'll come back to you, you wait and see. One way or another, you wait. Go on then." His words were of surrender, but he was beginning to struggle again. He screamed and then he went limp once more, Smiley still bearing down on him, unsmiling.

Luci said, "Easy, easy, old man. Today…is your lucky day. If it were up to me, there would have been…ultraviolence. In fact, I might have cut your cock off and fed it to you if not for the girl whom you've been referring to all evening as a whore. But no… we aren't going to kill you…are we, Priscilla?"

Priscilla sniffed at a cocaine drip, and said, "Nope."

"Nope, indeed," said Luci.

"Me and Maw Maw came up with a better idea. We got bigger plans for you," said Priscilla, sounding thrilled at the possibilities, and spinning in a literal circle.

"Lavinia! Lavinia!" Everett was getting desperate. "Get these niggers off me! Lavinia! All these…years! Help me! Lavinia!"

Lavinia sat at the kitchen table, watching absently, smoking a cigarette. "You made yer bed," was all she said, and she took a long, slow, Maw Scill-like drag off her cigarette.

Luci grinned, and looking deep into Everett's eyes, he said, "Are you ready?"

Everett's face was white as a sheet. Sweat poured from his scalp, and he was breathing in long drawn out heaves. His eyes darted, frantically.

Priscilla reached into her jacket pocket and retrieved a small green vile with a cork in it. She held it up toward the light for all to see. There was a small amount of liquid in the bottom. She said, "I fired up the old bathtub just for you, daddio…"

"Just for you," Luci echoed.

Then Priscilla looked back at her mother, gave her a wink, and using her teeth, she wrenched the cork free from the vile, and said, "Pry his fuckin' mouth open."

◆

There was some screaming, some convulsions, some cracking of bone, some blistering. Some contorting. Some anguish. Some crying. Priscilla hadn't intended physical harm, but now that it happened that way, she was glad for it. The fucker had it comin'. When it was all over with, the four of them—Priscilla, Lavinia, Luci, and Smiley—stood in the living room over a pair of dark blue work pants and a pair of stained white underwear. The clothes were laying in a crumpled heap on the floor. For several moments nothing happened. The clothes just lay there, motionless. But then, like a beating heart, or rather, a throbbing member, there was movement from within the underwear, and Lavinia said, "You gotta be fuckin' kiddin' me."

Luci and Smiley began to snicker, Smiley somehow doing so without smiling. Priscilla had just put a loving arm around her mother's shoulder when the movement inside the underwear took shape and hopped right out into the open. It had worked. It had actually worked. Everett was no longer big and scary and threatening, oh no. He was slimy, and green, and the size of a bullfrog. In fact, Everett was a bullfrog. Everett was a literal motherfucking bullfrog. Laughter broke out, as he hopped toward the kitchen.

"Holy shit," said Luci. "I've never actually seen that spell put to work. I'm honestly impressed."

"Good God," said Lavinia, holding a hand over her mouth.

"I told ya we wouldn't hurt him, Momma. Not too bad anyway," said Priscilla.

For several minutes they all stood there watching Everett attempting to acclimate to his new reptilian form. He would sit for a few seconds, then he would hop. Then he would sit, then he would hop. Eventually, Everett's hopping took on a clear path, and the four of them walked behind Everett as he hopped his way toward the back door of the kitchen, which was slightly ajar. When Everett hopped through the crack on to the back porch, Lavinia turned on the porch light, and they all followed him out.

"Aw, look at him hop!" said Priscilla.

"There he goes," said Luci.

"Good God," said Lavinia.

Smiley, characteristically, said nothing.

On the back porch Everett sat for a while, staring out at the massive expanse of his own backyard, at the old apple tree. Then he turned and looked up at the spectators, huddled in the door way. The look on the tiny frog's face was as close to bitter hatred as any frog's face could manage, and if Everett could have spoken, he surely would have said all sorts of terrible and nasty things, but he couldn't. So when his throat sac swelled up, the only thing that came out was "RIBBIT, RIBBIT" and everyone laughed. All but Everett of course, because he was now a bullfrog, and bullfrogs can't laugh.

As the humor faded, Everett began hopping his way down off the porch. He stopped for a while on the bottom step, and then he hopped into the snow. And just as Priscilla was about to say, "Well, good riddance," Lightning, from out of the shadows, pounced on Everett. All claws and teeth, she took hold of Everett by the frog skin, rolled over, and in one quick motion, ripped his little green body in two. Everett's blood and guts sprayed. Then the cat rolled over again, pawed at Everett's remains casually, and commenced to eating him, piece by piece.

There was silence from the porch. Only the wind moaned. Everyone, even Smiley, watched on with horrified expressions, some more amused than others. After five or ten seconds passed, Luci defensively said, "I promise…I did not see that coming."

◆

When Everett died, he didn't think about his family or his friends, or his parents, and though there had been some, the happy moments of his life did not flash before his eyes. Only good people are permitted to exit life in that way. It's a privilege. When evil people, or frogs like Everett, die, they don't spend their last moments thinking of their weddings or children, or their first kisses in the schoolyard. They die thinking about all the terrible things they've done. They die fixated on the moments in their life when they inflicted the most harm, the moments when they purged and gutted all kindness and love from their hearts, and gave into the darkest parts of their being. And why? Because of fear. Fear and recognition. Fear of an eternity spent suffering for the consequences of their actions, of God's wrath, and recognition that the moment of reckoning is upon them. When evil people die, they die terrified, and their last thought is of their worst deeds, shadowed by the distinct and undeniable certainty that Hell awaits.

Farewell, Everett.

◆

Luci wasn't only with Priscilla that evening. Being legion and all, he was spread out through space and time like a drug plate at a Doctor Hook after-party. In addition to being with Priscilla, he was also having dinner with Marilyn Monroe three days before her death, he was riding with Genghis Khan in battle, and he was begging alongside a starving child in eighteenth century London.

He was in Birmingham, and he was in Bangladesh. He was in Abudabi and Amsterdam. He was everywhere that fear and weakness prevailed over love and courage, and he was everywhere that pleasure took precedent over purpose. Everywhere the moment overcame eternity. Everywhere God wasn't. But in addition to all of those places, Luci, Lucifer, The Devil, he was also in Hell. He was in Hell, and he was seven thousand feet tall, with nine heads, and nine forked tongues, and fangs and claws, and he was bathed in fire and the blood of the wicked, awaiting Everett's arrival.

Having shed his amphibian form, Everett Carpenter was once again human, and as he stumbled naked and confused through the rot iron gates of Hell, Luci lifted one of his massive, nineteen-ton clawed feet, and let it hover for a second. Then he brought it down on Everett's unsuspecting head, crushing him flat, and splattering his blood and guts all over the entrance to Hell. All nine of Luci's cyclopse heads laughed triumphantly, "HAR HAR HAR HAAAR!" and then they all looked down at what was left of Everett Carpenter, and in unison, they roared, "WELCOME TO YOUR FIRST DAY IN HELL!"

◆

They were once again gathered around the kitchen table, Smiley now in Everett's old seat, silent and unsmiling as ever. Supper for two, uneaten and cold, was still in front of them. As can be imagined, Lavinia was filled with a multitude of questions following Everett's extraordinary demise, and one by one, over the course of an hour or so, her questions were answered. The conversation started with the topic of witchcraft, but needless to say, it evolved.

"So, yer the Devil, huh?"

"Yes."

"Hmm…I figured you'd be taller…" Lavinia pulled on her cigarette. There was dubious suspicion in her voice. "So, if yer the Devil, what is it you want with my daughter?"

"I'm here only to help. As she mentioned, she is quite the gifted witch. I want to insure that she flourishes."

"Buuullshit," said Lavinia. She clearly didn't believe Luci. "Great Deceiver, my ass. You don't think I see the way you look at her, the way she looks at you? Sheeit. I bet if I smelled yer fingers right now, I'd find my daughter."

"Momma!" said Priscilla, her cheeks burning red.

"I assure you, I have only the best intentions for your daughter."

"Oh I'm sure you do," said Lavinia, nodding toward Priscilla, "Especially with a set of tits like that."

"Momma! Fuck…"

"Priscilla Louise. Language." Lavinia notoriously disliked the words fuck and cunt, though she said each of them regularly. "You want me to bend you over and smack you on the ass in front of company?"

Priscilla lowered her head. "No mam…" she said, reverting back to a child's submissiveness.

Luci and Smiley eyed one another, as if to say, *I'd be into that.*

"That's what I thought," Lavinia said. "Now you mind yer cussin'. I'm just givin' Luci here a hard time. When Jesus asks me, the least I could say is when I met Satan face-to-face, I busted his balls a little."

"To hell with Luci, it's me yer embarrassin'. Damn, Momma."

"Yer right…I'm sorry, sweetheart. Yer right. Momma's feelin' a little crazy, but well, after all I did just see my…sorry excuse for a husband get turned into a frog…then get eaten by a cat. So I'd say I have some right to act out."

"I know, Momma… I know… I'm sorry too…"

"I love you, baby doll, all this just has me…well…" said Lavinia, her expression growing all of a sudden weary. She turned her eyes toward the floor, staring into the past.

"Rejoice, Lavinia. Everett is in Hell now…where he belongs. I see your lingering concern, and I assure you, this is a time for merriment. You feel like you've done something wrong, but you haven't. This was out of your hands. Yours and Priscilla's. Out of my own hands even. No one dies unless it is God's will. Simple as that," said Luci, gesturing toward the sky. "All things are God's will. The black flood that destroyed this valley, your birth, Priscilla's baby teeth, the changing of the seasons, Everett's abuse of you and your children. Your mother's arthritis. Even me, and my ongoing presence in your home…all God's will. So cheer up, my dear. You're a free woman now."

Lavinia eyed Luci as if she were trying to determine whether it was worth her effort to speak, but then she did. "It ain't that. Everett was a mean bastard. He deserved…well, he deserved gettin' turned to a frog, but…the cat, well…I don't know, maybe he deserved that too…"

"Then what is it," asked Luci.

And Priscilla added, "Yeah Momma, what's the matter? He's gone. We're finally rid of him."

After a few moments of contemplation, Lavinia looked harrowingly up at Priscilla, then at Luci, like only a woman who has been thoroughly abused in life is capable, and said, "It's just… it's life… We only get one shot at this, and God sure ain't make it easy… He… he ain't got no account for our sufferin'. No account for our tears. Even here, now, where's God?" Then she added, "I guess you wouldn't understand."

Luci seemed to contemplate Lavinia's words. Then he said, "I was God's third divine creation. A perfect angel. And he cast me from Heaven for being too, well…charming. So. I understand more than you know."

Luci's words must have struck some chord within her because Lavinia suddenly sat up straight and grew gravely serious. She said, "If you hurt my daughter… I'll hunt you down in Hell and… cut yer balls off. Perfect charmin' angel or not. You understand me?"

Luci's grin faded into something more solemn and sincere, and he nodded. "I understand."

"Well," said Lavinia, a faint but reassuring smile returning to her face. "This has been the weirdest damn day of my life." Her mind was clearly all over the place. "I could use some coffee. Anyone else?"

Priscilla stayed quiet this time. As did Smiley. Neither of them liked the taste of coffee. Luci said, "Thank you so much, but no, I have to be leaving. I have a long overdue meeting with the Sheriff." Then he stood, and to Priscilla, with a wink, he said, "Perfect Peach, Smiley will wait and drive you home. I'll walk. Be back no later than eleven thirty though or he'll turn into a pumpkin." Lavinia stood, being polite, and Luci took her by the hand and kissed it, saying, "Lavinia, it was an honor." Then he tipped his hat and left through the door like a normal person.

When he was gone, Lavinia looked at her daughter, and with her eyebrows raised, she said, "…Perfect Peach?"

Priscilla was a raccoon in the headlights. She stood up quick, and said, "Let me clear the table," and she began clearing the table. Priscilla could feel her mother watching her as she collected plates and cans, watching her squirm.

Then Lavinia winked at Smiley, and once again to her daughter, she said, "Perfect Peach?"

Priscilla turned red and blurted, "It's 'cause I like fruit so much, Momma. God." Then she stomped off to the kitchen with her arms full of dishes.

Lavinia grinned at Smiley, knowingly, and said, "Oh, the joys of havin' children."

There was homemade fudge, several pieces, and afterward Smiley sat quietly in the corner of the living room while Priscilla and Lavinia spoke in the kitchen. Lavinia sipped coffee. Priscilla smoked one of Luci's cigars. Twenty minutes prior to this, Lavinia, having only smoked cannabis once when she was a teenager, decided it was finally time to give it another try. And so, after stating as much, she politely snatched the cigar from between Priscilla's fingers and took a nice long, oh so overly confident pull. Back to now, as she sips her coffee, her eyes are red and heavy, and she is most obviously baked. Priscilla, too, is baked.

"So how long's this been goin' on with you and…Luci?"

"Only a couple days," said Priscilla. "Well, I mean, he started comin' to me in visions and dreams in the Fall, and he made me—well, but—only a couple days."

"Fuckin' hell… And yer certain he's the real Devil? Like the real, real Devil."

"I mean, I told you he took me to the crucifixion…and about turnin' a pineapple into a peach, but no, I'm not certain. I'm not certain of anything really, anymore. But I think he is. He has all sorts of magic."

"All men do in the beginnin'…" Lavinia said with a sigh. Then she said, "Good God, look at you girl. I can't believe how beautiful you've gotten. No wonder the Devil has his sights on you… Christ, listen to what I'm sayin'. I sound insane. Is this real life? Have I gone loony? We should be figurin' a way out of this and here we are talkin' like it's just another Thursday or whatever the fuckin' day is."

Priscilla understood what her mother was feeling. She felt it herself. Priscilla made her bed and now she would have to lay in it. "Ain't nothin' to do, Momma. I got myself into this, and we'll

just have to see how it goes. But I'll tell ya, I have a good feelin'
about it. I know how it sounds, but I think Luci really likes me.
And I know he's a zillion years older than me, and he's the Devil,
and all, but he's so, so nice and sweet to me, Momma. Like, so
sweet."

Lavinia's eyes widened with understanding, and her mouth
hung open, just slightly. She said, "You two are doin' it, ain't ya."

"Oh my God, Momma, no. No."

"Yer gonna sit there and tell me…yer mother…that you—"

"Alright. Alright, fine, we've done…some stuff, but not all the
way. He does this thing with his tongue, and…there was…there
was another woman there too, and she was usin' her mouth, and
oh my goodness, Momma, you would not believe—"

Lavinia cut her off in midsentence. "Thank you, I've heard
enough."

"Oh, okay…" Priscilla said with a wounded look on her face.
"Yer not mad, are ya?"

'Of course not. I could never be mad at you. There's just some
things a mother don't need to know.'

"Well, what is it then? You look upset."

Lavinia considered the question. Then she said, "Oh it's nothin'.
I just can't believe how much you've grown…and how much yer
like me. Lord help me, hearin' you talk about a man like this,
well… Yer just like yer momma… through and through." That
last part, she said with a mixture of pride and sorrow.

"You say that like it's a bad thing?"

Tears formed in the corners of Lavinia's eyes, but before she
could speak, Priscilla said what she knew, deep down, intuitively,
needed to be said.

"Momma, stop. Now, I learned a lot in the last few months—
like a whole lot, like Momma, God and the Devil are *real*. Heaven
is *real*. *Hell* is real. Other worlds with rollercoaster-gods holdin'

flashin' neon signs that say YA BIG DUMMY are real. Turtlebears are real, broom flyin', hypnotizin', multiple orgasms, colors that talk, magic potions—it's all real. And our lives, me and you and everyone, we're all… o small. Like so small. But we're still just mixed up in it, ya know? Along for the ride. And that's just how the world is. Good and bad. And we just gotta make the best of it." Here, Priscilla finally took a breath. Then she continued, "But I guess what I'm tryin' to say is, well, forget all the bad shit that's happened, Momma. The world is so far-out, and magical. And our mistakes, our past, where we were born, they ain't who we are. They don't even really matter at all. We are…what we become."

Priscilla continued, "So, forget everything that happened to us, Momma. Forget the fightin' and the drinkin'. Forget Everett. Forget it all. I don't blame you for none of it. I love you so damn much, Momma. So damn much. Ain't nothin' gonna change that."

Lavinia looked up at her and with a faint smile, she said, "I love you too…and I am so fuckin' high right now."

◆

Meanwhile, back at El Rancho Del Diablo, Sheriff White was growing impatient and cold. He'd been waiting in the woodline for three hours, and the big city nigger still hadn't come home. From where he stood, the Sheriff could see Deputy Knotts's silhouette peaking around the side of the house. Junior and Stanley were tucked up under the front porch. Everyone was in place, but their intended target was nowhere to be found, and Sheriff White was becoming particularly annoyed. But that was his lot in life, wasn't it. A slow, annoying drip. A cracked sewer pipe. A cocaine ravaged nostril. A busted knee. The Chinese water torture of the gods. Drip. Drip. Drip.

Leaned against a new maple, Sheriff White had a clear view of the better part of his sister's property, and what he couldn't see, Deputy Knotts could. When they first arrived, they checked the windows and doors. Finding the back door unlocked, Sheriff White entered the house alone, and to his surprise the interior of the place looked exactly as it had the last time he was inside it, ten years prior—abandoned. All of his sister's old furniture and boxes still occupied the small space. All of her pictures still hung on the wall. Cobwebs and dust covered everything. Rat shit littered the floors. It was as if the place hadn't been lived in at all.

Sheriff White was just beginning to reconsider his plan of attack when the front porch light turned on. He instinctively took cover behind the maple, then slowly, he reemerged, peering through the night. A moment later, an inside light was turned on, and he could see movement behind the curtains. And then he heard a noise. It was…music. It was…*Hound Dog*. It was *Elvis Fuckin' Presley*. It was playing loud inside the house, and there were even more shadows moving behind the curtains now. From where the Sheriff stood, it looked and sounded like there was a full blown party going on inside. And somehow, even though he was there before the party started, he had shown up late.

But how? He'd searched the house from top to bottom, and there was no way anyone sneaked past him. The only thing that made sense was that the coon bastard somehow slipped past Knotts. But it wasn't just one person inside. And why sneak in only to turn on the lights and throw a party? Sheriff White was baffled, befuddled, both feelings to which he was not accustomed, and he did not like it. Not one little bit. He was off his game, and that was rare, and it took him a few minutes to regroup before approaching the house.

Breath caught and heart rate slowed, he came out of the woods, motioning to Deputy Knotts, who began creeping along the side of the house toward the front porch. All four men huddled at the foot of the steps. Junior and Stanley, having climbed out from under the porch, were wiping snow from their pants and acting nervous. "What in the fuck is goin' on," said Stanley.

"Quiet," said Sheriff White in a whisper.

Deputy Knotts said, "Sheriff, ain't nobody come past me, I swear, I don't know how they got in there."

"I was afraid you'd say that," said Sheriff White, softly. "Alright, boys, I don't know what's goin' on here but we got a job to—"

Sheriff White was interrupted when the front door of the house suddenly swung open. And there stood the *jig bastard* himself, Black Lavender Luci, a silhouette, featureless in the doorway, Elvis Presley and red light pouring out around him. *You ain't nothin' but a hound dog.* He was tapping his foot to the beat. *Cryin' all the time.* Sheriff White, Deputy Knotts, Junior, and Stanley all stared up at him where he stood, and where he stood, he was naked as the day he was born, save the pick in his afro. And hanging there, his long, heavy dick seemed to be swaying to the music, dancing even. *Back and forth.* Like a phallic omen, *back and forth,* like a hypnotist's coin, *back and forth,* like a Seventh Veil belly dancer, *back and forth,* like a gypsy snake charmer, swinging *back and forth, back and forth, back and forth,* lulling, *back and forth,* and tantalizing, *back and forth,* the sheriff and his cohorts. Back and forth. Then Luci snapped his fingers.

The music stopped and the lights went out.

On instinct, Sheriff White and his men backed up a few steps. Luci was barely visible now, but for moonbeams catching him here and there. Sheriff White was glad for it too. If he had to look at that big black dick any longer, he wasn't sure what he would do. There was something about it that he hated, maybe even feared, something that inspired panic and awe equally in his intestines. Sheriff White was just about to say, *Alright nigger. I know it's you that's been causin' all the trouble 'round here so why don't you just come quietly and make it easy on all of us,* when Luci, from the shadows, said, "You're not very fond of niggers, are you, Sheriff?"

Sheriff White sucked in air, coughed, and sort of chuckled. His confidence was faltering. Not being able to see Luci on the porch was making him uneasy. It was like he was speaking to a void, or rather a void was speaking to him. He didn't like it. Sheriff White said into the void, "No…I sure don't. You got our women in there?"

"Yes…I sure do," said the Void.

There was silence, stillness. Darkness. Sheriff White moved his hand to the gun on his hip. Deputy Knotts did the same. Junior and Stanley backed up a little further. They both held shotguns but neither of them were aiming. They only held them, barrels toward the ground. Then the Void said, "All evening long…I've had to show restraint…self-discipline…mercy. But no more. We all niggas tonight, Sheriff. All of us."

And the Void snapped its fingers.

'The Black Swan Waits for No One' by Castle Grayskull plays

The first to go was Stanley. It was quick. The demon came barreling out of the night sky and ripped his head clean off his shoulders. Junior screamed. Blood sprayed from Stanley's neck as his decapitated body crumpled to the ground. Sheriff White and Deputy Knotts both spun around in time to see another bat-winged demon, like some grotesque living gargoyle, blackened and ravaged by fire, come swooping down out of the sky. Junior raised his arms in defense but the beast was on him. It forced him to the ground, clawing and biting at his face, screeching, shrieking, laughing. Junior screamed as the monster tore through his cheek and into his mouth, and began eating at his tongue. But it was of no use. His anguished howling quickly turned into a flat gurgling sound just before his life source was evacuated completely. Sheriff White and Deputy Knotts watched on, too stunned to move.

The other demon landed beside Junior's body, just as its twin was finishing up with Junior's face. On the ground they stood no more than three feet tall. The two creatures looked at one another, seemed to confer, then slowly they turned their bloody and menacing faces toward the sheriff and his deputy. Human carnage and thick coagulated mucus stringed between their lips and over razor sharp fangs, and their jaws snapped at the air, and clicked as they sniffed at the night. Their eyes were hollow black pits, but Sheriff White had no doubt about where their attentions were focused.

Surprisingly calm, Deputy Knotts said, "Run, Sheriff."

Until that moment, Sheriff White had been in a sort of trance. It had started with the Devil's dick going *back and forth, back and forth, back and forth,* and it was intensified by Stanley's decapitation, but it abruptly ended the moment he heard Deputy Knotts tell him to run. And he did. Deputy Knotts lit out for the woods, and Sheriff White followed him. He ran harder than he'd ever ran in his life trying to keep up. He ran and he ran. Bashing off trees, stumbling over rocks and roots, tripping, falling, sliding in the snow, Sheriff White ran like a scared animal. He ran like the dogs were after him. Like his life and freedom depended on it. Like lacerated scars lined his back. Like a runaway slave.

"Wait, goddamn it," Sheriff White yelled, trying to be quiet. "Wait!" The screeching had stopped. Sheriff White was doubled over, panting, and gasping for air. "I can't run no more. Wait."

Deputy Knotts reluctantly stopped, and looked all around, searching the sky for whatever demonic, murderous creatures were after them. After spinning in several circles, crouching low, and surveying the sky, he said, "I think they're gone." Then he held up a hand and said, "Wait, ya hear that?"

Sheriff White listened. He heard nothing, save the wind in the trees. The still rustling of stick on stick. Nothing. Only the forest at night.

Then he heard it. But it was too late. The sound, a high pitched whistle, like a tea kettle reaching its peak, was the sound of both the winged demons, latched on to one another, plummeting toward the earth at breakneck speed, and before Sheriff White could even think to say, *Look out!*, the demons came crashing down on Deputy Knotts, leveling him to the dirt. Without hesitation, they took hold of his head and torso with their claws, and the three of them disappeared up into the sky, his agonizing screams quickly fading as the demons took him higher and higher. And just like that, he was gone.

Deputy Knotts was gone and Sheriff White was alone. In the woods. In the dark. He was down on one knee, watching his breath form clouds in front of his face, waiting. Waiting to die. He wasn't ready, though. To die that is. He thought he would be when the time came, but he wasn't. For whatever reason, he wanted to live. But what could he do? Fear had him frozen in place, paralyzed even. He was sure that as soon as he tried to move, they would return, those hideous snarling demons, they would come screeching out of the sky to end his life. So he remained there, kneeling in the snow, a black smear of coal dust across his face, afraid to move, all night long.

◆

"So the frog idea was your Maw Maw's…Good Lord, that woman…wait till I see her."

"Mmhmm," said Priscilla. "All I could think of was nasty stuff. Cuttin' his pecker off, and stuff like that, but Maw Maw said I was thinkin' too hard about it. Witches turned people into frogs when I was a little girl, she said. And soon as she said it, I knew. It just felt right…OH MY SHIT, MOMMA. WHAT TIME IS IT? I gotta go. Smiley wake yer big ass up, we're late!"

"Well now, calm down, Honey. What's the rush, is there a fire somewhere?"

"No, Momma. Me and Luci got a date. And Smiley turns into a pumpkin at eleven thirty, remember. Smiley, wake yer ass up!"

Smiley, asleep on the couch, opened one eye, and used it to look around. Then he opened the other eye, stood up, brushed himself off, walked to the door, and stood there waiting. Priscilla pulled on her coat, arranged her hair and to her mother, she said, "Okay, I love you. I gotta go."

"Yer comin' back tomorrow, right?"

"Yep."

"To stay, right?"

"Yes, Momma. I promise. You can't be livin' here all alone in this old house. I'll be back tomorrow. To stay. I gotta go." Priscilla was standing by the open door.

"Priscilla?"

"Momma, I'm lettin' the cold in."

"Angel, I promise you, things is gonna be different, you won't never see yer momma touch another drop of alcohol again, after today. Okay?"

"Okay."

"You believe me, don't ya?"

"Of course I do, Momma."

"You do?"

"I believe you every time you tell me that, Momma. Now I gotta go. I love you. Bye. I'll see ya tomorrow." And Priscilla was gone.

◆

The ride back to Luci's was short and sweet. Priscilla sat in the back of the Wraith, and Smiley drove silently, avoiding pot holes to the best of his ability. At no point did he turn into a pumpkin.

In front of the house, Priscilla stepped out of the car, and into what she thought was a puddle of mud, which of course it wasn't. It was a puddle of blood, but it was dark so she didn't notice. She shut the door and Smiley pulled the car around the side of the house. Priscilla walked up the steps and in the front door of the abandoned house. It was eleven thirty-eight. Twenty-two minutes to midnight.

All was quiet inside the mansion. Priscilla hung her coat by the door, and kicked off her shoes. She found Luci, alone in the parlor, where she first met him, and he was once again hovering over the chess board. A music she had never heard was playing softly. The last thing Priscilla could remember saying was, "I'm not too late, am I?" The last thing she could remember being said was, "Hold on tight, little lamb. It's going to be one hell of a night."

Everything after that was a blur.

'Angel of the Morning'
by Merrilee Rush and the Turnabouts plays

It started on the floor of the parlor. Luci was on top of her. He smelled like cinnamon and coconuts, and something else, something…raw, like water and smoke. Priscilla inhaled it. Luci bit and licked at her lips, and face, and neck, and it felt as if he had a thousand hands, each one touching, massaging, caressing, and exploring her everything. Inside and out, two fingers here, one finger there, a hand holding firm under the arch in Priscilla's back. And then he was kissing her. Kissing her slowly but intensely, pressing and writhing, gripping and pulling, the only thing that stood between them was a single pair of red cotton panties.

Priscilla's mind began to swirl. She felt like she was on a drug. As Luci sucked at her bottom lip, the red cotton was slid off, and her thighs were spread apart. She could feel another tongue lapping at the sweetest bits of her, wet and soft, and then faster, until…until….mmm, yes, yes. Yes? Does he have two heads? Oh yes, all around them the room began to disappear, growing ever darker, as warm liquid leaked down her legs, and she moaned, and panted, and whimpered, until the room around her was cast in absolute shadow, and all she could see, eyes opened or closed, was Luci, only Luci, as though they were floating together in a sea of nothingness.

Then Luci was inside her. Considering his size, she expected pain, but there was none. Slimy, throbbing, and wet, Luci fit inside her like Cinderella fit into glass slippers. Far from discomfort, she felt only the warm oceans of release and satisfaction, pouring down on her like a honeysuckle waterfall. Eyes squeezed tight, now biting at her own bottom lip, she dug her nails into Luci's back like she was riding without a saddle. She pulled him into her, deep, and he reciprocated by thrusting, and thrusting, over and over, again and again, until Priscilla was breathless and covered with sweat. He pushed on and she gasped and moaned and purred like a kitten, her sounds seeming to reverberate and echo through the darkness surrounding her.

But then she saw them. As though her eyes were beginning to adjust to the dark, the emptiness around her, black and pure, began to come into focus, and the echoes and reverberations of her own ecstasy took on new dimension, and she saw them. She and Luci were not alone.

The hands were not all Luci's. The moans were not all her own. All around them, like a part of the darkness, were dozens upon dozens of naked and ecstatic girls and women—most of them she recognized. The bags had been removed from their heads, and Luci was having his way with each and every one of them. Some riding, some bent over, some on all fours, others star fishing flat on their backs. Two on one, two on two, three on four, Luci's replications of himself fucked and sucked, and pushed and pulled, kissed, licked, bit, slapped, and stroked all around the two of them, her and Luci, and yet he never moved from on top of her.

He was still thrusting into her, long and slow, in and out, but Priscilla was no longer focused on what was happening to her, but rather, what was happening around her.

The smell of cinnamon and coconuts was gone, and left behind were the raw, dank, unadulterated, oceanic odors of sex, and the hard packing, and squishing sounds of uninhibited, hedonistic fornication. The moaning and screaming growing louder and louder around her, and Luci pushing harder and faster, and the darkness growing brighter and brighter until the black emptiness was no longer an emptiness at all, but a hilltop in the middle of a forest. A shining, waxing moon hung in the night sky, illuminating gnarled leafless trees, and Priscilla was no longer on the floor of the mansion. She was in a strange forest, in the grass, and all around her the Bacchic, Satanic orgy continued.

Then came the fires. They began burning all around her, but from where the fires burned, she could not discern. The faster and harder that Luci went, the faster all the Lucis went, the hotter the fires burned, and the louder the squishing and moaning became. Priscilla's mind continued to swirl and swirl and was now taking the time to spin and flip, just for the bloody hell of it. Then, like emetic icing on a purgative cake, through the tangles and heaps of bodies, Priscilla spotted Daisy Layfield with her tongue down her sister Lilly's throat. Luci had Lilly's breast in his mouth, Daisy's pussy in his hand, and he was pounding away at Violet who was bent over a rock. Priscilla had to look away. It was too much to comprehend.

But looking away was a mistake of sorts. All around her was madness. The Layfield sisters were on her right, and to her left were two small creatures that looked like blackened flat-faced dragons with bulging eyes and ascending fangs, and they were watching her. They were watching her being fucked. With drool pouring from their gaping mouths, they were furiously masturbating cocks that were twice the size of their bodies. They were cackling, and making grotesque wheezing sounds. Priscilla looked away almost immediately, but she still managed to witness a shower of thick orange goo come spurting from the cock of one demon and onto the face of the other. Priscilla closed her eyes tight to the sound of the two demons' insane, perverted chuckling. She wanted it to be over.

But Luci continued sowing his seed. In her and all around her. There must have been nearly forty or more women on that hilltop, and at least twice as many Lucis. Some women were being taken by three of him at once. On her left, Luci was fucking the Layfield sisters, and on her right, voyeuristic demons with giant cocks were jerking off on each other, and what was above her, on top of her, inside her, she was no longer sure. She was afraid to look. Whatever it was, she could feel its jagged scales drag against her inner thighs with each and every thrust. She could feel the heat of its spoiled meat breath on the side of her face. She could feel the wiry tangled bristles of its hair, the flick of its corroded tongue, the pain of its claws digging into her skin, the rhythmless throbbing of its pronged organ. And then…nothing. True darkness. Unconsciousness. Sleep.

◆

Priscilla woke up the next morning alone in Luci's bed. She was beginning to notice a pattern.

A dark room. Aromas of incense in the air. Coals burning low in a fireplace. After analyzing her surroundings, she pulled back the covers to examine herself. She was nude, but there wasn't a scratch on her body, and nothing sticky between her legs. Strange. She got out of bed and stood in front of the mirror. She inspected her nether regions for signs of wear. Nothin'. She smelled her hands and fingers. Smoke. She pulled back her hair and looked for sucker bites on her neck. Not one. She sat down on the edge of the bed, and lifted her leg by the ankle to smell her feet. Stinky. Why she smelled her feet, she wasn't sure, and afterward, she felt silly for doing it. Then she put two fingers up inside herself and felt around. Everything seemed to be intact. Nothing unusual, anyway. As she dried her fingers on the pillow beside her, she couldn't help but wonder…had it all been a dream?

———◆———

CHAPTER EIGHTTEEN

When Joseph woke up he was feeling better. He had spent an entire day praying, self-flagellating, and begging God's forgiveness, and he was pretty sure he had covered all the bases. He prayed he had, just in case. And now, with the sun shining and the birds figuratively singing, he felt like maybe he could go on with his life, albeit following a much holier path. After he took care of his regular morning erection, and then prayed about it, he went downstairs where his father was sweeping the kitchen floor.

"Mornin', son," his father said.

"Mornin', Pops. Where's Momma?"

"I'd tell ya if I knew."

"You don't know where she's at?"

"No, she left about thirty minutes ago. Said she had to run a few errands. If I had to guess, she's over at Margerie's doin' her gossipin'."

"Yeah, yer probably right, knowin' her."

"You want me fry you up some eggs?"

"No thanks. I'm not feelin' real hungry."

"You alright?"

"Oh sure," said Joseph reassuringly. "I just ain't hungry is all."

"Just checkin'. Say Joseph, I want you to stay outta town today. When I got off work this mornin', there was somethin' goin' on."

"What do you mean?"

"Well…t'tell ya the truth, I ain't real sure. Somethin' about some girls disappearin'. I think it might have to do with the flood, but there was dang near fifty old boys outside the Sheriff's station when my shift let out, mad as all hell and hollerin' about some-thin'. Anyhow, you just steer clear of town."

"Missin' girls?"

"That's what Old Man Parmour said. I saw him comin' out of Layfield's. He was sayin' somethin' 'bout some girls, or women too I reckon, goin' missin'. And actually, son…I hate to worry ya but, he said Miss Layfield and her girls is some of the ones missin'."

Joseph found this information discouraging. The Layfield girls were mean as they come, but he still really wanted to see them naked. Then his father said something that nearly made Joseph shit in his pants. He said, "And you know Kathleen, that plays piano at church? Can't nobody find her neither."

◆

Sheriff White stood at the center of a mob. There were bags under his eyes, and a strained look was on his coaldust-streaked face. He'd spent the entire night in the woods. At day break, being still alive, cold but alive, he walked down out of the woods, scanning the sky as he went for some sign of the demons, or of Deputy Knotts, but there were none. He followed a stream downhill, and came out on top of The Knob, coincidentally enough. He walked down past the Scarberry farm, and the mill, and past the school where the Red Cross was busy unloading trucks. It was just after eight in the morning, and he had to get back to the station. It had been unmanned for nearly twelve hours, and between the missing girls, and the flood, God only knew what he was walking into. But it was worse than he had imagined. Much worse.

He heard them before he saw them. In addition to the flood relief traffic that was now a staple of Main Street, there were several dozen men, a hillbilly rabble, gathered in mob formation in front of the Sheriff's station. Even from a distance they looked angry. All Sheriff White had wanted was a few minutes to come down, to decompress, to organize his thoughts, and maybe splash a little water on his face. To warm his goddamn feet up. If he didn't have frostbite on any of his toes, he would be utterly amazed. But no time for any of that. Oh no, no time for recalibration. No time for weakness. Memories of a trench in the south of France flashed in his mind, and as Sheriff White approached the mob, he said to himself, "Mind yer bread, boys, the rats'll be comin'."

The mob parted, quieting to a dull roar, as Sheriff White limped into the crowd. He had slipped on an icy rock the night before, and was carrying his wounded arm close to his chest, as though he were pledging allegiance to a dying cause.

At the center of the mob he stood, contemplating his next move, what to say, and how to say it. After a few moments, he raised his good hand, and the mob fell silent. Then he pointed into the crowd, and said, "Paul McDaniel, this about the women?"

Paul McDaniel said, "Yes sir. Nearly every man here's missin' a wife or a daughter…or sister."

Happening past the mob with a fishing pole over his shoulder, Bob Smith shouted, "Yeah, and I'm missin' four of my girlfriends," and he continued on to the river.

To the crowd, Sheriff White said, "Alright. I figured as much. I need five minutes. I want y'all to elect four men to speak on yer behalf. I don't care how you do it. In five minutes, you send those four men inside the station. You understand? You all understand?"

All around him, heads nodded.

"Good," said Sheriff White, and he turned and made his way through the crowd. Inside the station, he went into his office, and sat with his elbows on his desk and his head in his hands, the warmth and solitude giving him some relief. But only a little. His mind was still plagued by visions of demons and decapitations, of dismemberment, and of Deputy Knotts screaming as he disappeared into the sky. Not to mention, the thought of making the call to Emma, Deputy Knotts's wife, filled Sheriff White with a sense of dread so pressing that it caused his hands to shake. Emma Knotts loved and adored her husband, and for good reason too, as far as Sheriff White was concerned. And she was seven months pregnant with their first child.

What happened the night before was something out of Sheriff White's worst nightmares. Beyond his worst nightmares. Never, not even trapped behind enemy lines, had he ever been this shaken. Men killing other men was one thing, but those things that came down out of the sky the night before were something wholly different to try to comprehend. Maybe the best thing to do would be to sneak out the backdoor, climb in the cruiser, hit the road headed South, and never look back. After all that happened it seemed a more than reasonable thing to do.

But there was just one problem, Sheriff White had never run from anything in his entire life. He'd faced death and destruction on numerous occasions, and not once had he ever turned his back. Not once had he surrendered. Retreated maybe, only to regroup and strategize, which is what he was chalking the previous night up to, but never had he given up due to fear. And he had certainly never been run out of town.

KNOCK KNOCK

There was a knock at his office door. Sheriff White lifted his head from his hands. There were four men standing outside his office, each looking weary and unsure, all but the man in the front. He looked furious. Sheriff White surveyed the men, momentarily, then waved for them to come inside.

The men were Erick Helmstetter, Toby Garret, and Mark Layfield. The furious looking one was Wetzle Diamond. Wetzle was an ugly, flat-faced man with brown, curly hair and a wide mouth, and he and his wife lived alone at the end of Drake's Holler. He worked in the mine, drove a beat up old truck, and once spent a night in jail for public drunkenness. Sheriff White knew little else about him.

Wetzle and Mark sat in the two chairs opposite Sheriff White. Erick and Toby stood behind them. For a long tense moment, they only stared at one another, the men and Sheriff White. Then Wetzle said, "Two days, Sheriff. Two days since I seen my wife. Now there's somethin' goin' on around here, goddamn it. We all know there is, and we want it solved. If we gotta go house to house, knockin' down doors to find 'em, then that's what we gotta do. Ain't no more waitin' around, Sheriff. I speak for every man out there, and these ones too. We find 'em today, and we put a bullet in whoever took 'em."

"My whole family…" Mark Layfield added, pitifully. Normally clean and kempt, he now looked as though he'd spent the day plowing a field in the rain. Ragged, worn, and wet, and his words came out sounding much the same.

Sheriff White stared at Wetzle, considering the man's words and his own response to them. Telling these men about the demons was out of the question. They would think he'd lost his mind. But if he didn't tell them, and they went out there and got massacred, then what? Either way, he had to say something.

"I know who has 'em," Sheriff White said.

Wetzle came up out of his chair, ready to kill. Through clenched teeth, he said, "Who?"

"Sit down, Wetzle. I'll tell ya."

Wetzle stood seething, his breathing heavy, but after a few second he calmed and sat back down. "Who?" he asked again.

Sheriff White said, "What's said here, stays in this office. Agreed?"

All four men nodded.

"I wanna hear you say agreed."

"Agreed," said all four men.

"Last night," Sheriff White began, "me and Deputy Knotts, and Stanley and Junior, on a hunch, went to see the nigger that bought my sister's place, the one that come in with the RedCross, and the rest of these yahoos, one that calls himself Black Lavender Luci... Y'all met him?"

Three heads shook. Mark Layfield nodded. "I met him," he said. "He came in a couple days ago with three other spooks just like him to buy liquor and candy. No food though…"

Sheriff White nodded. "Well, long story short, we went down there last night, and…boys, Deputy Knotts, Junior, and Stanley were all killed. I just barely got away with my own life." He decided to leave out the part where he spent the night in the woods covered in his own piss and paralyzed with fear.

Wetzle again came up out of his seat. "What in the fuck are we waitin' for then?" he shouted, and started moving toward the door.

"Hold it," said Sheriff White. The men all paused and looked at him.

"Last night we went out there heavily armed, and we got our asses handed to us. The last thing you boys need to do is go racin' off down there all halfcocked."

"Well, what in the fuck do you expect us to do?" said Wetzle. "Sit around and wait for him to set 'em all free? Are you out of yer fuckin'—"

Now it was time for Sheriff White to stand. He popped up out of his chair, and said in his most threatening tone, "I'd watch yer next words, Mister Diamond."

Wetzle seemed to relax, seemed to realize just who he was talking to, but he still said, "Then what, *Sheriff*? What do you reckon we ought to do?"

Sheriff White sat back down, adjusted in his seat, and looked up at the four men. "I want you to go out there and tell everyone to go home and get the biggest gun they have, all the guns they have, and if they ain't got a gun, tell 'em to bring whatever they can find. Two-by-fours, shovels, knives, pitchforks. You tell 'em to meet back here in two hours, and don't you tell 'em nothin' else. Nothin', you hear me? I don't want word gettin' back to Deputy Knott's wife and I don't want nobody goin' to that house on their own. Y'all understand?"

The men all nodded.

"Good. Now, go on. I got thinkin' to do."

As the men began shuffling out of the room, Sheriff White said, "And boys...tell 'em all to bring their Bibles...tell 'em to come ready for war."

◆

Joseph said goodbye to his father. He told him he would be back before dark, and walked out of the kitchen. The last thing in the world that Joseph wanted to do was go back to the Devil's house, or mansion, or whatever it was. But he had to. He had to warn Priscilla, or maybe even save her, he wasn't sure. He may already be too late. What if the mob that his father told him about was already there? What if they had Priscilla tied to a stake at this very moment, a hundred men with guns gathered around, ready to spark the match? What if she was already burning? What if he was too late? Joseph's mind raced with terrible possibilities, and the only things that it kept coming back to were the women who were stoned to death in the Bible, and the witches that he learned about in school, the ones from Massachusetts, and the end they all met. Without realizing it, he began running.

◆

"Spent his whole life hatin' women, and he was killed by a pussy… seems fittin'," said Maw Scill. She was referring to Everett. "Now I sorta wish I'd been there to see it…"

"Good Lord, Momma, I don't know how you can joke like that after someone dies."

"Are you shittin' me, that goddamned bastard weren't no someone. He was a…well, he was a toad. You said so yerself." Maw Scill couldn't help but smile at her own joke.

"You know what I mean," said Lavinia.

"Yeah…I reckon I do," said Maw Scill in a way that confirmed she understood, but didn't care to.

"I just can't believe you've known about all this for months and never told me," said Lavinia. She stood up from the kitchen table to pour herself another cup of coffee.

"Well," said Maw Scill. "I seen the beer cans pilin' up out back, and I figured you had enough on yer hands to worry about."

"She's my daughter, though, Momma."

"Yer daughter, sure…that I've damn near raised," Maw Scill said. Then she said, "Lavinia, you ain't been in the shape to handle no more stress. You ain't been up to see me in months. That's when I know it's bad, when you ain't visitin' me…"

Lavinia lowered her head. Reluctantly, she said, "Yer right, Momma…yer right….I'm sorry. I am… But things are gonna get better now. No more drinkin'. I swear it. Now that Everett's gone, I ain't makin' no more excuses." And she sat back down at the kitchen table.

"Well, I hope you mean it this time. I truly do. But as far as Priscilla's concerned, well, I wouldn't worry. I used to know this old nigger lady, name of Hagatha, lived up in Fairmont, used to practice Voodoo, and she was always real nice."

"I hate when you say that word," said Lavinia, sternly. "It's not nice."

"What word, Voodoo?"

Lavinia cocked her head to the side, an exasperated expression on her face. She said, "You know what word."

Maw Scill shrugged. "Old habits die hard. What can I say. You know I don't mean nothin' by it. I like colored folks as well as anyone."

Lavinia shook her head, and rolled her eyes, just as she had when she was a teenager, but unwilling to fight that old battle, she said, "Okay fine. But Momma, this ain't Voodoo. This is the real Devil she's messin' with. This ain't some old woman that—"

"Child, hush. Just hush, there ain't nothin' we can do now. We just gotta wait and see how things go. If it really is the Devil she's messin' with then… I don't know. Maybe we ought to get to prayin'…"

Lavinia slumped back in her chair. "Good Lord, I can't even believe we're havin' this conversation… We sound crazy. I swear, since last night I don't even know what life is anymore."

"That's 'cause yer young," said Maw Scill. "You ain't seen nothin' yet. Wait till you get to my age, won't nothin' surprise ya. Last night I had the choice of watchin' the tube or watchin'

Everett get turned into a frog. I chose the tube."

Lavinia couldn't help but laugh a little. "I'm sure yer right…
and if you ain't, I've heard it before… I just hope Priscilla's alright. At least with her movin' back in today, I can keep an eye
on her."

"Movin' back in, is she?"

"That's what she said last night."

Maw Scill didn't respond right away, but when she did, she
said, "You gonna report Everett missin'?"

"I thought about that…I was actually hopin' you would call it
in. It'll be easier." Lavinia grinned a little, and in a razzing way,
she said, "Big bad Maynard White would never question the word
of Miss Priscilla Fisher, the fairest damsel in all of Logan County."

Maw Scill gave her daughter a salty but not altogether unamused look. "I knew you was gonna say that. Hand me the phone,
goddamnit. Dial the numbers. The things I do for you…"

"Oh Momma, it ain't like I'm askin' you to blow him."

Maw Scill's eyes went wide, "Yer sure as shit yer not. Good
God, if'n I did, that man would never leave me alone. Now, get
the phone. Let's get this over with."

Lavinia gave her mother the phone, walked back to the wall,
and began turning the dial on the reciever. Three, **zip nahnah
click**, zero, **zip nahnahnahnahnahnah** click, four, **zip nahnahnah
click**. Then she pressed down on the lever, ending the attempted
call, and said, "Wait, what are we gonna tell him?"

Maw Scill said, "I'm gonna tell him my granddaughter turned
my son-in-law into a fuckin' toad, and the cat ate him, Lavinia. Dial
the damn numbers. *Bonanza* comes on in five minutes, Christ."

◆

Sheriff White watched the mob beginning to reform outside
his office window. Two hours had gone by like two minutes.

FIVE ZERO FOUR

There were already more than fifty men with all sorts of weapons, ranging from rifles and pistols, to garden spades and lengths of rusty rebar. He also saw several men with Bibles. Most of the lot were scraggly looking. Only a few of them looked to be formidable in the least. They were certainly not the finest group of soldiers that Sheriff White had ever taken into battle, but they weren't the worst either. In France, he was pinned down in a trench with a platoon consisting mostly of Italians for close to three days, and those men, they were the worst. *Those greasy, pasta eatin' son of a bitches, never knew when to shut up. All they did was talk about cookin' and their mothers.* But even then, he made it out alive.

Sheriff White holstered his side arm, and stared out at the crowd. After the previous night, he was in no hurry to see this thing out. If he were smart, and he surely was, he would leave. Turn in his badge, hang up his belt, and leave. Walk home, pack up a suitcase, load up his dog, and head to Florida. Leave Clockmaker in the rearview mirror, and only stop to piss and refuel. If he were smart, that's exactly what he would do. And he was smart. Smart as they come. So why was he still standing there? Was it pride? Was it contrariness? Boredom? Whatever it was, he couldn't put his finger on it. But it didn't matter. He was going to see this thing to the end if it killed him. That's just who he was. Wasn't it?

Then the phone rang. Sheriff White picked it up without thinking, and immediately regretted the decision, or lack thereof. He listened into the handset. When nobody spoke he sighed heavy, and said, "Sheriff White speakin'."

The voice on the other end of the line was the last one that he expected to hear, but it was also the only one that could have caused such a goofy and awkward grin to form on his otherwise empty face. The voice said, "Maynard, it's Priscilla Fisher."

"Oh uh, well, hello there, Priscilla. To what do I owe the pleasure? Ain't nothin' wrong is there?" After a pause, Sheriff White said, "Mmhmm…mmhmm, oh Christ…mmhmm." Then he said, "Well Priscilla, under most circumstances, I'd tell ya not to worry. He wouldn't be the first man to go out for cigarettes and never come back, but well… I don't know if I should be tellin' you this or not, but I'm goin' to tell ya anyhow. There's a bunch of folks gone missin'. I reckoned they was all women and girls, but it wouldn't shock me in the least to find out that's what come of Everett too." Another pause, and then, "Oh Lord, there's been a whole mess of girls comin' up missin' the last few days." Then, "Yeah, we got a lead, alright," and finally, "Well…this stays between you and me, but there's this new city coon done moved to town, moved into my sister's old place, and well…it's him. He killed my deputy and two others last night. One of 'em was Junior we went to school with. I got half the men in town down here with guns now, and we're 'bout to go light his ass up. And look, uh…there's a chance I might not make it outta there today, so I just wanted tell ya that I—. Hello? Hello? Priscilla?" She'd hung up.

Before giving up, Sheriff White stared at the phone for nearly five minutes, waiting for her to call back. When she didn't, he put on his hat and walked toward the door. For years, since he was a teenager, he had chased after Priscilla Fisher, and she never gave him the time of day, but that was no matter. Just hearing her voice, even all distorted through a telephone line, gave rise in him a newfound confidence, and as he walked out of the station to assemble his troops, he did so with a stride in his step, and a swagger fitting of a Texas Ranger. He now felt prepared to do what needed to be done.

'Found dead on a fence line' by The Davisson Brothers plays

———— ◆ ————

ChapTEr niNETEEn

Luci had been distant all morning. He popped his head in once, just after Priscilla woke, to say good morning and that he had 'Hell business' to tend to, but beyond that he had been altogether absent. In truth, what he was actually doing was arranging and rearranging chicken guts on an altar made from the skulls of angels. In a hollow vacant realm of Hell, he was slinging chicken organs around like he was rolling dice and working a marionette simultaneously. And he did so with the persistence of someone not searching but feverishly seeking an answer to a question long held. Organ, bone, blood. Organ, bone, blood. Organ, bone, blood. Organ, bone…

Priscilla didn't know all of that, though, about the chicken guts and what not. She just thought Luci was avoiding her. It seemed to her that he was aware of her desire to converse and was evading her purposefully. All she really wanted to do was talk to him about what happened the night before. Try to make some sense of it. It wasn't a big deal. She wasn't mad or anything. Not really, anyway. But he never did come back, and Priscilla sat alone. She called for Cupcake, but he didn't come. All the women with bags on their heads were gone as well. The mansion was as quiet as she'd ever heard it.

For a while, she sat around thinking. Then she read the 'original' Bible on the nightstand. After that, more thinking. Then she got dressed. She wanted to see Joseph. She wanted to tell him about the Layfield girls and about Everett's…unfortunate demise. The look on his face alone would be worth the long cold walk.

She decided on her cloak. It had been far too long since she'd worn it, and her mother had never seen it. She wanted to show it off. She did, however, throw on black jeans, and a matching sweater underneath. As much as she adored the rough feel of the cloak on her bare skin, it was a cold day, and when Priscilla opened a window, she could smell rain. And if it did rain, the half inch of snow on the ground would turn to slush. So from a dozen or more options, she chose a pair of tall black boots with deep tread to go with her outfit. As she laced the boots, she heard the sound of a fist coming into contact with the mansion's front door. BOOM! BOOM! BOOM!…

BOOM! BOOM! BOOM!…BOOM! BOOM! BOOM!

At first, she didn't know it was coming from the front door, or a door at all, she merely followed the sound. Over the last few days, she'd learned to navigate the mansion quite well. It wasn't easy. It took focus, but she was beginning to get it. Or so she thought, and with how quickly she found the source of the BOOM!ing, it seemed she was correct.

BOOM! BOOM! BOOM! The sound hadn't ceased since the moment it began. As she approached the door, she looked around the foyer for Luci, assuming she couldn't be the only one hearing this frantic pounding. With Luci nowhere to be found, Priscilla turned her ear toward the door and yelled, "Who is it?!"

"It's Joseph, open the dang door!"

Priscilla's mood brightened instantly. She intended on swinging

the door open and saying, "Hey you old pecker head, son of a
dime-whore, what's shakin'?" or something like that, but when the
door did open and she actually saw Joseph's state, she decided
to greet him with a little less spunk. She said, "Afternoon, uh, old
pal. What'd you do, run here?"

Joseph, hands on his knees, panting, and sweating in the cold
winter air, said, "Yeah, I did. We gotta get outta here. I think
there's men with guns comin'. I saw 'em all in front of the Sheriff
station on the way here."

"Men with guns, what for?"

"Why the heck you think? They comin' for him. For the Devil.
Now come on, let's get the heck outta here."

"Going somewhere?" asked Luci, appearing behind Priscilla
in the doorway.

Leaning his head back, Joseph closed his eyes, and let out a
sigh the could have blown the hood ornament off a Buick. In mock
politeness, he said, "Well look who it is. Right on time. So good
to see ya, always is. I was just tellin' Priscilla here, how there's
a whole bunch of fellers with guns, fixin' to come over here and
have a chat with you. So I do apologize but we're gonna have to
be goin'. It was…weird knowin' ya. Come on, Scilly."

"No need to rush off," said Luci, laying one ancient brown
hand on Priscilla's delicate shoulder. "Come inside, let's chat."

"No thank you,' said Joseph. 'I ain't never settin' foot in there
again."

"Nonsense," said Luci. "Come in."

"Ain't happenin', slick. I done got right with Jesus."

"Have it your way then," said Luci, and he nudged Priscilla
forward, on to the front porch. "We'll just chat outside in the
cold."

"Ain't nothin to chat about," said Joseph, backing away from
the door. "We gotta get the hell—heck—outta here. Come on,

Scilly, let's get to it." Joseph took Priscilla by the hand, she assumed, in an attempt to assist her in their escape, but as soon as he did Priscilla said, "Oh shit."

It was too late.

The first of a dozen or more cars, and trucks, each holding armed men in their beds, had crested the hill, some thirty yards away, and they were coming down the gravel road toward the house. In the lead was a cop car. They were done for. The distance between the house and the woods was too far. They would never make it without being caught. Or shot. The only options were to retreat into the house or face the mob, and since Joseph refused to go inside, it didn't appear they had much to discuss.

As the small fleet of mostly aged automobiles came to a rumbling stop in front of them, as car doors swung open and angry men stepped out on to the soft snow, as Priscilla unconsciously squeezed Joseph's hand, Luci said, "And now you see why I wanted to talk inside… But don't you two worry, I'll handle this."

◆

Riding alone, Sheriff White could see them on the porch as his car was descending on the house. He couldn't make out who the two white complected figures were at first, but as he drew closer that changed. The boy's first name he wasn't sure of, but he knew he was Jim Smith's kid, and the girl wearing the cape was Priscilla Carpenter, Priscilla Fisher's granddaughter. And the recently missing Everett Carpenter's daughter. Sheriff White had seen the two kids around town numerous times over the years, and he had a run in with the Carpenter girl's older brother a while back, but he'd never had any trouble with these two. *What in Christ's name were they doin' here?* He didn't know. But for that matter, *what was he doin' here?* Leading men to a slaughter was the only thing he could come up with.

He stopped his car two feet short of the steps leading up to the front porch. Deep down, he hoped they would run, scatter, but they didn't. The fact that the three of them only stood there on the porch staring at him, casually as they would a squirrel scampering across a tree limb, made him seriously hesitate in his approach. If they had run, he could have shot them. But this? They just stood there, staring. It was unnerving. But then something happened.

Just as Sheriff White was reaching for the door handle, he saw the black son of a bitch, in a far too familiar and endearing way, stroke the Carpenter girl's hair, and speak something he couldn't hear. And right away, the gears in Sheriff White's head began turning. Pieces of a puzzle that he had been trying to solve for months began to align in new and meaningful ways. *She was fuckin' him. And she had been fuckin' him. And the piss, and the fog, and the flood, it was her. That horror show on the Knob, it was her. It was all her. Well, not all her, it was the nigger too, and maybe the Smith boy, but it was her.* He didn't know how he knew, but he knew. He was certain. It was her.

Sheriff White stepped out of his car, and stood in the crook of the open door, one hand on his holstered revolver. Behind him, more automobile doors slammed, and men jumped from the bed of trucks, engines died, tension mounted, metal clicked and clacked as weapons were cocked and safeties were checked. Stomachs churned, hands shook. In front of Sheriff White was his future, the length of which he could not be certain. But there it was, his future, staring down at him like he was a forest critter. Silent and amused. Defiant. He said, "Yer grandmomma know yer here, little girl?"

A little voice came back from the porch, "I uh…I kinda do whatever I want."

"Is 'at right?" said Sheriff White. But what he thought was, *I bet you do. Oh I bet you do.* Then he said, "What about you,

Mister Smith? Jimmy know yer down here?"

The Smith boy didn't say anything at first. He turned to look at the girl, and she to him, and they shared a long visual exchange, but finally, and without looking away from the girl, he said, "No sir, but I don't wanna be here…and neither does she. We was just fixin' to leave."

"Not so fast, boy. What was you doin' here in the first place? Is there women in there?"

This time there was a quick glance between the boy and the girl. Black Lavender Luci only stood there watching, fascinated, a bag of popcorn fitting perfectly with the expression on his face. Even facing down an armed mob, he looked amused. But there was nothing after that. The Smith boy just stood there, quiet, looking guilty.

"Nothin' to say then, boy?" said Sheriff White.

The Smith boy reluctantly shook his head. He looked at the girl again, then back down at his shoes.

"I figured…" Sheriff White said.

Black Lavender Luci suddenly stepped forward, standing slightly in front of the Carpenter girl, and said, "You figured…? Please, nigga. You ain't figured a goddamn thing in your whole motherfucking life. Today is no different." Then he said, "I have noticed you've been watching the sky an awful lot though, *Sheriff.* You expecting rain?"

Sheriff White didn't flinch, although he had indeed been watching the sky, but not for rain. He was watching for winged demons, and the son of a bitch on the porch knew it. As much as Sheriff White wanted to blow *his goddamn black brains clean out of his goddamn black head,* he wasn't sure that was the best plan of action. Back at the station, his confidence had held steadfast, but now, standing mere feet from the spook bastard, Sheriff White was having second thoughts about escalating the violence.

If Black Licorice Luci, or whatever the hell his name was, unleashed more of those monsters on this mob, the casualties would be countless. Sheriff White, said, "Alright, look. Ain't none of us come here today to die. All we want is our women…our girls. Those are our wives and sisters and daughters you got in there. Just send 'em on out, so we can all go about our business."

"First of all, nigga, I was born in the dark, and I do mean dark, but it wasn't last night. Your bitches are my bargaining chips. You know it and I know it. Secondly…what makes you think they're alive, Sheriff…your wives, and daughters, and sisters? For that matter, what makes you think any of you are alive? I assure you, from where I stand, that is not the case. I see only dead men. I see not a hollow, but a mass grave. I see the end of seventeen bloodlines, all riding to the Abbey of Thelema as one. Do you understand me, Sheriff? Should I invite back my friends from last night? Is that what you want?" And then loud enough for all to hear, shouting to the point of almost screaming, his voice breaking in places he said, "Is that what you all want? To die? To fucking die?"

CLICK CLACK, CLICK CLACK, CLICK CLACK.

◆

When the guns came up, Joseph instinctively ducked, pulling Priscilla down on to the wooden decking of the porch with him. Scrabbling back a few feet, they were both now cowered together behind the Devil, with their backs against the house. Joseph was sure they were going to die. He thought of *Frankenstein*, the book Priscilla had forgotten in his possession. He had made it to the final chapter, and now he may never know the ending.

But it was far too late for literature. Staring out at what seemed like a sea of loaded weapons, Joseph did the only thing he could think to do, the one thing that, lately, had been coming to him quite naturally. He prayed to God.

◆

"Whoa, easy, boys! Stand down," Sheriff White shouted. "Lower your weapons!"

Priscilla could no longer see the Sheriff from where she and Joseph were taking cover, but she could see the back of the mob, and she watched on as they hesitantly, one by one, lowered their guns and pitchforks and whatnot.

Speaking to Luci again, she heard the Sheriff shout, "Alright, fella. Let's all just calm down. What do you wanna do here? You call the shots. How do you think this should go?" Priscilla could hear trembling in the lawman's voice.

The situation was growing tense, and Luci didn't seem to have any interest in rectifying the issue. On the contrary, he seemed to enjoy it. Mentally, he was sharp as they come, and so when his answers arrived slowly, Priscilla knew he was doing it on purpose, for effect. And they were arriving slowly indeed. He said, "Are you sure you wouldn't rather die, Sheriff? I mean look at you. Look at all of you. Look at your lives. Wouldn't that be easiest for everyone?"

"Please don't," came the Sheriff's voice, now so weak that it was barely audible. "Please don't do that. We all wanna live. There's no need. What do you want? What do you wanna do?"

At this point, Luci looked back at Priscilla. And he was still grinning. She couldn't believe it. He actually wanted this madness. He wanted there to be killing. He liked it. Here she was terrified for her very life, and he was getting his goddamn rocks off. But what did she expect? She called him Luci, but he was Lucifer. She was a fool for calling him by any other name, and it was time to face that fact. Sitting there on the porch, looking up at Lucifer, she did not return the grin.

Lucifer's expression hardened. Priscilla could tell that he was disappointed in her, probably because she wasn't having 'fun', but she didn't care. She wasn't sure that she liked him very much anymore, anyway. So she held her scowl.

Lucifer tilted his head to the side, gave an off-handed shrug, and turned back to the mob, but he did not speak. He held his response, surveying the gathered men as if he were contemplating each of their deaths individually, taking the time to make eye contact, pacing himself. Watching them watch him.

And in that moment, the sky suddenly grew dark. An ominous grey cloud engulfed the already hazy sun, and it began to sprinkle. The porch was only partially covered, and when the drops began hitting Priscilla's face, she pulled her cloak up over her head, and draped half of it around Joseph.

With the falling of the rain, Lucifer's grin returned, predatory in every aspect, and he repeated the Sheriff's question back to him, as if he were pondering it aloud. "What…do I want…to do? If you only knew how fascinating that question was, Sheriff. Let's see… Oh, I've got it. You'll like this one… How about I get down on my knees, here on the porch, in the rain. Like a good nigga. Never mind my suit. I'll put my hands behind my back, and you can come up here and put the cuffs on me. Drag me down to the station for questioning. How's that sound to you?"

There was a pause, then Priscilla heard the Sheriff say, "Yeah… good one."

"No joke, Sheriff," Lucifer came back. "I'll get down on my nigger knees and you can waltz right up here in front of your constituents and slap the cuffs on me. Make a big show of it. Guaranteed re-election."

Again there was a pause, and then, "I weren't… I weren't born last night neither…" the Sheriff said.

Lucifer began laughing, Priscilla assumed it was because of

the Sheriff's timidness. He'd spoken with such authority to she and Joseph, but now, talking to Lucifer, his words were shaky and tense. It reminded Priscilla of how she used to be around Everett.

As Lucifer's merciless chuckling came to an end, he put his hands on his hips, and took on a half serious expression, and he said, "Oh, Sheriff, you kill me. You really do. You are one charming cracker. But I couldn't be more serious." At this point he spun around, so the Sheriff could see, and put his hands behind his back, wiggling his fingers to draw attention. Then, facing Priscilla and Joseph, but speaking to the Sheriff, Lucifer, in the most casual and only slightly mocking tone, said, "Go on, Sheriff. Put the cuffs on. I wouldn't hurt you. If I'm lying, may God strike me dead."

Priscilla had no doubt that Lucifer was only trying to dig at the Sheriff, wind him up, and to her it sounded like an attempt at irony, but no sooner did the words 'strike me dead' leave Lucifer's lips, than a bolt of brilliant white hot lightning came down out of the clouds and blasted him right through his fucking skull. BANG! ZAP! POW!

Lucifer stumbled, but did not go down. His head was cocked at an uncomfortable angle and each of his limbs were tweaked at the joint, but he did not fall. He just stood there, smoke rising up off his burnt shoulders, his suit now ravaged and charred, his hair completely gone on one side, one eye aimed at the ground, the other aimed at the door just to Priscilla's left. He looked exactly how she imagined a person would look after being struck by lightning. Not good. Not good, at all.

Prior to this moment, Joseph's head had been resting against his clasped hands, but now Priscilla felt him stir beside her, and with his eyes now open wide, she heard him say, "What in the fuck, I mean heck…just happened?"

Priscilla didn't respond. Her focus was on Lucifer, who was sizzling like a piece of bacon right in front of her face. And she couldn't be positive, but despite the new angle of his eyes, Priscilla was pretty sure he was looking right at her. But after he spoke, well…then she was certain.

With smoke floating lazily from his nostrils and his mouth, and in a hoarse, barely audible whisper that sounded as though it had been dragged down a gravel road and been beaten with a shovel, Lucifer said, "You're…pregnant."

And immediately, he was hit by another bolt of lightning. This time the bolt didn't come straight down. It cut a diagonal path across the sky, then banked right and came at him from the side, nearly splitting him in two and boiling both of his eyeballs in their sockets. This time he didn't stumble. He only fell. With a crunch and a squelch, Lucifer was gone. Dead on the porch.

"Ho-ly fuck," said Joseph. Then he added, "Boy, I did not pick a good time to quit cursin', did I? Forgive me, Jesus."

Without taking her eyes off the smoldering pile of guts, and blood, and bones, and polyester that used to be the King of Hell, Priscilla shook her head. It was true, this was not a good time to quit cursing. Then Joseph said, "You catch what he said there at the last?"

Again, Priscilla shook her head. She lied. She'd heard what Lucifer said. She just didn't want to have to repeat it out loud. Not to Joseph. Not to anyone. Not now, not ever.

◆

After the second bolt of lightning hit, and the dust settled, Sheriff White had to draw his revolver to keep the mob from rushing the house. They wanted to find their lost loved ones, he understood that, but this was a crime scene and if there were thirty-five dead women in that house, he didn't want anyone going in there and contaminating evidence. That's what he told them, anyway. The truth was he wanted some time alone with the two kids. He wanted answers. Simple as that. So he sent all of the men home, and against their will, they went. Wetzle Diamond, not unexpectedly, put up the most fight, but in the end, even he too got in his truck and moved on.

With everyone gone, Sheriff White walked up the steps onto the porch. On the last step, he stopped. The two kids were sitting side by side against the house, and the evil nigger was dead, in a pile. Parts of him, his juices, were leaking between the floorboards of the porch. Sheriff White kicked at the pile, making sure it was actually dead. It didn't move. He kicked it again. Still nothing. So he stepped up on to the porch.

◆

Lavinia and Maw Scill spent twenty minutes driving lost down the backroads of Clockmaker, looking for Sheriff White's sister's old house, before they ran into the exiting mob. Maw Scill flagged down Mark Layfield as he passed in his truck, and he filled them in on what happened. He also gave them directions. And now, rolling up to the scene, Maw Scill and Lavinia watched through the windshield as Sheriff White stepped up on to the porch. He stopped there, likely having heard the sound of their car approaching, and he watched them as they pulled up in front of the house. Maw Scill and Lavinia both got out of the car.

The first thing out of Maw Scill's mouth was, "Maynard, where the hell's my granddaughter?" But that didn't matter, because as soon as she said it, whatever was laying on the ground at Sheriff White's feet reached up and grabbed his ankle. And whatever it was must have scared him, because he screamed bloody murder, and jumped and he spun away from whatever had ahold of him. And somewhere in all that his gun went off. KERBLAM!

◆

When Lucifer's crispy corpse reached up and grabbed Sheriff White by the leg, Joseph jumped too. He nearly shrieked. But it was the gunshot that really gave him a supreme fright. When the gun went off, Joseph didn't even think, he just tucked and rolled. At first, loud as it was, he thought lightning had struck again, but it wasn't lightning. It was Sheriff White's gun. It had gone off. Shook as he was, Joseph had no idea how much time passed before he realized Priscilla had been shot in the chest.

◆

Fuck. Fuck fuck fuck. Fuck. The corpse had grabbed him. Well, it sort of grabbed him. What actually happened was the hand sprang to life and fell against his leg, the untimely result of leftover electrical current trapped inside the remains, but either way, it had startled him. And either way, he damn sure did not mean to shoot the girl.

It was an accident. *A goddamn accident.* The truth was, he hadn't even realized he was holding his gun until it went off in his hand. But oh Jesus, what had he done? *What in the fuck had he done?* Sheriff White's thoughts swarmed as he stumbled and fell down to one knee against the railing on the porch.

He watched helplessly, silently, as Priscilla Fisher and her daughter ran up the steps. He watched the daughter drop to her knees, screaming, when she saw the result of his negligence. He could see her screaming but he couldn't hear her. All the sound seemed to have been sucked out of life. There was only a dull hum. He watched the woman of his dreams, the unrequited love of his life wrap her arms around her daughter, and she too began wailing, tears pouring down her cheeks. Then he saw the woman of his dreams look at him, and the look she gave him was made of pure venom, of battery acid and bleach, of sour milk and antifreeze. It was in that moment that Sheriff White knew that he was lost to Priscilla Fisher forever.

He stood. He wanted to speak, to say something, to defend himself, to explain away his mistake, but he knew without knowing that his words, no matter what they were, would ring hollow as any funeral bell. Even the Smith boy was sobbing now. So instead of speaking, Sheriff White ran. He ran down the steps, and just as he grabbed hold of his car door handle, the previously overcast sky opened up around him and erupted with light.

◆

Priscilla's mother had pulled her into her lap, and was holding her lifeless body. Her grandmother was knelt down stroking her hair. Her best friend was standing over her. All three of them were weeping.

And that's when it happened. That's when God came down from Heaven and resurrected Priscilla.

————◆————

A Word From Joseph

Y'all, it was like a nuclear fuckin' bomb done went off in the sky, it was so bright. Out of nowhere. All three of us had our hands up shieldin' our eyes. Hell, I still got spots in my vision from it. Floaters, the doc calls 'em. And the light, well…it overcome'd us.

See, I was standin' there, over Priscilla and her momma, and her grandmomma, and we was all sobbin' and cryin', and out of nowhere comes this light out of the sky. It flared up real big and bright and spectacular at first, but then it settled, and when it did I seen him comin'. I shit you not. I watched with my own two eyes, God himself descend from the sky. Reverse rapture. Naked as a newborn and wings like a fuckin' eagle he had, with a twenty foot span. And he was glowin'. Me and Lavinia, and Maw Scill, we was just frozen in awe.

He come down feet first, not slow, but not fast neither, and he landed real soft on the far side of the porch. Well, he ain't really land, his feet never really did touch down. He just floated there, bout an inch off the ground, and he looked at us. Now, I'll tell ya one thing, I ain't know what I expected God to look like. Up to that point I hadn't done a whole lot of thinkin' on the subject, but

I will tell ya what I didn't expect him to look like. Marvin fuckin' Gaye. But he did. He looked exactly like Marvin Gaye. Just like him. I mean he was the spittin' image. And I knew it back then too. My daddy was a fan. He kept his albums, and in sixty-eight, me and Daddy seen Marvin sing the National Anthem durin' game four of the World Series on television, so I knew what he looked like. And I am here to tell ya, on my momma's grave, God, thee God, thee one and only God, looks exactly like Marvin motherfuckin' Gaye. I mean, exactly.

Anyhow, I'm standin' there stunned. Maw Scill's stunned. Lavinia's stunned. We're all stunned. Priscilla, she's still dead in her momma's arms, and God, without a word, floats across the porch and hovers over 'em, not two goddamn feet from me. His wing damn near put my eye out. I was tremblin', I was so nervous, and Maw Scill, she must have been feelin' it too, cause we both backed up a couple steps. I mean, it was God, after all. Weren't no doubt about it. He was radiatin' a powerful damn energy. You could feel it, like the pull of a magnet. And I don't mean to go off on a tangent, but for the record, you ain't never seen a nicer dick than God's. God's dick alone will make a feller take a few steps back. I mean it was fuckin' magnificent, y'all. Magnificent. I mean, just from a structural point of view. It was like lookin' at a fuckin' Picasso, its composition, its form, its color. True Perfection… Not to mention it was damn near the size of my forearm. Praise Jesus.

But enough about dicks. For a while, he just floated there, lookin' down at Priscilla and Lavinia…God, I mean…but then all of a sudden, he kneels down…still floatin' mind you…and he reaches out with one of his big…chocolatey…divine hands and puts it right over Priscilla's heart…right over the spot where the bullet went in. Then he closes his eyes, and takes this long, drawn-out breath in and when he lets it go…Priscilla's eyes popped the fuck open. Just like that. She gasped for air, and kinda shrieked, and her back arched real hard, then she went slack in her momma's arms. Now, I'll be honest, she was *droolin'* a good bit, and her *eyes* was all glazed and wanderin'like a dope fiend, but even still it was a fuckin' miracle. It was a genuine, bonified miracle. She was alive again. It was like God breathed life right into her.

Now, with Priscilla breathin' again, he rises up and floats back a few paces, God does, and sorta just looks at us. And there was a moment where he looked me square in the eyes. Talk about a trip. Imagine…God lookin' you in the eyes. I tell ya, the feelin' it gave me, it was…well, it was sure powerful. It made my hairs stand on end. Beyond that, it's difficult to explain. The problem, I've decided, is there ain't words to describe it. They don't exist. But I reckon, I'll try one more time for the sake of this here story. Let's see…it was like all the beauty and love that ever existed in the world, or ever would, was all inside me. It filled up my heart first then just kept on with the rest of me…I was unburdened… Decrucified…I was set free…

That's the best I got, and that don't do it an ounce of justice. But I assure you…it was quite the feelin' indeed…

For fuck's sake, where were we? Oh right. So God's just lookin' at us, and he's kinda smilin', more with his eyes than his mouth, and I can hear Lavinia and Maw Scill fawnin' over Priscilla, tryin' to help her get reacquainted with bein' alive again, but me, I can't take my fuckin' eyes off God, ya know. He's got me enchanted. The face of God. The skin of God… The lips of God… I remember at that moment, I felt like such a fool. A fool for ever thinkin' that what was around me was all there was. There was clearly far more goin' on behind the scenes than on stage. And I was held fast in my revelation.

But then I heard Priscilla start to cry, and just when I did, God's mighty wings started flappin', and he starts risin' back up into the air. Instead of takin' off though, he gets about twenty feet up off the porch and hovers there, and he turns his head and raises his arm and finger until he's pointin' off the side of the porch, real stern like. And that generous look on his face, it was gone. He turned grim. Real grim. And at first I wondered what the hell is he pointin' at, but then I looked and seen Sheriff White standin' down by his car, and I knew. God was pointin' at him. And lookin' at the Sheriff, I could see he had the fear. But when God started shakin' his head real slow, like a disappointed father, that's when tears started streamin' down the old Sheriff's face and he collapsed against the side of his car, blubberin' into his hands.

I remember lookin' back and forth from God to the Sheriff and thinkin', *Woo boy, I'm glad he ain't pointin' at me right now.* Talk about late for church. But then God, he drops his arm and looks back at Priscilla, his eyes smilin' again, and he sorta nods at her. And I could tell he was about to lift off again, and I just remember thinkin', This might be yer only chance, Joseph. Yer one and only chance. Ask him somethin'.

Now, I wanted to think of a real good question, somethin' profound, like what's the meanin' of life, or where do dogs go when they die, and I couldn't come up with one, not on the spot like I was. But I had to say somethin', right? Right. So I did. I shout out, Wait! And he pauses, God does, and he looks down at me, and I says, Anybody ever tell you, you look like Marvin Gaye? And do you know what he says? Do you know what God says to me, as he's goin' back up in the sky? Without missin' a beat? Do you know? God says, *Bitch, Marvin Gaye look like me.*

You believe that shit? I swear on my momma's grave he did. Called me a bitch. Then he goes up a little higher and there's another big flash and he's gone.

You wouldn't believe, or maybe you would, the looks I get when I tell people I met God and all he said was, *Bitch, Marvin*

Gaye look like me. They can't wrap their minds around it. They forget all about the whole resurrection and get stuck on that last little part. Seems trivial to me, personally, but anyone who's ever heard me tell that story gets fixated. Which is a shame, cause there's a whole lot to be gained by distinguishin' the forest from the trees. Particular in this case. But oh well. That's life, ain't it? Everything and everyone just hangin' on by threads, and runnin' head first into trees.

Well, either way, I ain't told 'at story too often to too many people. They miss the goddamn point every time. But there you have it anyway.

Now, what say we all roll up another big fat one, pour out a little more whiskey, and see this thing through to the end…

———•◆•———

CCHAPTEr TWENTYYY

THE ANTICHRIST

After the resurrection, Lavinia and Joseph helped Priscilla down off the porch to the car. They passed Sheriff White, who was still crouched against his cruiser, sobbing into his hands. Maw Scill stopped and put a hand on his shoulder, and when the Sheriff looked up, his face resembling that of a child whose mother just died, she said to him, "I'd say you have some work to do, Maynard. Wipe yer tears." Then she climbed into the back-seat next to Priscilla and the car drove away.

At home, food was made, cigarettes were smoked, and conversations were had, but Priscilla didn't mention being pregnant or the things that she learned while dead. It seemed like a lot to lay on the table, especially after all they'd been through.

Eventually, just before dark, Joseph went home, and a little later Sheriff White showed up looking timid and humble as anyone had ever seen him. Too shaken to drive, he arrived on foot, and when he knocked on the door, Maw Scill answered. The Sheriff could hardly look her in the eyes. Maw Scill said, "You better have left yer badge and gun at home if you plan on steppin' foot in this house. The law ain't welcome here tonight."

"I gave up the badge and gun for good… I ain't here to cause problems…" he said. His vocal chords were ravaged from wailing and his voice had the tenor of a coffin door. "Would you mind, Priscilla…if I spoke to you out on the porch just a minute? I won't keep ya long."

Priscilla Fisher obliged Maynard White, and stepped outside with him for a word. For several seconds he didn't say anything, and Maw Scill watched him stare out at the few stars visible in the sky. But then he spoke. He said, "That was God, wasn't it…?"

"I think you know the answer to that, Maynard."

Maynard's face tensed as though he were about to burst into tears, but straining, he held back his emotions. He said, "Yeah… I do. I just wanted to hear someone else say it…that's all."

"Well," said Maw Scill. "Alright then. Yes, I reckon it was God, Maynard."

Maynard was quiet for a while after that. Then he said, "Farewell, Priscilla. It was my heart's pleasure to know you," and he walked down off the porch and disappeared into the night.

◆

For several weeks afterward, aside from getting sick every morning, which Priscilla hid from everyone, things were looking up. For the first time in her life, her mother wasn't drinking, and best of all, Everett was gone. Also, she and her mother had started eating supper every evening with Maw Scill, and when Jeremiah got back from his trip, he joined them. So for the first time in Priscilla's life, she felt like she belonged to a happy, normal family. But then her belly started to show.

◆

When Priscilla died, in the time before God brought her back to life, she was in Hell. Several different moments of her life, most of them with Joseph, flashed before her eyes, then there was blackness. Then she was in Hell, and there was Luci, Lucifer. She was back in his mansion and he was sitting on the bed beside her. Once again she questioned if she was dead or dreaming, but Lucifer assured her that it was the former. He even pinched her hard, on the ass, to prove his point. Then he drew the blinds so that she could see the lake of fire outside his bedroom window. It was actually very pretty.

In the short time that she was there, in Hell, Priscilla learned three important things from Lucifer. Number one, she hadn't misheard him on the porch. She was indeed pregnant with his son, and he would grow up to be the Antichrist. Number two, although she was now dead and in Hell, she would soon be brought back to life, and not just brought back to life by some doctor or faith healer, oh no, but brought back to life by God Himself. According to Lucifer, God had a plan, a prophecy to fulfill, and it required that Priscilla be alive so that she could birth Lucifer's child, and usher in the apocalypse, and ultimately Armageddon. And number three, Priscilla would die once again while giving birth. Then, without so much as a flicker, she was back, alive again, in Clockmaker, at an abandoned house, watching God ascend into the sky.

There was one another thing. While in Hell, Lucifer told Priscilla to make sure she dug up the book. And that she keep it with her. Apparently, for some reason, she was going to need it.

FIVE TWO NINE

And he may very well have told her why she was going to need it,
but that happened to be the moment God chose to intervene. So
she just had to take the Devil's word for it. Which she did.

◆

Once Priscilla's stomach began to grow, she had little choice but
to come clean about being pregnant, and after many long discussions between she and her mother, and Maw Scill, a decision was
made. And though it was a tough decision, it was decided that
given Priscilla's age, the mixed race of the child, and the father's
reputation around town, the best thing to do would be for Lavinia
and Priscilla to leave Clockmaker and re-establish in a more
enlightened and accepting area of the country.

The part about her dying during childbirth, Priscilla left out.
Again, not only did she not want to worry her mother and Maw
Scill any more than they already were, but she sort of refused to
believe it, herself, and saying it out loud made it true. Or, at least
it felt like it would.

Priscilla and her mother left Clockmaker, West Virginia, headed for upstate New York to stay with a cousin, on April twenty
sixth, nineteen seventy-two. Standing in the driveway before
heading out, Maw Scill kissed her granddaughter on the forehead
and said, "Don't you be scared, you hear. I'll be up to help you
and yer momma change diapers after you have the baby."

"I love you Maw Maw. Take care of Lightnin' for me if she
shows back up. She's a good cat."

Jeremiah said, "Well, yer gettin' run out of town for witchcraft
and fornication…" Then he winked, and sincere as he could be,
he said, "I'm real proud of ya, sis. Real proud."

"Thanks big brother. And remember, it's all chemicals and
motion…whatever the fuck that means."

Joseph showed up right as Priscilla was getting in the car to leave. His face was red and puffy, and tears leaked from his eyes, and he said, "Just don't f-forget about me, alright. That's all I a-ask. I'm…really gonna miss you."

"How could I forget someone ugly as you?" Priscilla asked him, trying to lighten the mood, but before she could get the whole question out of her mouth, she was also a sobbing mess. She threw open the door, jumped out of the car, and wrapped her arms around Joseph and squeezed him tight, and although neither of them acknowledged it, it was the first time in their nine odd years of friendship that they ever held each other that close for that long. After she made Joseph promise that he would visit as soon as he got his license and a car, and he made *her* promise to get saved and start going back to church, Priscilla, knowing that she may likely never see them again, waved goodbye to her grandmother, her brother, and her best friend.

'Into the Mystic' by Van Morrison plays

◆

On October twenty second, two weeks earlier than expected, Priscilla's water broke. And as they waited for the midwife, Priscilla told her mother she was going to die. She said, "Momma, I gotta tell you somethin'… I don't think I'm gonna make it through this. I think I'm gonna die havin' this baby."

Lavinia rolled her eyes. "Oh, nonsense. Yer hormones is just all over."

"No, Momma, the Devil told me. I'm pretty sure that…I'm gonna die, and I'm goin' back to Hell. I think it's…I think it's God's will."

"Priscilla, honey, don't talk that way," said Lavinia, tears forming in the corners of her eyes. "No, don't you talk that way.

Everything is gonna be fine."

"It's okay," said Priscilla. "There ain't nothin' to be done. Even after all the church we've been goin' to, he still comes to me in my sleep every night."

"Priscilla. But I—why wouldn't you tell me this?"

"I just hate to worry you… But my blood's in his book. He owns me, Momma. He owns my soul…and that's just…the way it is."

"Oh, sweetheart, please stop. Please. Tell me this ain't true. Please tell me. I just can't believe this. I just can't."

"It's true, Momma. I'm so sorry. If I'd have known…" At this point, they both began to cry.

Lavinia didn't speak for several minutes after that. She sat beside the bed where Priscilla laid, and stared out the window into the dark. Priscilla watched her, as she stared. Even in her grief, she was still the most beautiful woman Priscilla had ever seen, and the one thing that pained her the most about dying was the idea of leaving her behind. That was the one thing that really got to her.

Out of nowhere, her mother turned to her, a look of determination now on her face, and she said, "I want in."

"What do you mean," asked Priscilla, genuinely confused.

"I mean, I want in. I wanna be a witch. Put my blood in the book."

"But Momma…you can't."

"And why not?" her mother asked. "You said witchin' is for women only. Well, I'm a fuckin' woman, ain't I?"

"But Momma, I told you when I die, I'm goin' to Hell, like real Hell. No questions about it. I've been there. It's not a great place. I've seen it."

"Sweetheart, stop. I done decided."

"But what about Maw Maw and Jeremiah?"

"Knowin' them, they'll be right there with us. If not, they'll have each other in the clouds."

"Still Momma…I just…"

"When we was diggin' up that book, I asked you why we was doin it and you said the Devil told you that you had to do it, and you needed to keep it with ya, but you didn't know why. Well?"

"Well, what?"

"Well, this was why. You been carryin' it all this time for me."

"Oh no, but Momma…"

"No more buts. Just stop, sweetheart. I done thought about it. If yer goin', I'm goin'. End of story. I've screwed up too long. And I ain't doin' it no more. I'm yer mother. I love you too much to spend eternity without you. Besides, I have no desire to set foot any place my baby ain't welcome. Even Heaven. Now, hand me that goddamn book."

LIME GREEN SMOKE

◆

Priscilla died for the second and final time, on October twenty third, nineteen seventy-two, shortly after giving birth. Her last words, before drifting off forever, were, "Remember, don't skip steps… Sufferin' is part of the process… See you soon…"

Shortly after, there was a knock at the door, and in walked Smiley. Without a word, he took the baby from the midwife, slung Priscilla's lifeless body over his shoulder, and left. Lavinia and the midwife tried to fight him, of course, but it was no use. He swatted them away like children. He put Priscilla and the

baby in the back of the purple Wraith and, after tipping his hat
to Lavinia, he got in the car and drove away. The book, he left
behind.

———◆———

A Word from Joseph

Well, there ya have it. That's the story. That's how a little nobody girl from Nowhere, West Virginia ended up givin' birth to the Antichrist. It's also the story of how I lost my best friend. But that's not nearly as excitin', is it? Surely not. I'll tell ya this, it may not be book worthy, but if there's one thing I learned from the winter of seventy-two, it's the importance of friends. Real, honest and true friends, family, yer circle, however you wanna put it, they make life worth livin'. It ain't money or cars or booze, it's connection. It's carin' for one another, and givin' a call once in awhile just to chat, just to tell someone yer thinkin' 'bout 'em. That's the real shit in life. That's where the gold's at. Everything else is glitter and drugs. Everything.

It's wild to think about. The year now is two thousand and seventeen. I'm an old man, and the world is a different place. All the magic of my youth, metaphorical and otherwise, has long vanished. Hell, the last time I saw Dead Kid Cave, there was swastikas spraypainted on the walls. My long hair's done gone grey like my uncle Bob's, and although I go to church ever Sunday, I ain't seen God since I was a boy. And Marvin Gaye's own daddy shot him to death. But not a day goes by still that I don't think of

Priscilla and that long ago winter, and all the magic it held. In all these years, all the places I been, all the things I done and seen, I ain't never made another friend quite like her. And I reckon I never will.

But that's enough of my sentimental bullshit. I reckon it's time to wrap this thing up. Where to begin is the question. But I reckon we'll start with the star of this whole show. Not that there's much to tell. Ain't nobody seen or heard from Priscilla since the night she give birth. The whereabouts of her child are also unknown. I can only assume they's both in Hell.

As for Lavinia, she never did come back to Clockmaker after Smiley took Priscilla and the baby. I reckon it took her a few months to get her shit together but after she did, she traveled the world. I kept up with Maw Scill here and there until she died, and she kept me informed of Lavinia's adventures. Showed me the postcards. Last I heard, she was in Egypt. But that was decades ago.

But then, like I mentioned, Maw Scill died. Heart attack, I think. For whatever reason, Lavinia wasn't at the funeral. It was just me and Sheriff White. And Pastor Swan. At first, anyway. Then Mathias showed up with the whole Elder clan, and it turned into a big old party. I think we went through damn near eight gallons of shine that night, and a fifth of Beam just for Maw Scill. Beam was her favorite.

Mathias died in seventy-eight. Good Lord, that was one hell of a shindig. He ain't die blind though, or with a crow on his shoulder. Two days after Priscilla died the second time, him and his whole family got their sight back. They just woke up one mornin' and they could all see. No one knew for sure how it happened but we all had a feelin' we did. And I'll mention it, not that it fuckin' matters, but when Phuket got her sight back…well, she, uh, she moved on from me real quick like, but we remain friends to this day.

Jeremiah just died a few years ago. I'm not sure where he was buried. I never knew Jeremiah real well, but I ran into him on Dead Tour back in ninety-one, at the Omni in Atlanta, and after the show, he handed me a ten strip and I ate it, and he ate one too, and we went to the titty bar, and I bet he spent damn near ten thousand dollars. You ever hear of the Brotherhood of Eternal Love? Well… Jeremiah was one of the ones who managed not to go to jail.

The missin' women, Kathleen Gibbon's fine ass, and all the Layfield girls, who I never did get to see naked, but like I said, they all ugly as shit now, and all the rest of 'em, thirty-three in all I think was the final count, they all showed up back up to their respective homes a few days after the Devil got zapped. All of 'em unharmed, claimin' not to remember anything about where they'd been or how they got home. Go figure.

My uncle Bob, he ain't die till last year, at the ripe old age of ninety. The secret to his longevity, accordin' to him—raw liquor, and the occasional piece of ass. Seems unlikely, and a feller could argue, but the man did live to be ninety…so….

The Mire brothers, Merle and Kester, Priscilla's slaves, they turned up dead in eighty-one, when two kids who was fishin' found their skeletons standin' upright next to a creek bottom in Drake Holler. Their mostly intact skeletons were leanin' up against a tree that had the macabre words GOD FORGOT US carved into it. I read about it in the paper. Damn near spit my coffee out when I did too. Those poor bastards never had a chance.

Sheriff White, that motherfucker quit his job, found Jesus, started workin' with at-risk inner-city youth in Pittsburg and died a sort of folk hero. I don't remember what year. Nineteen eighty-somethin'. He was real old. You believe that shit? There's even a bridge named after him just outside town here.

FIVE THREE SEVEN

My momma died when I was thirty. Lost her hearin' first. Then a lung. It was tragic. I started drinkin' a little after that.

My daddy's still alive. He's in his nineties now. He can't hear for shit, but we go fishin' on the weekends, and most nights I'll sit down at the house with him and watch old westerns. Some new ones, but mostly old. My favorite's *The Hateful Eight*, his is *McLintock*. We regularly debate the merits of both.

Well, I think that's about it. Anyone else you give a shit about? Oh, how about Lightnin'? You remember her, don't ya? The serial killer kitty of Clockmaker, West Virgina. There was an article about her in the *Clockmaker Times* in seventy-nine, although it ain't mention her by name, but it was on the fourth page, buried under the classified ads, so you likely didn't see it. A buddin' young journalist by the name of Ryan Scarberry wrote five hundred words on 'The Missin' Mice Population of Clockmaker.' Apparently, according to the article, the population had been wiped out entirely. All and all, it was a fine piece, but it went largely unnoticed. As far as where Lightnin's at today, I have no idea. She could be dead, or she could be sixty-somethin' years old, killin' off mice in another county. Either way, I wouldn't be surprised.

So that just leaves me, I reckon. But ain't much to tell. Married twice, divorced twice, and I am most certainly on my way out. How the fuck I outlived everybody, I do not know. I ate all the drugs, drank all the booze, and never exercised a day in my life, and yet, here I am. Still smokin', still drinkin', still eatin' fuckin' bacon. Still not givin' a shit. And still livin'. But just barely though, I'm right outside death's door. I can hardly breathe most days, and I get these damn terrible headaches. But I'm alive, I reckon…somehow.

Yeah…why God ain't took me yet is a mystery. But I'll tell ya this, I sure am ready to go. I'm tired, and I'm ready. This life's been hard on old Joseph. It sure has…

To be perfectly honest, I ain't sure how to end this. I could ramble on infinitely. As I said, it is my nature. To ramble. A rambler. In life, and in verbiage. I could draw this thing out till the Apocalypse if I needed to, which with Priscilla's son pushin' fifty, could be any day now. Or I could transition into somethin' more poetic, and leave you feelin' all ooey and gooey. Like a dandelion in a summer field or some shit.

Or maybe I should end with somethin' profound. Somethin' deep. Leave ya thinkin'. Or…maybe I'll just keep it plain. Simple, like my daddy taught me… Yeah, that's it.

The world is strange beyond belief. And life is hard. So be kind to people. Be patient. Be compassionate. And make sure that you hug the people you love. Squeeze 'em tight. And don't forget to tell 'em you love 'em. Life goes by fast. You never know when someone's time is gonna come. Or yer own.

Oh, and don't forget to carry a knife.

The end.

———◆———

A final word from Joseph

Well, shit fire to save matches! You ain't never gonna guess who showed up today. I just come in from waterin' the garden, and waitin' for me, sittin' in my livin' room, drinkin' coffee like they fuckin' live here, was Priscilla Louise, Lavinia, and Maw Maw Scill. In the flesh. You believe 'at shit? All of 'em dressed like an Edgar Allan Poe tale, hands black as coal, and sittin' in my livin' room. With their goddamn boots up on the furniture.

They looked prettier than ever too, I might add. All three of 'em. Lookin' like they been bathin' in the fountain of youth for the last half century. Not a grey hair or wrinkle one. Maw Scill looked like she was twenty-nine and in heat, if that tells ya anything. I almost didn't even recognize her. They was on their first vacation from Hell, they told me. Stopped by to have a chat with yers truly. I was shocked as all shit, as you can imagine, but one thing did strike me. I says, Damn Maw Scill, you went to Hell too? And Maw Scill ain't say nothin', just sorta starts noddin' like she knows what's comin', and Priscilla, she chimes in and says, *Yeah this slick bitch thought she could get away with cheatin' on Paw Paw Fish seven times, not countin' hand jobs. But God ain't see it that way, did he, Maw Maw?* And Maw Scill just scowls at her with a defiant little twinkle in her eye, and real bitter soundin' she says, *Eh fuck you and yer momma, I regret nothin'. Them was desperate times.* Boy, how I laughed. How we all laughed. It felt just like the good old days.

But then Maw Scill looks at me all unimpressed and says, *Laugh all you want, old man, yer name's on God's shit list too. I seen it. You'll be gettin' a flamin' pitchfork up the ass 'fore ya know it.*

Now they all started laughin', but I'll be honest, I had a moment of panic. I never really considered I was still goin' to Hell. I figured all the good I did in life and all the prayin' and gettin' saved, and shit was gonna…save me. Ya know?

Fortunately, all that worry only lasted about as long as it took for the cacklin' to quiet. 'Cause then Maw Scill says, *Nah, I'm just milkin' yer fuckin' tits, old man. Relax. There ain't no list. It's a literal fuckin' dice roll every time.* So I went to cacklin' right along with 'em. And I says to 'em, I says, I gotta be honest, ladies—and I don't know why but I started to cry a little. Now, not alot. Just you know… I wouldn't really even call it cryin'. It was more like one tear. Like an Indian watchin' someone litter. It ain't a big deal. I don't even know why I brought it up. So, yeah…anyhow, I says to 'em, Ladies, I gotta be honest…I, uh, well I love you all…so much, and I missed you so much. And I am just so dang happy to see you. Overjoyed I am. I really am. Then they all says, Awwww, and gave me big old hugs, and I wiped away that one tear, and we all laughed some more. It was real beautiful. It sure was. The four of us…together again.

Next thing I know, Scilly, coal-black up to the elbow now, mind you, says, *Go get dressed, you old bastard, let's get the fuck outta here. And put on somethin' sharp. We're goin' to Disneyland.* And I says, Wait, really? And she says, *Fuuuuck no. But we do have reservations for dinner at Renee's in Bangkok, four years ago,*

*in thirty minutes, with Big Tommy, Mathias, his wife Khun Mae,
who you will love, Lucifer, who you will… get used to, Bernie
Mac, Chris Farley, Lucille fuckin' Ball, who, believe it or not, loves
cocaine, I call her Lucille Eight Ball, and oh yeah, Richard Pryor.
Then we're all goin' back to seventy-six to see Elvis do his last
show in Vegas. Now get to scootin'.*

My jaw dropped. I says, Are you shittin' me? And she says,
Not even a little bit. And so I says to Maw Scill and Lavinia, Is she
shittin' me? And they both just shook their heads. So I says, How
the fuck are we supposed to get to Thailand in thirty minutes,
four years ago? Now, of course, I realize in hindsight the question
was stupid, but that's the first question that came to my mind and
I lack a filter. So I asked it. It's a bad habit. And of course, Scilly
looks at me like I'm a dumbass, as is her custom, and she says, *I
snap my fuckin' fingers, Joseph. How do you think three gorgeous
dead women got inside yer house? Black Magic, Grandpa. That
Satanic shit. Now, come on, get it the fuck together. Get dressed.
Bring a toothbrush. I'll make ya look young again on the way.*

And at that point, I probably coulda kept quiet but I've grown
old and disoriented and curious over the years, so I had to ask.
Just in case I was losin' my mind, ya see. I says, Priscilla, how is
this possible? How are you here? I says, Yer all dead. Am I goin'
crazy? Am I dead?

And you know what happened? They all just laughed. All of
'em , all at once just started geekin' out, laughin' their heads off,
like school girls. And I just stood there watchin' 'em, amazed.

Once they gathered themselves a little, Lavinia says, *Yeah,
Priscilla, how is this possible?* And Maw Scill says, *Yeah, Priscilla,
how? How is this possible.* Like they was teasin' her, ya know.
Like an inside joke. Then they all started laughin' again. Like
damn school girls, I tell ya, all three of 'em.

But then Priscilla, she just looks at me with her big green eyes, and her wicked little grin and she answered my question, how is this possible? She says, *Well, old pal, that's the perks of bein' the King of Hell's baby momma. And you don't think I'm suckin' the Devil's dick for nothin', do ya? We can go wherever the fuck we want and we can do whatever the fuck we want. Time and space don't mean shit no more. Now go. Best Italian food in Asia, Elvis Presley resurrected, one night only, endless drugs, lavish hotels, fancy cars. Get dressed.*

Then they all cracked up again. Fallin' all over each other, laughin' so hard, they was cryin'. I tell ya, all the years I known them, all we been through, I ain't never seen them three happy as they were today. Not never. And boy, I have to admit, I ain't felt that complete in a real long time…maybe ever. What a joy it was.

Even still…much as it pains me… And I know this likely ain't what y'all wanna hear, but I had to send 'em on their way without me. I just couldn't go. That ain't the man I am anymore. I'm a righteous and principled man now. And besides, I don't wanna take any chances. Runnin' off with them three, powered by devil magic and drugs, ain't gonna do nothin' but damn my soul. Won't be nothin' but trouble. So, hard as it was, and it surely was hard, I had to send 'em on their way. And I'm takin' my sorry ass to choir practice, or Bible Study, or…confession, or damn somethin'.

Nah, I'm just kiddin'. I'm breakin' out the polyester, and headin' to see Elvis with my good timin' buddies! What else! Like I said, ain't nothin' in the whole wide world more important than friends and family. And I mean nothin'.

So, uh…yeah. I reckon that's all she wrote. See ya in Hell, motherfuckers!

'The Sign' by Ace of Base plays

———— ◆ ————

THE
END

BUFFALO CREEK DISASTER
One of worst floods in US occurred here 26 February 1972, when Buffalo Mining Co. impoundment dam for mine waste broke, releasing over 130 million gallons of black waste water; killed 125; property losses over $50 million; and thousands left homeless. Three commissions placed blame on ignored safety practices. Led to 1973 Dam Control Act and $13.5 million class action legal settlement in 1974.
WV CELEBRATION 2000
WEST VIRGINIA DIVISION OF ARCHIVES AND HISTORY, 2005

THE REAL MAW SCILL

1942-2021

A WORD FROM THE AUTHOR

My father, once upon a time, told me that the trickiest part of killing a turtle is they never really die. Decapitate it, rip off its shell, skin it, let it bleed out, and its legs will still be going. Clawing at the air. Flexing. Trying to escape death. Cut out the heart and sit it on a stump, and it will still be beating five days later.

I said all that to say this. When it comes to life, things are often not what they seem. What it is to be alive or dead is a mystery to me. And I don't know what God is, or what the one true religion is, or what happens to us when we die, but I am pretty darn sure there is something beyond this world, something far greater than any one of us could possibly imagine. Maybe we will find out what that something is one day. Maybe we won't. I can't be certain. However, I do know one thing to be absolutely true. Like the turtle, we as human beings may be killed. But we never really die.

Thank you for reading my book. Godspeed.

'Do You Realize' by the Flaming Lips plays

KOP KHUN KRAP

'Need All My Friends' by lynyrd skynyrd plays

First and foremost I want to thank my family for all of the love and support and inspiration. My father, my rock, James Lewis Toothman, my brothers, Lucas Allen and Jerrod Robert Toothman, all my mothers, Pamela Kay McQuain-Toothman, Aimee Denise Toothman, Shirley Jean Tennant. My sister, Lauren Hill. My uncle Robert Allan Toothman, BT, or Uncle Bob as you and I know him. My aunt Sissy, Cindy Ann McQuain-Amsden. My Uncle Arny, Arnold R. Amsden. My late uncle Jerrod Roy Moore. My grandmother Eleanor Jean McQuain. My late great grandmother, Genevieve Conrad and her threatening knuckle. My late grandfather James Edward McQuain Sr. My late grandparents Big Jim and Esther Toothman. My extended grandparents, Margaret and Jerry Moore, who do not call the law. My cousins, Andrew Toothman, Justin and the late Jeremy Smith, Ricky Amsden, Preston and Jason fuckin' Swann, Jamey and Collin McQuain. Gorf. Evan Tonkery and the Tonkery family for teaching me how to lay hardwood floors. And my late best good dog, Sunshine. Oh, and my great, great, great, great, great, granddaddy, Colonel Morgan Morgan.

And the list goes on, but in no particular order.

Etta James. The late Maw Scill, Priscilla Ann Turner of Backbone Ridge. Nicole Cooper, my best pal and confidant in all things and for Priscilla's Fungarium. Jeremiah Yates and Mathias Hickman for having my back and keeping me chained to the earth for the last twenty some odd years. Duane Richard Keenan for so many things. My Morning Jacket. Lea Morris, my oldest, dearest friend. My boy Saew in KohTao. Josh, Jason, Jeff, and Lisa Fluharty. Seth Yates for Hateskrape. Chris Yates for the Tiger Maple. JB Tennant for letting me break down my first QP at your place back in the day. My boy Jesse KONG Freeman, for letting me write in your chair. Brianna Reising for getting me to my mother. Joedan Hite for giving me a leg up when I really needed it. Brent Hoel. Bernie Mac. Scott Ratner for keeping a roof over my head and then some. AJ Macedonia. Amanda Martin. Jimmy Chan! Bitemyfuckingfist Alyssa Oliverio for the space to write and all the amazing food and love. Alexis Dezaro. Jake Haney-Hedley. Big Kid. My Sweet Lucille in Chicago. Club Vinyl and the world famous Shotgun Willie's for keeping me out of the poorhouse. Patrick Apostle. The Marevlous Marv and the entire Frick Frack Black Jack project. Jonathan Bienko. Quentin Tarantino. Colton and Jonathan at the Blasting Room. Anna Marie Scarberry. Matt Riffee. Joe Parsons. Katrina Rundle. Panos Cosmatos. Taylor Vangilder, I'm still sorry, honey. Mike Buege. Amanda Wotton for the art. Mr Jennings. Party Liberation Front. John Gay for the art. Jessica Powers, the best editor in thhe wrld. Captain Josh motherfuckin' Rice. Kinsley Maggard. Jessica McMillan. John Pericles perk, my blood, my werewolf brother. Beat Kitty. Erick Fields. Dickman. Snoop Dog. Lisa Goddamn Diamond. My nigga Osa for all the laughs when I needed them most. Jaron Drucker, White Zombie forever baby. Naomi Russel. The Sugarkube.

Unchong Shin for Jesus healing my arthritis. Sweet lady Hannah Marie. Clive the Jew. Kaydee and Mae. Austin like the city, Taz like the devil. Casey Sutton the Fire Felon. L fuckin' T. Curtis Shaffer. Zeni in New York. George Rollins for so many things. Pink Floyd. David Gilmour, the Rock-God. Love you too Roger. Clarence Milton. Matt Heston. Jamie Janover. Steven Hanson for showing me how to be a gentleman and make proper gin and tonics. Bandy the drunken fire master. Castle Grayskull. Hunter Thompson. Donald Pollack. Blais Bellenoit. Kasey Docherty. Justin and Jenna Zonts. The Main Squeeze, Billy Strings, and the String Cheese Incident for all the good tunes. Pantera. Marilyn Manson. Tom Fields. Chuck Palahniuk for Guts and Rant. Captain John Ross Cramer. Abraham Smith. The lovely and irresistible Dakota Sue Willy. Big Boi and Andre Three Thousand. Jacob Riddle. Kady Ortiz. Jayme, Jimbo, and Debbie Ferguson. The dreamy Adysun Hawkins. Neal Bronsac and Travis Bronsac. Melissa Hickman. Dr. Hook. Lauren Morgan. Jiri Cechak. My boy Facundo Camps for teaching me to dive in Thailand. Fuckin' Cahill. Got dang Navawan Wan, Momma Jim at Jim's Guest House in Kanchanaburi. Sarah Carpenter-Davis. Jim Righter. The Grateful Dead. Elynn Lay. Lynzi Cottingham. The late great Ronnie Van Zant. Ken West. My girl Lollipop down in the keys. Coda Burdette. Jess and Joel. Dr. Mark on little crick. Kylie Fernandez. Miss Megan Romine. Rich Jones. Curt Tucker. Ben Swiger. The Bordas Bros. The Foo Fighters. Be Bell, DJ Way Up High. DJ Kitana. Ashley Helmstetter. Jordan and Alyssa Ween. George Strait. The late Aaron Joel Mitchell for the most introspective acid trip of my life. Cathy DeBellis. Will Davis. Ghost. Cody Rizner. William Wright. Brian Kopulos. Zac Riedel. Christian Breeden. Dan Summers. Russell Currey. Jack Henry and Annie Bee. Emily Ferguson. Lee Swoope. Dillon Endico. Anurag Bhattarai. Christopher Lee. Angie Shaffer. Charlie Letts.

Marta Corbin. Tots. David Westfall. Kristina Koay, wherever you are. Charles J. Berger for that pack of reds. Jen Verta. Natalie White for a wonderful week in the Keys. My boy Hog down in the Keys. Rhandi Lores. Angie Naomi Geis. Robert Eggers. Harmony Korine, The Beach Bum is my favorite film of all time. Ari Aster. Everett Sailsbury. Extra Gold. Pete Natthapong. Haley Mckinley. The late Mike Dean. Kristina Moffitt. Scott Taylor. The late Jeremy Abel, and the whole Abel family. Kelli Frye. Matt Jacoby. Naomi Russell. Trent fuckin' Marshall, my Tasmanian twin. Kazzy who gave me DMT for the first time in Charleston. Insane Clown Posse. Jarred at Lost Sailor. Nate Bee. The late DMX. Savannah Cosby for turning me on to Tom. Pinja Kauhanen, we'll always have Bangkok. Korn, Monkey has the prettiest eyes on acid. Nolan and Ashley Merrifield. Also, fuckin' Mrs Merrifield, what a great woman and educator. Chris Starcher. John Lorenz. Jake Burkhart. Alexis Etchison. The Davis twins. Tool. The late Erik Rundle. Nikali Heeter. Ryan Pujals. Kate Atkinson. Ron White. Carla Ware. The late Nicholas Young, CUZO. TJ Rogers. Robby Hoye. Gabby Blassou. Miller and Hayden Smith. Erica Skinner. The late Michael K McDonald. Fuckin' Galaxy Girl, Celeste. Clay Strawderman. Pickle. Hump. Zachary Boyce. Travis Hudson. Matt, Kermit, Cliff, Justin, Josh, Worm, Iris, Jim, and Rob. Richard Prior. Matt Sanders, for that trip to Vegas so that I could see what real evil looked like with my own eyes. Chris Titley. Adam Lefkowitz. Chris Tony and his brother Jeffrey. Adam Danger Smith. Adam and Kelly Musgrove. Mike Diaz. Fuckin' Slade. Sexy Jesus. Dustin Davis. Gazda. Dirty. Scott Starn, for being friends with me when I was uncool. Shane Spadafore. Greg Heyman. Cole Holbrook. The Davisson Brothers Band. Wim Hof. Joe Rogan. Zach Linn. Joey Diaz. Lee Cyrankowski. Keisha Hunt. Emily Kell. The late Tracey Harland Vincent, who was the first person to show me Stephen King movies. Stephen King. Cormac McCarthy. Tom Robbins. Mary Shelley. Gabrielle Garcia Marquez. Lindsay Elftinge. NiggaWolf. CJ McQuiston. Tiona Kapnicky. Jessica Miller-Harmon. Joshua and Justin Malott. Dean Koontz. Dave Chapelle. Rob Zombie. David Allan Coe. Doug Stanhope, Conway Twitty. Andy Griffith. The entire U.S.A. experiment experience. Ray Sawyer and God.

If you're on this list, then at some point you brought goodness to my life, and in one way or the other influenced the writing of this book. Lots of love to you all. Living and dead.

Anna and Trevor, you get your own paragraph because this book would have never seen the dark of night without you. Also the time you saved me from dying of exposure in the desert. Thank you so much.

—◆—